continued . . .

···ORPHANS OF EARTH

······ **SEAN WILLIAMS**
AND SHANE DIX

ACE BOOKS, NEW YORK

This is a work of fiction. Names, characters, places, and incidents either are the product of the author's imagination or are used fictitiously, and any resemblance to actual persons, living or dead, business establishments, events, or locales is entirely coincidental.

ORPHANS OF EARTH

An Ace Book / published by arrangement with the authors

PRINTING HISTORY
Ace mass-market edition / January 2003

Copyright © 2003 by Sean Williams and Shane Dix.
Cover art by Chris Moore.
Cover design by Judy Murello.

Visit our website at
www.penguinputnam.com
Check out the ACE Science Fiction & Fantasy newsletter!

ISBN: 0-441-01006-7

ACE ®
Ace Books are published by The Berkley Publishing Group,
a division of Penguin Putnam Inc.,
375 Hudson Street, New York, New York 10014.
ACE and the "A" design
are trademarks belonging to Penguin Putnam Inc.

PRINTED IN THE UNITED STATES OF AMERICA

10 9 8 7 6 5 4 3 2 1

For Simon Brown,
fellow boggler.

CONTENTS

ADJUSTED PLANCK UNITS: TIME

Old Seconds

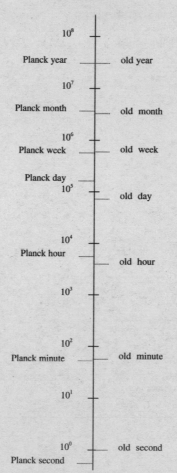

NB: For more information about Planck Units, see Appendix 1.

ADJUSTED PLANCK UNITS: DISTANCE

Old Meters

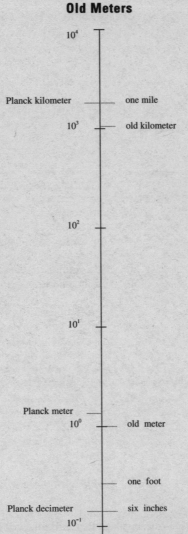

	10^4
Planck kilometer	one mile
10^3	old kilometer
	10^2
	10^1
Planck meter	
10^0	old meter
	one foot
Planck decimeter	six inches
10^{-1}	

WHAT CAME BEFORE ...

2050 A.D.

The United Near-Earth Stellar Survey Program dispatches 1,000 crewed missions to nearby stars in an attempt to explore terrestrial worlds identified by Earth-based detectors. Instead of sending flesh-and-blood humans, UNESSPRO crews each mission with simulations called engrams that are intended to behave as, and function as though they in fact are, the original scientists. A core group of sixty surveyors is duplicated many times over to cover all the missions.

In each mission, UNESSPRO plants a single control crewmember who has been altered to ensure the crews follow strict operation guidelines. These controls unknowingly possess directives that come into play when certain conditions arise. One of them is to immediately contact Earth should any evidence of extraterrestrial life be discovered. Twelve years after the missions are launched, all transmissions from Earth cease. Without explanation, Sol System falls silent. Cut off from UNESSPRO, the missions continue as planned, hoping that whatever fate befell the home system will not follow them also.

2163 Standard Mission Time

Aliens come to the system of Upsilon Aquarius in the form of giant golden spindles that build ten orbital towers around the *Frank Tipler*'s target world, Adrasteia. When the towers are complete and connected by a massive orbital ring, the aliens disappear, leaving no clue as to their intentions or origins.

Peter Alander, once a highly regarded generalist but now a flawed engram barely holding onto sanity, is sent to explore the orbital towers by the mission's civilian survey manager, Caryl Hatzis. Within them, Alander finds AIs that identify the towers as gifts to humanity from a powerful star-faring civilization. The Spinners are secretive and mysterious, but their gifts are to die for: a detailed map of the Milky Way, featuring details of other alien civilizations; a surgery containing exotic medical technology, such as a perfectly transparent membrane designed to keep its wearer from harm; a means of instantaneous communication with a range of 200 light-years; a faster-than-light vessel that defies known scientific laws; and so on.

The gifts are too much for the crew of the *Frank Tipler*. Testing the ftl communicator and the hole ship severely stretches the crew's resources; a detailed examination of all the things they have been given will take decades. They need help. Amid a crisis brought about by the UNESSPRO control, Peter Alander decides to take the hole ship to Sol to see what has become of Earth. If anything remains of UNESSPRO, he will return with the resources they need or, at the very least, instructions on how to proceed.

What Alander finds in Sol, however, is a civilization bearing little resemblance to the one he left. A technological spike shortly after the launch of the UNESSPRO missions, 100 years earlier, resulted in a war between nonhuman AIs that led, among many other things, to the total destruction of the Earth. A small percentage of humans have survived, in highly modified forms, to create a new society in Sol System called the Vincula. The posthumans regard Alander's arrival with suspicion and some disdain, since engrams are now regarded as a very poor cousin to the sort of minds that have evolved from the ashes of Earth.

A much-expanded form of Caryl Hatzis, the sole survivor of the original UNESSPRO volunteers, is pressed into service. Alander has disturbed the fragile equilibrium between the Vincula and its main opposition, the progressive Gezim. Confused by his reception, Alander tries to hail Adrasteia for more instructions but receives only silence in reply. As war breaks out in Sol System, the expanded Hatzis sends her original with Alander to Adrasteia, both to attest the veracity of his claims and to see what has happened in his absence.

They arrive in Adrasteia to find the colony and the gifts destroyed. Something has swept through Upsilon Aquarius and erased all trace of the *Frank Tipler*. Stunned, Alander and Hatzis retreat immediately to Sol System, only to find the same thing happening there. A fleet of vastly superior alien vessels destroys the Vincula and the Gezim with equal prejudice, along with every last trace of humanity. All the resources and technology of the AIs can do nothing to stop the destruction. Within a day, there is little left but dust. Reeling from the double whammy, Hatzis and Alander retreat to the edge of Sol System to avoid destruction at the hands of these new aliens, the Starfish. The feeling that the gifts should have heralded a golden age of humanity only enhances their grief and shock. They have never been friends in any form, and the tension between them is not helped by the revelation that Alander himself may have inadvertently brought about the destruction of humanity. By following the hails of another colony contacted by the Spinners, they determine that the Starfish home is on the omnidirectional signals broadcast by the ftl communicators provided in the gifts. It was Alander's attempt to call Adrasteia from Sol System that drew the Starfish to the Vincula.

This pattern, they realize, will only be repeated as the Spinners sweep through surveyed space, dropping gifts as they go. Colonies must be contacted to warn them against using the communicators in a way that will bring the Starfish down upon them. A severely traumatized Peter Alan-

der and the original Caryl Hatzis, very much alone
without the rest of her distributed self, make it their mission to save what remains of humanity: the orphaned
UNESSPRO mission engrams scattered across the stars.

1.0.1

2160.9.02–03 Standard Mission Time

Everyone has to have a reason to be. Mine, I think, is to appreciate the subtlety of the Spinners' work.

Subtlety? From creatures that do in a day what humanity would struggle for decades to do? Who flaunt their technological superiority as we would wave a stick in front of a dog before throwing it to watch him run?

Yes, subtlety. When we retrieve the stick, we find the hand that threw it long gone, utterly disinterested in whether we found it or not. There has to be something subtle at play there, or else the universe truly is incomprehensible—and that is something I cannot believe.

The Spinners have been here for what feels like an eternity, and we have found no obvious explanation for their mysteries. So I place my faith in subtlety, and in my all-too-human inability to see it.

For now, anyway. I guess I'll just have to keep looking.

Hatzis has gone off to powwow with the bigwigs from the other colonies, and we don't know when she'll be back. That's fine with me. She's so damned strict about system resources. At least while she's not here, I can fast-track to talk to people without inconveniencing them too much.

Ali Genovese has been left in charge. When I spoke to her today, she looked tense. It's understandable. Our current situation is more than a tad iffy. Psi Capricornus is

smack-bang in the middle of the hot zone. If anyone's
going to be attacked by the Starfish, it's likely to be us.
And I'm not just being dramatic, either. Every broadcast
brings news of another colony lost. Yesterday it was
Balder; tomorrow it could be Inari. I feel like we're sitting
on top of a volcano.

"I vote for firing up the engines and leaving the system," I told Ali when she dropped by.

"Leave Inari? You can't be serious, Rob."

"We're sitting ducks here. If they hit us, we'll never
get away. Not without the hole ship."

"Even with the hole ship, we probably wouldn't get
far," she said glumly. "You heard what happened to Adrasteia."

Adrasteia was the first on a list of names I didn't want
Inari to join.

"Ah," she said then. "It's because you're bored, isn't
it? You want your old job back."

"Would you blame me if I did? There's not much use
for a pilot around here."

"You're working on *something*," she said. "I see your
data flow. It's all inbound, all about the gifts. Are you
doubling up on our research, Rob?"

"Tiptoeing across the cracks."

She pulled a sour face. "Sometimes I think there's nothing but cracks," she said.

"Then I'm not wasting resources."

"No. You have my blessing to keep poking around."

She didn't leave then, although she could have. I had
what I wanted, and she had more important things to at-
tend to. But she stood for a moment in the low-
maintenance parlor I whipped up for guests, gazing idly
into space. She's letting her blond hair grow out—or pre-
senting the illusion of growth, at least. I like it better that
way, even though I can never tell what's going on under
it.

Eventually, she blinked and returned. "Sorry about that,
Rob. Got stuck thinking about home."

I nodded understanding. We all do, sometimes.

1.0.2

By the time Lucia Benck realized her friends were dead, the blue-shifted photons that had carried the news were already a month old. Although she fought to comprehend what the images were telling her, searching for the remotest possibility that her interpretation of the data could somehow be wrong, she'd had enough experience with distance and relativity to know this was no illusion that she could simply brush aside. Her powerful rejection of what she was seeing had more to do with not wanting to accept her impotence than not believing what she saw. She wanted to reach out across the vast gulf of space and time that separated her from her crewmates and warn them, to save them from the fate they had already suffered.

Deep down, she knew there really was nothing that could be done for the *Andrei Linde*. All she could do was watch, accept, and consider what was to be done next.

The first thing she did was return to *Chung-5*'s clock rate. During the approach to pi-1 Ursa Major, she had been gradually accelerating her perception of time from the deep rest she experienced between targets to something approximating normal. Even so, she had been severely behind at that point in the mission, experiencing barely one second for every ten of the probe's. Once she was back in synch with the probe—albeit still dilated with respect to Earth and the *Linde*—she wouldn't waste days pondering her options. She had the luxury of time, if not resources.

The second thing she did was examine the data in meticulous detail. Could those flashes of light have been the signs of an accident? Was there any chance that the emissions encircling the planet were atmospheric disturbances? Could a sudden flare-up of pi-1 UMA have caused the things she saw across the system? But it was all just speculation, and the absence of any definite answers to her questions only frustrated her further.

While doubt remained, her options were unclear.

Prior to receipt of those images, her mission had been proceeding as normal—or as close to normal as she had decided to maintain, anyway. *Chung-5* had been coasting headlong toward pi-1 Ursa Major, where the crew of the *Andrei Linde* had established a beachhead around the fifth world out from the primary star. She assumed that her crewmates had christened it with the name they had agreed upon prior to leaving Sol—Jian Lao—so this was how she referred to the planet in her own mind. Apart from that, she really didn't know a whole lot more. The *Linde* and its crew had arrived almost exactly on schedule, Mission Time, seventeen months earlier. She'd seen the braking flare of the ship's atomic engines reflected off the planet's moon and upper atmosphere, and she occasionally picked up faint echoes of carrier waves not aimed at her.

With *Chung-5*'s main dish expanded as wide as possible, and with secondary baseline dishes spread out in a vast array around her, she had eagerly absorbed the data coming in from the target system. It boasted eleven major planets, six of them gas giants. Two of the giants had ring systems to rival Saturn's, large enough to be just visible to her interferometers. She couldn't detect asteroid belts, but she did discern a comet passing close to the sun, its tail impossibly faint against the deeper darkness of the background.

As for Jian Lao itself, its emissions indicated an Earth-like world. In fact, as she watched it slowly resolve, she realized it couldn't have been more like Earth. From the vaguest suggestions, she imagined its blue oceans and green forests, dreaming of the Eden she was giving up. As with all of the survey ships, the *Linde* had the capacity to build new bodies for its crew, and she pictured herself standing under an alien sky with the wind on her skin and Peter at her side. It was a reunion she longed for sometimes. How many other couples could boast surviving a separation of not only normal years, but light-years as well? It was hard not to want to complete the circle, to connect the dots.

"The tourists outnumber the truth seekers," he had said back on Earth, the night before their engrams had woken. She was a committed tourist, and she knew it; that was why she was riding a glorified rocket forty-five light-years away from home, alone. But there was a haunting, tempting truth to the image of her and Peter that was hard to deny.

Then had come the flashes from around Jian Lao and its moon, closely followed by smaller disturbances across the system. Each flash had been brief but frighteningly bright, reminding her of an antimatter containment failure she had witnessed once, back in Sol. She'd watched the flowering of small pockets of annihilation across the system, thinking of the work the crew of the *Linde* would have been doing in the years since its arrival: the satellites that would have perhaps been placed around the moon and the nearest gas giant, and maybe even the solar poles to watch for prominences; the installations on Jian Lao itself; the geosynchronous orbit of the *Linde* . . .

Christ. Geosynchronous orbit is where she would have put the *Andrei Linde,* and that was where the biggest flash of all, the first, had come from. If the flashes really were explosions, and if that first flash had been the *Linde,* all hope that she might ever stand in that Eden with Peter was gone forever.

She was surprised by how much the thought hurt her, how much the dream had meant. She might not have intended to go back to him, but it had been important that he was out there somewhere, waiting for her. The source of such feelings had to be other than genetic—since she no longer had any actual genes—but she couldn't rationalize it.

UNESSPRO wouldn't program the desire to reproduce into a *machine,* surely? Perhaps they would. She wouldn't put anything past UNESSPRO. If they thought something would increase the chance of the missions succeeding, they'd probably do it.

Whatever. The origin of her confusion was just a smoke screen for her deepest concern. Peter was gone, the need went unfulfilled, and she grieved. In the empty spaces of her virtual coffin—she had long ago dismissed all but the most basic conSense illusion in preference to the company of stars—she cried tears that felt real but weren't.

The truth sank in. She was proud of herself for not flinching. It would have been easy to switch off, metaphorically or literally. Instead she reexamined new data obsessively, looking for clues. Although the stray signals from the *Linde* had ceased with the flashes, there were other signals she couldn't interpret. Over the course of a real-time week, drawing 100,000 kilometers closer with every passing second, she watched as numerous other energy sources flared and died with irregular rhythms across the system. The smallest of the rocky worlds disappeared; the infrared signature of one of the gas giants changed.

She was too far away to tell who might be responsible. A hostile Earth government, perhaps, much advanced in the decades since the *Linde* had left Sol? The possibility that someone would break the lightspeed barrier and beat them to the target worlds had been one seriously considered by the UNESSPRO bigwigs, but out here it was pure speculation. It could just as easily have been aliens. All she knew was that, whoever it was, their talent for destruction was startling, and the more she saw, the more nervous she became.

Then, without warning, everything stopped. The energy flares faded and died; the small, rocky world reappeared, and the gas giant returned to normal. It was as though nothing had happened, as though everything she had watched had been an illusion, after all—or perhaps a glitch in her instruments.

But there was one small difference: there were no longer any human signals coming from the system.

"Okay." She imagined herself pacing to and fro in a small room. "What have I got here?"

Not much, she told herself. It looked like someone had flown into pi-1 UMA and blown up the *Linde*, but she had no way of confirming that.

"And then what?" she asked herself.

Someone might have screwed around with the system for a while afterward, but she couldn't be sure about that, either.

"So what now?"

Everything was back to normal, no different than it had been a month ago.

Except for the *Linde*.

The silence from the mother ship was complete. No echoes. No stray beacons. No engine flashes.

"Shit." She stopped pacing and worried at a virtual hangnail. The only way to confirm what had happened was to get closer, which she was already doing. In twenty days, whether she wanted to or not, she would flash across the system at a sizable percentage of the speed of light. If there was anything there, she would see it clearly enough. But it might also see her, and that was the problem.

She had a bad feeling that had nothing whatsoever to do with genes. But what was she supposed to do? Her options were limited. If she was wrong about her gut feeling and she went out of her way to act on it, what was the worst that could happen? She might feel foolish. Whereas if she ignored her gut feeling, then whatever killed the *Linde* and her friends might kill her also.

The thought was a sobering one and made the argument pretty clear cut, from her point of view. No one else had to know if she was wrong. And if she was right, she would still be alive.

Simple.

The problem was that the only way to be sure she wouldn't be noticed was to switch herself off.

She thought back to her days on Earth spent training for her mission to the stars. In reality, she was going on many missions at once, since she consisted of over 200 duplicates all kitted up in nearly identical probe vessels, each craft little more than engines with instrument packages attached. While the main missions would go directly to the target systems, the various versions of herself would make a flyby of the numerous smaller and failed stars along the way, surveying brown and white dwarfs, protostars, and stellar remnants, seeking out curiosities rather than Sol-like environments. She was proud to have been chosen for these missions, since they were the dangerous ones—both physically and psychologically. She would be alone for the entire time, completely out of contact with Earth and her crewmates. If something went wrong, there would be no one to help her.

That thought had never bothered her before. She had learned to rely on herself and was as independent as a person could be. In the end, on this particular mission, she had come to like it—being alone on the new frontiers, seeing things no one else would see. The thought of going back had in fact filled her with a kind of dread. Once the novelty of watching sunsets with Peter wore off on Jian Lao, what would she have to do?

Risking suicide wasn't something she'd planned, though. Shutting herself down certainly hadn't been on the agenda. She could build a simple molecular timer and switch that would power herself back up again, but nothing was perfectly reliable. What if it failed to restart the systems? What would happen to her then? The question was meaningless. Frozen in time like an old photo, doomed to decay into stardust, she would no longer exist. She would never even know what had happened to her. But who was she, anyway? The solo missions incorporated three hard copies of the driving personality into the hardframe, in case of degradation or damage, and she knew that at least one of hers had been compromised in the past. At best she was a piecemeal version of herself; at worst, a completely new template seamlessly taking over where the old one had left off. Not even her memories of life before the program were really hers in the first place.

Try as she might, whichever way she looked at it, she could come up with no reasonable argument against disconnection. She didn't believe in God, so the idea of suicide certainly didn't pose any moral dilemma for her. And on the balance of things, surely it was better to go that way than at the hands of some interstellar murderer.

And that was that.

Decided, she didn't waste any more time. She started immediately with a detailed inventory of the *Chung-5*'s system and resources. Although she had left Sol sixty-seven years earlier, relativity meant that the probe had only aged about forty. (She herself had aged barely a year, which made it hard to remember, sometimes, how long it had actually been.) Radiation had damaged a thousand little things in those forty years, and she needed everything to be working when she shut herself down.

What she could do without, she switched off, concentrating all her resources on several key areas and letting the rest lie dormant. Nanorepair systems could look at those later. If the engines never started again, that was a fair trade to ensure that she didn't die.

With eighteen days to go to Jian Lao, she retracted the wide-array gain antennae that doubled as the probe's transmitter and receiver, along with the baseline dishes. She converted their mass to an extra layer of porous material around the probe and radically restructured the interior. When she finished, the most precious parts of the probe were protected from the outside by more material shielding than before. Nothing would stop a direct hit, but this would take some of the sting out of turning off the magnetic deflectors. She wanted be as sure as she could be that she wouldn't be torn apart on the way through the system.

Next, in one randomly chosen corner of the probe's new shell, she hollowed out a small crater, little more than a pockmark on its rugged, gray surface. At the bottom of the crater, she placed a small camera, the design for which she had dredged out of the UNESSPRO archives. Its non-reflective lens, metal shutter, and silver halide film seemed almost ludicrously obsolete compared to the instruments the probe had once possessed, but she didn't want to use chips or CCD arrays. Anything more than dead matter might give her away. A mechanical trigger would activate the camera at key points in the coming days. The pictures it took would be her only record of the probe's journey through pi-1 Ursa Major.

She gave the probe a slight tumble. This, combined with its irregular shape, low density, and lack of electrical activity, would, she hoped, convince a casual observer that the *Chung-5* was a perfectly ordinary lump of rock drifting through from out system. She converted the outlets of the thrusters when the tumble was established and added its mass to the shielding, thinking, *What if I'm wrong? What if I'm being paranoid? I could be burying myself alive for nothing!*

But there was no point going down that path again. Such a train of thought was counterproductive. For peace of mind, she had to assume that she was being prudent. If she woke up and viewed the pictures and found nothing out of the ordinary, then she could call herself foolish and paranoid. She could laugh about it later, when it was over.

Once her disguise was in place, there was only one thing left to do.

Before that, though, she took a moment to say good-bye to the stars.

Pi-1 Ursa Major was growing brighter every day and easily outshone the brightest of its neighbors. If that was the last thing she ever saw, she didn't really have any right to complain. At least she had a chance of surviving, unlike the crew of the *Andrei Linde*. And if she did survive, the universe was her oyster. Originally, she had planned to keep going to Muscida, the next major star out from Sol, but her ambitions hadn't been satisfied with that thought for long. A course change or two could take her out to rho UMA, then by a number of stars in the Hipparcos catalogue, and on her way out of the galaxy. If the probe held up—and she wasn't really naïve enough to hope that it would, although the dream was romantic—the end of that journey promised Bode's Nebula and the galaxies M82, NGC3077, NGC2976, IC2574, millions of light-years away.

Although she didn't pray as she shut herself down for the long sleep through pi-1 Ursa Major, she did express a hope to the universe in general that she might at least survive.

For you, Peter, she thought, as darkness closed around her. *For all you truth seekers. I hope we get to compare notes, one day.*

1.1

PLANETS IN THEIR STATIONS

2160.9.3 Standard Mission Time
(30 July, 2163 UT)

1.1.1

The Head was setting with a wild profusion of purples and blues into the western horizon while Achernar, a brilliant blue star, watched coldly from the north. To the south auroras whipped through the upper atmosphere, humming and crackling with startling energy. Opposite the sunset, setting around the far side of Athena, was the glint of light that was all that could be seen of the *Mayor*; directly above that hung another speck of light: the alien installation designated Spindle Nine. In between, at the summit of a mighty chunk of rock and ice thirty kilometers high, stood Peter Alander.

The potential extinction of his species had never concerned him less than at that precise moment.

Athena was an unusual world—but then, he thought, they all were. In most respects—radius, mass, density, gravity, etc.—this one was up the scale from Earth. Its sun was the B3V star called Head of Hydrus, bluer and more intense than Sol. Athena's magnetic field was bombarded by all manner of radiation and particles every one of its seventeen and a half hour days, and Alander would have been dangerously exposed to the interplanetary elements so high up in the atmosphere, had he not been wearing a Spinner Immortality Suit, or I-suit, as they were increasingly being called. Several hundred kilometers to his left crouched the base of the orbital tower connecting the planet to the spindle above. Where he stood, on the highest point of the planet, was just one of several very large and very tall mountain-islands girdling the equator. But for the solar weather, Athena could have been made for skyhooks.

The planet's signature quirk revolved around those mountainous islands, jutting out of the surface of the planet like strange volcanic growths. Over many millions of years, the seas had evaporated into the upper atmosphere and deposited themselves as ice on the mountains, increasing their bulk even more. As a result, most of the planet's water had been trapped in solid form, leaving only a thin, salty scum of an ocean behind. Life blossomed around the bases of the giant islands in strange, linear landscapes. Caught between salt and ice and separated by great distances, each coastal biozone had become home to enough wildly diverse phyla to keep a whole army of xenobiologists busy for centuries. A handful of them that had been scooped up and examined by robotic probes from the *Michel Mayor* had shown such unique chemistry that they would have caused a scientific revolution back home—had the Earth existed any longer, that is.

Alander watched the sunset fade from deep purple to black. Stars were starting to poke through the growing darkness, twinkle-free in the thin air. He had seen nights fall on more than a dozen different planets, but this one beat them all for sheer splendor. The night sky was so vivid that if he stood absolutely still and tilted his head back so that all he could see were the stars, it felt as if he was actually *in* space.

"You cooled off yet?" said a voice in his ear.

He didn't allow himself a smile. Cleo would note the expression from his bioreadings, and he wasn't going to give her the satisfaction.

"This isn't just a bad mood," he said. "You realize that, don't you?"

"I realize more than you give me credit for," she replied. "You hate being outvoted, for one."

"I'm glad you noticed. That's one of the few human traits I have left."

"Not so few. You also hate feeling like an idiot."

He shivered from purely psychosomatic cold but didn't say anything.

"And you love a good argument for its own sake," she went on. "You *love* picking fights—and I dare you to tell me otherwise!"

He swallowed an automatic retort. "I think you're mistaking me for Caryl Hatzis."

"Some people would take that as a compliment, you know."

"Would you?"

He heard a faint noise from behind him and turned to see her image walking to join him across the crusty high-altitude ice pack. She wasn't really there, being the product of a conSense illusion piped into his artificial nerve endings by the processors on the *Mayor*, but he would have been hard pressed to tell the difference, had she still had a physical body to compare it to. He could even hear her feet crunching in the ice as she approached.

"You know how I voted," she said, coming to a halt in front of him, her blond hair buffeted by the wind. She was wearing a khaki oversuit sealed at wrists and ankles; her face was exposed and caught the light of the auroras in a convincingly eerie way. "Doesn't that count for anything?"

"After Adrasteia—"

"I know what you're going to say, Peter," she interrupted. "After Adrasteia, you don't trust anyone. Well, that's something you need to get over, pal. With UNES-SPRO gone, there are no traitors in the system anymore. You know that. They either owned up or went psychotic. And if it's me you're worried about—"

"It's not you, Cleo," he cut in quickly.

"I was going to say that if it was me you're worried about, then you can go to hell," she said. "Because even if you didn't already know that Otto was the rotten apple in the *Michel Mayor* I think I've proved myself a dozen times over. I'm on your side, Peter, except when you're obviously wrong or just being an idiot."

He raised one hand to brush the hair out of her face. Although she was nothing more than an illusion, his fingers registered every pressure, texture, and temperature he would have expected of the real thing.

"*Am* I being an idiot?"

Her expression softened. "In the long run, no, I don't think you are," she said. "But things are changing too fast for the rest to focus on anything but the short term—the present. Christ, Peter, in a single day, the Spinners came and gave them gifts beyond their wildest dreams. Then they heard about the Starfish. First, they were given everything, and now they're being told they've lost everything. You can't blame them for not liking what you've got to say—or at least for being resistant to it. They want a future." She paused to sigh. "Besides, I don't think they're even listening to what you have to say; they're just hearing the voice of the person saying it. It's you again: the oracle of doom and gloom. Believe me, Peter, pushing isn't going to help."

He knew she was right, and she knew he knew, too. He could see it in her expression. There was no point arguing when they were both, more or less, on the same side.

She leaned in close to put her arms around him. He wanted to hug her back, but conSense hadn't quite perfected a convincing full-body squeeze. Her illusory warmth was enough to take some of the chill out of the brisk night wind, and he was comforted by the contact, even though part of him still thought of Lucia with regret, and probably always would.

"This could be our home, if we let it," she said, her voice slightly muffled by his shoulder. "We can expand the existing bases, put habitats down on the strands, build more bodies—"

"I know how it goes, Cleo. Dig in, delve into the gifts, build up resources until we're able to diversify, disseminate the human race across the stars." The four Ds made perfect sense on the surface, and he felt their calling more deeply than maybe even Cleo imagined. The argument was fundamentally flawed, though; it assumed that nothing would get in the way of the dream becoming reality. "But can we do this with the Starfish still out there? Would you be prepared to take a chance on raising children here without ever really knowing whether or not they'll be back to finish us off?"

"Children?" She pulled away from him so she could look at his face. "Who's talking about children?"

"Some of them are," he said.

"But *I'm* not one of them." She frowned. "I thought that was already established. I just want a little time to heal."

"I'm not denying anyone that."

"Yes you *are*, Peter. You want us to make a decision that will affect the rest of our lives. You want us to avoid settling down on the grounds that it might not be safe. But what are you offering instead? Can you tell us when it *will* be safe?"

He shook his head, tight lipped.

"I think I know what my decision will be," she went on, "but I'm not ready to make it right now. Not yet. I don't want to commit myself to anything before I feel as though I can support it one hundred percent. Especially something like this, which will affect my entire future."

"If we have one—"

She cut him off with a sigh. "Save the speeches for the next meeting," she said, letting go and stepping back.

"I'm sorry."

She hugged herself, rubbing her arms as though cold. On another world, in another time, her lean frame, broad face, and high cheekbones would have lent her enough of a Nordic air that he might have been surprised by her apparent chill. On Athena, though, seventy light-years from the remains of Earth, at thirty below freezing, Alander was very aware that, his hypnotized nerve endings aside, he was interacting with little more than a phantom, invisible to anybody else but him.

"If you need to talk to me about anything else," she said, "you know where I'll be."

"Thanks, Cleo," he said, meaning it.

She walked around him, having learned the habit of vanishing when she was out of sight so as not to disorient him. His mental state was still disturbingly fragile at times.

"By the way," she said at the last moment, "Caryl wants you to bring the hole ship back. There are some emissions she wants you to check out."

He shook his head, amazed by the woman's arrogance. "I'm not her goddamn dogsbody, Cleo," he said without facing her.

"Neither am I," she said. "Nevertheless, here we are."

He turned then, expecting to see her standing there smiling at him. But she had already gone, her disappearance leaving him seemingly isolated on the giant mountaintop, although in reality he was no more alone than he had been before.

Slowly, reluctantly, he returned to where he'd left the hole ship. Apparently unaffected by gravity and whiter than the snow it hung above, the enormous spherical mass of the craft floated over a shallow rift about a hundred meters away. The black cockpit was ready for his return with the light from its open airlock now easily the brightest thing in the landscape around him.

He briefly considered complying with Caryl Hatzis's wishes and returning immediately, but then he decided against it.

To hell with her, he thought. There was no cause to hurry. The aurora was particularly spectacular tonight, and making her wait half an hour while he enjoyed it wasn't going to kill her. God knew he'd certainly earned the break.

The emissions were coming from a point roughly seven AUs from the Head and twenty-five degrees above the ecliptic. They consisted of a semiregular pulsing in the

upper microwave band and didn't correlate to any satellite, active or inactive, placed in-system by the *Mayor*.
Hatzis had thought it might be a piece of Spinner flotsam,
which warranted checking it out. Alander agreed.

The more the Spinner artifacts were investigated, the
clearer it became that the spindles were built by machines,
that the Spinners themselves had had nothing actually to
do with it. Alander thought that mapping that single fact
onto humanity's experiences with AIs might be mislead-
ing, but even he couldn't resist the assumption that something would inevitably go wrong with any automated
process. Somewhere, eventually, the Gifts would make a
mistake and leave something behind, some clue that
would speak more about their origins than they had ever
been willing to reveal.

The question of whether the Gifts would let him return
with anything like a clue occupied his mind as he instructed the hole ship AI to take him to a position closer
to the source of the emissions. They were programmed
not to reveal the origin of their makers; indeed, at times
it seemed as though they didn't even know it themselves.
But were they also programmed to keep that knowledge
a secret if the humans were to stumble across it? How far
would they go to protect their makers? Alander didn't
know, and it worried him.

"We've had word from Sothis," Hatzis had said to him
when he'd checked back in for duty. "They've found three
more drops."

Drops. Alander remembered his first sight of a Spinner
skyhook unraveling its way from orbit and thought the
term very apt. Not every Spinner drop had the same number of towers, but the method was the same in each, as
were the number of the gifts.

"Any joy?" he asked.

"Two markers," she answered. "One contact."

A *marker* was the euphemism for a destroyed colony,
so called because of the strange, inert sculptures left behind in systems visited by the Starfish. These artifacts
seemed to serve no function, and some had taken them to

be the equivalent of death markers or gravestones. Who planted them, however, remained a mystery. They seemed to employ a similar technology to the hole ships the Spinners left behind, but beyond that, nothing was known.

"What's the contact?"

"Beta Hydrus. Borderline senescent, but the Gifts managed to reactivate some of the archived engrams." She hesitated before adding, "You weren't one of them."

"That was the *Carl Sagan*," he said dismissively. "Not one of my missions."

Even if it had been one of his missions, the chances of his persona remaining intact for so long would have been minimal. All of the engrams were unstable, but his was particularly so. He would've been lucky to last a year, let alone the seventy-four years since the *Sagan* had arrived.

"Who did they choose this time?" he asked.

"Neil Russell. Deep-time physicist; kept himself in extreme slow-mo to observe changes on a larger scale than the human. For him, only a few hours had elapsed since the mission arrived. He wasn't happy about being dragged back up, apparently."

Alander could imagine. He remembered Russell well enough, although they'd never been friends. He'd gone through entrainment on a hard science ticket, whereas Alander had strictly generalized. When he pictured him in his mind, he saw a tall, scraggy man with black, wiry hair, prone to long, furiously defended silences.

Another difficult contact, Alander mused. If it wasn't functional unreliability, as in his case, the Spinners seemed to look for people with inbuilt restrictions on information flow. More often than not, they picked the traitors UNESSPRO had insinuated into the missions. How they identified them, though, no one had yet managed to work out.

"What else did Sothis say?" *Have you and the other members of your little cabal voted me out of the loop yet?*

"I'll fill you in when you get back," Hatzis said. She rarely appeared in conSense transmissions beyond the confines of the mother ship, but he could hear the smile in her voice.

"Caryl . . ." he began.

"Screwing with your head is one of the few pleasures left to me, Peter," she said. "At least grant me that."

He allowed himself a laugh, then, as she fed him the coordinates and he relayed them to the hole ship AI. The Starfish might have decimated the human race, but there was still hope left. That was what the settlers—the ones who wanted to take what humanity had left and hunker down in the few habitable worlds they'd found—were feeding on. Down that route, the only source of conflict would be between the survivors themselves. Hatzis and Alander were the most prominent of those: the first person to establish contact between one survey team and another, and the sole survivor of Sol. Perhaps it would be best, he thought, to ease back on the arguing—in public, anyway.

At least she was offering the public something, whereas he had nothing but nebulous fears and equally nebulous plans. Until he had a clear alternative, he supposed that Cleo was right and that he should, perhaps, cut her some slack.

His train of thought was broken by a sudden lurch of the ship that almost threw him off the couch. The stomach of his artificial body leapt to his throat as the ambient gravity in the cockpit shifted wildly beneath him.

"What—?" he started, clutching at his seat to keep himself upright.

"We have arrived," said the hole ship the same instant the wall screen cleared. Alander saw a wild profusion of angular silver shapes ahead of them: many-pointed stars spinning and exploding in a rush of energy out of a bright central light source coming toward him.

"Get us out of here! Now!"

The view went black as the hole ship jumped. It lurched again, only this time the entire ship shuddered violently. The noise in the cockpit and the vibrations he could feel through the floor suggested someone was scraping a giant saw across the alien vessel's smooth hull.

"I have suffered minor damage," announced the hole ship blandly.

"Can you still relocate?"

"Yes."

"Then take us back to Athena—quickly! If we're lucky, we might still be able to beat them there."

He got up from the couch, every muscle in his body quivering. Adrenaline coursed through his body as he replayed the fleeting image of the silver ships over and over in his mind.

Starfish.

Despite only getting a brief glimpse, he had no doubts about this. There was no mistaking the knife-slim lines of those ships; even measuring kilometers across, they were lightning fast and as maneuverable as anything Alander had ever seen. The emissions were either a trap or a side effect of their arrival in the system. But where had they come from? What had brought them to Head of Hydrus? And why now?

The journey back, as with the journey there, would only take less than a minute, but for Alander it was an intolerably long time. He paced about the cockpit, racking his brain to understand what was happening while waiting impatiently for the wall screen to clear. This was the only indication that they were at the end of a journey. During the jumps themselves, there was no actual suggestion that the ship was even moving at all. He was protected in the heart of the ship like a mollycoddled child, ignorant of just about everything important to do with the world around him.

When the hole ship did finally emerge from wherever it went between locations in the real universe—some physicists had coined the term *unspace* to describe the state—Alander was rigid with tension, holding his breath as he stared at the wall screen. As soon as he saw the silver and black framework of the *Michel Mayor* hanging before him, apparently undamaged, he was gesticulating, boiling off his excess energy in a vain pretense that it

would make a difference to how quickly things happened
next.

"I want a line opened *immediately* to Caryl Hatzis!"
Maybe there was still time—*if* they moved quickly
enough.

Her image appeared in the screen: dark, stocky, and
frowning.

"You're early," she said with surprise. "I thought—"

"The Starfish are here!" he cut in urgently. "We need
to upload the *Mayor* immediately!"

"Starfish?" Her frown deepened. "But we haven't used
the communicator. They couldn't have—"

"Let's not analyze this now, okay, Caryl? They're on
their way, and I don't know how much time we have. We
need to move, Caryl—*now!*"

Time was moving so slowly for him that when she
hesitated just for an instant, as though she was about to
question his judgment, he found himself balling his fists
and wanting to scream his frustration at her: *Move it, or
you'll all die!* But then she was suddenly moving faster
than he, ramping up to four times the natural clock rate
of the *Mayor*, spouting orders in unintelligible gibberish
too fast for him to even follow.

A window opened in the wall screen, indicating that
information had started to flow from the *Mayor* to the hole
ship. He glanced anxiously at it and found biological and
astronomical data, not people. He almost called Hatzis to
say, *What about the people? Get them out first!* But time
was of the essence, and he had no idea how long it would
take to upload the contents of the survey vessel's memory
banks to the alien storage devices. Perhaps it would only
take minutes. Or perhaps, he thought, the gifts could do
it more quickly. A minute was a long time under the circumstances; any time he could save might be crucial.

He was halfway through the first syllable of an inquiry
to the hole ship when the first of the Starfish appeared
around Athena.

The screen flickered as the hole ship announced: "Taking evasive action."

"No, wait—"

The view changed as they jumped to a higher orbit, away from the survey vessel. The upload from the *Mayor* ceased, broken in midflow. Alander gripped the back of the couch as the first Starfish killing vessel was joined by two more. The three of them streaked around the blue white globe below them in a display of fearful energy, peppering the biosphere and inner orbits with red darts that burned white when they exploded. The ten orbital towers of the gifts with their golden spindles in geosynchronous orbit came under heavy fire, three of them blossoming in quick succession like short-lived nova.

"Take us back to the *Mayor*!" Alander shouted. "We have to do something!"

The hole ship relocated just in time to catch the edge of one of the darts. The screen went blue, then black. The hole ship seemed to roll end over end for an instant, then relocated again.

"Taking evasive action," the hole ship repeated.

"What happened?"

"The *Michel Mayor* has been destroyed," the AI replied shortly. "We are under attack."

The hole ship bucked beneath him. Battered, disoriented, Alander clung to the couch as though it was a life jacket.

"Caryl?" he called. "Cleo?" It was futile, he knew, because they were already dead—as he would be, too, if he didn't get out of there fast.

The screen flickered back to life. For a moment he saw nothing but stars—just long enough to think that they might have outrun the alien ships—but the brief peace was shattered by the arrival of a weapon last seen in Sol system: a sphere of oddly shaped silver missiles popping into existence around the hole ship, high-energy weapons at the ready, closing in like white cells around an invading virus.

"Taking evasive action." The hole ship's mantra was barely audible over the deep rumbling that shook the entire craft. It felt to Alander as though the walls were being torn apart around him. "I have suffered damage."

It was all happening too quickly. Alander's thoughts were disjointed and confused. The hole ship was in real danger of being destroyed if he stuck around any longer. Should he run? Save his own skin? *Could* he run, given that the Starfish seemed to be following him everywhere he went in the system? How far did their light cone spread? he wondered. He might jump into another trap— and just one more might be enough to finish off the damaged hole ship. He would have to jump a long way to feel safe, and that would take time. And while he was jumping, he couldn't send a message.

There was only one reason to stick around that he could see. It was vital, too, but was it worth dying for?

While the hole ship jumped through unspace, he thought about the sunset from the high point of Athena. Perhaps if he hadn't stayed there so long, if he had investigated the emissions earlier, as Caryl had asked, they might have had more time to do something about the Starfish attack. He might have saved the others. The thought that he had brought about the deaths of his friends and colleagues simply by being stubborn made him feel nauseous, but it also helped him with his decision about what to do. He would have no more deaths on his conscience.

"Send a message to Sothis," he instructed the alien AI. "Tell them . . ." He stopped to think. Timing was everything. He didn't know how long the hole ship would last if he told it to stay put long enough to send a message. They were getting only a second or less between each relocation. He would have to keep it brief.

"Tell them the Starfish have attacked Head of Hydrus without provocation," he said. "Their tactics have changed." He added, "No one is safe anymore," before instructing the hole ship to compress and send the message next time they relocated.

He didn't have long to wait. The screen cleared to reveal scenes of wild energy release. Strange forces roiled around the hole ship, tossing it like a soap bubble in a hurricane. Around him, Alander felt rather than heard the gonglike ringing of the ftl communicator as the message was sent, as though he was in the middle of a giant church bell. The ringing stuttered momentarily, and the interior illumination of the cockpit dimmed. Then the hole ship seemed to gather itself and the ringing resumed. A second later, it was done.

Alander's uncertainty cleared that very instant. He had done his duty. *Now* he could get the hell out of there.

On the screen, vast silver shapes overlapped like scales as they swooped in for the kill.

"Get us out of here!" he shouted. "As far away as you can!"

"Taking evasive action," said the hole ship. "Sustaining damage." Alander lost his grip on the couch as internal gravity failed entirely. "Concentrating available resources on emergency priority maintenance. Unable to take evasive action. Sustaining—"

The screen flickered and died at the same instant as the hole ship's voice. The lights turned red. One segment of the cockpit tore away, leaving him exposed to the blistering energies of the attack.

The last thing he saw was the invisible membrane of the I-suit boiling away under a purple light and his right forearm melting painlessly back to the bone.

1.1.2

*Sixty-seven light-years away, but at the very same mo*ment, the message from Athena arrived. The hole ship permanently stationed in the heart of McKenzie Base, Sothis's main habitation complex, resonated like a drum and conveyed Peter Alander's voice to the one person listening.

Caryl Hatzis felt her legs lose their strength for a moment, and she sat on the couch to listen uneasily to Alander's troubled words.

"The Starfish have attacked Head of Hydrus without provocation. Their tactics have changed." A slight hesi-

tation conveyed any number or emotions—tension, fear, determination, perhaps even resignation—then: *"No one is safe anymore."*

And then silence.

Hatzis clenched her flesh-and-blood fist and brought it to her chin.

"Fuck," she said after a few moments of thinking it through. The message had been intended for her, she was sure, but it had also reached every ear within two hundred light-years. There was no recalling it now.

The hole ship resonated again as another message suddenly thrilled through the hole ship's chassis.

"This is Gou Mang." It was Hatzis's own voice, belonging to an older engram from the system 58 Eridani. "Message received."

Nothing more was said.

The message was brief and to the point, but it was all the Starfish would need to get a fix on their location. She just hoped that her engram from Gou Mang hadn't been fool enough to have called from anywhere important. But then, if she couldn't trust herself, who could she trust?

She waited in silence for a response to come in from Head of Hydrus, from the colony called Athena. But as the seconds ticked by into minutes, she knew there would be no reply from Alander. He was already dead, along with everyone else in the colony.

She also knew that Gou Mang, or maybe even someone closer, would check out the Head as soon as possible to verify the contact. The earliest she could expect such verification, though, would be in a few hours. The closest colony was in HD203244, thirty-odd light-years away. Even at a hole ship's impressive rate of speed, it would take half a day to get there.

For now, she would have to take Alander's message at face value. Everything had changed, and no one was safe anymore.

"Fuck," she said again, driving her fist into the couch.

Out of the 1,000 UNESSPRO missions, barely 100 had been catalogued in the two weeks since the fall of Sol.

To date, there had been 60 failed missions; 21 Spinner drops; 13 Starfish kills, complete with markers; and six missions that had arrived intact and been untainted by alien contact. Nine missions had experienced anomalous contacts that were still under examination. With every Spinner drop discovered, the facility of the human remnants to examine the status of the remaining survey missions increased dramatically, and the job became that much more achievable— if not still daunting, in the face of the odds. Even with alien technology on their side, and with the number of catalogued systems increasing rapidly, they were still only a handful of survivors in various states of decay.

And the Starfish front kept rolling onward, snapping at the heels of the Spinners and destroying everything touched by their gifts. The colonists on Athena were just the latest victims of the Starfish attacks.

What made this one more unsettling for Hatzis was that she had been there only within the last few days. One of her engrams had been on the *Michel Mayor* and she had spent a full day with her, discussing the issues confronting the human race. To date, she had found a dozen copies of herself among the colonies. All were equally precious, although the older ones, like Gou Mang, tended to be more obsessively fragile, closer to senescence and therefore better for dangerous missions like the one to Athena. She was happy to indulge them, but at the same time unwilling to risk any part of herself. The Starfish detected every message sent via the Spinner ftl communicators; anything in the vicinity of the transmission would be destroyed if it remained behind long enough. That was how the Starfish had found Adrasteia and Sol— and Varuna and any of the others unlucky enough to test their communicators before being contacted by the survivors. It was all a matter of timing, catching the colonies post-Spinner and pre-Starfish. Until now, anyway . . .

Heavy footsteps resounded along the gantry leading to the hole ship hangar. She looked up.

"You heard?"

"Yes." Peter Alander strode through the hole ship's air-lock and into the cockpit without breaking stride. His was a very old genus of vat-grown body that had been standard issue on the UNESSPRO missions; more robust and slightly stockier than a natural human body, its skin had a faintly olive hue and sported no body hair at all. He inhabited his body permanently, cogitating exclusively, when required, through a series of processors installed in the body's skull instead of operating it from remote as was originally intended. Over it he wore one of the gray habitat jumpsuits they had found on Sothis, and over that was the ever-present shimmer of the Spinner I-suit. Her eyes, modified long ago to see in a much wider spread of frequencies than many of the UNESSPRO scientific instruments, had no problem discerning it.

She couldn't help but think of him as the closest thing to genuinely human company she had left—although that might have simply been because she had known him longer. The first and only engram to contact Sol prior to the Starfish invasion, he had been on the verge of a complete mental breakdown when they'd met. A slight scrambling of his internal processes by a random element she had introduced—a procedure she had conducted without his knowledge—seemed to have quashed some of the more dramatic symptoms, but she could never quite tell what he was going to do next. Maybe that was why she tolerated his company over that of the other engrams.

"What should we do?" he asked, coming to a halt before the hole ship's wall screen as though experiencing some sort of revelation from the alien vessel. "Should we withdraw everyone from the area?"

"Who do we have there?"

He fell silent for a few moments as he consulted the mental checklist that he, like she, kept of every colony the survivors had contacted. His thoughts moved with glacial slowness compared to her own, but she liked to keep him feeling useful.

"There's the *Sagan* in Beta Hydrus, of course."

She nodded; that was the latest colony they'd found, the one called Bright. Alander still tended to think in terms of missions rather than worlds named, whereas she preferred to acknowledge them by their colony name. "Then there's the *Davies* in Zeta Reticuli, the *Chandrasekhar* in Alpha Mensa, the *Tarter* in BSC8061, the *Smolin* in HD113283 and the *Bracewell* in HD203244. I think that's it."

She did her own quick mental check and nodded in agreement. The area around Athena that Alander was referring to, less than fifty light-years across, represented not quite 1.5 percent of the thirty-three million cubic light-years of space covered by the UNESSPRO survey. They'd been lucky to find so many active missions within that space. Four of the seven, including Head of Hydrus, were Spinner contactees; there were others Alander hadn't mentioned, which had already been destroyed by the Starfish.

"I don't think we have the resources to move all of them quickly," she said.

"Who says we have to move quickly?" asked Alander. "It could be days, even weeks if the Starfish are searching stars systematically."

"We don't know *what* they're doing, Peter. This could just have been a fluke, an unlucky accident."

"Don't give me that." His expression, when he brought it round to face her, was one of extreme skepticism. "You know what the odds against it are like."

She did. On an interstellar scale, solar systems were minuscule things, more scarce than fish in Earth's long-gone deep seas: the odds of hitting one at random, let alone one of the few inhabited by humans, were vanishingly small, as pointed out ad nauseam by the mid–twenty-first century's anti-SETI movement.

"Then somehow we screwed up," she said. "We let something slip. The Starfish can't be idiots. They'll be looking for mistakes."

"Exactly. And they're listening to everything we say."

"There's no evidence to suggest they've managed to translate our transmissions," she shot back.

"Maybe there is now," he said, cheeks flushing slightly.

"You're arguing for evacuation?"

"No, not until we have more data, at least. Where would we put everyone?"

"Sothis has room."

"And what if the Starfish come here, Caryl? What then?" His lips tightened. "We won't be safe *anywhere*."

"Better an acceptable risk than being dead," she said soberly, holding his stare long enough to reinforce the challenge, then dropping her gaze.

This was where they differed. Each of them had a clear idea of what was acceptable and what wasn't. It was just that, at the end of the day, she thought *she* was right.

"So we're supposed to sit here and wait? Is that it?" He paced around the cockpit like a caged animal. "Caryl, one of me just died."

"You weren't alone, Peter." She felt annoyed that he was claiming the attack on the *Michel Mayor* as some sort of personal tragedy. "There was a Caryl Hatzis on that mission, too. As well as a Cleo Samson, a Kingsley Oborn, a Michael Turate, a—"

"For Christ's sake, Caryl," he snapped. "I *know* that. That's not what I'm saying."

"Then what *are* you saying, Peter?"

"There's more of you than there is of me," he said. "You're—"

He stopped, his mouth left hanging for words that seemed to have stuck in his throat.

Although there had been more Peter Alanders sent by UNESSPRO, the fundamental instability of his engrams had reduced their effectiveness. The Alander sent to the Head of Hydrus was so far the only other one that had survived any length of time, so in that respect, she could sympathize with him. Nevertheless, she was curious as to what he'd been about to say she was.

"I'm what, Peter?" she said. *Lucky? Ungrateful? Spoiled?*

"It doesn't matter."

She sighed. "Then tell me what is it you want to do about this."

"I don't know." He exhaled heavily, shrugging. "We don't have many options."

"That's been the case all along," she pointed out.

"So nothing's changed. Is that what you think?"

"Not at all," she said. "I simply disagree that the change is as fundamental as you think."

He looked at her from beneath furrowed brows and shook his head. "Bullshit."

With that, he turned and walked from the cockpit, his footsteps booming as he crossed the gantry and headed back into the habitat. She didn't need to hack into his senses to work out where he was going, but she did anyway.

The observation platform overlooked the dried-up bed of a sea that would have been roughly the size of two Pacific Oceans, before it boiled away. Sothis was a dead world that had once held life. The fierce illumination of Sirius, blazing high above on its slow arc across the sky, had stripped the planet of its water just as significantly complex organisms had appeared. The salty crusts left behind by the oceans held the remains of numerous kinds of single-cell life-forms. According to the experts, given a less harsh climate, another billion years might well have seen creatures walking Sothis's rocky shores.

But those same experts who had first studied Sothis were themselves now extinct. The McKenzie Base habitats were all that remained of a senescent engram colony, sent from Earth in 2050 along with all the other UNESSPRO missions. Sirius's close proximity to Sol meant that the *David Deutsche* had arrived less than sixteen years after it had left Sol. Nearly 100 years had passed since then, and the engrams who had established a base on the system's one Earth-like world and seeded the system's other planets with monitoring stations had all degraded.

The only things that remained of the colony were their machines. Even the numerous artificial bodies with which they had populated the habitats had died, one by one, as the minds behind them had ceased giving them orders to eat and repair themselves.

Engram breakdown wasn't pretty to watch, and Hatzis had avoided studying the colony's records too closely. She had made sure Alander had seen them, though. Engrams might have been adequate copies of the mind of a human being for short missions, but they simply weren't adaptable enough to survive more than a few decades. They couldn't cope with the changes that inevitably came as a by-product of life. As small errors or random mutations built up in the code that generated them, higher definitions resisted the subtle new pathways each mind wanted to follow. Instead of adapting, the engrams clung to the way they had been, to the selves they had left behind on Earth years ago. Psychosis was inevitable. If they weren't shut down from the outside, they entered a state Hatzis had heard described as brainlock and ceased to function. When they reached that point, there was no repairing them. It was, she supposed, a sort of natural death for this particular sort of artificial mind—so the term *senescence* seemed particularly apt. Whether it was possible to reverse the aging process, she wasn't sure. Alander's continued existence suggested that maybe the randomizing was doing him good, but the experiments she was conducting with various copies of herself had yet to yield any clear-cut results.

All she needed was time, though. Only thirteen days had passed in the real universe since the destruction of Adrasteia, but for her, thinking faster, that was the equivalent of several months. She had shown her engrams ways to cheat the processing budget on the survey missions, so they were working faster, too. Combined, her extended self was working inefficiently but exhaustively on various projects designed to ensure humanity's long-term survival. All she had to do was live through the coming weeks by avoiding the Starfish as much as possible, and then everything would work out. She would solve the senescence problem, she was sure; then, using Spinner technology, she would unite all of her various parts and commence working on what she would ultimately become. Whatever that was . . .

Alander's eyes tracked across the dust-filled basin of the dead sea. Upraised rib cages of long-dead sea beasts, Hatzis mused, seeing what Alander saw, would have been much more evocative of the life that had died here than the occasional footprint preserved in the salt crust near the habitat's egress airlocks. The structure was large enough to hold a community of several dozen people and boasted two shuttle landing pads and the base of what might have been, given time, an orbital tower.

Sothis wasn't a Spinner contactee; by the time the aliens had appeared, the very last of the colonists—Faith Jong—had been dead for almost thirty years. Hatzis remembered Jong as a petite software specialist interested in bonsai and late twentieth-century popular music. It was hard to picture her as the crazed engram that had loaded herself into the operating system of a small fusion reactor and sent the contained nova within critical in order to drive out the darkness creeping over her mind.

Faith Jong's memorial was a crater two kilometers wide on the far side of the planet. Thankfully, the explosion hadn't harmed the main installation, which now served as the counterintelligence base for the remains of humanity. It combined Spinner and human technology, the latter a mix of 2050 and 2150, depending on what resources were available at any given time. It orbited a star that wasn't typical for human habitation and sat slightly ahead and to one side of the projected Spinner advance. It had a population of two, but if circumstances had their way, that figure would rise considerably.

"I know you're watching me," said Alander.

Close, she thought. Through his senses she could see not only the view but hear the whisper of the wind brushing outside of the habitat, feel the cool smoothness of the nanofactured metal rail Alander was holding with both hands, smell the dusty air that had circulated the lifeless habitat for three decades before their arrival, and taste the saliva in his mouth. She couldn't see him, but she could experience him a thousand times better from the inside. She could even read his thoughts if she wanted to. Only the fact that such familiarity would ruin what little companionship he offered stopped her from doing so. And the fear that his resistance to her plans would turn out to be built on sand. She needed a devil's advocate as much as she needed her other selves.

"Perhaps this does change everything," she said, placing her voice as a whisper into his ear, "but at the same time, it changes nothing."

"Of course it does," he said. "It changes the way we feel about things, Caryl."

"Peter, until this happened, our greatest fear was that someone would make a mistake. Just one transmission from the wrong place would bring the Starfish down on us. But if the message from Athena is right, then we could be damned either way now. It's out of our hands. There's no point in running anywhere, because nowhere is safe."

"There's no sense digging in too deeply, though," he said less stridently than before. "We need to be flexible, to be able to move fast if we need to."

"Oh, I agree," she said. "And I'll draw up contingency plans while you're gone."

That surprised him. "You're not coming?"

She shook her head—unnecessarily, she realized, as he couldn't see her anyway. "No," she said. "I think it's best that one of us stays here to coordinate things. When Thor comes with the hole ship, she can go with you instead. That'll save you dropping her off on the way."

She felt his brow crease into a frown. "And Thor is . . . ?"

"HD92719." She indulged the question, even though she was sure Alander knew very well which system the Thor colony was in. Given the number of different versions of her she had to deal with, she had adopted the posthuman custom of calling them by the places they had come from. To the others, she was Sol, the sole original human remaining in the universe.

"Will you work with her?" she asked.

"Will she be up to it?"

"Of course she will, Peter," she said tiredly, thinking, *She'll be a damn sight more stable than you.* "And she has her own body, so you won't have to deal with conSense."

She waited while he mulled it over. The question of what the colony of Thor would do without its hole ship was begging. Would he bring it up? she wondered. She would hate to have a dead colony on her conscience, if the Starfish came calling on them, but Thor was far away from Athena, and the work she hoped to do was important enough to justify the risk. And with Alander gone, she would have full access to the hole ship *Arachne*. It would obey her orders, unlike the Gifts, and there were plenty of versions of her out there that needed to be contacted, Spinners and Starfish notwithstanding.

From her higher processing rate, he seemed to take forever to think it over. He stood watching the view, one hand toying with the pendant he wore around his android body's neck. It consisted of a simple disk made of densely packed carbon, one side reflective, the other carved with barely a dozen words. It read:

LUCIA CAROLE BENCK

2130.05.17

"Bliss was it in that dawn to be alive."
(WORDSWORTH)

Alander had found it orbiting 53 Aquarius, an empty solar system between his home colony, Adrasteia, and Sol. He carried it with him out of loyalty to Lucia's memory, she supposed, although his hope of ever seeing her again must be dwindling. She had yet to reach any of her target systems, out of all the solo missions she had been on.

Or perhaps, she thought, the slow turning of the disk in his fingers was a gentle reminder of mortality.

Eventually, he grunted his consent. "Whatever," he said. "You're getting hard to tell apart, so I guess it makes no real difference to me who comes along."

He let go of the rail and stalked off through the habitat, perhaps assuming that this would put him beyond her observational range. It didn't, of course, but she chose not to go with him.

Returning to herself, to her self-imposed isolation in the hole ship *Arachne*, she looked down at her hands, where they lay folded in her lap. They were flesh and blood, or the closest thing to it that had survived the Spike in Sol system; they weren't composed of cells grown in a soup and assembled en masse, differentiating as they went. She was *human*.

That set her apart from all the others. She felt it keenly. As much as she played it down when she encouraged them to work together, the truth was impossible to ignore: she was the product of 150 years of experience and biological technology a century in advance of anything UNESSPRO had had. She simply wasn't the same as them.

But Alander had the gall to suggest that he couldn't tell them apart . . . ?

She smiled. *Ah,* she thought, realizing: *An insult.* That was good. He wouldn't normally resort to personal attacks when he couldn't get what he wanted. The fact that he had this time suggested she must have been getting to him. Was it the argument, she wondered, or the randomizing of his thoughts she had introduced? Either way, it was an interesting development.

Sol uploaded the change of plans the moment Thor arrived in the secondary dock. Thor wasn't happy about it.

"This is bullshit, Sol," she said, trying to keep a lid on her annoyance but failing. "I didn't come all this way to baby-sit."

"Try to think of the bigger picture, Thor." The original Hatzis's voice was placating. "It makes more sense this way."

Thor glowered at the image that came with the words via conSense. The Caryl Hatzis who had survived Sol had done so with a grace her UNESSPRO engrams had never known. She was slimmer, her skeleton was better structured, and she carried herself with confidence. Compared to the circus freak body Thor had been decanted into, she looked like perfection, damn her.

But envy aside, Sol was right. It made sense that she should go with Alander. It also made sense that she be mobile in the same way he was. It was just her bad luck that she had drawn the short straw.

"No word from Athena yet?" she asked, deliberately moving on from the subject. Sol had told her about the message they'd received from Head of Hydrus on her arrival. She hadn't heard the transmission from the dying colony while in transit.

"Gou Mang should be there soon," said Sol. "Before you leave, why not wait with me over here for news? Then, if we do need to broadcast instructions, you can make a detour along the way."

With the lack of anything better to do, Thor accepted Sol's invitation and made her way from her own hole ship to *Arachne*.

The Sothis habitat was spacious and airy compared to the underground structures her crewmates were building on their colony world. Thor was mainly ocean, apart from two diamond-shaped continents and a smattering of islands. The storms were ferocious. She had thought she might welcome Sothis's arid bleakness, but she was already finding herself missing the distant howl of the wind and moisture in the air. Here the air smelled of nothing but mummification.

Arachne was identical to the vessel she had flown from HD92719. It had the same cockpit interior, right down to its smell. The AI, when it spoke, had the same voice. She experienced an odd feeling of *jamais vu* as she walked through the airlock to find someone different there, as though returning to a home she now found unfamiliar. Her original was sitting on the couch in exactly the same pose as the image she'd seen in conSense.

She looks like a queen waiting to receive guests, Thor thought, resisting an urge to genuflect.

"So, where is Peter?" she asked.

"Getting ready," replied Sol.

Thor frowned. "Packing? What does he think he's going to need?"

"He places great importance on his physicality. It anchors him. I find it simpler to indulge him than to fight him in this instance."

Thor snorted a slight laugh and shook her head. "I remember him from entrainment camp," she said. "They indulged him there, too. He was their favorite son, their star pupil. He could have gotten away with murder if he'd wanted to."

"I think you'll find he's different now," said Sol. Her eyes were gray, almost disturbingly human-looking. There was no hint at all of the furious processing taking place behind them. "Besides, we must be tolerant. He just lost his only active copy, and we need him on our side."

"Not as much as we used to," she said. "The Gifts have shown they're prepared to talk to others, now."

"Yes, but only in the absence of Peter," Sol returned, admiring her own copy's narrow-mindedness. Alander was a hero, at the very least, for getting off a warning in time.

"The contact for your mission was Donald Schievenin. He was also the UNESSPRO spy, right?"

Thor nodded and shrugged at the same time. "Nobody's perfect," she said. "But *Peter* . . . ?"

"Quiet. He's coming."

Sol stood as Alander's artificial body walked up the access ramp and into the cockpit.

Thor's body was a match for his in size—both dwarfed her original—but hers had retained the XY body type that was a hangover of the artificial genome's male origin.

Some effort had been made to sculpt the final result into forms resembling their original shapes, but they had ended up with the same eye and skin color. They looked to Thor like brother and sister. *Frankenstein's twins,* she thought wryly.

"Hello, Caryl," he said, shaking her hand. Her name sounded oddly out of context with her original standing beside her. "Welcome to Sothis."

She nodded stiffly. "Thank you, Peter."

"If it makes you feel any better," said Sol, "he's not happy you're going either."

Alander looked as unnerved as she felt by the admission. "Let's just say," he said, "I don't like last-minute changes of plans."

"You've had hours to get used to it, Peter," said Sol. "And since when have any of our plans ever been written in stone? Like you said earlier, the Starfish force us to be flexible."

"Not just the Starfish."

"All right. The Spinners, too. We need a better idea of where they are as much as we need to stay alive."

"Agreed. If that was your only motive for sending me away, maybe I'd trust you."

Thor felt as though she had walked into the middle of an argument. "Fuck that," she said. "Is it going to be like this all the way to Groombridge?"

He turned his attention to her. "Don't worry about me," he said. "I'll behave. It's not you I have a problem with. Not yet, anyway."

She was about to tell him precisely what he could do with his attitude when *Arachne* began to vibrate with the ringing tones of an ftl message.

The cockpit fell silent as all three stopped their bickering to listen to the transmission the hole ship was about to relay.

"This is Gou Mang in Head of Hydrus," the message began. "Athena is dead. I repeat: Athena is dead. The gifts are down, and the *Michel Mayor* is gone. There are no signs of surface life, no observatory beacons—*nothing.*

Not even a death marker. Everything's just . . . dead."

Gou Mang hesitated, and Thor heard all manner of unspoken tension in the silence. *What is it like to see a colony destroyed?* she wondered. Alander had seen it, as had Sol. Sol had witnessed all of that and more! The destruction of Earth during the Spike, then the destruction of its magnificent remnants by aliens—

Gou Mang finally came back with: "There's nothing we can do here. The Starfish can't be too far away, either, so I'm getting out of here in case the fuckers home in on this transmission and come back to clean up."

The transmission ended there, but the silence in *Arachne* extended until Sol let out a heavy and troubled sigh. It was only then that Thor realized she, too, had been holding her breath.

"That's it, Thor," said Sol sullenly. "We have visual confirmation: the Starfish have changed their tactics."

"What about the missing marker?" asked Alander. "Could that be significant?"

They both stared incredulously at him. His concern for the marker seemed trivial, given what they had just learned. Then again, she thought, perhaps it was easier to focus on something like that than the death of an entire colony.

"I don't know, Peter," said Sol, coming around the cockpit and putting the couch between them. "Maybe Gou Mang arrived too early." She shrugged. "The most important thing is still to plot the progression of the Spinners. We have enough hole ships now to continue surveying the systems around us. We can afford one to jump ahead, to see how far the leading edge is from us. If we're going to warn the Spinners about what's going on, then we have to know at least roughly where they are."

"Especially if the Starfish are starting to eat into us from behind." Alander ran a hand across his eyes.

He was tired, stressed, that much was obvious. Was he unstable, too? Thor didn't like the idea of spending a week or two cooped up in a hole ship cockpit with some-

one constantly on the edge of a nervous breakdown. But
then, her original had done it and survived, so she figured
she could also. Perhaps it would become some kind of
rite of passage that every version of Hatzis would one day
have to endure.

"The sooner we get started, the better," she said, more
in response to her train of thought than anything else. "I'm
ready whenever you are, Peter."

He nodded once. "Then let's get this over with," he
said, turning and walking out of *Arachne* without looking
back.

Thor tore her eyes from his receding back to look over
to her original. "Is he always this charming?"

Sol shrugged slightly. "And then some," she said.

Thor extended her hand, and Sol took it gently in hers.
The contrast of olive artificial skin and pale human flesh
was shocking, as was the discrepancy in size between
their limbs.

I'm a freak, Thor mused as she followed Alander to
her colony's hole ship. *And she's a goddess, in more ways
than one.*

1.1.3

Six days later, Alander was regretting his promise to be-
have. As *Pearl* relocated without incident for the twentieth time that week, in a system classified as AC +48
1595-89, he found himself wishing for an excuse to start
an argument. It would certainly have helped the time pass.

AC +48 1595-89 consisted of a G-type star corresponding almost precisely to Sol, right down to the sun-
spots creeping across its face, plus seven planets
occupying various positions along the spectrum between
rock and hydrogen. There was a fat gas giant with rings;
there were numerous moons; there was an asteroid belt
and a cometary halo; there were deserts and clouds and
ice; there was an Earth-like world in the habitable zone.
But there was no sign of the mission sent to study it.

Pearl, like every hole ship, was equipped with standard radio and laser broadcast equipment. Alander scrolled through the visual data while Hatzis went through the motions of trying to hail the mission.

"This is Caryl Hatzis of UNESSPRO Mission 154, *S. V. Krasnikov*, hailing UNESSPRO Mission 707. *Frank Shu*, do you read me? This is UNESSPRO Mission 154 hailing Mission 707. If you can hear me, Vince, please respond."

Vince Mohler was the civilian mission supervisor of Mission 707, in charge of operations once the survey vessel had arrived in-system. He had also been in charge of the *Paul Davies*, one of the first successful missions Alander and Hatzis had found following the destruction of Adrasteia. They had encountered him in various roles in a number of other systems as well. It was hard to imagine him being dead, let alone feel any sense of loss, when he was still noticeably active in so many places.

That was the problem, Alander thought. There might be hundreds of missions left, each with thirty crewmembers, but all those people were really just the same sixty people copied over and over again. He was beginning to feel suffocated, one of the very few singular people left. With the death of his sole remaining stable copy in the Head of Hydrus, he was alone again. *Would anyone miss me if I died, too?*

"No sign of any gifts," he said, shaking the thought. Once he would have lingered over the data coming in from the planets in the system, but he was becoming desensitized to the thrill of exploration. He had seen dozens of similar systems in the previous weeks, and many of them had been dead, like this one. AC +48 1595-89 was a time waster. It would be catalogued with the others; its suitability for future colonists would be noted, so Hatzis and her supporters would have somewhere to live when the settlement faction got their way; the failure of the mission would be a footnote added somewhere at the bottom of the file. Then he could move on.

"Do you think we should bring *Pearl* in closer?" Hatzis interrupted her broadcast to look at the screen.

"I don't see the point," replied Alander. "There's no one here."

"What about the Starfish?" she asked. "Any evidence of visitation?"

Alander shook his head slowly as he examined the data. "No debris, no hot spots, no suspicious gas clouds, no death marker."

"Damn it," she said, then cycled through the message one more time before resigning herself to the fact that there was no one around to hear the message anyway.

He could understand her frustration. The exploratory mission to the Spinner front had generated ambivalent data at best. *Pearl*'s first two ports of call, near neighbors Groombridge 1830 and 61 Ursa Major, had contained successful missions untouched by either Spinners or Starfish. Alander and Hatzis had ejected messenger buoys in each system, microsatellites designed to bring the UNESSPRO missions up to date without requiring *Pearl* to stick around too long. From there, *Pearl* took them to numerous other systems along the projected front. Many of them had either failed from senescence or simply failed to arrive altogether, including those sent to Tau Ceti, BD+14 2889, Altair, Mufrid, and a high-profile mission sent to Castor and Pollux. Half of the double mission to Procyon and Luyten's Star had succeeded, and it had been contacted by the Spinners. Gamma Serpens and BD+14 2621 were likewise Spinner drops, thankfully caught in time before they brought the Starfish down upon themselves. Apart from those few active colonies, though, there was just an automated monitoring station around Barnard's Star to report. Alander doubted any of it would help pin down the Spinners' progress with much greater accuracy than they already knew.

He performed a quick mental calculation.

"We have an hour to the next transmission," he said. "I suggest we wait to hear it, send our own update along with the usual warning, then get the hell out of here."

"In that case, we might as well spend the time collecting as much data as we can." She shrugged. "Has to be better than sitting around twiddling our thumbs, right?"

Alander didn't argue; it was her call. They had spent their time in the hole ship so far trying their best to maintain both distance and politeness. He didn't know what her original had told her back on Sothis, but she hadn't brought up the issue of colonization even once, and he had no intentions of rocking the boat now. Not until he'd come up with an alternative, anyway.

He found himself missing his copy from Athena more than he had expected to. They had met on only a couple of occasions, but that had been enough to cement their relationship. The same but different, they had both struggled with Overseer processing problems and were trying to keep their thoughts together as best they could. Their plans to discuss Sol's intention in more detail had been put to a dramatic end by the Starfish, and Alander sometimes wondered if his other self had experienced any blinding revelations at the last moment, if suddenly everything had become clear.

Hatzis instructed *Pearl* to take them to a medium polar orbit around the fourth planet and, moments later, the hole ship had relocated smoothly to this location. They performed a cursory sweep for transmissions of any kind from their new position but quickly gave it up for a lost cause. Instead, they concentrated on gathering data about the planet, adding it to the many other examples they had of worlds that might one day be capable of supporting human life.

The globe was unevenly split between land and sea, with only a few small oceans in the northern hemisphere. The southern hemisphere was richly vegetated, relying on deep reserves of groundwater to preserve the water cycle. They christened it Ea, a Babylonian deity whose realm had been the sweetwater ocean under the Earth. It seemed appropriate, Alander felt, as did claiming it in the name of Sol, rather than either of the UNESSPRO missions. Alander didn't know when there would next be an active government residing in the human home system, but he wasn't prepared to give up on the idea just yet.

The familiar ringing of the ftl communicator brought an end to their brief survey of the planet. The broadcast was scheduled to coincide with midday on Sothis, although it might be broadcast from anywhere, and more often than not, it contained little of interest to their mission. But they listened to it when they could, anyway, to see if anything had changed.

Caryl Hatzis, the voice of hope for many, began the transmission with her usual spiel: "This is an open broadcast from McKenzie Base, Sirius, to all UNESSPRO missions within range of this transmitter. Do not reply until you have read the entire contents of this message. We are the sole survivors of the human race, and we are united by the goal of rebuilding. Our primary task at the moment is to locate those colonies that have survived and been contacted by the alien race known as the Spinners. All life is precious. All resources are valuable. To ensure that nothing else is lost, we *must* cooperate in this venture—even if it is to be our last."

There followed the standard introductions to new colonies that might have received the gifts but not been contacted by other survivors, warning them not to use their communicators except from their hole ships in positions well away from their home systems. After that, there was the plea to both Spinner and Starfish, requesting the opening of diplomatic channels as a matter of some urgency. Until either of the aliens talked to the humans whose paths they were so dramatically crossing, there was little the survivors could do to prevent the ongoing catastrophes. The long-term goal for all species was peaceful coexistence within human-surveyed space.

Attached to the message were data files containing the current state of the human survivor network. Alander glanced at it and saw that their last update had been included, along with data gathered from the fringes of surveyed space, where other missions were exploring. A handful of new Spinner drops were also highlighted. Starfish attacks were noted, too, as was their change of tactics, although not in any great detail. A careful perusal of the

latest attacks suggested that three more systems had fallen
to surprise invasions, one of them the mission found in
Beta Hydrus, the *Carl Sagan*, yet there was no talk about
evacuation. Alander wondered if Hatzis was trying to play
down the new development in order to further her own
plans or whether she genuinely wanted to avoid an over-
reaction.

Also embedded in the data was something intended
specifically for them: "We have a message from Groombridge saying that the Spinners arrived two days after you
left. The colony on Perendi did everything your messenger buoy told them to do, and everything went smoothly.
Yesterday, though, they were buzzed by one of the anomalies and managed to capture an image. See for yourself,
but I think it looks like one of our friends from Varuna."

The transmission carried a picture of a modified hole
ship, its black cockpit encrusted with strange growths similar to barnacles or coral. It was shown silhouetted against
the bright gold hull of one of the spindles, blurred as
though in fast motion.

The message went on, "As usual, the anomaly departed
when hailed, but not before giving the colonists a bit of
a fright. They'll keep an eye on the colony in 61 UMA
to see if the Spinners or the anomalies go there next. Who
knows? We might be able to get the jump on them, this
time."

"And do what?" said Alander dubiously.

Hatzis didn't reply; she was listening to the continuing
message: "Peter, in your last report, you expressed a degree of uncertainty for the benefits of continuing your
mission. But I'm asking you to seriously reconsider coming back too soon. We need scouts along the front—now
more than ever, in fact. You are our closest agents to 61
Ursa Major and a possible Spinner/anomaly occultation.
Please stay in the area for a while longer. If we do get
any news, we may need to act quickly."

And that was that. There was nothing more he could
do, unless he planned to hog-tie Thor and take command
of *Pearl*. He waited restlessly as she broadcast a brief

reply to accompany the little information they had discovered on the system. When she had finished, he sat down beside her on the couch.

"So," he said, "where to next?"

"You choose," she said. Her mood was subdued and morose. "Somewhere nearby, though. I don't want to be too long out of contact."

Yes, he thought, *mustn't disobey orders.*

"I need a change," she said. "All these systems are starting to look the same to me."

He consulted the star chart in the hole ship's memory and compared it against the UNESSPRO mission register. One name stood out. He changed the view to external cameras, then panned around until he had found the direction he was looking for.

"There," he said, pointing to the brightest star in the sky. "That's where I want to go."

"Vega?" she said, frowning. "But there won't be much to see. Any proplyd would have been dispersed long ago—"

"I know that," he said. "And UNESSPRO knew that, too, but they sent a mission just the same. The truth seekers won out on this one, I guess."

She was about to say something, but he cut her off. "Anyway, that's my decision, Caryl."

She shrugged. "Data is data, I guess."

"Exactly," he said. Then, not wanting to give her the chance to change her mind, he addressed the ship's AI: "*Pearl*, take us to Vega, twice standard orbital insertion." He didn't know the habitable zones of a blue A0V variable, and he wasn't about to take any chances. They were still unsure just how much punishment the hole ships could take. "Advise ETA."

"Two point nine hours," the AI reported. "External."

"Okay, *Pearl*," he said. "Do it."

The screen went blank as the hole ship got under way. He turned to Hatzis next to him, wondering what she intended to do during the three-hour trip, and caught her staring vacantly toward the empty screen, her gaze lost somewhere between her and it.

"Are you all right?" he asked.

She came to life, then, meeting his eyes. "What?" she asked distractedly. "Oh, I was just reviewing data."

"Are you sure?" Even though he had known several incarnations of Caryl Hatzis, Alander found it hard sometimes to read the woman as an android. The muscles of the face were a profoundly complex and subtle barometer of personality; and the slightest change could have a profound effect. Half the time he didn't recognize her at all, let alone know what she was thinking. Or when she was lying.

She stood. "I'll be in my cabin."

"Reviewing the data?" he asked.

"That's right," she said and walked from the cockpit.

Alander came to get her before they relocated. He had spent the jump lying on the cockpit couch listening to a selection of music from various alien races, courtesy of the Gifts' Library, piped directly to his ears from the hole ship's AI. He wasn't so much enjoying the unusual sounds as fascinated by how much they differed from what his own species regarded as music.

She opened her eyes when she noticed him watching her from the archway to her tiny cabin.

"You look relaxed," she said.

"Just conserving my energy," he said. It sounded better than *bored out of my mind.*

She laughed lightly. "For what?"

He shrugged. "Who knows what we might find in Vega?"

"It's an astronomical curiosity at best," she said. "We'll be lucky if anything remains of the cloud it coalesced from."

He rolled his eyes and went back to the cockpit, calling over his shoulder: "We'll be there in five minutes!"

He was performing stretching exercises when she appeared. Sitting on the couch while he utilized the empty space behind her, she crossed her legs and waited.

"The *Matthew Thornton*, wasn't it?" he asked, fishing for conversation.

She nodded. "Registered as UNESSPRO six six six, believe it or not."

"Really?" He hadn't noticed that. "How would you feel getting *that* mission?"

"Out of 1,000 missions, one of them had to have that number; 23 Boötis got unlucky thirteen. It doesn't mean anything."

He touched his toes. "Maybe the devil himself will be there to greet us."

Hatzis didn't comment. She just kept her attention fixed on the screen.

"Relocating," said *Pearl*.

Vega blossomed on the screen, a powerful blue white star with a highly variable output that peaked every three hours or so. Alander couldn't tell if it was on an up- or downswing of its cycle, but was nonetheless impressed with its brightness. Hatzis had been right, of course: with that sort of energy blasting through the solar atmosphere, it was unlikely the cloud of gas it had condensed from would have been stable enough to form planets of any kind.

But that doesn't mean the system won't be of interest, Alander mused silently as he viewed the various images the hole ship had taken in the seconds since its arrival. It was a thought that proved true more quickly than he could have imagined.

"What's this?" he said, unnecessarily taking a step closer to the wall screen. The image was of a tortured blob of gas off to one side of the star.

"*Pearl*," said Hatzis from the couch behind him, "zoom in on that feature."

"What the hell is it?" asked Alander, taking a step back again as the image on the screen magnified.

"It looks like a dust cloud," said Hatzis. "Falling into the star against the solar wind."

It did have that look about it—like a sail collapsing slowly to the ground on a windy day. But there was a dense core that made him think it contained more than just gas.

"And look there," he said, indicating another image from a more distant part of the system. "Another one."

This blob had a definite solid core but still trailed a wispy cloud through the intense radiance of the star. It looked almost like a comet.

"Planetary fragment?" Hatzis suggested.

"Perhaps." He called up other images, touching the screen as though it were a manual keyboard. Even up close, the resolution was perfect. "Jupiter mass, maybe not native. A protostar with a solid core that drifted into the system and is being torn about by tides. Do you think it's possible?"

"Possible, yes. Likely?" She shrugged. "I don't know."

Within five minutes, they found four more fragments of varying sizes and a spreading band of rubble that might have become an asteroid belt in an ordinary system. Here, the intense and variable solar wind was causing all sorts of havoc. The fragments were being blasted by radiation and particle winds more dense than anything the planets of Sol would have experienced, even during the worst solar storms. The larger fragment closer in was being blown apart by the wind as much as by the tides, while those farther out were in the process of losing significant percentages of their atmosphere every hour, hence the striking tails trailing away from the primary. Within a few decades, it would all be gone; Alander and Hatzis had timed their visit just right for a truly cosmic spectacle.

It was only while studying the details of the rubble cloud that Alander noticed the tiny flashes of light winking and darting through the debris.

"Do you see that," he asked, "or are my eyes playing tricks on me?"

This time, Hatzis got up to take a closer look at the expanded image. "Little ships," she said breathlessly. "Fuck, Peter, there's somebody here!"

"But that's not possible, surely? I mean, none of the other missions *built* ships like that."

Their eyes met for a second; she wasn't alarmed yet, but she was ready to be. "Perhaps you should start broadcasting your hellos, now."

Before she could open her mouth, an alert sounded.

"Proximity alert," said *Pearl*, its voice even-toned but urgent.

"Where?" Hatzis demanded.

The view changed to point at the sun, but there was nothing visible.

"*Pearl*, what the hell are we meant to be looking—?"

"Wait," said Alander, taking her arm. "There!"

At the center of the star was a slightly different white from the rest of its surface, and the discolored patch was growing rapidly, spreading like a stain. It looked to Alander as though something impossibly white was rushing toward them. Or—

The hole ship exploded out of the screen, perfectly white and perfectly spherical, completely visible only once it had grown larger than the star behind it. The smaller, black sphere of its cockpit spun around it like a bola, trailing sparkling motes in its wake.

"Impact alert," *Pearl* warned.

"Can we dodge it?" asked Hatzis, staring fixedly at the screen as the hole ship swelled to fill it.

"Taking evasive action," said the AI. *Pearl* relocated, but not before a swarm of motes emitted by the attacking hole ship rattled across its hull. There was a sound like hail falling on a tin roof.

"Are we damaged?" she asked, alarmed.

"No."

"But we were attacked?"

"From the data available," reported the AI, "the best answer to that question would be yes."

"What the hell is going on?" said Hatzis to no one in particular. She was prowling anxiously around the couch, glancing at the screen in anticipation of them reentering real space. When they did, it was barely a kilometer away from their departure point, and the hostile hole ship was nowhere to be seen.

"*Pearl*, broadcast the following message," said Hatzis. "This is Caryl Hatzis of UNESSPRO Mission one five four hailing UNESSPRO Mission six six six. We are peaceful envoys representing the survivors of Sol system. Do you read me? I repeat: we are peaceful envoys representing the survivors of Sol system. Please cease all hostilities immediately, or—"

The hole ship reappeared at frighteningly close quarters, emitting another wave of the sparkling darts. They struck with the same furious staccato as before but again did little more than cause the floor to vibrate beneath them.

"Or what?" asked Alander dryly.

Before Hatzis could reply, the attack abruptly ceased. The attacking hole ship stopped dead before them, its midnight black cockpit orbiting rapidly around a pristine central sphere.

A male voice issued into the cockpit: "You're human?"

Hatzis's jaw dropped open in surprise.

"Of course we are," Alander said. "What were you expecting?"

There was a pause that felt much longer than it actually was.

"*Pearl*," Alander said. "That transmission—it came from that hole ship, right?"

"Not as such," was the reply—not from the AI, but from the male voice that had spoken before. "I've temporarily linked our ships—made them semiindependent nodes of the same mind, if you like. That makes it easier to communicate."

"How—?" Hatzis started.

"Hole ships have the ability to cross-talk when sufficiently close. You didn't know they could do this?"

"No. Who *are* you?" she asked, looking around the cockpit as if the answer to her confusion might be found there. "And how the hell do *you* know?"

"The name's Axford," he answered. The voice held a

mixture of amusement and challenge. "General Francis T. Axford. And now's not the time to stand around chatting. Even if you hadn't just told me, I'd know where you came from. Only a bunch of incompetent scientists like you would go about things in such a crazy, half-assed fashion."

Alander's memory worked furiously. The name rang a bell, but it wasn't on any of the mission registers he had memorized, and he didn't recall a ranking general qualifying for the survey program. All the military officers were trained for administrative command. Unless . . .

"Frank the Ax?" he asked incredulously.

The man let out a low chuckle. "My reputation clearly precedes me," he said. "Or outlived me, depending on how you look at it. Either way, I'm—"

"But you can't be," Alander cut in again. "It's not possible."

"Can be, is, and I am," said the man. "Listen, I don't particularly like sitting around in the open for long, so if you want to continue this conversation, then I suggest we go somewhere less conspicuous."

"Where exactly would that be?" he asked.

"Your hole ship has the coordinates, Dr. Alander," said Axford. "I can't actually command its guidance system, but I can tell it where to go. Just give the word, and it will take you there. Don't bother asking it for the exact destination, because I've already instructed it not to tell you."

Alander frowned. "Wait a minute. How did you know that I was—'?"

"Your expression. Like I said, the ships can cross-talk," he replied with obvious irritability. "They can exchange data. But I haven't got time for this right now, people. If you want to talk, then you've got to instruct your ship to follow me in."

"*Where*?" said Hatzis.

"Hermes Base," he said. "My headquarters. Can't you see it?"

Both looked simultaneously at the hellish solar vista on the screen.

"No," said Alander after a moment.

"Good," said Axford. "That's just the way I like it."

1.1.4

*It took some convincing to get Hatzis to follow the ex-*general after the hole ship on the wall screen disappeared. Alander appreciated her apprehensions (making a blind jump into God only knew where, he said, didn't much appeal to him, either), but he argued that the presence of the hole ship indicated that there had been a Spinner drop, and they should find out what they could about it—especially given the fact that nowhere else in the system had they found any evidence of the Gifts. There were no normal planets around which to anchor orbital towers, so they must have used a new design. At least in systems containing alternate gift configurations, the Spinners had had a solid planet to work with. But it was the presence of Axford—former military cost cutter, then senior financial advisor to UNESSPRO—that seemed the greatest lure for Alander. Everyone who had argued for funding prior to launch had crossed swords with him, usually to their loss. There had long been rumors about shady deals and favoritism—but Axford had never been on the survey team register. He hadn't been at entrainment camp. There was no way Hatzis could think of that could have brought Frank the Ax to Vega. Alander, of course, had to hear the explanation.

"It'd be criminal not to," he said. "We have to know what he's doing here—and how he knew about the hole ships merging. And the weapon systems he has . . ." He stopped, waved his hands as though lost for words. "The system is a Spinner drop," he said instead. "We're obliged to make contact."

That was an argument she could accept, if not whole-heartedly. "*Pearl*, you have a destination?" she asked.

"Yes, Caryl."

"Can you tell us where it is?"

"I have been instructed not to."

She shook her head, resigning herself to the fact that she couldn't leave in good conscience. "Take us there, then."

Barely a minute later, they relocated in hell.

*Light of every frequency assailed the hole ship. Giant up-*wellings of gas or liquid—Hatzis couldn't tell which—circulated around her with surprising turns of speed. If the information Axford provided was accurate, then the scale of what she was seeing was enormous. And while she didn't believe everything he said, she was sure he had no reason to lie about this.

Hermes Base was *inside* the largest planetary fragment, close in to the pounding brightness of Vega. Its immediate surroundings consisted of a turbulent mix of elements, stirred by the tides and its own internal collapse. Torn between coalescing into a new planetoid and breaking apart altogether, it seemed the most unlikely place in which anyone would ever consider hiding a base. Which was exactly why Francis Axford had chosen it, she imagined.

She and Alander followed him via conSense deep into the fragment's churning interior, letting him take her on a sightseeing tour designed more to impress than to actually inform. Hermes Base turned out to be not so much a base as a distributed network of work points that combined to perform all the functions of something more rigid. Parts failed constantly, but there were so many replacements at hand, and more constantly being built by nanomachines, that the loss was barely noticed. The fierce melting pot of the fragment was a rich source of elements and energy for the manufacturing process.

"I've been here over seventy years," Axford was saying as he showed them around. His image was of a slight, gray-haired man dressed in a loose-fitting black suit, with a lined face that belonged to someone's grandfather, not a high-echelon hatchet man. "Seventy years; remember that. I had all of this in place long before the Spinners arrived."

"And when was that, General?" asked Alander.

"Two weeks ago," he said.

Seventy years, Hatzis thought, *and not a trace of senescence.*

"What happened to the crew?" she asked.

"They never even made it on board," he answered. "It was all faked. We made it look like the *Thornton* left with a full complement, but there was no one else aboard except me and the others, and I soon got rid of them."

The offhand manner in which he spoke about killing sickened Hatzis. "You make it sound as if you did little more than delete some unwanted data."

He laughed at this. "Well, it could hardly be regarded as murder," he said. "They were only copies, after all. Look, this was a one-man mission from the start; that was the way I'd originally intended it, and I indulged attempts to change my mind only as a temporary measure."

"So you're basically a stowaway and a mutineer, is that it?"

He laughed again. "Absolutely," he said. "But I prefer to think of it in terms of expediency. We were all in this for ourselves. I just acted first."

"Who *were* the others?"

"Entrainment techs, policy makers, a senior ministerial aide, a dozen or so people from within UNESSPRO itself. No names. I needed them to get me aboard the program. After that, they were irrelevant. One ship was all I asked for, and that's what they gave me. It didn't matter *where* I was going; I just wanted to get out before the Spike hit."

"You saw it coming?" asked Alander from the hole ship. Still unable to withstand conSense for too long, he was following their progress by less intrusive means.

"Everyone with eyes did," said Axford drolly. "It's just that no one knew what to do about it. That's partly why UNESSPRO was founded, you know: to get *something* out before the crunch came. But there was only so much we could slip past the serious science payloads. A few missions out of the thousand aren't what they appear to be. Don't ask me which ones, because I don't honestly know; the idea was to keep them secret so no one or no *thing* could follow. If the others survived their journeys, they'll be working out what to do next, just like me."

Hatzis thought of the anomalies seen by such colonies as Perendi in Groombridge 1830. Everyone had assumed that they were of alien origin. Now she wondered whether they could be the work of one of these pre-Spike human outposts. But she doubted it. The first had appeared in the very early days, when only a few Spinner drops had been recorded. That didn't give anyone enough time to find and modify hole ships in the way that had been observed, and it still left the motive behind the death markers hanging.

"This is what I wanted to show you," murmured Axford. They zoomed through an incomprehensibly large gobbet of molten rock and into a startlingly clear space. "This is my hangar, if you like," he explained. "I keep *Mercury*, my hole ship, here. Before that, it was a materials repository. The walls are reinforced with a flexible membrane designed to bend with the pressure but not burst. No matter what shape the space within assumes, it's perfectly safe."

Six golden structures occupied the center of the bubble, linked together and anchored to the walls by delicate-looking strands of black material. There was no doubt they were essentially the same as the gifts found elsewhere in surveyed space, different from the others only as a result of their different environment. Their shapes were just as intricate and mysterious, and Hatzis was sure that the contents would have been the same also.

"You're telling us that *you* built this place, not the Spinners?"

"You don't have to sound so surprised," he said with a smile. "Seventy years is a long time, and I didn't have to put up with interdepartmental arguments to get things done. If I wanted to do something, I just did it. End of story. I actually started redesigning the *Thornton* in transit. By the time I arrived, I had patterns for fifty of myself ready to transfer into hardware. The first thing to do was find raw material and exploitable energy—and as you can see, Vega has plenty of both. Within a year, all fifty of me were running at triple time, all following the same agenda: better, more, faster. I mass-produced probes, mining vessels, and processors to run them all. I seeded myself everywhere to avoid catastrophic breakdowns. I burrowed into the planetary fragments to diversify as much as possible. Vega is pretty volatile, and even down here, I've had problems. But it's nothing I can't recover from. I'm spread far and deep enough to bounce back from almost anything. Got three bases now: Hermes, Apollo, and Terpsichore. I hope you won't take offense if I don't tell you where the other two are."

"You're the contact, then," said Alander. "The Spinners chose you when they came?"

"There was no one else to choose from," said Axford with a sly grin. "They had to talk to me."

Hatzis shook her head, still trying to come to terms with what Axford was telling them.

"So you're a group mind?" she said. "A gestalt?"

"Absolutely not," he said indignantly. "They're all me. I don't want to be anything I'm not. That's the surest way of losing control." His expression sobered. "That's how I noticed the old-age problem, you know. It showed up very early on because I was fast-tracking. My earliest copies started to behave improperly. The later ones worked out what was going on and erased the corrupted ones, the failures. Kept the memories, of course, and installed them in fresher copies, so I haven't lost anything. We're a team, here, and we don't tolerate weak links."

They paused in their wild flight around the gifts long enough for Axford to lean in closer to Hatzis and to part his hair, revealing a numeric tattoo on his scalp.

"That's my iteration number," he said. "One thousand twenty-second Francis T. Axford to roll off the production line. You can have any color, as long as its blood is pure."

"But you're—" Hatzis started, but was quickly cut off by Axford.

"I'm talking metaphorically here, Caryl," he said in a tone that suggested he was disappointed he'd had to point this out. "And I'm not racist, either, in case you're wondering. The only ideal I believe in is *me*."

So I see, she thought.

"What are your long-term plans?" asked Alander.

Axford smiled innocently, as if to say, *What makes you think I have a plan?*

"To survive, of course," he said. "Isn't that what everyone wants?"

"Yes, but not everyone uses the same methods," said Alander.

Axford laughed. "You're wondering if I'm going to stay put here in my little pocket of space, is that it? Or whether I might burst out of here like a cancer and spread like a contagion across your own region of space." His smile widened. "I'm tempted, you know, just to see your reaction. And how you would deal with something like that. If you handle me as badly as you're handling the bug-eyed monsters, I'd be all over you within a decade."

"What does that mean?" asked Hatzis.

"Ever since I turned on my communicator, I've been listening in on your broadcasts. How you guys have managed to last as long as you have is beyond me. They're slaughtering you out there."

"So, how *should* we be handling this, then?" said Hatzis with irritation. His smugness was rapidly starting to piss her off.

Frank Axford didn't answer straightaway. Instead, their inward plummet came to a halt—or seemed to, anyway. The journey had been entirely conSense-generated; Hatzis's body was still in *Pearl*, sitting on the couch. The hole ship itself was docked next to Axford's *Mercury* in the very bubble they had just reached, virtually.

The illusion folded around them, became a spare, gunmetal-gray room, as bare of personality as an interrogation room, with two aluminum chairs for them to sit on and a 3-D tank for Alander. Axford's physical presence was slight compared to Hatzis's artificial body, but his personality more than made up for that.

"To start with," he said, "the Spinners gave you gifts, which you have used to blithely announce your presence to all and sundry throughout the galaxy. You might just as well have sent a message saying, 'Here we are, please come and get us.' It was the stupidest thing you could have done."

"We've been extremely cautious with the messages we've been sending out lately," Hatzis said, defending Sol automatically.

"Yeah, but only after you had your butts kicked a couple of times," Axford shot back. "And look at the cost of your recklessness! Those Spinner installations are enormously valuable—more valuable than the colonies, if you want my opinion. Humans can be copied; the gifts can't. What's the current estimate of the leading edge of the Spinner migration, 61 Ursa Major? At that rate, they'll be gone in weeks. And once they're gone, it seems pretty clear that they're not going to be coming back. If we lose what we have, that's it. Mommy's not going to take pity on us if we drop our ice cream in the dirt, no matter how unfair we think they're being.

"The BEMs you call the Starfish don't care about us, either. And they're not stupid. For whatever reason, they want us gone—totally and unequivocally *gone*. They don't even wait anymore for your invites; they're actively seeking us out, and *that's* a scary notion. These are superintelligent beings, remember. It's not like they're going to miss a system here and there. They are not going to stop until we've been eradicated from every single system. Yet you guys jaunt about surveyed space like you're on some divine mission and don't do a goddamn thing about it! You're ignoring the real problem, and until you *face* that problem, it's just going to keep coming back and biting you on the ass."

Hatzis did her best to keep a lid on a rising tide of resentment. "So what's your solution? Wait it out? Hide while everyone else suffers? Great scheme, Frank."

"Hey, don't knock it, lady," said Axford with a smile. "It sure beats sitting around like ducks and painting little targets on yourselves. Besides, I'm talking to you now, aren't I?"

"And we're listening," said Alander, casting a cautionary glance in Hatzis's direction. Axford's chair creaked as he sank back into it. "Okay, good, because I have an opinion I'd like to share with you. I think you're wasting valuable opportunities—or at least you *seem* to be, if the information in your broadcasts is anything to go by. None of you are treating the situation as a military threat, which is precisely what this *is*. And until you do, you're always going to be at a disadvantage." Glancing over to her, he quickly added, "I'm sorry, Caryl, but it's true."

It was his tone that bothered her more than anything else, she decided, and not necessarily what he was actually saying.

"Go on," she forced herself to say.

"Okay," he said, shifting his position to fully face her. "Look again at the Spinners; bug-eyed monsters number one." An image of the drop in Vega appeared behind him, rotating to highlight key points as he spoke. "Ten obvious gifts, among them a communicator, a hole ship, a library, an art gallery, a map, a surgery, a science hall, and a materials lab. The hardware makes up the rest of the gifts: the Gifts themselves, a machine for making the skyhook cables, the instantaneous transport system. But what's all this stuff *for?* What's it supposed to teach us? Judging by your transmissions, you lot look at it and see knowledge for its own sake. You search the library for answers to questions, rather than solutions to problems."

"But the Gifts don't know anything about the Starfish," she protested. "We've already asked."

"A number of times, actually," Alander added.

"As did I," said Axford. "But that doesn't mean they *can't* help. Look." He leaned forward. "Me, I'm an old army man, right? I've been trained to think certain ways. That makes me one-eyed and obsessive, agreed, but it also gives me a tremendous focus in situations like this. Whether you like it or not, this *is* a military situation, and it needs a military mind to cut through it. When I look at the hole ship, I don't see a convenient means to contact neighbors and issue invitations; I see a scout vessel that is superbly designed for covert operations. When I browse the materials lab, it's not to marvel at strange forms of matter and energy we barely suspected existed; I'm looking for something as hard as the spindle hulls, just in case we ever need to get through one of them. And when I search the library, it's not for information on alien cultures or the black hole at the center of the Milky Way; it's for anything I can use to throw at the enemy, whoever they are and whenever they come. Because, believe me, they *will* come. And when they do, I want to be as ready for them as humanly possible."

Something like revulsion rushed through her. "You're using the gifts as weapons?"

"Absolutely," he said without shame or apology. "Where did you think I got that trick with the darts I used on you when you arrived here? It didn't work, but it might have. Give me another day, and I'll have something else. There are hundreds of me working simultaneously on this: researching, building, testing. Laser batteries I already have—in fact, I've had them since 2080, just in case something came this way after the Spike. In a week, I'll replace them with something much more powerful. Something, maybe, to make the next visitors I get think twice about staying."

"You can't really think that fighting the Starfish will work," said Hatzis.

"I'm not talking about the Starfish right now."

"Then who *are* you talking about? One of the other colonies?" she said. "You're in contact with someone else?"

"He's not talking about the other colonists," said Alander, a look of realization on his face. "Tell me, General, just who exactly did you think we were when you attacked us earlier?"

"Exactly?" said Axford. "That I don't know. Do you?"

"What the hell are you two talking about?" Hatzis asked irritably.

"The anomalies," Alander answered. Then, to Axford: "If we're talking about the same thing, then yes, we've seen them—but we have no idea who or what they might be. We think they leave artifacts behind in systems that have been destroyed by the Starfish."

"And they've been here?" Hatzis asked.

Frank the Axe nodded. "Even tried to take my gifts," he said. "They didn't manage it, of course, but I thought they might try again—maybe even come back with reinforcements. Then you two appeared. I was better prepared this time. You were lucky I called off the attack when I did."

"You *fought* them?" Hatzis exclaimed.

"I had to," said Axford. "The bastards were trying to take what was mine. Just because I was lying low, waiting to see what they were, they thought I wouldn't be able to resist. But they were wrong. I don't like people who prey on the weak."

Hatzis wondered if there was anyone Axford *did* like.

"Would we be able to look at your data on their hole ships?" Alander asked.

"I'll do one better than that," said Axford, the sly grin returning. "I can even let you take a look at the sample I managed to capture."

1.1.5

The hole ship looked little different than any other. It appeared in the far reaches of the system, hung there for a second as though looking around, then relocated closer in. A twisted, strangely modified cockpit issued from its side, orbiting in a disconcerting ever-changing fashion. It radiated an air of readiness, like a fencer shifting restlessly, with sword upraised.

Then it moved. With no noticeable emissions, it went

from standing still to blurring motion in less than a second. The image wobbled as its source tried to keep the hole ship in view. It failed just as the craft's destination came into view: a blue black world under a yellow sun.

"Impressive," said Alander. "We've been looking for attitude controls in the ones we have."

"You won't find them," said Axford, freezing the view. "They have to be added. But it isn't as difficult as you might think. The hole ships actually have an inertialess switch you can activate to make it easier to push them around. Although I'm guessing you haven't found that, either?"

Alander nodded. There was no point lying. One look at *Pearl* would have told Axford that already.

"Where was this footage taken?" asked Hatzis.

"Van Maanen 2," said Axford. "One of the inner systems; not far from your McKenzie Base, in fact—"

"I know it," said Hatzis. "We've been there."

Alander didn't correct her. He and her *original* had been there in the very early days, when scouting for a location for their headquarters, but this version of Hatzis never had. Van Maanen 2 was a dwarf G-type star not far from Tau Ceti and Sirius.

"The mission was dead," Alander elaborated. "But we left a beacon in case someone else came through."

"They did." Axford switched to another image. This one showed the same planet but from another position. In the foreground was one of the golden spindles left by the Spinners. "The usual configuration," Axford went on. "Ten towers, ten installations, one orbital ring. They must have revived someone to act as contact. From your reports I've listened in on, I gather they do this sometimes."

"They do," said Hatzis. "We've had the occasional response from colonies given up for dead. Not this one, though."

"No, you wouldn't have." Another image, another point of view. This one showed an orbital installation of human origin. "This is what they turned their ship into."

"The *Steven Weinberg*," Hatzis supplied.

"As you no doubt saw, they were busy before they died out," said Axford. "But they died out just the same. Watch."

The strange hole ship flashed into view, heading on an apparent collision course with the human installation. A split second before impact, however, it vanished.

"See? The hole ship was trying to get a reaction from the colonists, to see if anyone was home." The recording continued behind Axford's narration. "Clearly, they got no response. For whatever reason, whoever was in there wasn't paying attention. So the hole ship comes back. . . ." The hole ship appeared again, no longer moving aggressively but jockeying to dock with the station.

"How come they ignored *you?*" asked Hatzis.

"I was lying low," explained Axford. Then, seeing their blank expressions, he laughed out loud. "You haven't even worked *that* out yet? Ha! I swear, it's a miracle you lot have survived as long as you have."

Hatzis was clearly about to respond to this when Axford continued with: "Your hole ship doesn't have to arrive completely at its destination before you can start looking around. You can be half in, half out of real space, and the sensors will work. When you're in that state, your profile is reduced to about thirty percent. You can't move, but it's handy if you just want to check things out without being seen."

Alander turned back to the display, more reassured than ever that they stood to learn a lot from Frank the Ax. He watched in fascination as the hole ship's modified cockpit managed to attach itself to the installation. The point it had chosen to adhere to wasn't an airlock, however. The coral-like growths surrounding the cockpit seemed to reach out with droplets or tentacles to adhere to the installation's exterior, anchoring fast to the metal and carbon.

"Looks like they're getting ready to tow, doesn't it?" said Axford.

It did, Alander thought. The cockpit retreated until it was close to the larger, central part of the hole ship and stopped rotating. There was a moment of stillness in which he imagined the alien machine muscles flexing in readiness, then—

"Bang," said Axford softly as the hole ship vanished altogether, taking a sizable chunk of the installation with it. The remains shuddered violently, losing their center of gravity and almost disappearing for a second in a bright gust of frozen air. Then it was tumbling, dead, through its orbit around the planet.

The image froze as Axford spoke again. "It took them six trips to take the lot of it," he said. "By then, of course, someone *had* noticed. There was some ground activity; a satellite changed orbit in order to get a better look. But there wasn't much they could do. Whoever the contact was, they clearly didn't have time to get into the spindles and explore the gifts. The Roaches timed it perfectly."

"Roaches?" asked Alander, turning away from the screen to face Axford.

The ex-general shrugged. "That's what I call them, anyway," he said. "Because they scavenge, just like cockroaches."

"You think that's what they were doing?" asked Hatzis. "Scavenging?"

"Absolutely," said Axford. "When the main installation was gone, the hole ship came back to pick off a few of the larger pieces of junk floating around in orbit. Then they started stripping the gifts themselves. One thing you may have noticed about them is that they're not terribly reducible. You can't take them apart; you can only remove their contents—and then only in places. Your Immortality Suits, for example, are transportable, as are some of the safer materials in the Lab. The art in the Gallery is as well, obviously, but then I personally wouldn't waste my time with such stuff—and from what I've seen, I don't think the Roaches are overly concerned about it, either. They focus on the things that are practical. Things they can *use*. And to that end, the biggest prize is, of course, the hole ships."

He indicated the new image display before them. It

showed two bright circles moving in tandem across the planet and vanishing at the same time.

"They took it," said Hatzis, staring at the screen with her eyes wide. "No wonder we didn't hear from the colony. They would've listened to the beacon we left and known—"

"Don't be so naive," Axford cut in quickly. "The beacon was the first thing the Roaches took out. Whether or not your contact on the planet had the time or the brains to listen to it beforehand, we'll never know. As the Roaches left, they signaled the Starfish."

"What?"

Axford seemed to be enjoying her reaction. "Within a day, all evidence was gone," he said, nodding. "Listen to this." A sound like two bells colliding rang through them. "That's the transmission I picked up through the hole ship just before they left. Sound familiar?"

"It sounds like a transmission we picked up in Upsilon Aquarius," said Alander, "when we were testing the communicator for the first time. After a couple of primary transmissions, we received something in reply, but at the time, we just thought it was just noise or some sort of reflection."

"There have been several such pulses recorded," said Hatzis. "We ignored them for the same reasons. They don't seem to contain any information."

"The Roaches are sending them," said Axford. "I mean, who else could it be? If they were reflections, we would've heard more of them. If it was just noise, the hole ships would have filtered it out. There's no evidence to suggest that the Spinners or the Starfish use this means of communication. And why would they, when there's no way of choosing who you talk to? I'm guessing that such a means of communication would be too primitive for intelligences as advanced as they seem to be. No, these transmissions don't contain any information because they don't *need* to. They just need to be heard."

"And you're that confident it's the Roaches?" said Alander.

"Nothing else make sense," said Axford. "It *has* to be them."

"Those sons of bitches," said Hatzis. Even in conSense, her face was pale. "They're sending entire colonies to their deaths!"

Alander nodded, although he preferred to defer his moral judgment until he had more information. "This would mean they've been active since before Adrasteia was destroyed," he said. "There must have been other systems they've approached for us to have heard their bait signals."

"Exactly," put in Axford. "Who knows how many systems these scabs attacked before you started to get your shit together? Now it's harder for them because you have some vague organization up and running. There are fewer cracks for them to slip through. Even without me to help you, you might eventually have noticed them. And then where would they be? My guess is they don't like to fight if they can avoid it, otherwise they wouldn't be skulking around like this, letting the Starfish do their dirty work."

"Parasites," Hatzis spat. "They're nothing more than fucking parasites."

"*Intelligent* parasites," Alander said. "Let's not forget that. They've worked out how to modify the hole ships. They look different, behave differently. It'd be foolish to write them off completely."

"I agree," said Axford. "When they came here, I stayed hidden, thinking they'd move elsewhere. But they detected the gifts somehow and came in here to get them. The element of surprise only lasted so long. Before they came, I'd have bet good money that no one would get out of here if I didn't want them to, but they *almost* managed. It was too close for my liking."

"What happened?"

Axford smiled. "Now, now, Dr. Alander," he chided playfully. "I'd be a fool to let you know exactly what I'm capable of, wouldn't I? Let's just say there's one less Roach ship to worry about, shall we?" He faced Hatzis.

"You like the sound of that, Caryl? Does that appeal to your all-for-one moral code?"

She looked uncertain for a moment. "I don't approve of violence, if that's what you're wondering."

Axford rolled his eyes. "I don't give squat for your approval, Hatzis," he said. "I did you a favor, narrowed the odds a little. Can't you be pragmatic enough to at least acknowledge that? Would a small display of gratitude be too much of a stretch for you?"

She glared at him as though thanks was the farthest thing from her mind.

"You two deserve each other, you know," said Alander wearily. And they did: multiple bodies, long-term agendas for the human race, definite ideas about morality and their place in the universe.

Hatzis turned her glare on him, then returned to Axford. "What about this sample you said you had? Are you ever going to show it to us?"

"That depends on what's it worth to you."

"Oh, for fuck's sake." Hatzis stood. "Do we have to put up with this bullshit?"

Alander indicated that she should sit back down. "What exactly do you want?" he asked Frank the Ax.

"An ally," was the simple and surprising reply.

"Someone else you can sacrifice when you no longer need them?" Hatzis snapped. "Forget it."

"Not this time," Axford returned evenly. To Alander, he explained, "Look, if the Starfish really *are* going from system to system now, then I'm not safe here anymore. If the Roaches could find my gifts without any problems whatsoever, then I'm guessing that the big players in this game will be able to as well. I need a contingency plan. I need more resources. Ideally I'd like another hole ship— or a whole fleet of them, preferably—but I'm not likely to find one on my own. So I need allies. Specifically, I need someone to help me do something—something I think you might be interested in."

"And you think we should put our differences aside so we can work out a trade?" said Hatzis.

Axford nodded, ignoring the sarcasm in her tone. "I'll give you what information I have on the Roaches in exchange for your help."

Hatzis looked like she was about ready to leave, just to deny him, but Alander couldn't let that happen.

"Well, we can't deny that we need that information," he said. "So unless you're planning to do something we can't agree to, then I think you've got a deal."

Hatzis's face settled into a mask of distaste, and he knew she understood. They *did* need what Axford had; there could be no denying that. Besides, she must have realized that Alander had saved her from making the decision herself, so if anything went wrong, the option of blaming him would always be open to her.

"I want something more substantial than promises to share information," she said. "What about this sample you've been promising to show us? Is it a piece of one of their hole ships or something?"

"Oh, much better than that, Caryl." His smile was wide and predatory. "Hole ships don't blow up, you see. They dissolve like they're made of nothing but air, piece by piece. When you hit one hard enough, when they die, everything on the inside spills out—and if you're careful, or lucky like I was, you can time it just right to make sure none of it gets damaged."

Alander glanced at Hatzis and saw understanding dawn in her eyes, but it was he who managed to speak first. "You caught one of their *bodies?*"

"Even better than that." The view of conSense before Alander began to darken as Axford talked. "Remember, they have access to Spinner technology, just like us. They have hole ships and ftl communicators. In fact, they probably use the libraries to locate suitable stars for our colonies and scout them until the Spinners appear. I'm sure they dipped into the library as I have, seeking new ways to modify their hole ships. But more importantly for us at the moment, they have—"

"I-suits," finished Alander, staring at the figure materializing before them in the darkness.

Axford didn't try to hide his pleasure. "Caryl Hatzis, Dr. Peter Alander, I'd like you to meet my guest, the first alien I've ever had the good fortune to meet in person. I call him Charlie. You'll have to forgive him if he isn't very talkative, though; he really hasn't been himself since he arrived. In fact, I think he might even be dying."

Alander stared in amazement at the gangly, frail looking alien that appeared on the screen. A long silence ensued as neither he nor Hatzis could speak, and it was only broken when Axford glibly muttered, "I don't suppose either of you would have any idea what these bastards might like to eat, by any chance?"

The alien was, to all intents and purposes, right there in front of Alander: living, breathing, solid, but as motionless as a stuffed museum exhibit. He didn't doubt for a second that it was real. After all, what would it benefit Axford to fake something like that? It was too important, too critical a moment in the evolution of humanity. Not even someone like Frank the Ax would invent something like *this*—although there was little doubt that he would use it to his advantage.

But that didn't matter to Alander right then. At last, after many frustrating weeks of dealing with the nebulous Spinners and Starfish, here was a creature he could actually *touch*.

The image rotated so he could see it from all angles. That Charlie was a biped was immediately obvious, but its proportions were all wrong. Its legs were much longer than a human's, compared to its trunk; long, tapering shins flared upward past the knees into enormously strong-looking, triangular thighs. The knees were bent so it looked like it was crouching. Its trunk was barrel-shaped, almost literally a cylinder, with strange, pouchlike folds and flaps in waxy, gray green skin. Partially hanging from this was a coarse-looking vest, while covering upper parts of its legs was a kilt fashioned from the same material. Alander assumed that the garments were decorative, as they offered no real protection. Much like his own, beneath the I-suit.

The creature's forward-mounted arms were folded protectively across its chest, rising and falling with every rapid breath—the only movement Alander could discern. The hands were small and thin, and had several digits sprouting from each, but it was unclear how many there were or how precisely they were jointed. Two flat plates extended from its back. *Vestigial wings?* Alander wondered. They were more like an insect's wings than a bird's, or the sheaths that might once have covered them, at least.

When the image rotated around to the front again, its face captured his full attention. The head was roughly the same shape as a biscuit barrel and seemed smooth all over. There were no obvious protuberances. Instead, it had a marked pattern of pigmentation across its face: stark black lines with a perfect vertical symmetry that reminded Alander of a Rorschach blob. The line of symmetry gave the face a protonose; on either side were blobs that might have been eyes, nostrils, and ears, while a line that stretched from one side to the other could have been a mouth. It was impossible to be certain. For all he knew, the alien could have been wearing a helmet.

"He's an odd-looking fellow, don't you think?" said Axford. "I ran him through the gifts when I picked him up, but there's only so much you can tell without invasive surgery. We'll have to wait for him to die before we can do that, I guess."

Alander caught Hatzis's look of disgust at Axford's comment, but she didn't say anything. She was probably as much in awe of what she was seeing as Alander and wouldn't spoil it by arguing with Axford.

"His biology is very complicated," Frank the Ax was saying. "Some of it might even be enhanced by nanotech or implants. He has analogs of cells and DNA and blood and stuff, but it's all slightly skewed. His genes have six bases, for instance, and his blood is sort of yellow."

"Do the Gifts recognize his species?" Alander asked.

"No, they don't," he said, frowning. "And I find that a bit odd, actually. Either the Spinners deliberately kept him and his kind out of the library, or the Roaches themselves wanted to be kept out of it for some reason. For all we know, he could be a renegade Spinner stealing back some of the booty."

Alander nodded thoughtfully. It was an interesting suggestion. If there were factions within the Spinner race, then maybe they weren't as all-powerful and mysterious as once thought. In fact, they might be no different than humans.

"Where are you keeping him?" asked Hatzis.

"In the hole ship. The *Mercury* has set up an isolated environment for him, based on what we picked up in the surgery, and is keeping him relatively safe. It's not perfect, but the I-suit is doing the rest. For now, anyway. I'm not sure how much longer he's going to last. I think he might be in a coma."

"You keep saying 'he,' " interrupted Hatzis. "You're sure that's its gender?"

"Take a look for yourself."

A series of anatomical images flashed against the darkness behind the alien, settling after a few seconds on a close-up of the creature's genital area.

"Two . . . ?" Hatzis was clearly as amazed as Alander.

"Like snakes," said Axford. "Whoever these guys are, they take symmetry to the extreme."

"What about communicating with him?" Alander asked.

"I tried," he said, nodding to the image display. "See what you can make of it."

More footage appeared. In it, the alien was awake and active, restrained in a small room. It was pacing backward and forward, its legs moving with a disturbingly jerky gait that left no doubt in Alander's mind that it wasn't human. *A person in a suit pretending to be an alien couldn't move like that,* he told himself.

It was clearly agitated. The wing sheaths growing from its back flexed and snapped. This, combined with its long, angular legs and relatively short arms, reminded Alander of a giant grasshopper. But the creature was clearly warm-blooded, and it lacked the carapace, compound eyes, and mandibles of an insect.

Its face was the most startling thing. Transformed from a lifeless biscuit barrel, it was almost unnaturally mobile. Muscles under the skin flexed the patterns of pigmentation into new shapes, breaking the symmetry then re-forming it with unnerving speed. Its eyes, opened, revealed glassy orbs with internal lenses that constantly changed position, like the inside of an antique camera. Its mouth was the slit he'd identified earlier, but it wasn't that of a lifeless dummy. It was extraordinarily mobile, opening and shutting in shapes that had no parallel on a human face. Behind narrow lips Alander glimpsed a yellowish tongue and two rows of protrusions that might have been teeth. And its voice . . .

Alander put his hands over his ears when Axford cranked up the volume. It sounded like a fight between two giant parrots, dropped in pitch.

"Two sets of vocal cords that operate simultaneously," Axford explained, reducing the volume again. "It's not so strange when you think about it. There were species of birds back home that sang this way. You can cram a lot of information into the combined sounds, using not just pitch and timbre but interference and counterpoint as well. I'm sure under other circumstances, it could be quite beautiful, but at this point, Charlie wasn't trying to endear himself to me, I'm afraid. He wanted out. That much was obvious."

"Did you communicate with it at all?" Hatzis asked. Her expression was one of cautious fascination as she watched the alien pounding on the walls of his cell, shrieking in harshly dissonant tones that echoed through *Pearl*. She flinched every time its double voice reached a new peak of intensity.

Axford shook his head. "The language is simply too complicated," he said with obvious disappointment. "Besides which, I didn't get enough of it to make a detailed study. I've had a dozen of me working full time on it, but so far we haven't had any breakthroughs."

Alander looked at Axford in mild surprise. He kept forgetting that there were hundreds of the man scattered across Vega, and yet most of the time he spoke as if there was only one of him. But then, as the original Hatzis had said, that was the problem with engrams: it didn't matter that they were simulations run on software, they were all essentially locked to their original state and could not change. Even if there were a million Axfords, they would all still behave like the original. Deviation would simply not be tolerated.

If only *his* engram had been so robust, Alander thought. Just two out of all the systems they had surveyed wasn't very good odds at finding someone else he could trust.

The symmetry of the alien continued to bother him. "Could it be an artificial body," he suggested, "like ours?"

"Possibly," Axford replied, nodding. "But then, I'd have to see an original before I could tell the difference."

"And that's where we come in?" Hatzis asked. "You want us to go looking for you? To find out where they come from, perhaps?"

He shook his head again. "Frankly, where he comes from doesn't particularly interest me," he said. "It's what he's doing *now* that matters."

A star map appeared, showing Vega and its near neighbors. Some were UNESSPRO targets—including Altair, Kruger 60, and Gamma Serpens—but there were others Alander wasn't familiar with.

"Your clone on Sothis," Axford went on, "she said in her last broadcast that the Roaches had bothered a system not far from here." The map moved to show Groombridge 1830.

"Perendi," said Hatzis, automatically naming the colony. She didn't seem to take offense at her original being referred to as a clone.

"Whatever. You also spotted a number of kills, through here." Axford indicated an area between Vega and Groombridge 1830. "Now, there have been two unsuc-

cessful Roach attacks in the last week, but the bait signals
I picked up suggest they must have been successful elsewhere. And given that it's all happening in roughly the
same spot—cosmologically speaking, that is—I can't help
but wonder if they have a base somewhere nearby."

"But we haven't seen evidence of any alien installation
around here," said Hatzis.

"Nor would you if you were looking in the wrong
spot," said Axford. "But maybe the aliens don't like G-
type stars. They could like M- or K- or F-types instead.
For all we know, they might even go for brown dwarfs,
drifting through interstellar space."

"Surely they wouldn't be able to support life?" said
Hatzis.

"They can support life if their cores are still active,"
offered Alander.

"Maybe," said Hatzis. "But they'd still be damn near
impossible to find."

Axford shrugged. "I'm just thinking out loud here," he
said. "I'm not really suggesting we go on a Roach hunt
just yet. I have another idea."

Alander had thought ahead. "61 Ursa Major," he said.

Instead of looking annoyed that Alander had stolen his
thunder, Axford seemed delighted. "I'm impressed, Doctor."

"Please don't call me that."

Axford frowned. "But that's your title, isn't it?"

"Just Peter will be fine," he said.

Both Hatzis and Axford stared at him for a moment,
Hatzis with curiosity, Axford in puzzlement. The protest
sounded childish and irrelevant even to his own ears, but
each time he heard the title, he felt as if everything he
had done to make his new self stable was being undone
again. "Dr. Alander" had died on Earth in the Spike; he
wasn't entirely sure who *he* was, yet, but it felt inappro-
priate to be addressed by someone else's title. He didn't
think he had earned that right.

If not for us, then for whom?

He had rarely thought of his last conversation with Lucia Benck since the destruction of the post-Spike civilization in Sol system. It didn't have the same resonance as it used to, in the context of the new, hostile universe he'd been thrown into. What did it matter who you were, he thought, when you were only one of a bare handful of humans left anyway?

Axford shrugged. "Okay," he said. "If that's what makes you happy, then Peter it is." He turned to Hatzis. "And what about you, Caryl? Anything in particular you like to be addressed as? Madam President, perhaps? Or maybe I should be swearing allegiance to your Congress of Orphans?"

"How did you—?" Hatzis stopped with a furious flush on her face.

Axford's laugh echoed through *Pearl*. "You really should tell your mother superior to find a better way of broadcasting her secrets," he said. "I'm sure she doesn't want just anyone listening in, does she?"

Hatzis's gazed flicked to Alander, then back. "I've no idea what you're talking about," she said.

Alander observed the exchange with fascination. What had Axford caught Hatzis doing? And not just this Hatzis, but *all* of them. Whatever the Congress of Orphans was, and however the information was being disseminated, he obviously wasn't supposed to know about it. He would have to take a closer look at the broadcasts from Sothis in the future.

"When you two have finished," Alander said, deliberately playing down the matter, "do you think we could get back to the business of 61 Ursa Major?"

"Right." Hatzis was obviously relieved that he was changing the subject.

"If the Spinners are progressing the way we think they are," Alander went on, "then they'll be arriving there any time—with the Roaches not far behind them. So, my guess, General, is that you want to set an ambush, right?"

"Of sorts." Axford brought the image of the alien back into the foreground. "We have here an important piece of intelligence, but he's no use unless we can figure out how to talk to him. The Gifts have no record of this species and therefore no record of their language, oral or written. We could try digging magnetic electrodes into its brain— the regions that were most active when it was shouting before might tell us *something*—but that's a desperate measure, and a short-term one at best. If Charlie dies, for whatever reason, then we're right back where we started."

"Then what *are* you proposing?" asked Hatzis.

"Well, I'm presuming that their hole ships speak to them in their own language and know something about their physical needs," said Axford. "If we can get close enough to one, I can merge the nodes of the AIs and get my hands on that information. Once we've got *that*, I can use it on Charlie here to make him useful."

"You mean torture him?" she asked with distaste.

"If reviving him, feeding him, and asking him a few questions about where he comes from counts as torture, then, yes, I guess we'll be torturing him." Axford's eyes flashed dangerously. "What do you take me for? I'm not in the CIA anymore, you know."

"Yet you deliberately wiped out your crewmates and—"

"Okay, okay," Alander cut in. "Once we talk to it, what then?"

"Then we see what it has to say, I guess." Axford leaned back into his chair with a sigh. "Who knows who these people are? Or what they want? *That* information is our priority, not what we do with it once we've got it."

"But they haven't tried to communicate with us before now," said Hatzis. "Who's to say they'll want to communicate with us at all?"

"I'm aware of that," he said. "But I don't see that we have much choice right now." His gaze studied both of them in turn. "So what do you say? Are you in, or not?"

"What exactly is it you want us to do?" Hatzis asked after a moment's consideration.

"Well, for a start, surveillance will be a whole lot easier with two hole ships rather than one," he said. "We'll need to keep a low profile, otherwise they'll think the gifts have already been opened and move on. Once they *are* there, then you can distract them while I move in. I don't know how long it'll take, so I don't know how long we have to pin them down for—"

"Do you even know whether it's going to work?"

"Of course not," he said. "But I figure it's worth a try. I didn't know I could merge the AI lobes, either, until I tried it with you. It was just an idea I picked up from something in the library. It paid off, and this might, too. If it doesn't work, then what's the worst that can happen?"

Hatzis stared balefully at him. "They'll know how to modify their hole ships, too," she said. "They might also have weapons."

"They do, but they're not invincible." Axford indicated the alien with a smirk. "Charlie is proof of that," he said. "And anyway, they've shown a marked tendency to run when confronted. Unless we force them into a corner, as I did here, then I doubt they'll even want to fight. Like I said, they're nothing but scavengers."

Axford glanced significantly at Alander, and Alander wondered what he was trying to tell him. There was a whole other level to the conversation, all of a sudden.

"Excuse me," he said. "I need a break. The disorientation . . ."

Axford nodded. "Come back when you're ready. Caryl and I will work out the finer points together."

Hatzis looked annoyed but didn't say anything. "What steps do you plan to take to guarantee the safety of the colony?" she asked Axford as Alander disconnected his presence from the virtual conference. There followed a small jolt of dislocation, then he was back in the smooth emptiness of *Pearl*'s cockpit, alone apart from Thor's inert body.

"She's a slippery character," said a voice from behind him, startling him. "You'll have to keep an eye on her. Or, I should say, *them*."

Alander turned on the couch to see Frank the Ax near to the exit, leaning against the wall of the cockpit.

"Tell you the truth," Alander said, standing, "I'm more

concerned about you right now than I am about Caryl."

Axford's brow creased. "What do you mean?"

"I think you have your own long-term objectives," said Alander. "Objectives that might not match ours."

"And just what *are* your long-term objectives, Peter?" Axford straightened and took two steps toward him. "Where do *you* see yourself in a year from now? Or a decade, even? A *century?*"

Alander laughed dryly. "I have trouble seeing ahead a month."

"That's not true," Axford replied curtly.

"Maybe not," said Alander, "but it feels like it, sometimes." He glanced at the android of Caryl Hatzis, sitting motionless on the couch. "Are you sure she's not listening to us?"

He nodded. "Four-oh-six is keeping her occupied."

"I thought his number was ten-twenty-two?"

"It was originally," he said. "Then eight-ninety-two took over negotiations when you arrived in Hermes. Perfectly seamless. I'm three-fifty-eight," he said. "The numbers are chronological, so I'm one of the older iterations. I can feel my algorithms getting a little creaky. When I start making mistakes, they'll be replaced."

"You mean *you'll* be replaced, don't you?"

"Not at all," said Axford. "I am nothing but the sum of my memories and my personality. The personality is identical in its primary form, and the memories can be copied perfectly from engram to engram. There will be no loss of identity."

"But it won't be *you,* will it?"

Axford laughed at his confusion. "You're grappling with philosophical questions that were of no concern to the original Francis T. Axford. Therefore, as you are well aware, they're of no concern to me. I'm the ideal person to found a society like this, you know, because at no point am I bothered by such meaningless concepts as the soul. I am a product of what I do and what I remember. There is nothing else."

Alander put aside the problem for a moment; perhaps,

as Axford suggested, the distinction of who was who—
If not us . . . ?—was irrelevant.

"Anyway," said Alander, "I'm more interested in what it is you're doing rather than who exactly it is doing it."

"And so you should be." Axford's expression sobered as he came around the cockpit to face Alander.

Axford was a product of conSense, but he seemed perfectly real. And surprisingly short in person, Alander thought.

"What exactly is it that concerns you, Peter? You should tell me now, before we agree to work together, because I don't want an ally turning on me in the middle of a tricky maneuver."

Ally, Alander noted. *There's that word again.*

"You said these Roaches are reluctant to fight unless cornered," he said. "I'm assuming you must have trapped them in here when they came to steal the gifts."

"That's right," Axford replied. "There are ways to impede a hole ship's ability to relocate, you see. The exterior of this habitat bubble has been treated to prevent anyone escaping—"

"Anyone?" Alander cut in quickly.

Axford smiled casually. "I haven't said that you're prisoners, have I?"

Alander held his gaze steadily. "So *are* we?"

"Well, let's see what happens when you try to leave," said Axford, his smile widening. He was enjoying the game, splitting hairs with the precision of atomic force microscopy. "We have a very democratic process, here," he continued. "We all come to the same decision because we're all the same person; the votes are invariably unanimous. Could you say the same about your own ragtag collective?"

"There's strength in diversity," Alander defended.

"I know," said Axford. "Which is why I want your cooperation."

"And if we don't want yours?" asked Alander.

Axford smiled faintly. "Unless you seriously disagree with me on matters of policy and the implementation of the same, then you'll leave here unimpeded."

Alander snorted a derisive laugh. "Is that a threat? Agree or be incarcerated?"

"Not at all. I would never waste resources keeping you prisoner for long. It'd be much more sensible to kill you and use your hole ship myself."

Alander could see that Axford wasn't joking. There was no trace of humor in the man's gray eyes.

"But I'm not intending to threaten you, Peter. I'm simply stating a strategic reality: if we can't agree on the basic terms, then it simply wouldn't be safe for me to let you leave. You know things about this establishment that I can't afford to have disseminated—that it exists at all, for a start. If the Roaches or the Starfish ever learned what I have here—"

"They won't even *talk* to us," interrupted Alander. "How the hell are we supposed to pass on vital information about your base here?"

"You actually have to ask that?" He shook his head as if disappointed. "The way you people spray information around, I'd say being paranoid about it would be the most prudent response. Listen, Peter, you people give away tactical information on the location of your bases, your core population, your resources—everything! All you need is for someone with a communicator to crack your encryption, and you're in deep shit, my friend. I have no intentions of being dragged down with you."

As much as he didn't want to admit it, Alander knew Axford had a point. He had once been a staunch supporter of daily broadcasts designed to alert new colonies to the dangers of using the Spinner communicators. But they had changed in content to become something completely different from what he'd originally envisaged. They were becoming bloated tracts of policy and—as Axford had rightly pointed out—tactical information. And if his earlier comments about the Congress of Orphans weren't simply a cheap destabilizing tactic, then maybe there was something else in them, too.

"Why would you bring us here at all, then," said Alander, "if you felt it could be such a risk? In fact, why are you even talking to me *now*?"

Axford smiled. "Your friend here . . ." He nodded to Hatzis on the couch. "She thinks I want to take over the galaxy—spread through it like a plague or something. And maybe she's right: maybe one day I *would* like to do just that. But I know that strength of numbers isn't everything. There could be a billion of me, swarming over your colonies, and all you'd have to do was devise a virus that targets a chink in my personality—and *bam*, you've taken me out overnight. So when you say there is strength in diversity, you're absolutely right. There's a balance, somewhere, where there's more than enough of *me* and just the right amount of everyone else to make us all strong. At the moment, I'm simply trying to find the balance."

"And who, exactly," Alander asked, "is 'everyone else'?"

"That's the billion-dollar question, isn't it?" said Axford, although he didn't offer to elaborate.

Alander stared at him, furiously trying to work out what Frank the Ax could possibly want that he didn't already have. It wouldn't be something as general as safety or security, because Axford thought in terms of specifics. He must have some specific goal in mind, or else taking such risks as inviting Hatzis and Alander to his main base—regardless of what he said about them being unable to escape—made no sense. He needed them to help him do something. And if he was making Alander work out what it was on his own, and without Hatzis present, then the chances were it was something—

The truth hit him midthought and, when it came, he didn't know whether to admire the man's audacity or fear what he could bring down upon them all.

"When you talk about *allies*," Alander said slowly, "you're not just talking about us, are you?"

Axford smiled, clearly pleased Alander had worked it out.

"You're talking about the Roaches," Alander went on.

"You want them to help you do what you can't do on your own."

Alander hesitated on the brink, thinking: *Ultimately it is about security, and there's really only one way to be totally secure.* But it could also be about revenge. "You want them to help you attack the Starfish."

Axford's expression became serious as he nodded and said, "Yes, I do. And if I get it right, it won't be suicide."

1.2.0

EXCERPTS FROM THE PID (PERSONAL INFORMATION DIRECTORY) OF ROB SINGH, UNESSPRO MISSION 639, TESS NELSON (PSI CAPRICORNUS).

2160.9.4–11 Standard Mission Time

The gifts are amazing. Sol has researchers in every colony poking into hundreds of different niches, but I doubt they're even scratching the surface. I remember when I was a kid and people used to talk about the entire Earth's knowledge compressed into a single SSDS unit the size of an apple. Well, I bet the Spinners use something a lot more sophisticated than that to store their data, and the Library is simply enormous. Even with our clunky old memory storage devices, there's enough physical space to hold data from a billion Earths. We could tunnel through such a repository for centuries and not come out the other side.

Nevertheless, we continue to dig away. And at the same time we send robots through the Gallery and collate the images they send back (the layout of each Gallery is slightly different in each colony, for some as yet unknown reason). We chart the stars and planets in the Map Room and marvel at worlds we might one day visit. We poke our noses—gingerly—into dark and dangerous spaces in the Lab, scratching our heads at scientific theories we don't even know how to read, let alone understand.

We are apes let out of our cages and set free to wander the streets of New York. Is it any wonder I feel lost?

The Gifts themselves don't make it any easier, picking just one person from every colony to interact with and refusing to speak to anyone else. Is that evidence of a higher purpose or simply designed to frustrate us? I don't know. But poor old Neil is swamped with requests. He longs to go back into deep time mode and sleep out all the fuss. This isn't his thing at all, poor sod.

Would I feel any different if I were in his shoes? I don't know that, either. All I can do is submit my questions with the others and wait as they inch their way to the top of the list. And then, when I get the answers, I'll probably be as much in the dark as anyone. But it's not as if I don't have enough data to get on with. Everyone has access to the research pool. I can browse freely through Nalini's astrophysical data or Owen's report on the likely load-bearing properties of the orbital ring material. We didn't bring an ethnologist, not expecting to find life anywhere near as advanced as us, but Jene, my fellow pilot, has a secondary specialization in that area. She's making some interesting extrapolations on the races we're finding in the Library. It doesn't tell us much about the Spinners or the Starfish, but it does us good to learn something about *someone* out there.

My secondary specialization is in comparative religions. Right here and right now, it isn't really much use. The gods of Earth are dead. We're just going to have to make up some new ones.

Today I found my first error. The Library lists a culture called the Esch'm (or something approximating that) originating around a type-G supergiant we call 22 Vulpecula, in the constellation of the Fox, about 4,075 light-years away from Sol. There are examples of the Esch'm's art in the Gallery; it looks like someone blew up a beanbag full of multicolored Jell-O, caught the explosion on camera, then sculpted it upside down and hung it from the ceiling, many times over.

I don't get it. The images Gallery Droid 9 brought back remind me of scuba diving under a floating mat of seaweed.

But this has nothing to do with the art, except for what

the label attached to it says. It clearly states that the art
is from 22 Vulpecula and is by the Esch'm. When you
look up 22 Vulpecula and the Esch'm in the Map Room
and Library respectively, you find they are recorded. The
trouble is, the Map Room says that 22 Vulpecula has no
solid worlds, just a close companion star, and the Library
says that the Esch'm actually come from another G-type
supergiant called Azmidiske, in a completely different
part of the galaxy. So, a hole. That makes one. Perhaps
it's not surprising or even noteworthy. Think of all those
billions of Earths' worth of data those gifts must contain!
I keep trying to imagine just how many cross-referencing
errors would be in there if *we* had compiled it. But I don't
think the Spinners are the sort to make mistakes. Either
someone's fooled them, or the data is wrong for a reason.

Lies or honest mistakes? Either way, now that I know
errors exist, *they* have become my reason for being.

Ali came to visit again. Neil had some answers for me;
nothing unexpected, unfortunately. On other fronts,
though, the news is good. The boundary of stealth attacks
moves ever forward—*past* us. It seems we've been
spared, after all. This is a huge relief. Caryl still hasn't
returned from Sothis, so we've had no means of escape,
no matter how unlikely, for three days now.

"The burden of command getting you down?" I asked
Ali. She looked tired.

"You want to swap places?"

"No, thanks." There are other versions of me running
missions in other colonies, but I am deciding that I like
my spare time. "The slower I run, the longer I live."

"Not subjectively. From your point of view, you'll have
just as many years all up. Outside, they'll be smeared over
more time, that's all."

"That's good enough for me. I'm stockpiling, if you
like, against the possibility that we don't get blown to
smithereens. Instead of trying to cram as much as possible
into what few days we might have left, like you, I'm

taking it easy. I'll want them later, if we live."

She found that amusing, I think.

"I thought you gave up gambling," she said.

"I did, but only over trivialities. When my life is on the line, it's a different story."

"It changes everything, doesn't it?" she asked seriously. "Senescence, I mean. Sometimes I wonder why we're struggling so hard when in the end it won't make any difference. We'll still degrade and break down."

"We're programmed to keep fighting. It's that simple."

"You think so?"

"There's always hope of fixing us, remember. The Hatzises will see us right—according to the propaganda, anyway."

"Do you really believe that, Rob?"

"Why shouldn't I?"

"They had engrams after we left, on Earth. They all died, even after the Spike. You'd think the Vincula, or whatever it was called, could have fixed them if it could."

I opened my virtual mouth, but no words came out. She had a good point. She left me with it, and for once I was truly glad that I've been shunted aside, processing-wise, so that others can think faster than I. While they fall apart, I get to hang on a little longer. The Spinners not-withstanding, I tell myself, I'll have the last laugh. Or sob, or gasp, or whatever.

Here's something. It's not an error, but it is interesting. I found it in the data Caryl Hatzis from Sol provided us with. It seems the equivalent of SETI in the early 2080s picked up a series of alien transmissions from the part of the sky containing the constellation Sculptor. Never trans-lated or repeated, the transmissions ended as abruptly as they began. Their source was never determined.

My first thought was that they comprised evidence of the Spinners' passage through space, toward us. As Sculp-tor is in roughly the same direction as Upsilon Aquarius and the other first-hit colonies, it seemed reasonable to assume that the mysterious transmissions could have been the last gasps of a civilization attacked by the Starfish. At last, I thought, we have clear evidence going back more than a few weeks of where the Spinners came from.

Sadly, it isn't so simple. The math doesn't work out. The Spinners are traveling through space much faster than the speed of light; they would have rapidly overtaken such a plea for help. The transmission must have left long before the Starfish arrived for us to have heard it so long ago—which, obviously, doesn't make any sense.

Unless the transmission was intended for us, of course. It could have been broadcast by the far vanguard of the Spinners. If they'd known where they were headed, eighty years ahead, they could have been seeking responses from anyone in the area so they'd know what awaited them. Maybe they sent a probe ahead, like a beacon, to test the water. The trouble with that theory is this: my estimate of where the main Spinner migration must have been at the time those transmissions reached us, given the migration's current rate of movement through surveyed space and assuming it traveled in a straight line, gives an outside guess of 160,000 light-years, almost twice as far across as the galaxy. That's mind-boggling. Who thinks *that* far ahead?

Error number two. This one was so big I would have missed it completely had Nalini not brought it to my attention.

One of the great things about the Map Room is that it shows us the far side of our galaxy, which is normally hidden from our view by dust. We have no way of checking if the stars the map shows us are actually there, but there are some things we *can* check—such as X-ray sources, for example. We've been mapping them for decades. They show up in the Map Room data as black holes, neutron stars, and so on. Most of our guesses were right, which is a relief. At least some of our theories check out.

The trouble is this: there are dozens of X-ray sources in the Milky Way, and all of the ones we knew about check out—except three. Those three don't appear in the Map Room data at all. According to the Spinners, they don't exist. As there is no mistaking an X-ray point source for something else, or missing it, this comprises another hole in the data. Nalini doesn't concur that there has to be something sinister going on, though. Given a choice between blaming the Spinners for fudging the data or thinking we must somehow have cocked it up, she goes firmly for the latter. And I sympathize. I can't imagine what the Spinners are doing out there that needs covering up (using black holes for wormholes? Spinning down neutron stars to generate power?) but I can't let the thought go. Two mistakes could be coincidence. Or it *could* be just one step away from a conspiracy.

1.2

THE COMPANY OF STARS

*2160.9.11 Standard Mission Time
(10 August, 2163 UT)*

1.2.1

The golden light of alien industry played like flames across Caryl Hatzis's face. She'd heard eyewitness reports and seen conSense footage, but this was the first time she was actually *seeing* the Spinners with her own eyes. *It's like watching God in action,* she thought.

Sixty-one Ursa Major boasted no Jupiter-sized gas giant, so the inner system was a mess of post-planetary formation rubble. The major terrestrial world, Hera, had several smallish moons and suffered constant bombardment. A smaller world in a nearby orbit, Eileithyia, had probably been knocked from Hera at some point in the distant past. Hera's surface was a mess of impact craters distorted by tectonic movement and volcanic activity. It was a world of fire, from the furious swirling of its magnetic field to the rumblings of its still-hot core.

Hatzis had anchored herself to one of Hera's small moons. It had an orbital period of nineteen hours with a high eccentricity and was presently the closest solid body to the fourth spindle being built in Hera's geosynchronous orbit. The hole ship was hidden in a nearby fissure. She sat on the outside of the moon, protected by an I-suit and using the senses of her modified body to view the act of creation taking place above her.

The spindle seemed to be growing out of the vacuum: great sheets of golden matter spread and overlapped, creating cavities that seemed—before they were closed from her view—to be filling up with gray masses of creeping technology. Silver cables snaked across yawning gulfs to snap home on distant surfaces to create unusual conjunctions of planes and curves, while around the planet's equator, the incomprehensible length of the orbital antenna reached for the next spindle along. Somewhere above all of this lurked a small mountain of hyperdense material that would act as the tower's counterweight—a dark counterpoint to the awesome golden spectacle below.

No, she decided on reflection. This was *better* than God. Miracles needed no explanation beyond divine grace, whereas science could be explained. She'd seen vast works performed in Sol during and after the Spike, and they, too, had filled her with wonder. The Spinners might have been on a completely different level than the rogue AIs of Sol, but what they were doing here was no miracle. This level of science *was* achievable; the fact that she was watching it now was proof of that. And if it could be done once, then there was no reason why it couldn't be done again.

She nodded quietly to herself as she continued to look on at the unfolding extravaganza taking place on Hera. This was what she wanted for humanity, to attain this level of sophistication, not to be scratching out an existence from the ruins of her civilization. She wanted something *permanent*.

In fact, she wanted more than what the Spinners had achieved here. To look at their wonders being created, it was almost inconceivable that they could ever be destroyed, and yet somehow the Starfish had managed to do just that with seemingly little effort, suggesting a level of technological advancement that paled into insignificance the efforts of the Spinners. If humanity was going to survive and prosper in this harsh universe, then it was to the Starfish that they would need to aspire.

For now, though, she'd be happy to just be able to make contact with either of these two superspecies.

She'd seen what happened to satellites that had strayed too close to the spindles: they were destroyed out of hand.

That, she suspected, was an automatic reaction, no different in essence from the survey vessels' automatic meteor defense systems. But there had to be *some* form of intelligence driving construction, even if it was artificial. If she could disrupt construction in a nonlethal but significant way, she might be able to attract attention to herself. And would the minds behind the building then stop in their relentless push through surveyed space just because of one failure out of the many systems contacted? She could only hope so.

But how was she supposed to disrupt construction? Take *Arachne* and relocate into the heart of one of the spindles? She didn't know if the hole ship could withstand the furious energies it might find in such an environment. It probably wouldn't even allow such a jump if there was the possibility of risk involved.

And if she could get in there, then what? Transmit a message? Deposit an explosive device that might hopefully bring a halt to the whole construction process? She simply didn't know. With every new contact with the Spinners, she felt less as though humanity was being favored by some alien benefactors and more as though they were merely ants trying to attract the attention of a passing human who hadn't realized that the bag of sugar they were carrying was leaking.

Part of her wanted to take the hole ship *now*, to end the frustration of waiting and wondering. If she was killed, then so be it. At least it would be over. Humanity would be reduced to little more than a few scattered engrams, marking time until they died. The responsibility of wanting to preserve and re-create would be gone, for there would be no one left to carry the torch. The race would be effectively finished.

But she didn't move. Her eyes remained fixed on the golden splendor unraveling before her while her fingers grasped comet dust and primordial ash. Her body hadn't needed food for many decades, but right at this moment her insides were burning with a terrible hunger.

If only I could transmit this feeling to the Spinners, she thought. *Surely someone among them could understand this hunger for knowledge.*

Midday on Sothis arrived, and the transmission went out on schedule. She had left Gou Mang, still wide-eyed from the stealth attacks on Athena and the other colonies, to maintain the service. She returned to *Arachne* when the hole ship signaled that all the reports were in. Settling back onto the couch, she flicked through them, one by one. There had been two new Spinner drops, not counting Hera. Five more colonies attacked by the Starfish, three of them without provocation, and nine other senescent or failed colonies had been found close to Sol. Statistical analysis conducted by one of her older engrams confirmed that the Spinners were following a slightly curved path through surveyed space, so their origins couldn't be extrapolated with any great precision. The Starfish stuck to that path like deer to a track—except for the recent stealth attacks, and the attack on Sol, which had taken them many light-years out of their way. The new attacks concentrated on the trailing edge of the Spinners' path, as though the Starfish were systematically searching for colonies where their concentration of kills was the highest. That made sense, she thought, in a grim sort of way.

Three transmissions created a new connection in her mind. Gou Mang reported that a hole ship sent to investigate the forward flank of the Spinner advance had failed to report back on time. She couldn't pin down the exact location of the disappearance, but her best guess was that it had vanished somewhere in the vicinity of pi-1 Ursa Major. Hera was in 61 Ursa Major. The similarity of system names made her automatically check her mental star map. Pi-1 Ursa Major was thirty light-years away. The missing mission—piloted by a version of her from Eos in BSC7914—had been due to finish the previous day. That it hadn't returned or reported was unusual (after all, she was nothing if not reliable), and she couldn't dismiss the possibility that she had arrived during a Starfish attack and been unable to escape in time.

The second transmission concerned an increase in anomalous contacts along the front and flanks. Someone was dogging new colonies, buzzing close enough to be noticed but never sticking around when contact was attempted. They made no overtly hostile moves, but their dogged lack of communication had ominous overtones

The third transmission was the most interesting and possibly the most worrying. It opened a whole new swath of possibilities which, when combined with the other two transmissions, cast everything in a very different light.

Hatzis sat through it twice to make sure she absorbed everything correctly. The reports from her other selves came in densely packed files readable only through the Engram Overseer platform on which all the UNESSPRO missions ran. She literally dived into the heads of the person reporting to experience it firsthand. It was a far cry from the multinode consciousness she had experienced in Sol, but it was a step in the right direction, at least. When surveyed space was empty of dangerous aliens, the possibility existed that she might open the channels of all the hole ships, allowing herselves to communicate in real time, even though separated by dozens of light-years. That would be the beginning of something truly amazing, she thought.

Another reason to use the Overseer files lay in the need for caution. She didn't know if Alander had noticed that the gifts could receive more than one signal at a time and transmit while receiving, but she didn't want to make it too easy for him to pry into her affairs if he did. Given his tenuous grip on reality, he might balk at the idea of diving into someone else's mind.

But then, his disapproval was the least of her worries right now.

From the mind of herself from Thor, whom she had dispatched with Alander to explore the front itself, she learned that she had much more pressing matters to deal with: sabotage of UNESSPRO, deliberate destruction of colonies using the Starfish as an unsuspecting weapon, a legion of Francis Axfords, *and* a race of alien scavengers with two penises, for fuck's sake! She would have happily dismissed it all as a hoax had the information not come from Thor herself—and she had seen it with her own eyes. Aliens stealing gifts before humans could use them, increased anomalous activity, a missing hole ship—and now Axford, Alander, and Thor were planning to ambush a possible "Roach" attack in 61 Ursa Major, the very same system that she was in. She sighed in frustration. Surveyed space seemed a much more dangerous place, if that was possible: being able to predict where the Spinners might strike next was supposed to make things easier, not more complicated.

At least Thor had managed to warn her beforehand. If humanity was going to declare unofficial war against *another* alien species, she supposed it was best if she was there as well. Axford had been reluctant to let her stop midjourney simply to listen to the Sothis update, but she'd convinced him otherwise. *Not* sending a report of her own, she'd said, would only make Sol suspicious, so she had posted a rather bland description of the systems they had visited, not including Vega. Behind that report, she had managed to send a private Overseer transmission that filled in the blanks. Axford, who obviously knew about those transmissions, hadn't tried to stop her, and Alander had said nothing about it at all.

Maybe he was being coy, she thought. But she doubted it. It wasn't like him to keep a lid on his disapproval, and the Council of Orphans was almost certain to garner *that*. She'd always known it would have to go public at some point, but she would have preferred if it had happened at another time. She wasn't in the mood for a civil war right now.

Sol turned her attention to the data flowing in through *Arachne*'s sensors. The gifts around Hera were almost complete. Thor, Alander, and Axford would be in 61 Ursa Major soon—and so too, perhaps, would be these "Roaches" Thor had mentioned. She tried to think of a way she could call for backup, but calling via the ftl transmitter would not be an option until the next Sothis report. And if Eos hadn't gone missing, she might have been able to jump to one of her systems and bring her back.

She silently cursed the Spinners for handing them a means of communication that spoke to *everyone* each time they used it. It was obviously supposed to teach them the principles of such technology instead of just handing it to them on a plate—but fuck, it made life hard! Sometimes she imagined how things would have been if the Spinners had never come—or if they'd come to Sol first. She wondered what the Vincula would have made of the gifts. Perhaps, with luck, they could have used the technology to communicate with or even repel the Starfish. With a million superior minds working on the problem, rather than a few thousand flawed engrams, things might just have turned out very differently indeed.

Hera's primary survey vessel, the Fred Adams, *had as-*sumed a cautionary orbit well away from the gifts. In the sixty years since the mission to 61 Ursa Major had arrived, the crew had set up a network of low-orbital facilities around the volcanic planet as well as establishing mines on various asteroids. All were put on alert following the message buoy Thor and Alander had dropped some days ago, but they still weren't as prepared for their encounter with the Spinners as Hatzis would have hoped. Perhaps the fact that half of the colonists were on the fragile edge of senescence had something to do with it.

The colony itself was run by a sturdy climatologist by the name of Tarsem Jones. His personality breakdown was well established, almost certainly as a result of spending too much of his time thinking faster than the normal clock rate. *The pressures of command,* Hatzis thought wryly as she addressed the man.

"The Spinners are going to choose one among you to act as a contact," she explained.

The colony's engram of Alander was locked down in

memory, too unstable to wake even for a day, and there
was also no version of her available, either. "This person
will probably be a UNESSPRO plant psychologically
modified to ensure the mission runs according to regulations. One of those regulations is to report to Earth as
soon as alien life is contacted. But you must not let them
do this." She spoke carefully, wanting to impress upon
him the importance of doing precisely as she said. "Shut
them down as soon as you find out who they are. We'll
deal with that problem later."

"But surely we should at least *talk* to them." Jones's
expression was one of intense indecision. "I mean, they've
gone to so much trouble to come here in the first place."

Hatzis thought again of her analogy of a person dropping sugar for ants to collect.

"Maybe they have," she said distractedly. "But there's
a bigger picture here, Tarsem. You need to do absolutely
nothing for a couple of days. Do you understand? Just
ignore them. Go about your business as though they
weren't even there."

"This is the biggest thing that's ever happened to us,
and you're asking—"

"A lot," she cut in. "I know. But bigger things could
yet happen." She thought for a moment of all the action
this system might soon get to see—assuming Thor and
Alander were right about the Roaches. "You're just going
to have to trust me on this, Tarsem. But I assure you,
you'll be perfectly safe."

Or so she hoped, anyway. From what she understood
of the Roaches, they had had so far shown no malice
when it came to systems that had already appropriated
their gifts. They didn't bring the Starfish down on people
they hadn't stolen from. But all of that might change if
they were ever attacked and expelled from a system by
force—especially if Axford's AI-merging idea failed to
work and they realized that their data had been stolen.

The weirdest thing—and in many ways the hardest to
accept—was that Axford might actually be right. She and
the other UNESSPRO colonists weren't the best people

to be dealing with situations involving hostile alien races. They were scientists and civilians; they weren't used to thinking in terms of military strategics or threats. He had viewed the gifts as an opportunity to make himself stronger; she had seen in them the chance to glean knowledge about the builders themselves. She wasn't, however, about to hand over charge of the human survivors to the likes of Frank the Ax just yet. That would be suicide.

Encrypted laser channels conducted all communications between her and the colony, so no one else knew she was present. If Axford was going to try anything, she wanted to see it with her own eyes. When the Spinners finished building the gifts and everything went quiet, she had Hera turn all available instruments to searching for signs of hole ships—*any* hole ship at all. Somewhere out there she was sure that Thor's *Pearl* and Axford's *Mercury* would be snooping around.

"Just who exactly are you waiting for, anyway?" asked Jones down the secure line. "I still don't understand. Are they enemies or allies? I have frightened people here, Caryl; what am I supposed to tell them?"

"You can tell them to be calm," she said. "Whatever happens, Tarsem, they're not going to get hurt, okay?"

On the screen before her, the ring of gifts girdled the planet like a thorny crown, glinting brassily in the golden sunlight.

"I'd like to believe you," said Jones. "But I can't help feel as though we're caught in the middle of something here."

You are, she said to herself. *We* all *are.*

But as much as she would have liked to tell Jones everything about the Spinners and the Starfish, in the end she simply didn't have time. Vector alarms rang loudly and suddenly, indicating that the near-Hera radar monitors had detected objects on impact trajectories. There were two of them, coming from wildly different directions. She fed the data to *Arachne* which promptly produced much clearer images of both objects. They were hole ships, definitely, each a white point gliding smoothly against the black. As they approached, their cockpits appeared: warped, distorted, alien-looking. Both ships belonged to the Roaches.

When the cockpits were completely free, the hole ships began to change course. This was something she hadn't seen before, although information in Thor's report suggested it was possible. The strange additions to the cockpit clearly gave the hole ships some degree of maneuverability, enabling them to swoop in close to the gifts and assume the same altitude without relocating. Still traveling much faster than orbital velocity, however, they swooped around the alien installations as though conducting a rapid survey.

Inspecting the booty, Hatzis thought. *Waiting for a response.* Axford's retaliation in Vega must have made them cautious, hence their traveling in pairs. The colony remained passive, broadcasting nothing more than a plea for identification: "This is Tarsem Jones of UNESSPRO Mission 538, *Fred Adams.* Please state your origins and intentions. I repeat: this is Tarsem Jones of UNESSPRO Mission 538 . . ."

The hole ships didn't respond, but they did change course again. One angled close to the seventh orbital tower—the one, Hatzis presumed, containing Hera's hole ship. The other made a close pass over the installation the *Fred Adams* had evolved into.

"*Fred Adams* to unknown vessels: we are not a military installation!" Singh's protest had become shrill. "Our meteorite shielding is purely defensive. If you won't identify yourselves, then at least maintain minimum safe distance!"

The hole ship closest to the *Fred Adams* completely ignored the pleas. On its second pass, it braked with astonishing suddenness and came up alongside the installation. The cockpit came around to a point close to the installation. The coral-like protrusions that marred the perfect smoothness of the alien vessel began to stretch, sending pseudopods across the open space that separated it from its target.

"Hatzis." There was a quiet panic in Singh's voice. "You promised . . ."

Although it was difficult, Hatzis held back from attempting to rescue the colonists. She *had* to assume that Axford, Alander, and Thor knew what they were doing. But if these people died because they left her hanging . . .

Just as the pseudopods had gained a firm grip on the *Fred Adams*, something happened. Hatzis watched as a second hole ship began to swell into existence at a point close in to the first. The Roach vessel went to withdraw, but the pseudopods held it fast. The second hole ship— *Mercury*? *Pearl*?—attained full size and had extruded its cockpit before the first was able to disengage from the human installation and attempt to relocate. Or perhaps it simply wasn't able to. Perhaps the close proximity of the two ships prevented it from using that means of escape.

The cockpit of the second hole ship had been modified, although its additions seemed minor in comparison to the first. It swept after the alien vessel, matching vectors with inhuman precision. The Roach ship soon proved its superior maneuverability with two seemingly suicidal swoops into Hera's atmosphere. The friction didn't even bring a glow to the alien hulls.

When they emerged from the second pass, the Roach had a considerable lead on the second craft and, having achieved that lead, its cockpit began to withdraw as it was clearly opting for escape over a course change.

The second hole ship beat it to the jump, however, relocating in an instant to match velocities again.

It was only then that the Roach hole ship retaliated. An angular shape grew out of the side of its cockpit and spat a fiery trail of darts at the hole ship on its tail. The darts sparked where they hit its hull, producing a fiery ball of gas from the extrusion attached to its cockpit.

The extrusions are engines, Hatzis realized. *And weapons!* They'd been added to the original designs in much the same way people back on Earth used to add extensions to existing houses. That way, they didn't need to interfere with or even understand the original design.

The Roach ship pulled away and readied for relocation. Undamaged but unsuccessful in its mission to raid the colony around Hera, it was quickly attempting to beat an early retreat. Did that count as a victory for the humans? It would depend, Hatzis imagined, on whether or not the hole ship harassing the Roaches had had enough time to steal the information they needed.

A sudden blast of noise came over the cockpit's speakers, startling her. Someone had broken radio silence! Hatzis searched the data displayed on her screen for the source of the transmission.

"What the fuck is going on?" she muttered, barely able to believe what she was seeing. During the skirmish around the *Fred Adams* installation, she'd totally forgotten about the second Roach hole ship. It had placed itself in a high polar orbit, watching while its twin had gone about its business. It had done nothing to assist its partner, probably assuming that it could handle itself against the relatively poorly equipped human hole ship. It had simply waited, just in case it was needed. Perhaps the incident at Vega, when they had lost one of their ships to Axford, had made them more cautious.

Only now *it* was under attack. A bright light played across its hull while its cockpit swung in erratic circles. Strange tremors vibrated through it, as though a mighty and invisible hand was shaking it. The transmission sounded like a roomful of very large, very angry birds all screeching at once, presumably the Roaches within, calling for help. Then the impossible happened: a *second* cockpit grew out of the side of the ailing hole ship. It spun in an increasing arc to match orbits with the first, while behind it, the core body of the hole ship seemed to swell in size.

"Oh, my God," she mumbled in growing disbelief. Somebody had relocated a ship *inside* it.

And she knew instinctively that there could only be one somebody fool enough to try something as dangerous as this: General Francis T. Axford. It had to be.

The screeching from the Roaches reached a higher note

as the two cockpits chased each other around the violently merged body of the hole ship. Hatzis kept track of them but only with great difficulty. Axford's ship might not have been the best equipped, but he'd made up for that with surprise.

Two rapid course changes brought his cockpit in contact with the Roach's, and suddenly it was all over. The alien vessels merged into one like two droplets of oil colliding. Once the meniscus was breached, there were no longer two vessels. There was just the one. And then the screeching stopped. A minute later, the other Roach hole ship—which had hung to one side, observing—disappeared.

Hatzis couldn't see what was taking place inside the new, larger cockpit. No doubt Axford was taking control of the situation as best he could. Despite his lack of a physical body, she had no doubts that he was, nevertheless, quite capable of attacking the unprepared Roaches. She smiled to herself as she pictured him as he might have looked in olden days, swinging on a rope between tall ships with a cutlass clasped between his teeth. He was a modern-day pirate, to be sure.

Would he take prisoners, this time? She imagined that would depend entirely on how much resistance they offered.

If he did win, there could be no denying that this was a major coup. Not only had he realized the alien AIs could merge, but he'd taken it one step further to attempt to merge the actual physical aspects of the hole ships, too. She was impressed, but she wasn't necessarily surprised. Spinner technology was so advanced, after all; why shouldn't they be able to merge materials and structures like they were made of putty? Whether it was the result of nanotech or a deeper comprehension of the nature of matter, she didn't know. Nor did she care right now. The end result was the important thing.

And Axford had planned it from the beginning. Merging AIs had been a good enough plan—and a convincing one. It would have been enough to satisfy her. But he'd had bigger stakes in mind. This way, he not only got his hands on the information they needed, but also on a—

What? Just what exactly did they have here? A *super–hole* ship? What, she asked herself, could this one do that the others could not?

The new, combined hole ship was similar in shape to the ordinary ones, except for the double-lobed configuration of the cockpit. In cross section, it would look like a figure eight on its side. The extrusions that both Roaches and Axford had added were looking very much the worse for wear, as though they'd been melted, then frozen again. Whether it could perform any advanced maneuvers, she couldn't tell—nor would she be able to until it was properly tested. And that would only happen if Axford won whatever battle was taking place inside between himself and the Roaches.

The configuration stabilized. The light and vibrations faded. A long minute passed while everyone in the system—the colonists of Hera; Thor and Alander, Hatzis presumed, in the other hole ship; and Hatzis herself—waited to see what the combined hole ship would do and who would emerge the victor.

Hatzis steeled herself for a confrontation. If the Roaches had won and they attacked the *Fred Adams* again, she would defend it herself with what little she had. If they summoned the Starfish, she would do everything in her power to ferry the engrams elsewhere as quickly as possible. If it was a war, she couldn't just stand by and watch it happen.

A click announced the beginning of a new broadcast. Hatzis physically leaned closer to the screen, as if doing so would somehow make it easier to hear. Old habits died hard, even for her.

She jumped when a harsh double shriek echoed through the cockpit. Dissonant, rapid-fire syllables wound around each other in an insane duet, less like mutated birdsong than like a tortured opera recording. It sounded like someone was screaming out of both of them at once in maniacal triumph.

Two sets of vocal cords, Thor had said.

Then it stopped, and her ears seemed to ring in the sudden silence.

"That's Roach for 'mission accomplished,' " said Axford, and Hatzis sighed at the sound of his voice. "More or less, anyway. Thanks for your cooperation, Peter and Caryl—both Caryls, actually. I suggest we take this powwow back to Hermes and discuss in private what to do next. Axford out."

The double hole ship vanished.

"*Both* Caryls?" repeated Alander over the same frequency. "What the hell is he talking about?"

"Would someone first like to tell *us* what's going on?" asked Tarsem Jones.

Hatzis shook her head and decided to leave them to it.

"*Arachne,*" she said. "Take me to Vega."

As the view of Hera faded from the screen, she settled back into the couch to reflect upon their triumph—as well as to consider what to do about the Axford problem.

1.2.2

Two brilliant points of light swept across the half yellow, half black sky, dragging Alander's attention with them. When they were gone, the vista above had fallen into place.

He was standing on the moon of an enormous gas giant. It was larger than any he'd ever seen before, almost certainly a borderline brown dwarf. It probably had numerous moons, with the one he was on having an atmosphere capable of supporting life. The gas giant clearly occupied an orbit somewhere in the habitable zone of its parent star.

Alander didn't know which star it was or what the world he was standing on had been christened. He didn't even know the mission name that had been sent to it. But he did know whose eyes he was seeing it through.

Fighting disorientation every second he stayed in conSense, he scanned the contents of the Overseer file that

one of Hatzis's many copies had sent during the daily
broadcast from Sothis. Axford's comment to Hatzis earlier
(*You really should tell your mother superior to find a
better way of broadcasting her secrets*) had piqued his
curiosity and sent him browsing through the previous
transmissions. It hadn't taken him long to uncover what
Axford had been referring to. Many such transmissions
had been broadcast from all over surveyed space and
marked for the sole attention of Caryl Hatzis, so the interface software wouldn't allow anyone else to stumble
across them. At first, the exact nature of the files had
eluded him; none of the various encryption codes he used
to crack them had worked. It was only on his way back
to Vega when he'd had more time to study them that he
realized exactly what they were.

He had enough trouble dealing with his own engram
without delving into someone else's, but if this was the
only way he could find out what Hatzis was up to, then
that was what he would do. Clenching his teeth, he concentrated on what he was seeing, all the while trying to
make sure he remained himself throughout the process.

A yellow gas giant roughly ten times larger than Jupiter, a moon world, and, if his guess was right, two space
vehicles breaking orbit. A name: *Donald Schievenin*. And
a thought (his or hers; it was hard to separate the two):
He'll be perfect.

The file ended abruptly with an intense rush of something he could only describe as *Hatzis*. The first time it
had happened, it had left him dazed for almost an hour.
Now, he knew better and pulled out from the files before
the rush peaked. Still, he was left blinking and disoriented
by brief but powerful glimpses of another person's inner
life: an apple orchard somewhere on Earth, before the
Spike; a weathered man sitting behind a desk, toying with
a paperweight; a dog's body, cut neatly in half and placed
in a cardboard box; a feeling of sorrow so piercing it
didn't leave him for ten minutes.

He sat on the edge of his cot in the berth *Pearl* had
provided him, breathing deeply as he fought to suppress

the residual effects of having dipped into Hatzis's mind. It was difficult, he found, to sift through her feelings for the relevant information, but he was sure the name *Donald Schievenin* was the key or point to the transmission. All of the five files he'd so far checked had mentioned names, so it had to be important; he simply didn't know *how* important. Or why, for that matter.

When he had once again established where *he* began and the memories of Caryl Hatzis stopped, he tried another file, dipping under the surface of her experience with all the nervousness of a new swimmer.

This time, a double star. No colony world, only dead stations scattered throughout a widely dispersed halo of comets. And a thought: *Barren, but the resources should be useful.* No name.

Alander timed it better, opting out of the file before the rush of Hatzis came on. He seemed to have tapped into some sort of catalogue of colonies, but he couldn't figure out why she was conducting it in secret. What the hell was she trying to hide?

The next and last—he could feel the cracks in his mind spreading each time he dipped into her—took him to a world that was almost the spitting image of Earth. Blue skies, white clouds, 70 percent ocean. His/Hatzis's heart ached to see it from his/her position in geosynchronous orbit. The gifts stood out as golden glints of light in a sparkling starscape, illuminated by a yellow sun that could easily have been Sol, as long as he/she didn't look too closely.

Another Cleo Samson, came the thought. *At least we know what to expect from her.*

Then the rush, and he was carried away by feelings of resentment and annoyance. Samson and Hatzis were polar opposites in many respects, and Alander found it strange that so much of his recent life had been bound up with either or both of them. Neither was a romantic entanglement; the one person he longed to see again, in that context, was the one they'd yet to find in any target system: Lucia Benck. His hand reached for the pendant hanging against his chest. *Bliss was it in that dawn . . . ?* Lucia's absence was increasingly puzzling for Alander, and it did nothing to ease the ache in his heart.

Cleo Samson's name stayed with him as he came down from the recording. *At least we know what to expect from her.* Hatzis's words echoed in his thoughts. What had she meant? What was special about Samson in the mission he had just visited? In Adrasteia, he'd been forced to erase her engram when she sabotaged the mission. Driven to psychosis by orders buried in her subconscious by UNES-SPRO itself, she had been compelled to attempt to force Alander to return to Earth in order to notify her superiors of the discovery of alien life. The overpowering conflict between her orders and those of the mission supervisor, Caryl Hatzis, had split her mind apart like a walnut, almost killing everyone in the process.

No one had known who the traitors were at the beginning of each mission. Some had frozen when news arrived that Earth had been destroyed, unable to operate around orders insisting that they report to superiors that no longer existed. Others were still unknown. Alander didn't doubt that out of the thousand survey missions, he himself could have been one such UNESSPRO operative. It could have literally been any one of the sixty surveyors—even Hatzis, although he was sure she would see herself above such treachery.

Donald Schievenin . . .

Maybe this wasn't a catalog of colonies and colonists, after all, he thought, but rather a roll call of traitors. Was *that* what Hatzis was disseminating among the various versions of herself?

He had thought that the Congress of Orphans Axford had referred to might be the beginnings of a group mind composed of the fragments of her engrams. The original Caryl Hatzis had, after all, been a part of a much larger being in Sol, a being composed of many diverse parts and as far beyond his comprehension as he was to a dog, so it wouldn't have surprised him if it turned out she wanted to establish a similar network again. But this didn't seem to have anything to do with it—unless that was what the emotive rush at the end was all about? He shook his head firmly. No. The Congress *had* to be something else.

He didn't know. Whatever these files were cataloguing, it was unlikely he'd find any answers in a hurry. The version of Hatzis from Thor had already informed her original that he knew about the secret transmissions (he had scanned her report and found that out all too easily, confirming his suspicion that she had been doing much more than "reviewing the data" after each midday broadcast), so chances were that it wasn't going to be so easy in the future to access such information. He idly considered confronting either or both of them with what he had learned but decided that would gain him little at the moment.

Arachne patiently put the transmissions back into storage for him to access later. Not arguing with Thor throughout their mission together had probably confounded her expectations, and not coming out firing over this would no doubt do the same. There were better ways, he decided, to get her back up.

"What the hell were you thinking?"

He did his best to sound angry as he walked along the pressurized gangplank that Axford had rigged up to connect *Arachne* to *Pearl*. Still wary of the ex-general, Sol had refused to enter the main compound in Hermes, fearing a trap similar to the one that had disposed of the alien hole ship that had attempted to steal Axford's gifts. Instead, their host had provided an unused base in the middle of nowhere, rapidly refurbished by nanotech to accommodate the two hole ships.

The original Caryl Hatzis looked up from her habitual position on the couch. "I don't have to explain anything to you, Peter."

"You put the exercise at risk," he growled. "As well as yourself! I mean, what if they'd seen you? What if we'd thought you were them? It was stupid and irresponsible!"

She tried to affect a casual, dismissive shrug, but he could tell she was annoyed by his attack. "What can I say? Curiosity got the better of me, I guess."

"Don't give me that shit," he said. "I want to know what were you doing there in the first place. There's no way you could've come from Sothis in time. You must've been there already—or at least in the area. Don't you trust us to do our work properly? Is that it? Were you snooping around, checking up on us?"

That point struck a chord with the Hatzis from Thor, who followed him into *Arachne* and stood sullenly behind him, her arms tightly folded.

The original Hatzis stood. "Since when is it your right to question what I do?"

"Since you started putting other people's lives at risk," he shot back. "There are precious few of us left as it is, without you pulling that sort of crap."

"You don't need to remind me about how few of us are left. I remember that better than you *ever* could."

"Meaning?"

"Meaning that your world was gone the day you left on the *Frank Tipler*. You turned your back on everything you knew quite willingly and with no hope of ever returning. But I had everything ripped out from under me—and not once, but *twice*." Her eyes blazed. "So don't ever accuse me of not appreciating how little is left, Peter, because I know better than anyone exactly how much has been lost."

The intensity of her response startled him. He walked around the cockpit, shaking his head.

"Listen, Caryl," he said patiently. "I said I'd behave before I left Sothis. How about you? If you expect me to believe that you truly have all of our interests at heart, then you're going to have to start caring about more than just yourself."

Her glare intensified; he'd obviously hit a nerve.

Before she had a chance to respond, however, a small chime announced the arrival of Axford's hybrid hole ship, *Mercury*, on the far side of the modified hangar.

Just far enough away so that the AI lobes can't merge,
Alander thought. *He thinks we're going to try the same
trick he taught us.*

"Greetings!" Axford's voice issued from the hole ship's
internal speakers. The screen behind Hatzis showed a
multi-angle view of Vega, with close-ups on the planetary
fragments and Hermes in particular. Suddenly, in the center, a new window opened from where Axford's face
beamed. "And a special welcome to you, Caryl Hatzis of
Sol. It's a pleasure to finally meet you. Although I ex-
pended a large amount of personal energy trying to avoid
the Spike, I'm genuinely fascinated to be meeting one of
its by-products."

Alander could see that this comment from Axford only
riled Hatzis even more.

"I'm not a product of the Spike," she said frostily. "I'm
a victim of it."

Axford laughed. "That's a fine distinction, don't you
think? One might even be tempted to call it pedantry."
He raised a hand to ward off an angry retort, continuing
quickly with: "I've been listening to your reports with
interest, Caryl, and I feel I've gotten to know you quite
well. But I'd consider it an honor to have the opportunity
to get to know you even better, and to that end, I'd like
to invite you over here to join me in *Mercury.* It would
give you a chance to meet my guests, too."

She shook her head. "There's no way I'm leaving this
hole ship, Axford," she said. "Not with you anywhere
nearby."

"Are you certain?" He didn't seem to have taken offense at her comment. "This will be a historic occasion,
after all."

"Peter and Thor will go," said Hatzis. "History can remember them instead."

Alander smiled, amused by the interplay between Axford and Hatzis. He had no doubt that Frank the Ax would
love to get his hands on the subtle technologies present
in the original Cary Hatzis's body. She knew it, too, and
she wasn't going to give him the opportunity. He might

have feared the destructive transition of the Spike itself, but Alander was certain that he wouldn't have had any qualms about reaping some of its benefits.

"Once again, we're the ones going over the top," Alander said dryly.

"This isn't trench warfare, Peter," the original Hatzis said irritably.

"But it's still our lives being put on the line, isn't it, Caryl?" He made the point more for Thor's benefit than for Sol's. Truth was, there was no way he'd *want* to miss the opportunity to speak to an alien species. Nevertheless, it did peeve him that the original Hatzis had felt it was her place to speak for him and her copy.

He waved Thor toward to the exit. "After you."

Thor nodded stiffly and led the way out of *Arachne*. Another pressurized tube had formed, connecting the first tube to *Mercury*. They tugged themselves along it in free fall, their artificial bodies having no problems with the lack of gravity. Inner-ear design had been a major consideration when their genomes had been tailored for space. Alander vividly remembered—or felt that he did— his first orbital flight while training for the UNESSPRO missions. He'd thrown up almost immediately and spent the rest of the flight nauseous. Being able to enjoy the absence of gravity was something, at least, that he could appreciate about his new life.

The airlock of *Mercury*'s hybrid cockpit hung invitingly open. The massive bulk of its central sphere, twice as voluminous as before, hid *Arachne* and *Pearl* from view. Alander had a strange feeling of stepping into the unknown as he walked across the threshold. At first glance, the cockpit interior appeared much the same as any other hole ship, except that there were two couches and two screens. The original design was perfectly adaptable, though, so that was no great change. There was simply a greater capacity for space, Alander assumed; if they wanted more room, it could be easily accommodated. A section of his field of view shimmered, and a conSense projection of Francis Axford appeared before him.

"Thank you for your help," he said. "Your assistance was absolutely crucial in the success of this plan."

"You were intending to do this all along," said Thor. "Weren't you?"

"Of course he was," put in Alander. "Overlapping AIs would have been too modest an objective for Frank the Ax. Right, General? Especially when records in the gifts told you that so much more was possible."

Axford smiled and shrugged. "They did suggest it, yes," he admitted. "Although I didn't know for certain. But I suspect that a much deeper understanding of matter is at play here—as well as energy. The hulls of these ships deny analysis. Who's to say they're made of matter at all? And if they're not, why can't they be manipulated as easily as we would mould a magnetic field?" His voice reflected his obvious excitement. "These hole ships are like building blocks! Aren't you curious to see just how much larger they can go?"

Thor nodded. "Of course we are," she said. "But you can keep your eyes off ours."

He laughed with good humor. "Somehow I *knew* you'd feel that way, Caryl," he said. "But I assure you, at this stage, I have no designs on what you consider to be yours."

Alander took little comfort from that statement, and he knew Hatzis wouldn't, either. "The rest of the mission was a success, I gather?" he said, moving the subject on. "You have the data?"

"I have *some* data." Axford's expression became serious. "The easiest to access is the language. *Mercury*—or should I call it *Mercury-squared*?—can act as a translator between our species. But there's still a long way to go with the translations. I mean, the words are okay, but the meanings are complicated. It's difficult to tell what's telemetry report and what's a history text, you know? Do the Roaches create and read fiction? I don't know yet." He shook his head. "There's a lot of information to sift through, and I've put my best minds on it."

Alander smiled at the intended joke.

"What about math?" he asked. "There must be some overlap there, surely?"

"Naturally," said Axford. "But that tells me little more than I already knew. Their operational techniques are much more advanced and use divergent philosophies. They grasped quantum gravity much sooner than we did." He shrugged again. "I don't know, maybe their fundamental symmetry gives them an intuitive grip on the concept of superposition. It's hard to say for certain."

"So why don't you just ask them?" said Hatzis. "Now that you know their language, why speculate?"

"They're not terribly communicative," he answered. "You'll understand that when you speak to them."

"And what has Charlie's response been to the new arrivals?" asked Alander.

"Charlie died," said Axford. From his expression, Alander could have sworn the man was actually upset by this. "There was nothing I could do about it. He weakened dramatically since you saw him, and the trauma of the maneuver finished him off. I haven't mentioned this to the others yet, and I suggest you refrain from doing so, too. We have no idea how they might react."

"And what did you learn from him?" asked Alander. "I'm assuming you conducted an autopsy and didn't just dump him out the airlock?"

"Of course, and I found a great diversity of genetic material, which could mean he was biomodified, as I originally thought."

"Or it could mean that you simply don't understand how their genetic analogue works yet," put in Hatzis.

Axford smiled at her cynicism. "Very possibly," he conceded. "The structure of his nervous system was fascinating. I'll be working on that for some time to come yet. It does appear that it had suffered from severe plaque formation. There were signs of repair in many places, however, which I took to mean that he was quite old."

"How old?" asked Hatzis.

"Any estimates will be exceedingly rough at this point," replied Axford evasively.

"Then give me a rough estimate," Hatzis persisted.

Axford met her stare evenly. "Possibly centuries. But like I said, at this stage it's all hypothetical."

"Better than nothing."

"But not as good as meeting the real thing. Speaking of which . . ." He turned to face the wall behind him, which immediately peeled away to reveal an adjoining chamber of roughly the same size. It was separated from the cockpit by an invisible boundary, made visible only by a yellowish tinge to the air on the far side. The aliens, two of them, sat with their backs to each other on a saddlelike couch, their long legs bent at disconcertingly sharp angles. Their faces moved differently from how Alander had imagined after seeing the recording of Charlie in action: instead of flexing like rubber masks, sections of their skin appeared to slide in and out of view, changing the symmetrical patterns dramatically when they spoke. No doubt the changing patterns expressed emotions of some sort, as did their postures and oddly graceful gestures, but it was all lost on him.

"Can they hear us?" asked Hatzis in a hushed tone.

"Not yet," said Axford. "Nor can they see us. I thought I'd give you time to adjust first."

"What did they evolve from?" Alander asked, fascinated by the shoulder plates hugging their spines. "Lizards? Insects? Birds?"

"Your guess is as good as mine." Axford shrugged. "Without knowing more about their original environment, it's hard to be sure."

"So you haven't translated that part of the information yet?"

"Not even close, I'm afraid."

Alander wondered how true this was. The knowledge had little strategic value, certainly, but he wouldn't put it past the ex-general to be automatically guarded when it came to data of this nature.

"Shall we begin, then?" he suggested.

"Caryl?" Axford asked.

Hatzis was staring fixedly at the aliens from a point

very close to the invisible boundary, her eyes following their every movement. She took a deep breath as she nodded faintly. "Okay. Let's do it."

The sound of the aliens' voices came over the cockpit's sound system. Alander tried not to make subjective judgments, but it was hard to avoid an automatic wince. Each of the aliens simultaneously emitted two series of piercing whistles chopped into fragments with recognizable intonations. Thankfully, at least, there was none of the screeching he'd heard during the attack. The pitch of each whistle was close to the other, so that the beating between the two frequencies conveyed additional information. That was all very well, Alander thought, but what he heard was a sequence of irritating dissonances, as though two flautists were arguing over who could play the highest note. Even at a low volume, it was an almost painful sound that could have been specifically designed to irritate a human ear.

One of the aliens looked up, its vestigial wings flexing. It raised a bony arm, and the conversation between the two of them ceased. Both heads turned to face the humans. Black, unblinking eyes regarded them closely. The patterns on their faces assumed almost identical expressions. The shoulder plates of first one and then the other rose slightly, perhaps in a reflex action to make them look larger.

"Can you hear us?" Hatzis began the interrogation cautiously, uncertainly.

The alien on the left uttered two strings of syllables at once, its mouth making strange, triangular shapes.

"We *you* hear sound *you* strange," came the translation from the *Mercury*. Clearly only one had responded, but two message streams were coming through simultaneously, causing whatever the alien had said to come out as gibberish. One of the vocal streams was softer than the other, almost as if it were the less important of the two statements.

"Can we avoid the overlap?" she whispered to Axford. He nodded. "*Mercury*, allow a time lag whenever the aliens issue more than one statement at a time. Try to keep the vocal streams separate." To Hatzis he said: "Have another go."

She turned back to the aliens and said: "My name is Caryl Hatzis." She placed a hand on her body's broad chest. "And this is Peter Alander."

A string of alien speech mimicked her own inside the alien's chamber. To Alander it sounded like two harpies having a shouting match in the house next door.

"*There is no telling you apart/our eyes see nothing,*" the same alien responded. The hole ship gave the alien a female voice, a contralto rich with exotic undertones. Alander wondered if it had based the gender on biological information they hadn't been privy to; to him, this alien looked no different than Charlie, who Axford had suggested was male.

"We are having the same problem," Hatzis said. "We're not getting the visual clues we're used to."

The aliens didn't respond in any obvious way. Their expressions didn't change; their eyes could have been looking anywhere.

"How should we address you?" she asked. "Do you have names?"

"We are—" Instead of a human word, the hole ship inserted a modified version of the double syllable uttered by the alien.

Alander shook his head. "I'm never going to get my tongue around *that*."

"I've isolated the phonetic components," said Axford. "The first is *yuhl,* a syllable that has no translation. The second is *goel*, which translates, as near as I can make out, to mean *predator.* I think it might be some sort of rank or class title, although they seem to use it as a general term for the species, as well."

"They certainly don't look like predators," Hatzis mumbled under her breath. "No claws, no canines—"

"But their eyes are forward-facing, and their legs are strong," said Alander. "So don't be too quick to judge."

"We've lost our claws, don't forget," added Axford. "That doesn't mean we're not dangerous."

"They can't hear us now?" Alander had noted the absence of a translation in the alien's chamber.

"Only when you address them directly."

Alander stepped forward. The heads of the aliens turned to face him.

"We'd like to learn about your species." He spoke slowly, stupidly believing that this might somehow make him less threatening and more affable. "Has Axford—" He indicated the ex-general. "—asked you where you come from?"

The same alien whistled something in reply.

"I have no clear analogue for that expression," said *Mercury.*

"Display what you *can* translate, then."

A string of Roman characters appeared on the screen:

WE DO NOT TALK TO THE [UNKNOWN].

"The word breaks down into two components," said Axford. "One means *bodiless,* the other *prey.*"

"Is he talking about us in general or you in particular?" asked Hatzis, glancing at Axford's conSense illusion.

"The latter, I suspect," replied Axford. "The boundary separating you from them is providing an illusion of my presence. I made the mistake of explaining that it *was* just an illusion, and they immediately stopped talking."

Alander chuckled. "How unfortunate."

"It's only a temporary setback," the ex-general defended. "I'm working on a body as we speak. In the meantime, you'll have to talk to them for me."

Alander kept his eyes on the alien who had last spoken. "I am flesh and blood, like you, and I have no intention of being anyone's prey. Can we speak as equals—as intelligent beings seeking common understanding?"

"*Why?/We do not understand.*"

Both vocalizations came out at the same volume, which

Alander assumed to mean that both utterances were of equal emphasis.

"To broaden our minds, of course," he said, "To learn how to understand each other."

The alien spoke. "*To* you *we have nothing to say/are different.*"

"Yes, we're different," said Alander, "but I still think there are many things we can tell each other. For instance, my species has never had the chance to compare its ethical codes with those of another. The same with religious beliefs, artistic tastes, modes of thought, and scientific methods. Our culture is still very much defined by primitive urges such as consumption, reproduction, and death. It colors the way we think and act on almost every level. Is your culture the same, or have you found a way around this problem?"

The first alien stared blankly back at him while the other remained as silent as before.

"To hell with this, Peter," Hatzis said, shaking her head. "They don't give a damn about this shit, and neither do I." She roughly shouldered her way in front of him. "Tell us why you're attacking our colonies—and what you know about the Spinners. If you call yourselves predators, then why are you behaving like *scavengers*?"

The alien closest to her turned its head to face her, but it was still the other one that spoke. "We are the *Yuhl/Goel.*"

"Spare me that crap," said Hatzis angrily. "Give me a straight answer, or I swear I'll hand you back to the bodiless prey, here. I'm sure he'd love another specimen to dissect."

The alien's wing sheaths flicked upward momentarily. "*We will lose* nothing *you can do.*"

Hatzis narrowed her eyes as if this might help her to understand what the alien was talking about. "What?"

"They have nothing to lose?" suggested Alander. "There's nothing we can do?"

"Our culture *is dead/has died*," the alien said. "We are the *Yuhl/Goel.*"

"When it said 'our culture,' " Alander said, "I thought I heard that *yuhl* syllable again."

Axford's eyes drifted as he consulted the hole ship's translation programs. "That's right."

"That must be their name," said Alander. "The Yuhl."

"And perhaps the *goel* addition indicates a subculture."

Axford nodded. "I think you're spot on."

"Open the line again." He faced the aliens. "If your culture was called the Yuhl, and you are the Yuhl-slash-*goel*—" He heard the hole ship insert the correct pronunciation in the final version. "—then who are *we*? If our culture was called humanity, what will you call us?"

"You are—" Buried in a dissonant alien whistle was a rough approximation of the English word he had used.

"We are humanity-slash-*riil*," interpreted Axford with a shrug. "That's the same word they used for prey before."

"Predators and prey," Hatzis sneered. "They're stuck in a stratified worldview. If that's so," she said, addressing the captives, "where do the Starfish and the Spinners fit in? Are you trying to *become* them? Or maybe even beat them at their own game?"

The alien addressing them stood and stepped forward. Its mottled orange skin (or was it a bodysuit? Alander still couldn't tell) gleamed under the thin membrane of an I-suit. It was very tall, standing almost a meter higher than Alander's and Hatzis's artificial bodies. The sides of its chest expanded, leaving a depression in the center large enough for a human fist, and the pigmentation on its face and upper body faded to a brown yellow.

"We are the *Yuhl/Goel*," it said. "That is *all you need to know/ all you will learn from us. Release us/kill us.* It makes no difference to the *Yuhl/Goel* or to you. Your fate is already decided."

"What does *that* mean?" asked Hatzis.

"You are *humanity/riil*. You are *already/dead*."

The alien sat down again, folding its enormous legs back up to its chest and turning away. It was a clear message: their discussion had ended.

"Well, they've got guts, I'll give them that," said

Hatzis. "They're not exactly in the best position to be threatening anyone at the moment."

"I don't think he needs to be," said Axford. He seemed uncharacteristically worried.

"What do you mean?" asked Alander.

"I question *Mercury*'s translation of that last word," he said. "I don't believe that *dead* is quite what our friend here meant to say."

"What, then?" asked Hatzis.

"I think the word *Mercury* was looking for was *extinct*."

1.2.3

Extinct.

The word echoed dully in Thor's mind. It struck deep, at the heart of her uncertainty, as well as her fear. If humanity really was *extinct*, then what would happen to Sol's dreams and aspirations? What of immortality? What of ascending to the technological heights of the Spinners or the Starfish? What of becoming . . . ?

She let the thought go, suddenly angered by the alien that had turned its back on her. She refused to let the argument end there; refused to allow these *scavengers* to dictate when the discussion had finished. They were her prisoners, for fuck's sake!

"What the hell do you know about us?" she said angrily. "Who are you to tell us that we have no hope? Extinct? You bastards will go before we do!"

The alien didn't respond. Its wing sheaths remained upraised, as though blocking her out, which only angered her more.

"Look at me, you fucker!" She pounded on the invisible barrier with both her fists.

A hand touched her shoulder, gently pulling her back.

"Take it easy, Caryl," said Alander. There was a hint of amusement in his voice that didn't do anything for her temper.

She wheeled on him. "These fucking parasites have

been stealing our resources and destroying our colonies," she yelled in his face. "Don't tell me to take it easy! If we die, it'll be because they—"

"Hey, can it, Caryl," said Axford. She was about to turn on him as well until she saw him staring at the aliens. "Look."

She looked to where he was pointing and saw the second alien raise its hands and press them to its temples. It spoke for the first time, keening a long phrase in its piercingly dissonant language. Its eyes might have looked at her, but she couldn't tell. They were black, bottomless pools staring out of a fractured face.

"What's it saying?" she demanded.

"I have no clear analogue for that expression," said *Mercury*.

"Display it, then," said Axford.

Words appeared on the screen to Hatzis's left.

THE SINGING OF THE ᴬᴸᴿᴱᴬᴰʸ/ᴅᴇᴀᴅ HURTS
MY EARS.
STRIKE THEM NOW, [UNKNOWN], AND
SPARE THEM THEIR [UNKNOWN].

Hatzis faced Axford. "Well? Any ideas?"

"Bear with us, Caryl," he scolded. "This isn't easy. It's like decoding two languages at once." He thought for a moment. "The third term combines concepts of mourning or despair and anticipation; grief-in-advance, perhaps?" He shrugged. "I'm guessing the second term is a name, comprising perhaps both benefactor and malefactor. If I had to pick a human term, it would be *Ambivalence.*"

"The *Ambivalence*?" Hatzis scowled. The phrase sounded ridiculous.

"It's the closest I can get."

" 'The singing of the already-dead hurts my ears,' " Alander repeated.

" 'Strike them now, Ambivalence,' " Axford went on, " 'and spare them their grief-in-advance.' "

"The Lord giveth and the Lord taketh away?" Alander offered with a wry smile. "Cute."

"Are you telling me," Hatzis asked, "that they think the Spinners and the Starfish are the same things? And they're *worshiping* them?"

"It kind of makes sense when you think about it," said Axford. "They have a keener sense of dichotomy than we do—if their math is anything to go by—so a god who provides gifts *and* destroys those that use them might make sense to them."

"I don't trust your translation," she said bluntly.

"Or you don't trust me," said Axford with a smile.

Hatzis glared at him. "If you're fucking with us, so help me, I'll—"

"Why would I do that, Caryl?" He opened his arms innocently. "I call them as I see them. We're in the same boat, here, remember?"

"Yeah, and according to these guys—" Alander gestured at the aliens from the position he'd taken up on the couch. "—that boat is sinking damned fast."

Hatzis bit her tongue. She didn't know who she was more pissed with: Axford, Alander, or the goddamn Roaches.

The Yuhl. A voice broke across her thoughts. She was so startled that for a moment she didn't recognize its source as her original in *Arachne. They have a name. If we're going to understand them, then we should use it.*

They're monsters, Thor returned. *They don't care about us. To them, we're nothing but walking corpses!*

Maybe so, said her original, *but we still have to establish communications with them. Let me take over.*

Thor balked at the invasion but then surrendered control without argument. It would probably be much easier to observe for a while, anyway; give her chance to calm down. She wouldn't have to make any decisions; she wouldn't have to worry about Sol always looking over her shoulder . . .

An odd sensation passed over her as her original took control of her body while she adopted a conSense fix-up inside a nonrepresentational virtual space. She had to have something to hang onto, or else she would suffer severe disorientation similar to Peter's.

This way, at least, she felt as though she were floating voluntarily along with her body's movements, rather than enslaved to them.

"Tell us about the Ambivalence," she heard herself say in a voice that was confident and self-assured, free of all the anger it had possessed moments earlier. "We wish to learn everything you know about it: where it came from; when you first encountered it; how you've managed to survive it."

The second alien removed its hands from its head. It fluted a short passage that, once again, the hole ship failed to completely translate.

THE AMBIVALENCE [UNKNOWN] HAS AL-
WAYS [UNKNOWN].
[UNKNOWN] WE PRESERVE YUHL [UN-
KNOWN] SANCTUARY
IN DEPTHS ETERNAL.

"I can't make this one out at all," said Axford.

"Sounds like ordinary religious gibberish to me," said Alander. "My guess is we've got ourselves a priest, here."

"And the other guy is military." Axford nodded enthusiastically. "That would certainly appeal to their sense of dichotomy."

"You visit systems that have been destroyed by the Ambivalence," Sol continued through Thor's body. "Why is that?"

The answer was relatively clear-cut:

WE LEAVE [UNKNOWN] TO THOSE BE-
YOND.

"I think that's 'tribute'," said Axford.

"Beyond hope? Beyond reach?" Alander frowned. "I

can't work out if they're mourning the lives lost or the gifts destroyed with them."

"The latter, I'd imagine," said Axford.

"We are grateful to you for that service," said Sol, taking Thor off guard not just with the words but also with a simple bow. "Your customs seem strange to us. But we are keen to learn more in order to prepare us for what will come."

The alien priest— if that truly was his role— seemed to study Sol carefully through the invisible barrier. When it spoke again, it was without the ambiguity that hampered their previous attempts to communicate.

"It is always this way," it said in terms *Mercury* had no trouble translating. With both sets of vocal cords working in synch, the words came out loud but not as shrill.

"What is?" Sol asked.

"There is no point fighting the Ambivalence," the alien's vocal cords continued in unison.

"But why not?" said Sol. "We don't understand."

"*Cannot fight gravity*," came the reply, with the softer vocal stream following a second later: "*All things fall to blackness.*"

"What goes up, must come down," suggested Alander.

Hatzis turned to face him. "If you're not going to take this seriously, Peter, then why don't you just get back to *Pearl* and leave it to me."

Alander looked genuinely indignant. "Identifying philosophical congruencies is an important part of learning to identify with new cultures," he said. "If we don't—"

"All right." Sol waved a hand, motioning him to silence. "I just thought you were being flip, that's all." She turned back to the alien, still not sure that Alander was completely with her. "How long have you known the Ambivalence?"

"The *Yuhl/Goel* has attended it for five *hundred/years*."

"Five hundred years?" said Sol. "That's a long time."

"I don't think that's right," said Axford. "Both sets of vocal cords uttered the number 'five,' but they were from two separate sentences. I think the overlap could be a form of multiplying—such as, they've been in attendance for five times five hundred years."

"Two thousand five hundred years?" Sol exclaimed incredulously.

"That's if my guess is right," said Axford. "It could be five hundred times five hundred. Either way, it's a long time."

"By our standards, that would be many generations," Sol said to the aliens.

The alien's head dropped slightly into its shoulder plates in an almost mechanical fashion. Perhaps, she thought, it was their equivalent to a shrug. "*Less than the snap of a wing sheath/to the Ambivalence.*"

"The blink of an eye," Alander offered from the couch.

"I got that one, Peter." To the alien priest she said, "If you've been following the Ambivalence all this time, why has it spared you?"

"We are the *Yuhl/Goel.*"

"Could humanity-slash-riil *become* humanity-slash-goel?"

The pattern of pigmentation on its face shifted. "*Humanity/goel?*" it exclaimed. Then it uttered a short burst of noise like a roomful of game show buzzers all going off at once.

"I think that was intended as an insult," said Axford.

Alander shook his head. "We seem caught between military practicality and religious dispassion."

"Is there anyone else we can talk to?" she asked the captives.

"We are the *Yuhl/Goel,*" said the other alien, without turning. "You are the *already/dead.*"

Sol turned to face the others. "This is getting us nowhere," she said, frustrated. "These aliens have been following the Spinners and Starfish for twenty-five hundred years or more. This is a prime opportunity for us to finally learn something about them—and all they want to do is play word games." She ran a hand across Thor's android's smooth scalp. "Any suggestions? I don't think we can afford to give up on them just yet."

"It sounds like they're giving up on us," said Alander dryly.

"Can you blame them?" said Axford. "They see it as their only chance at survival."

Sol frowned. "How so?"

"Well, assume that what the Yuhl have told us is true, and these Spinners and Starfish have been playing destructive game of interstellar tag for the last two and a half thousand years or so *at least*. In that time, the Yuhl might have witnessed many species standing up to the Starfish and being wiped out totally. Perhaps they attempted it themselves to start with but decided that it was hopeless. The only way to survive, they could have concluded, was to not get involved."

"Stay in the middle, you mean?" said Alander. "Play it safe?"

"Safer even than that," said Axford. "In the middle, you could get caught in the cross fire—and for someone like the Yuhl, or anyone trapped between two superpowers, there wouldn't be much left in the end." He shook his head. "No. I'm betting the Yuhl are on the sidelines, watching from a safe distance. In their minds, anyone attempting to go up against the Spinners-slash-Starfish are already dead. Taking sides is a quick path to destruction as far as they are concerned."

"That doesn't make sense," said Sol. "Why not just settle somewhere once the Starfish have gone by? They must have come across thousands of possible planets they could colonize over the years."

"They can't," said Alander. "Because they can't be sure that the Starfish wouldn't come back." He looked at Axford. "Right?"

The ex-general nodded. "Maybe. If there's a mighty whale swimming through the ocean gobbling up every fish that gets in its way, where would be the safest place? Near its tail, of course. That's all the Yuhl are doing. If they hang back, how do they know the whale won't turn about and come back for them? While they're at the tail end and keeping up, they'll never get eaten."

"Nice imagery, Frank," said Sol, "but meanwhile, they're exploiting all of the other races that stand in the path of the Starfish."

"I didn't say I approved," Axford responded. "I just said I could understand where they're coming from. To them, survival is the most important thing—not fighting and dying."

"That's as may be," said Sol. "But it doesn't help us much, does it? If we're to stand any chance against the Starfish, then we're going to need all the information we can on them *and* the Spinners. And so far, they haven't told us anything that might be useful."

"Look," said Alander, "it's too early to jump to conclusions. I mean, these two can't possibly represent their entire race. Maybe they're extremists—the only ones fool enough to volunteer for seek-and-destroy missions such as this. And if they are extremists, then what are the moderates like? Would *they* be more inclined to talk to us and help us? Instead of wasting our time here, maybe we should be looking to talk to others that might be more cooperative and sympathetic."

Sol nodded. "If we only knew where they were . . ."

Axford cleared his throat for their attention. "The records in their hole ship are locked with some sort of numerical key I can't get around, yet," he said. "However, I can tell you their destination after 61 Ursa Major. It's Alsafi—a K0V star not on the main mission register. Main sequence but older than Sol, and not far from here. They had it programmed in case they needed a quick getaway."

"I know it," said Sol. "The mission to Dsiban had a scheduled flyby. But why there? It's not even close to Hera."

"I have no idea," admitted Axford. "I'm just telling you what was in the hole ship AI when it merged with *Mercury*."

"We could check Dsiban to see if the survey team arrived there," suggested Alander. "The *Geoffrey Landis* wouldn't have flown by Alsafi itself, but its secondary mission would have."

"Who piloted that one?" asked Sol. "Lucia, I suppose?"

"It was," he said. "But that's hardly relevant."

"Her track record is far from irrelevant, Peter," said Sol. "We have no record of her *ever* arriving at her target system, so why should she be at Dsiban?"

"There's always a chance, Caryl," he said. "You can't afford to ignore the possibility that she might have useful data."

Thor stirred in her insulated, virtual space but didn't intrude upon the argument.

"You're forgetting something," said Axford. "It would've only taken her twenty-five years to get there. She would have been long gone by the time the Roaches even arrived."

Alander looked at him, then nodded. "That's true," he said. "I guess we have no choice but to jump in blind."

Axford's grin was wide. "Any volunteers?"

The rolling resonance of an ftl transmission rang through the expanded cockpit. On the far side of the invisible boundary, the alien captives looked up, chittering between themselves as if in alarm.

Or amusement, thought Thor. *Are they laughing at us?*

"Time for the daily bulletin already?" Axford said to her. "My, doesn't time fly when you're entertaining aliens?"

Sol ignored the comment. When the transmission was complete, *Mercury* played its contents in full. It began the usual way, with Sol's plea for cautious contact between the colonies and the various alien races traveling through surveyed space. Several new drops had been discovered as a result of all the exploration taking place along the Spinner front. Failed missions were downplayed, as were the latest Starfish kills. Hatzis felt herself grow cold when the figure appeared. Nine dead colonies. Not all had died in the previous twenty hours—they were still finding the ruins of colonies unlucky enough to have missed the warnings—but not all of them were old, either. A significant number of them must have been victims of sneak attacks.

She skipped to the bottom of the transmission, to the roll call of dead systems. The coldness in her gut turned to stabbing ice as she read that one of them was HD92719: her home system.

Thor felt herself lift out of the illusion that she was Sol as she reviewed the Overseer files that had come in at the same time as the Sothis transmission. Grief flooded through her as she fought to comprehend the simple but painful truth: everyone on the *Krasnikov* was dead! Rob Singh, Vince Mohler, Donald Schievenin, Nalini Kovistra, Angela Wu—*everyone.* The planet of Thor, if the other destroyed systems were anything to go by, lay in ruins right now, its biosphere traumatized by the falling of the orbital towers tethering the gifts to the ground.

And she hadn't been there because Peter Alander needed baby-sitting.

Flashes of memories from the other engrams filtered through her via Sol. She experienced new worlds and old ones, felt fresh insights from distant facets of her own mind, learned the names of more Orphans . . . But it was all meaningless to her.

Then a new memory burst across her mind: she saw golden machines bursting in two while sheets of unimaginable energy brighter than the sun effortlessly tore great holes in a small, green planet's atmosphere. Silver star shapes, rotating like the blades of giant saws, gathered energy and then hurled it back at anything within range. She recognized the fear of the mind witnessing it and knew also that she, *Caryl Hatzis,* was sacrificing herself in order that others might see more closely just how the Starfish operated.

This is 64 Pisces, called the mind of the dying woman. *This was Ilmarinen; this was my home . . .*

Debris rained down upon the helpless world, while fire burned its sky. The work of the aliens was almost done. She felt the ringing of the hole ship around her as the aliens closed in for the kill, wondered if the transmission was still continuing, forced herself through the onset of personality breakdown as her engram found itself thrust into experiences her original had never anticipated, gathered her resolve around her—she *would* survive; she *would* see it through; if it saved one life, *if it saved Sol,* it would be worth it—and—

The transmission from Ilmarinen ended abruptly and in blackness. A tag had been added to the file, and Thor watched as Sol read it. The Overseer file from 64 Pisces had been broadcast while the kidnap mission had been en route to Vegas from 61 Ursa Major, and had gone out with no thought to subtlety. The final thoughts of Hatzis of Ilmarinen had been detected by every colony within two hundred light-years. There was no mistaking the transmission for what it was, given that it came on its own. The deathbed experiences, even secondhand, were sparking panic all across surveyed space.

"There's a problem," said Sol, pushing forward through Thor until she was back in full control.

"So I gather." Axford didn't look smug, and she was grateful for that.

Alander looked confused for a moment. "What's going on? Is this to do with the transmissions you—?"

"I can't explain right now," she cut in. "It'll take too long, and I have to go."

Then Sol was gone, and Thor was thrust back into her artificial body before she was entirely prepared. Her confusion overrode automatic balance systems, and she pitched forward onto her knees with a gasp.

"Are you all right?"

Alander was halfway across the cockpit before she was fully aware of what was happening.

"They're all dead," she said through gritted teeth, brushing aside his outstretched hand. "Thor is dead."

"Your colony?"

She nodded, using the couch to help her climb to her feet.

I will not cry. I will *not cry.*

Alander straightened with her. "I know how that feels, Caryl," he said.

She shot him a sharp glare. "You patronizing little fuck," she said viciously.

He took a step back. "No, I didn't mean it like—"

She shook her head, and he shut up, throwing his arms up in defeat and turning away from her.

"That's a whole heap of trouble old Sol is going back to," Axford mused. "People will be howling for evacuation and resettlement. Hole ships will become the most precious commodity on the market. Everyone will be looking for somewhere safe to hide. And guess what, people? There's nowhere safe. You either fight or you die. They're the only options. It's survival of the fittest, dressed in spaceships not bearskins."

"Or we could do what our alien friends here have done for the last twenty-five hundred years," suggested Alander. "Tail the Starfish and not let ourselves be seen, scavenging what we can, when we can."

It was only intended as a quip, but it gave Hatzis the urge to strike out at him. She knew her anger wasn't really for him, though. As much as he pissed her off at times—all the time, these days, it seemed—lashing out at him simply wouldn't satisfy the fiery emotions she felt needed immediate release.

Sensing movement behind her, she turned to see one of the aliens staring at her through the invisible barrier. Its faceplates moved in odd ways, creating a shifting series of line-drawn expressions, none of which made sense. Its mouth changed shape several times until it became an upside down triangle, stretched far out into each cheek. Inside the lipless mouth, sharp projections slid into view at the front. The plates around its eyes narrowed, and its black eyes glinted in the light.

She narrowed her eyes. "Is that thing *smiling* at me?"

Alander stepped up beside her and peered closely at the alien. "It certainly seems to be," he said. "But smiles aren't necessarily friendly. Those teeth look *sharp*."

She ignored him, turning to Axford. "Drop the barrier," she said. "Let it out."

"As you wish," said Axford with amusement.

"What—?" was all of the objection Alander managed to get out before the sudden rush as air pressures equalizing indicated that the barrier was down.

"This isn't funny, General," said Alander nervously. From the corner of her eye she could see him edging away from her. "Bring the barrier back up!"

The plane delineating the former boundary blurred as the yellow-tinged atmosphere the hole ship had provided for the aliens spilled into the human section. Once Thor was sure the boundary was completely gone, that Axford wasn't simply baiting her, she leaped. The Roaches had necks that looked flexible but sturdy, so she went for the place in its chest where the soft-looking hole had appeared. She put all her strength behind the blow, lunging at the alien in the hope of freeing all of her emotions as the images of her dead crewmates flashed before her eyes.

Nalini, Donald, Vince, Cleo, Susan, Angela . . .

But the alien was too fast for her, and one of its mighty legs kicked up and out before she got anywhere near its chest plates. Rigid toes dug into her stomach and flipped her aside.

She smelled iodine as it went past in a blur, leaping for Alander. The sound it made was like two trains shrieking by in both directions.

She hit the wall hard and went down near the other alien, the "priest." It was slowly coming to its feet, its movements jerky, cautious, perhaps. She wanted to kick out at it, but the intense pain in her midriff forced her into a gasping ball.

"Axford!" she heard Alander bark as the creature came at him, its arms raised in readiness to rain blows down upon him. Before it could, however, a deafening crack split the air, and the barrier was back, curved in ungainly ways to separate human from alien.

The attacking alien bounced off it with a roar, kicking out in anger, its wing sheaths snapping up and down in rapid movements.

"Ambivalence take you!" it screeched.

"I think it just told us to go to hell," said Axford as his

conSense illusion strolled over to where Hatzis lay gasping on the floor. He leaned over her. "You okay?"

"Of course she's not okay!" Alander snapped. "What
the hell did you think you were doing?"

Axford shrugged with a self-satisfied smirk. "She
wanted the barrier lifted," he said innocently.

Alander knelt beside her, reaching under her shoulders
to help her up. She half managed to stand, hunching over
the terrible burning in her gut. Every movement caused
her pain.

"Those bastards are dangerous," she muttered, wincing
as she spoke.

"And never forget it," said Axford from off to one side.
"I-suits can only do so much."

Alander glared at him. "That's why you did this? To
teach her a lesson?"

"Come off it, Peter. She wanted that barrier down.
She's been busting for a shot at these aliens all along. She
needed to get it out of her system, that's all. And now,
hopefully, she's done just that."

She knew he was right; she had, quite literally, asked
for it. Nevertheless, his smug attitude was seriously rubbing her the wrong way.

"Come on," she heard Alander mumble. "Let's get you
back to *Pearl*."

Over his shoulder she could see the alien priest, its
black-and-white expression completely illegible. It was
impossible to tell where its all-black eyes were actually
looking, but she knew it was watching her every step of
the way.

"How are you feeling now?"

She was lying on the couch in the cockpit, with Alander
crouched beside her. She nodded slightly in response to
his enquiry. It was the best she could do at the moment.

"There's no blood," he said. "Nor any wound, for that
matter."

His reassurances didn't help. She felt as though her digestive tract had been turned to jelly.

"There wouldn't be," she said. "The I-suit stopped the blow from killing me, and it'll repair what damage did get through, I'm sure."

"Would you like me to take you . . . ?" He stopped before finishing the sentence, looking pained on her behalf.

"Home?" She laughed, but it was empty and humorless. "How, Peter?" The enormity of her loss welled up in her with greater urgency than the pain of her injury. For the first time, she truly had an inkling of what Sol had felt when the Starfish had destroyed the Vincula.

He hung his head, embarrassed. "Earlier on," he started. "I didn't mean to be insensitive—"

"I know," she said. "We've all suffered losses. The only thing we can do about it is get on with life. Move on. Right?"

He shrugged. "If you believe Axford, then yeah, I guess so. Darwin and all that."

"Do *you* believe that?"

He raised his head and looked at her. "I believe that, as things stand now, if it came down to a face-off between us and the Starfish, I'm pretty sure we'd lose. They'd squash us like bugs and wouldn't even think twice about doing it, either."

She thought of the ants scurrying after the careless giant, too small to do anything to avoid every crushing footfall. Did the giant even notice the ants it crushed?

"I don't like what Axford says."

"He's not stupid, Caryl," he said. "He's ruthless, yes, but maybe we need someone like him right now. Christ, he's had the gifts barely a couple of weeks, and he's already discovered things we had no idea existed. It would be wrong to turn our back on him."

The idea of ignoring Axford sent a chill through her. Turning your back on a man like that would be like turning your back on a rabid dog. He might not bite immediately, but he would always be thinking about it.

She exhaled from what felt like the very depths of her

soul. It was hard to think past Thor and concentrate on the things Sol would want her to consider. And how could she? She was only human—or trying to be, at least. Alander was no better. For all his apparent logic and reason, he was as much caught up in his own problems as anyone. Who was he to lecture her about dealing with grief? He who was alone and was dealing with it so stoically . . . ?

"There's something you should know," she said. "It's about Lucia."

Instantly on the defensive, his expression froze. "What about her?"

"Sol mentioned that you'd never found her, from any of the missions you'd checked."

"That's right."

"I wasn't aware of that until she mentioned it," she said. "Lucia was on my mission—as were you, although your engram failed on start-up. Lucia's mission was in *Chung-9*, and she had the usual job of scouting the lesser bodies along the way: the red dwarfs, the failed stars, the stellar remnants; all the things that we missed on our journey because we didn't have the time or the delta-v to change course."

"She was the tourist," he said, nodding thoughtfully. "It was what she always wanted to be."

"I know," she said. "But I don't think any of us understood just what that really meant, though."

He frowned. "What do you mean?"

"We received a transmission from the *Chung-9* five years after we arrived at Thor."

Thinking of her former colony made her throat ache, but she persevered, concentrating on the burning in her gut instead. "It was a long burst containing all the data it had gathered throughout its journey. It took an enormous amount of energy and forethought. This wasn't some last-minute, spontaneous gesture; it was planned, right down to the last detail. She wanted us to have access to everything she'd seen and done."

His eyes tightened. "Do you know where she was when she sent the transmission?" he asked hopefully.

"The transmission had a red shift suggesting she was accelerating for nu Hydra, maybe phi-3 Hydra. She didn't say. If she keeps going in that direction, she'll eventually come near a nebula called Ghost of Jupiter—and from there it's just stars and galaxies forever." She paused for a moment to let it sink in. "Do you understand, Peter? Lucia was enjoying being a tourist too much. She didn't want to stop."

"But—" He didn't finish the sentence. When he tried again, she suspected it wasn't the same one. "We didn't receive any such transmission in Upsilon Aquarius."

"Maybe it's still on its way. It all depends on how close her flyby came to your colony. You were only there for ten years before the Starfish came. If she was eleven light-years away when she sent her data package, it won't have arrived yet."

"Her mission might have failed."

She nodded. "It might have. That's still a possibility. But *all* of them? I'd sooner believe in missed transmissions than a complete failure of all her secondary missions—and only hers. After all, other secondary pilots succeeded in their missions. And it really was just luck that we picked up her broadcast at all. If we hadn't been looking in that direction, we might never have seen it."

He didn't say anything for a long while, and she tried to imagine what he was feeling. Grief? Jealousy? Anger? Betrayal?

She loved the stars more than she loved you, she wanted to say, to hammer the point home. *Don't give me any philosophical crap about accepting loss, or I'll rub your face in this every chance I can get.*

He sighed heavily through his nose. "I guess there's no point checking with the Dsiban mission to see if she arrived, then." His voice was even, almost *too* even. "She wouldn't be there. She'll be Christ knows where by now, heading off all wide-eyed into infinity."

Don't hide your pain behind poetry! she wanted to scream at him. *Don't be so fucking pragmatic! You've been in love with her ever since the mission started, and you've never given up hope you might see her again. And now you know you never will. Is that how you're going to get over it, Peter, by being practical? Is that what you expect me to do?*

"Okay." He stood, wiping his hands on his shipsuit. "Thanks for telling me. If you're going to be okay, I'll go and talk to Axford to see what he has in mind."

Show me some emotion, you goddamn robot! She forced herself to emulate his behavior; she wouldn't be the first to crack.

"I'll be fine," she said smoothly. "You go do what you need to do."

He nodded and, without looking at her, walked out of the cockpit and along the gangway.

She sagged back onto the couch and listened to his footsteps recede into the distance.

Far away, she thought. *We're light-years apart, even when we're sitting next to each other.*

The thought dismayed her. No matter how awful it must have been for the twin of her in 64 Pisces—her sister on Ilmarinen—to die so distant from the people she was calling, at least she had died knowing that someone out there understood her, was part of her. But how could Alander bear it, being alone in this universe? First his sole sane twin died with Athena, and now the woman he loved had rejected him hundreds of times over. How was he going to survive?

That he *would* survive she had no doubt at all. He wouldn't have lasted this long if he didn't have the will to keep going. Her purpose wasn't to destroy him, anyway. It was to make sure he didn't make *her* life any more miserable than it already was.

1.2.4

"I'm beginning to wonder if she's a liability," said Axford.

"Is that why you tried to have her killed?"

Alander was in *Mercury* with Axford, discussing what

they should do next. *Arachne* had left an hour earlier, with Sol. Thor remained in *Pearl*, resting while her I suit went about whatever repairs were needed after that single, disemboweling kick from the alien. The alien captives themselves were once again hidden behind an opaque bulkhead, which suited him for the moment. After the incident earlier, he'd be happy to keep his distance from them for a while—both physically and visually.

Axford laughed diminnively at Alander's accusation. "Come off it, Peter," he said. "She was itching for a shot at those aliens; she needed to get it off her chest."

"Or to be put in her place, perhaps?"

Axford shrugged unapologetically. "Either way, it's out of her system," he said. "Now she might be a bit more levelheaded."

"I'm sure she'll perform splendidly," said Alander wryly, "once she's able to walk properly again."

"Tell me, who is it you're most concerned for? Hatzis or yourself?"

Alander creased his brow. "Huh?"

"I rid myself of all of my crewmates," Axford said. "I loosed that alien upon Caryl. You must be wondering right now how far you can trust me."

"I daresay you're wondering the same about me."

Axford smiled noncommittally. "Whatever," he said with another shrug. "The point is, I'm not sure she's going to help us achieve our objectives at the moment."

Even though it made him feel as if he was betraying her, Alander had to agree with the ex-general. There were negotiations Axford would find easier to perform without Hatzis in the exploratory mission to Alsafi, but the loss of *Pearl* would make things more difficult for them. Splitting the *Mercury* back into two and housing the aliens in Hermes would increase their flexibility, certainly, but it also took away any tactical advantage of showing the Yuhl just what they had learned about the hole ships.

"Well?" pressed Axford. "What are your thoughts on this?"

"At the moment," he answered slowly, reluctantly, "I guess I'd be happier if she wasn't part of our plans." Her comments regarding Lucia still stung, as she had undoubtedly intended them to. He wasn't sure just how level-headed either of them would be working together. "At least in the short term, anyway."

"And what about in the long run?" Axford's bearing was conversational, but Alander didn't doubt that he was being carefully scrutinized. Just because the conSense illusion of the man wasn't looking at him didn't necessarily mean he wasn't being closely watched.

"In the long run?" he said thoughtfully. "I don't think we'll survive without her. *All* of her."

Axford nodded. "I agree."

It was ironic, Alander thought, that the future of humanity should rest in the hands of identities like Axford and Hatzis, whose uniquely multiple viewpoints set them apart from anything humanity had been beforehand. In a very strange way, he realized, out of all the engrams, he himself was the closest thing left to a traditional human. To the best of his knowledge, he was the only copy of himself alive at that moment. The other UNESSPRO programs had been multiplied almost beyond comprehension. He wondered if the only way for humanity to survive was to allow it to become something it was not: a society of identical clones, like Axford, or a self-obsessed group mind like Hatzis. There *had* to be another possibility, surely?

If not for us, then for whom?

He'd asked Lucia this in a completely different context, but it was as applicable now as it ever had been. And perhaps her answer was equally applicable: *It won't be us, Peter. And yet it will be. I try not to get tangled in the metaphysics of it all.*

The thought of Lucia in her tiny probe ship—all the copies of her in many such ships—radiating outward from Sol on independent missions of exploration, boldly defying UNESSPRO mission guidelines and thumbing her nose at her fellow surveyors, gave him a warm feeling. It was exactly the sort of thing she would have done: impulsive, yet requiring extraordinary effort and planning. It was also typically self-centered, and the part of him that missed her, the part of him that had grieved for her in Upsilon Aquarius, assuming she was dead, wanted to use the hole ship now to find her. He wanted to take her by the shoulders and say: *It's not for me, and it never was. How could you have led me on like that?*

But it was an idle thought, a foolish thought. She was as lost to him as she'd ever been. Finding her would be as difficult as finding a single grain of sand in a thousand oceans. And there were much more important things to consider.

"So we go to Alsafi," he said, shaking her image from his head. "Without Caryl. And then what?"

"Then we see what happens." Axford's image clasped his hands together as he spoke, reminding Alander of an excited schoolboy. The idea of jumping into the unknown clearly thrilled the man.

"What about Caryl?" said Alander. "Is there any damage she could do here?"

"I'll keep an eye on her," he said. "If the Roaches couldn't get me, she sure as hell won't, either."

Alander nodded, keeping his head bowed slightly, unable to meet the ex-general's eyes. He knew it was the right thing to do, but he felt guilty for it, nonetheless. Plus he wasn't looking forward to being the one to bring the news to her—

"Ah."

Axford's exclamation intruded upon Alander's introspection. "What is it?"

"I think the matter of Caryl Hatzis has just become a moot point."

One of the screens in the cockpit lit up, showing the section of gantry where *Pearl* had docked. The cockpit had swung free of the walkway and was already falling into the central part of the ship. When it was gone, the hole ship began to shrink. Before Alander had chance to consider calling out to her, it vanished altogether.

"What the hell is she doing?"

Axford chuckled softly. "Beating us at our own back-stabbing game," he said, shaking his head. "Damn. You just can't trust anyone these days, can you?"

Alander turned away from the screen after a moment, fighting a feeling of foreboding that was developing in his gut. As difficult as things could be at times with Hatzis, he would have preferred to have her in front of him, where he could see what she was doing.

"I guess it's just you and me now, partner," said Axford.

"Yeah." He nodded numbly. "I guess so."

Alsafi was less than fourteen light-years from Vega. Had Axford's home star not been such a fluctuating show-off, it would have been one of the brightest stars in the sky. It still staggered Alander that, thanks to the generosity of the Spinners with their gifts, they could now cross such vast distances without even feeling as if they were traveling. Unspace, as someone had recently quipped, was a nonevent.

During the four hours they spent in transit, he and Axford went over the resources they'd brought with them. The merging of the hole ships gave them a little more than double the capacity for haulage. Frank the Ax, naturally, had used that extra space to load up on exotic weapons and defensive systems. Much of the equipment that had come with the Yuhl had been ditched. Until Axford had time to examine it more closely—or until he returned and communicated with the copies of himself who would do so while the newly embodied Axford went to Alsafi—he wouldn't even be able to tell which pieces were damaged and which were supposed to look that way. The coral structures that had adorned the original Yuhl cockpit now had a half-melted look.

The Yuhl prisoners remained on board, however, and although they were still hidden behind the bulkhead, their presence on the ship unsettled Alander. He kept thinking of what the one had done to Hatzis in that brief fracas, and how it had come for him, too.

Nevertheless, on a couple of occasions through the trip, he did attempt to open a dialogue with them. They remained stubbornly silent, even between themselves. In the end, he contented himself with conducting a noninvasive exploration of their anatomy instead, using the subtle senses of the hole ship to examine the aliens' bodies from the inside out. It felt good to lose himself in science and forget about everything else that was going on, even if it was just for a short time.

"I think you got the genders wrong," he told Axford at one point.

Frank the Ax's new body—a sleeker version of Alander's but with an identical hairlessness and a closer resemblance to his original—looked up from an internal rumination. "Oh?"

"The structure you identified as a penis is more likely to be an ovipositor. Female insects and some species of fish use such organs to lay their eggs on—"

"I know what an ovipositor is, Peter," he said. "But what makes you think we have one here, rather than a double penis? Double-barreled species aren't unheard of, back home."

"The ducts servicing the organ lead to structures more reminiscent of ovaries than testes," Alander said, indicating finely detailed scans taken of the more passive alien's interior. "See? Large numbers of identical cells, not a production line like you'd see with most males. Whereas this alien—"

"We have *both* sexes here?"

"I think so," said Alander.

"Fancy that," Axford mused. "Hey, if we ever find a way to house-train these Roaches, maybe we should look into breeding them."

The humor was in poor taste, Alander felt, so he didn't honor the comment with a response. "This one has a stunted version of the same external organ," he went on, "indicating that it is perhaps a variant on the other's basic genotype—just like human males are of human females. This organ has numerous pores connected to vesicles containing exactly the sort of cellular powerhouse you'd expect of the species' male. My guess is the pores open under stimulation to release the spermatic analogue—"

"They sweat semen?"

"Only around their sexual organ."

"Where the female lays the egg?"

"Maybe," said Alander thoughtfully. "Or perhaps there could be an intermediary involved. A host."

Axford stared at him for a long time. "Are we talking parasitic wasps, here?"

"I don't know," Alander admitted. "I'm just trying to understand them at their most basic level. How their hearts beat is just fluid mechanics; but how they reproduce will have a bearing on every aspect of their psyches."

"Makes sense, I guess," said Axford indifferently.

Alander kept his attention fixed on the images before him. "I think they're infertile," he said after a few moments' reflection. "Either that, or they've deliberately suspended their reproductive activity. You'd expect that of an advanced species."

He stopped when he realized that Axford wasn't really listening anymore. The ex-general was clearly only interested in science he could use, and Alander left Axford to his thoughts. The joint thrills of discovery and the unknown kept him occupied for most of the remainder of the trip. Only when they were due to arrive did he put aside the images and concentrate on what Axford considered to be more important.

"We don't have much of an idea what we're going into." Axford directed Alander's attention to the partly decrypted data from the Yuhl hole ship that was flowing in streams down the screens. "I'm going to bring us in well out-system," he said. "And then only briefly. If they've dug themselves in, they could have all sorts of counterintelligence defense systems in place."

Alander faced him. "Does the system have planets?"

"I checked the map in the gifts before we left," he said.

"It shows a couple of large gas giants in close orbits, but nothing more than that. But that's not entirely conclusive, either. I agree with your survey team when they said that the data in the maps represent a quick glance rather than a detailed exploration. Given the Spinners' technology, they might have compiled the data while they were kiloparsecs from here. Or farther. We have no idea how far they've come."

"Or how they're traveling," Alander added. "I mean, we can't assume they're using hole ship technology. No one's managed to locate the actual front yet, so we have no idea *how* they're getting around."

Axford shrugged: irrelevant, for now. "My guess is that Alsafi is a staging base for the Yuhl, designed to service this area of the front. It won't contain anything too permanent," he said. "And not because it's especially dangerous, either, but because they know we're scouting around here. The longer they can delay a confrontation, the better. I'm willing to bet their actual base will be somewhere else. Not behind, because that's where the Starfish are. It's more likely to be to one side of the front—and possibly around a non–G-type star, like Alsafi, since the Gs are where the Starfish will be concentrating their search for us. Somewhere out of the way."

"Somewhere we'll probably only manage to find them by stumbling upon it by chance," said Alander.

Axford nodded. "Exactly."

Alander thought of the hole ship that had gone missing near pi-1 Ursa Major and wondered if someone already had.

"We're not going in to attack, are we?" he asked. "We're going in to try to open communications, right?"

Axford's expression was hard to read. "I'm not going to try anything crazy, if that's what you're worried about. This is my only hole ship, remember."

And this is the only version of me, Alander wanted to add.

"Relocation in one minute," announced *Mercury*.

Alander took a calming breath and told himself to relax.

A wave of dizziness rolled through him. The more debilitating effects of his engram instability had eased off in recent weeks, and he experienced only occasional attacks of vertigo. There were times when he almost forgot how crippled he had been on Adrasteia, when any moment might have brought on the forgetfulness or disorientation, to the point where he had feared for his very sanity. Those days seemed awfully long ago, but the return of his symptoms made them feel fresh again.

Or perhaps it was just a feeling of going into the unknown, as he had that first time with the Gifts, not knowing who or what might be waiting for him on the other side.

Mercury's screen cleared, and he caught his first glimpse of the Alsafi system.

Two gas giants: the gifts' maps had been right about that, at least. Of roughly equal size, they were locked in resonant orbits, the innermost straddling the system's habitable zone, taking precisely half as long to circle the system's primary. Each had a number of small moons, but none had any significant water or oxygen emission lines. There seemed to be no terrestrial bodies in the system.

"Anything?" Alander asked.

From Axford's glazed expression, he suspected that the ex-general had found a way to interface directly with the hole ship's senses.

"Not yet. Everything seems quiet. Unless . . . Hold on. We're jumping again."

The screen faded to black for a minute, and when it cleared, it showed a much closer view of the second gas giant out from Alsafi. To someone who had seen dozens of gas giants in recent weeks, it was unremarkable in almost every way: the usual tumultuous atmosphere, swirled in orange, gold, and red; intense electrical activity lighting up the night side; a powerful magnetic field blasting out radio waves as it interacted with the solar wind. It was almost too huge to comprehend and too fluid to get a grip on. As with most gas giants, its satellites provided the foreground landscape against which it simply loomed large in the background.

The view depicted on the hole ship's screen jumped from satellite to satellite, zooming in on cratered rock, fractured ice, bubbling volcanoes, smooth plains of solidified lava . . .

"Want to tell me what we're looking for here?" Alander asked edgily. He still wasn't sure what Axford was up to.

"I'm not sure exactly," the ex-general replied. "I picked up some unusual emissions from around this area, but they've stopped now. Everything seems quiet."

"*Too* quiet?"

"Perhaps. I'm going to jump again, just in case. It doesn't hurt to keep moving."

They reappeared on the far side of the giant. Three more moons hove into view, each as unremarkable as the next. Two were little more than captured asteroids, whereas the third was a smooth, icy ball roughly 800 kilometers across. A routine scan revealed a faint magnetic field, suggestive of a liquid ocean somewhere under the bright surface.

"Damn," Axford whispered after a moment. "I think they've gone to ground."

"They know we're here?"

Axford didn't respond immediately, which didn't help Alander's growing anxiety. When he did finally speak, it was slowly, thoughtfully, as he said, "Something's tipped them off."

"Could they have detected us when we first arrived?"

"It's possible." Axford shrugged. "The hole ships trigger all sorts of space-time distortions when they relocate. I've a rudimentary detector myself back in Vega. Unless they have advanced . . ." Axford trailed off.

"What is it?"

The view in the hole ship screen zoomed in on the icy ball before them. "Why, those sons of bitches."

"You've found them? Where? On that moon?"

"Look *again*," Axford demanded, although he didn't give Alander a chance to see whatever it was he was meant to be seeing before he added, "They *are* the god-damn moon."

"What—?"

Alander watched in amazement as what looked from a distance like an innocent high-albedo rock resolved into a perfectly smooth, white sphere, identical in every respect to a hole ship—except, of course, for its immense size.

"It can't be," he muttered, fighting back his apprehensions.

"Don't forget they've been following the Starfish for *twenty-five hundred years*," said Axford. "Think how many hole ships they could've stolen in that time! Imagine what that might look like if you added them all together!"

Alander didn't need to imagine; the evidence—barely comprehensible though it was—floated in space before them.

"What do we do?"

"Maybe we shouldn't do anything," said Axford. "Maybe we should just let them make the next move."

"What if they attack us?" Alander was thinking of how Axford had taken over the Yuhl ship in 61 Ursa Major. If the Yuhl performed the same maneuver, they could be inside *Mercury* before they even knew it.

"Relax, Peter," he said, obviously sensing his anxiety. "I'm keeping an eye on them. I'm fairly confident there aren't any other ships loose within the system, otherwise we would have spotted them moving by now. And if anything from this mother tries to come at us, I'm pretty sure we'll notice. There's a correlation between the number of component hole ships and the size of the final vessel. Take one away, and you change its radius."

"Very slightly," Alander pointed out, thinking of the immense number that must comprise the moon.

"It would be enough for *Mercury* to notice." Axford turned to look at Alander. "Want to say something to them?"

"It seems the next logical step. But what?"

"Perhaps we should ask *them*." Axford inclined his head in the direction of the bulkhead behind which was housed the two Yuhl captives.

Alander knew the importance of what their first words here could mean to future relationships with the Yuhl, and the weight of that responsibility increased a hundredfold when Alander remembered what had taken place earlier with their captives. It occurred to him that their brethren might not be too impressed to learn of how they'd been attacked—even if Hatzis had come off second best.

The barrier separating them from the captives faded away. The more aggressive of the two was seated in very much the same position it had been hours earlier; it didn't react to the change. The other was pacing and looked up when the wall cleared.

"Do you want to go home?" Axford asked it. The hole ship automatically translated his words.

Its reply appeared on the screen.

[UNKNOWN] NO LONGER EXISTS.
WE HAVE NOTHING BUT [UNKNOWN], AM-
BIVALENCE WILLING.

"The first term is probably the name of their home planet," Axford said. "Or government or system or something. And the second term loosely translates as *mantissa*."

"Could that be the name of their ship?" Alander directed the alien to the image of the massive ship on the screen. "*Mantissa*?" he asked. "Your ship?"

The aggressive alien snarled something untranslatable, but its partner remained calm as it answered: "*Our ship is* Mantissa *is what you see.*"

"How do we hail it?" said Alander.

"Speak, and it will hear," both vocal streams chorused smoothly.

Alander looked at Axford, who shrugged and said, "I guess we've nothing to lose."

He opened an all-frequencies broadcast and addressed

the alien vessel, instructing *Mercury* to translate it into the alien language. "This is Francis Axford of Earth calling the Yuhl-slash-Goel vessel *Mantissa*," he said. "We have two of your people aboard, as well as the body of a third in storage. Please respond."

The response came quicker than Alander had expected, almost as though the Yuhl had been anticipating the communiqué.

[UNKNOWN] REQUIRES IMMEDIATE RETURN OF HOSTAGES.
THE ᵞᵁᴴᴸ/ɢᴏᴇʟ DO NOT TRAFFIC WITH THE ALREADY-DEAD.

"Smug bastards," Axford muttered. To the alien vessel, he said, "I never said your two friends were hostages. I just said I had them on board. But should you attack me, then I won't hesitate to use them as a shield. Do you understand?"

YOU WILL NOT BE HARMED BY THE ᵞᵁᴴᴸ/ɢᴏᴇʟ.
[UNKNOWN] REQUIRES IMMEDIATE RETURN OF HOSTAGES.

"Sure," Axford snorted. "We hand over your friends, and you call in the Ambivalence. That's how you guys like to fight your battles, isn't it?" This time, he didn't even give them a chance to respond: "Listen, if you want these two back, then 'trafficking' with us is exactly what you're going to have to do."

The response took longer that time.

[UNKNOWN] DOES NOT REQUIRE US TO COMPROMISE.
RETURN THE HOSTAGES IMMEDIATELY.

"What's this 'unknown' it keeps referring to?"

"I'm not sure." Axford looked thoughtful. "The word seems to mean something along the lines of common sense, but it also appears to be a reference to an entity rather than an actual concept. Call it the Praxis for now, then we'll see if we can work it out later."

"Perhaps this is just their way of telling us it's common sense to hand over the captives," Alander suggested. "I mean, it's not as if we have much to bargain with, especially if they don't have the moral sense as we do."

Axford shook his head. "I don't buy that. If that was the case, they would have simply attacked by now."

"Okay, then what about an exchange? Split the ship; we take one each. One of us goes in while—"

Axford's laugh cut him short. "It's a good idea," he said. "But you won't catch me putting my hand up to volunteer."

"No, I didn't think you would," said Alander.

Axford's disposition sobered quickly. "Hey, it has nothing to do with me being afraid, if that's what you're suggesting. *Mercury* is the only hole ship I have, and I'm not prepared to give it away yet; that's all."

Alander shrugged dismissively. "Okay, then. If someone has to go, I guess it's going to be me."

Axford's artificial body faced him in an almost challenging pose. "With the express intentions of opening communications, right?" he said gruffly. "Nothing else?"

Alander forced a smile. "I can't decide what I'm going to do until we know more. This is a fact-finding mission, after all. I'll follow my own counsel, taking your wishes into account. That's the most I can promise."

Axford held his gaze for a handful of seconds longer, then released it with a slight nod of his head. He returned his attention to the Yuhl. "Okay, this is what we're prepared to do," he said. "We'll split our ship and one of us will come over there with one of your friends here. Then, if things go well and my crewmate returns unharmed, we will release the second one to you."

The delay in response was even longer this time.

THE PRAXIS IS SATISFIED.
YOU MAY PROCEED TO [UNKNOWN].

"And just what the hell is *that?*"

"I think that last part was meant to be *dock*," said Axford. "But there's no literal equivalent. Perhaps what they mean is—"

He stopped when he saw the appearance of the giant vessel begin to change, as hundreds of black bumps suddenly emerged and started to skim the bright surface. Axford zoomed in closer and revealed them to be hundreds of hole ship cockpits of varying sizes, all of them modified to some degree or another by the Yuhl technology. Some were encrusted with growths like the ones they'd already seen; others trailed flexible threads dozens of meters long that left glowing streaks in empty space; still others were bulbous shapes formed by combining many ordinary cockpits into one structure. One such Alander estimated to have been built from at least fifty cockpits. The interior must have been large enough to hold a couple of hundred people.

"Peter?" said Axford. It was only when Alander heard his name that he realized he'd been asked something.

"Huh?"

"I said that you'll have to merge the central portions but keep the cockpits separate. I'm guessing this is what they want us to do, anyway."

"Is that safe?" Alander asked. "I mean, will we be able to leave?"

Axford shrugged heavily. "Your guess is as good as mine, I'm afraid," he said. He studied Alander for a couple of moments. "Are you having second thoughts?"

Alander stared at the screen, at the massive construct formed from centuries of predation on Spinner contactees. He didn't dare believe that they'd show him or humanity any more compassion than they'd shown others, but at the same time he supposed it was worth the risk. Here was a chance to increase humanity's resources and knowledge exponentially. Plus, forming some sort of strategic alliance, even if it didn't go as far as the one Axford desired, could indeed make all the difference between survival and extinction. When seen in that context, personal sacrifice was an acceptable risk. More so: it was a necessary one.

He shook his head, but he could tell even as he did it that it lacked conviction. "I'm okay," he lied. "And I guess we shouldn't keep them waiting."

Axford gestured to their alien captives. "Which one do you want?"

Alander automatically indicated the passive one. "I'll take him," he said. "Or her. Whatever."

Axford nodded his approval. "Good choice."

The aggressive alien stared balefully at them, its masklike face completely unreadable, as a second force wall divided the cockpit into quarters. A tremor ran through Alander's feet as the union of the two cockpits began to reverse. The walls puckered and began to stretch along the half containing himself and his captive, leaving him with one of the screens and the alien version of the couch. The tremor became more noticeable as the floor formed a lip and began to pull apart. It was like watching a recording of cell division—from the inside.

"Call me if you need to," said Axford. "If I don't hear from you within an hour of docking, I'll assume the worst."

"Then what?" Alander asked.

"Then I kill this one and go for reinforcements."

Alander noted that his words were being translated for the benefit of both their passengers. A wall was forming between the two cockpits, stretching like taffy to separate their interiors.

"Don't do anything hasty," Alander put in quickly as the wall closed in.

"Or you, Peter," said Axford with a nervous half smile.

Then he was gone, and the tremor became a faint rocking sensation as the one craft became two. Watching on the main screen, Alander studied the separation with fascination. The material the ships were made of was so fluid, an impressive demonstration of the superiority of

the Spinners' technology. And this was, he reminded himself, the stuff they gave away! The hole ships were like
plastic building blocks given to a young child, a toy with
which they couldn't possibly harm themselves. And from
that perspective, the giant ship before him—the *Mantissa*,
if Axford's translation was correct—was little more than
a building block castle. It didn't necessarily show any
greater understanding of the technology than humans already possessed. The Yuhl had simply had longer to
gather the blocks and put them together.

Remembering the language issue, Alander decided to
test out his ship's own translation capabilities.

"Do you understand what we're doing?" he asked the
Yuhl in the cell next to his.

"I am *returning to Praxis/alone*." The reply was surprisingly
clear, although Alander reminded himself that there might
be subtleties to terms like Praxis that Axford's arbitrary
translation might hide. The alien's expression shifted so
that the black lines on its face resembled a geometrical Jap-
anese gigaku mask. "*This was not* supposed to be *different*."

"Why not?" he started, but was confused by the two separate statements. "I mean, how? Different in what way"

The alien didn't reply.

"Do you always travel in pairs?" Alander persisted.

The alien's reply appeared on the screen.

ONLY THE [UNKNOWN].

Without Axford to work on the translation, Alander was
forced to do the research himself. Using basic conSense
tools, the most he could handle without risking disorientation, he took the undecipherable term and teased it apart.
The components of the double sound had meanings relating to servitude and bureaucracy, and the English word
that first came to mind was *hierodule*, the name for a
temple slave in ancient Greece. It was, however, often
associated with temple prostitutes, so he settled on *helot*
instead, another Greek term referring to unfree men of a
higher status than the lowest possible slave.

"Do the helots have names?" he asked.

"Yes."

He touched his chest. "My name is—"

"*Peter/Alander*," said the alien. Plates on its face shifted back and forth in quick succession.

A nod? Alander thought.

"*Caryl/Hatzis* told *us/me* earlier."

The sound of his own name and Hatzis's in the alien dialect surprised Alander. He hadn't been sure that the alien was paying attention back then. At that point, the more aggressive of the two had been dominating proceedings.

"Then what is *your* name?"

There was a long pause. The alien moved to its couch and sat astride it, its head moving in an unusual manner. A strange whistling noise came from both its vocal chords; since the ship's AI didn't offer a translation, Alander assumed the sound was the Yuhl equivalent of humming or some other meaningless conversation filler.

When it stopped, though, the alien looked up, and the lines on its face were aligned in a series of near-perfect squares.

"*Ueh/Ellil*," it said.

"Ueh Ellil, huh?" The first name sounded like Huey without the *H* and with a more guttural vowel at the end. "Well, Ueh, I'm . . ."

What? Pleased to make your acquaintance? Awed to be in the presence of an alien species? Christ, what was he supposed to say to this creature? Ever since the arrival of the Spinners and the Starfish, he'd been pondering the existence of aliens. But to actually be standing in front of a real, live flesh-and-blood one was something he was finding very hard to get his head around.

Before he could decide, Axford's face appeared in the cockpit screen, and his voice came over the hole ship's communications systems: "Okay, Peter, we're fully separated, and you should now have control over *Silent Liquidity*. I duplicated the *Mercury*'s AI when it split into yours, so it should have everything this ship does."

Alander frowned. "*Silent Liquidity?* That's its name?"

Axford lifted his shoulders. "According to the *Mercury*'s translation," he said. "I guess the Roaches aren't averse to a little pretension."

"Either that or they appreciate the tactical importance of these ships." He shrugged himself. "Whatever. You say I should have access to everything your ship does now?"

Axford nodded. "Except that I removed everything about Vega," he said. "And I suggest you do the same for your colony worlds. You never know what they might use it for."

"To be perfectly honest," Alander said, "I don't blame you, but I'm not going to follow your example. I've got nothing to hide from these people."

"They're not people, Peter."

"No, they're not," he said. "I imagine they'd resent such a comparison."

"Very funny," said Axford flatly.

"I'm serious, actually." Alander hadn't closed off communications between him and his Yuhl passenger, but *Ueh/ Ellil* stayed perfectly silent. His attitude was frozen, as if he was almost afraid to move. "They're significantly more advanced than us. Think about it: they've been traveling through space long before we nailed Christ to the cross."

"As scavengers, though," said Axford. "Don't forget that."

Alander dismissed the matter with a shake of his head. It wasn't the time to be entering into such an argument. Certainly not with Axford, either. The man clearly had his feelings on these aliens, and no amount of arguing was going to sway him from that opinion.

"Have the Roaches given you any instructions about docking yet?" asked Axford.

Alander knew that referring to the *Yuhl/Goel* as Roaches was the ex-general's way of having the last word on the matter, dismissing the aliens as little more than insects, but he didn't rise to the bait.

"Nothing yet."

"Then tell *Liquidity* what you want to do and see what happens."

Alander nodded. "Wish me luck."

"I don't believe in luck, Peter," he said.

No, thought Alander, *you wouldn't.*

"*Silent Liquidity?* I want you to dock with the *Mantissa,*" he instructed. "But I need you to keep our cockpit separate. Do not allow any form of intrusion unless I authorize it. Understood?"

"Understood, Peter." The hole ship's voice was the same as all the others': smooth and melodic without sounding artificially so. He wondered if it sounded the same to a Yuhl's ears.

Before the screen showing the *Mantissa* went black, he caught one last glimpse of the massive vessel hanging before him. Its incredible size staggered him, as did the perfect smoothness of its surface. It looked like a giant, ivory marble. Only the constant dance of the swarming cockpits—some of them skimming the surface in rapid, swooping arcs, others drifting lazily several kilometers above the surface—gave it any form of identity. The blacks specks created patterns that formed and faded like bees crawling across a hive.

Then, absently, the hole ship was relocating, and it was too late to turn back.

What have you got yourself into this time, truth seeker? he asked himself.

1.2.5

The Spinners may not have visited Sothis, but evidence of their gifts was everywhere. The tragedies resulting from the Starfish sneak attacks were uniting and mobilizing the human remnant much more quickly than Hatzis had expected—or hoped—prompting a convergence on Sirius that she hadn't dreamed would occur for weeks yet.

There were over a dozen hole ships in parking orbit above McKenzie Base, taking part in a crisis meeting that spanned 150 light-years. Their names reflected the interests of the people who had discovered them, ranging from the purely descriptive (such as *Soap Bubble* and *Cue Ball*) to the biological (*Oosphere* and *Egg*). The notion of mythical spinners and weavers touched upon by *Arachne* was revived again by *Klotho*; legend also brought forth the names of numerous culture-givers, among them *Huang-di*, *Prometheus*, and *Koyote*. The newest edition was from the colony rescued by Alander, Thor, and Francis Axford in 61 Ursa Major; its freshly minted hole ship had been dubbed *Kirsty* for no clear reason Sol could see, although she suspected that the senescence of Hera's mission supervisor, Tarsem Jones, might have had something to do with it.

Sol parked *Arachne* in its usual dock. Gou Mang, whom she had left in charge during her absence, had had the sense to leave it free. The rest was clearly beyond her, however.

The hole ships above had ferried their physical passengers to McKenzie Base's rarely used conference room, while their human pilots—most of them copies of herself—were currently doing nothing but waiting. The first thing Sol did was organize a rotating roster enabling them to jump to random broadcast points in order to relay the events on Sothis to the rest of surveyed space. The number of inbound transmissions was rising; there had to be some sort of response to quell the developing panic.

She ensured that the link to *Arachne* was clear, then went to join the meeting. Strictly speaking, her physical presence wasn't required, but she knew it would have an impact. Since the destruction of her home, she had rarely left the security of her hole ship. As she strode along the tubular access ways to the conference, she adjusted her outfit to reflect the severity of the situation, changing from an imitation UNESSPRO shipsuit to a black and gray ensemble cut in the style of a 2050 business suit.

When the door opened on the conference room, the sound of voices greeted her like a slap in the face. In the three weeks since the destruction of the Vincula, she had rarely met anyone in person apart from Peter Alander. The engrams ran as simulations in virtual worlds; only in recent times had the impetus to house minds in permanent physical bodies become more urgent. The need to be mobile, and therefore able to escape if necessary, was now a priority—especially for the people Sol considered absolutely necessary. These naturally included the various versions of her scattered across the colonies, as well as those individuals contacted by the Spinners to act as interfaces with the Gifts. Unfortunately, it also included some of the mission supervisors with whom she would have preferred not to have to deal directly.

When she entered, all noise in the room abruptly ceased, but the argument she had clearly interrupted still simmered in the air. The pressure of eyes suddenly on her was an almost physical force that made her feel immediately uncomfortable. In total, there were only twenty people in the room, but at that moment, it felt like a multitude to her.

"Thank you for joining us here," she said without preamble, as though she had been the one that had requested the meeting. "I came as soon as I could."

"Where have you been?" challenged Otto Wyra of Pan straightaway. "Why weren't you here when you were needed?"

She met his accusation squarely. "There's simply too much work to do and not enough people to do it. I can't be everywhere at once. As impressive as the hole ships are, they can't perform miracles; they may get us to our destinations quicker, but they certainly can't provide instantaneous transportation."

"But—"

"I'm only *human*, Otto," she said firmly. "Please remember that."

He spluttered into silence. *Only human* was something he could never hope to be. Even in a flesh-and-blood android body, he was still just an engram. They were *all* engrams, apart from her, a fact that wasn't lost on them— nor one would she ever let them forget.

"I was busy observing an attack on a new colony," she explained. "As Tarsem may already have told you, Hera, our latest addition, engaged a third alien species seeking to obtain its gifts by force. There can be no doubt that this species is the source of anomalous encounters in colonies such as Perendi; they are also responsible for the death markers found wherever the Starfish have struck. It turns out that some of these strikes have been deliberately encouraged by this new race in an attempt to cover up their thefts." She stared levelly around the room. "It may or may not be something you particularly want to hear right now, given everything else that has been happening, but the fact of the matter is, my friends, that we are being preyed upon." She shrugged.

"That is what I have to report. I hope you will appreciate that I haven't been wasting time."

Her gaze settled meaningfully on Otto Wyra as she said this last part. He looked away uncomfortably.

"Now," she went on, "I've personally interviewed members of this alien race and will share that data with you later. But first I want to know what's going on here. You were discussing some issues when I came in . . ."

She let the sentence trail off as an invitation for someone to elaborate.

"There's only one issue," said Wyra, looking up to her again. "The Starfish. They're picking us off one by one."

Sol nodded. "And what do you suggest we do about it?"

This time it was Ali Genovese of Diana that spoke. "That's what we're here to work out."

Sol faced her. "And what have you come up with so far?"

"We have three options," she said evenly. "One: we do nothing."

"Which would be tantamount to suicide," Wyra pointed out irritably.

"Two," Genovese went on without addressing his comment. "We move."

Sol frowned. "But where?"

"That's the problem," said Genovese, nodding. "The Starfish seem to be scouring surveyed space reasonably thoroughly, but they tend to concentrate around the loci containing their most recent kills. That is, every time a colony slips through our fingers and uses the communicators, they jump elsewhere. That's how the colonies neighboring Athena managed to escape, we think. If the Starfish had been *truly* thorough, they'd be dead now."

"Thank God for small mercies," breathed Donald Schievenin of Fujin, one of the spared worlds.

"That doesn't mean they won't come back, though," Genovese added. "We've some evidence of back-filling, although the data really is too patchy to be certain. Some of us are under the impression that no one will be safe as long as we're anywhere that's likely to be targeted by the Starfish."

"So you think we should leave surveyed space entirely?" Hatzis asked her. "Migrate to another section of the galaxy entirely?"

Genovese looked uncomfortable. "Not in the short term, no. I was thinking more of moving the colonies at risk to the sites the Starfish have already struck. I doubt they'd return to a system they've already wiped clean of life, so the risks would have to be greatly reduced. As long as no one breaks communicator silence in one of those systems, we should be safe."

Wyra sneered. "Dead systems," he said.

"Why not?" Genovese retorted. "Adrasteia, Varuna, Athena, Thor—there are plenty to go around, and most of them are habitable. Yes, some have sustained long-term environmental damage, but that's not necessarily a problem."

"Maybe not for you," Wyra said. "For me, it'd be like sleeping in someone's grave."

"But isn't that better than dying yourself? Besides, it'd only be temporary. Once we're sure the Starfish have gone, we can move back to what's left."

"I'd rather set myself adrift in interstellar space, thanks. No one would find us there."

Sol nodded. "That's a possibility," she said. "But, Ali, you said there was a third option."

Genovese hesitated, a look of uncertainty passing across her face. She glanced at Donald Schievenin, on Hatzis's right, his artificial body taller than most, his features elongated in a rough approximation of his normal face.

"You're not going to like it, Sol," he said.

"Well, drawing it out isn't going to help." Again she looked around the room. "Is someone going to tell me?"

"Secession," said Wyra, the slight sneer on his face giving the word the emphasis of an insult.

She hesitated for a nanosecond, an instant too small for any of the engrams to notice, even if they were fast-tracking their processing speeds. She knew exactly what he meant by that single word, but she feigned innocence to give herself time to think.

"Secession from *whom*, Otto?"

"From everything," he said. "From the Spinners; from *you*."

"What difference is that going to make? Ignoring us won't stop the Starfish from killing you."

"They can't kill us if they don't know we're there," said Genovese. "So far, they've only attacked colonies using the gifts. They haven't visited or harmed the rest. Maybe that's not a coincidence. Maybe they home in on more than just the communicator broadcasts."

"If that was the case," said Sol, "then we'd all be dead right now."

"Maybe it's the Gifts themselves they see as a threat." Wyra waved his arms for emphasis. "People are dying out there, Caryl, and we don't know why. But if we drop the Gifts now, then maybe we can at least give them a few more days to live."

"Crap, Otto," Sol jumped in incredulously. "The Gifts aren't some hot potato you can simply put down because you're fingers are getting a little burned."

"Don't throw these trite aphorisms at us, Caryl, please. We're talking about *people* here, not—"

"I know that," said Sol forcefully. "All I'm saying is that you can't abandon something just because people are dying right now. Where would we be if humanity had turned its back on electricity following the first electric shock? Or dismantled the telephone system after the first obscene phone call?"

He scowled at her. "Downplaying the magnitude of this isn't helping either. We're not talking about someone getting a goddamn—"

"You came here in *Prometheus*, didn't you?" she cut in.

Wyra stopped, blinking in confusion at her abrupt change of tack. "So?"

"What would humanity have been like if we'd refused his gift of fire?"

He became instantly angered, knowing full well he was being mocked. "To hell with you, Caryl. Some of us don't have your confidence in the Spinners. They don't care what's good for us. They just toss us these baubles to make themselves feel magnanimous as they pass by, on their way to God only knows where! They don't give a damn whether the gifts end up destroying us. Why should they? There must be thousands of other species out there. Who'll miss us?"

Sol stared at him tight-lipped during his rant, wanting him to get it out of his system before she said anything else. In her head, she conducted a hurried, nonverbal conversation with Gou Mang:

WHY DIDN'T YOU WARN ME ABOUT THIS?

THERE WAS NO TIME—

YOU DON'T NEED TIME. USE THE OVERSEER CHANNELS. TALK TO ME LIKE THIS.

I'M SORRY. I DIDN'T—

IT DOESN'T MATTER. IT'S NOT YOUR FAULT I HAVEN'T WORKED OUT HOW TO FIX SENESCENCE YET. JUST REMEMBER WHAT WE'RE TRYING TO DO HERE, AND BE ON THE BALL. BE AN ASSET.

I'LL TRY, SOL.

"—can't expect us to sit here like idiots while you—"

"That's enough, Otto." She felt like a pale midget surrounded by green-skinned giants, but when she spoke,

Wyra fell quiet, and she knew she had all of their attention. "Your simplistic analysis of the situation has a certain persuasiveness, I'll admit, and I'll certainly be interested to know who the others are that agree with you. I'll also be quite happy to accept whatever gifts you're planning not to use while you bury your heads in the sand waiting for your asses to be kicked."

Wyra and a couple of the others bristled at this, but she went on without giving them chance to voice their indignation.

"Because that *is* what will happen, people, I assure you." She stared around the room, daring any one of them to defy her. "If you aren't prepared to do anything now, then you aren't doing humanity any favors, believe me, because clearly what connects you *to* humanity in the first place has already left you. You're not human anymore. You're just some nth-generation copy waiting to be erased. You're just echoes of the real thing. You might as well just get the Starfish on the blower right now and have them put you out of your misery. You sure as hell aren't any good to me anymore."

In the silence that followed, she breathed heavily through her nose, delivering oxygen to an anger that burned with more heat than even she had expected. "Look, you can do what you want to, Otto, but I'm not going to sit around and watch humanity die again. If fighting for survival means sacrificing a few individuals along the way, then so be it—even if one of those individuals is *me.*"

Everyone in the room remained silent, as if hanging on her every word, which gave her the confidence to go on: "I'll be the first to admit that at this moment in time I haven't got the faintest idea of what we should be doing, or how we can possibly overcome the odds stacked against us. But I do know this: today I spoke to an alien whose species had been tailing the Starfish for twenty-five hundred years. If they can survive that long, then there's no reason why we can't as well."

"But in all that time," said Wyra, in a tone that was

more subdued than before, "they haven't managed to find a solution to the Starfish problem, have they?"

"No," said Hatzis simply. "But that's not to say there *isn't* one, either. Look, I'm not trying to tell you that this is going to be easy. It's not! But I believe it can be done, and to do it I'm going to need all the help I can get. Everyone else, everyone who wants to stand around crying about how unfair life is, you can all go and get the fuck out of here right now, because your whining isn't helping the situation. If anything, it's holding the rest of us back. You're wasting my time, and I don't need you. None of us do."

They stared at her for a good twenty seconds before someone spoke. It was Cleo Samson, of all people, of Hammon.

"Otto doesn't speak for all of us, Caryl," she said. "Most of us are willing to do whatever it takes to overcome this problem. Just tell us what to do, and we'll do it."

Sol forced herself to be calm, slowing her heart rate and reducing the levels of some of the primitive fight-or-flight hormones rushing through her bloodstream.

"Okay," she said after a few seconds. "Then this is what I want. Our biggest problem at the moment is communications. We're too spread out, and there aren't enough hole ships to plug the gaps. We're also vulnerable the way we are, spread out at random across surveyed space. I do agree with Otto in that respect: I simply don't see the point in making us even *more* vulnerable, though. I think Ali's second proposition has some merit, too: we've yet to see any Starfish activity in systems that have already been attacked, so they might be good havens, if only temporarily—until the threat has passed."

"That would mean leaving the gifts behind," said Samson.

Sol nodded. "But I'm not suggesting we abandon the gifts entirely. I know we can't afford to do that." She thought as quickly as she could, formulating a blueprint for survival on the hop. "We're going to tackle this three

ways. One: colonies at risk will up ship and regroup in
two or three of the dead colony systems. No more than
that because we need to reduce the number of hole ships
we have committed to communications. I know it'll take
time to find a way to move the Overseer cores and any
other hardware we need, so I suggest we get moving on
that right away. Two: any colony that has a problem with
occupying a dead system will come here, to Sothis. And,
three: there are holes in our knowledge of the gifts. That's
become obvious to me in the last day. We'll need to conduct an intensive search through the Libraries for more
practical applications of the Spinner technology. I suggest
we concentrate that research in one system close to the
front, where the Starfish have yet to reach. Juno, perhaps,
in Gamma Serpens. You're from there, right, Jayme?"

Jayme Sivio stirred at the rear of the gathering from
where he'd been watching the argument. "That's right,"
he said. "And I'm sure you'd be welcome there."

"Who's your SMC? It's not me, is it?"

"No, it's Donald." Sivio nodded at the version of
Schievenin from Fujin. "Our contact is Kingsley Oborn."

And he's also your UNESSPRO traitor, Hatzis confirmed to herself. "Perfect," she said aloud. "While the
evacuations are under way, all volunteers for this project
should make themselves known. We can reclaim Overseer
resources from the senescent colonies, so processing time
shouldn't be a problem. We must make sure, however,
that everything is mobile so it can be pulled out at a moment's notice. While it's all very well to make the leap
to permanent bodies—" She indicated the crowd of similar faces before her, cursing Peter Alander for setting the
precedent. "—I still think we need to remember that we're
more at risk this way. Legs can only run so fast; free
engrams can travel at the speed of light. Any questions?"

"What about the other aliens?" asked Wyra, his posture
and tone no longer so confrontational. "You haven't told
us how we're going to deal with them, on top of everything else."

"I've already taken steps to explore that problem, and

I expect word to come soon." *Assuming Axford doesn't cock everything up,* she added to herself. "We have a report on our books of a hole ship that went missing near pi-1 Ursa Major. I'd like to send a mission to investigate the disappearance. If there are more, they could constitute evidence of direct aggression. We might have already been at war for some time without even knowing it."

She thought of the systems supposedly raided by the Yuhl then destroyed by Starfish that had come following their call. If this was true, the Yuhl had a lot to answer for. But she didn't know how far she could trust Frank Axford. He might have reasons for encouraging aggression between the human survivors and the Yuhl. Perhaps he hoped to pick up the pieces once everything settled down.

The eyes of the small crowd were still on her. "Otto, if you or anyone genuinely don't want to be part of this, I'm not going to force you. You know that. I'm not a tyrant. You are all free to follow your own counsel. Just remember this: we are all that's left of the human race. If we fail, everything dies with us. Not just our hopes for the future, but the memories of the past as well. Everything that makes us unique will end up as a footnote in a Spinner Library for some other alien species to read about someday—and I don't want that. If we can survive this, we can survive anything the universe throws at us." Heads were nodding. *Enough of the rhetoric,* she thought. "We have work to do, people."

The crowd broke up into smaller groups, muttering among themselves. Not everyone was satisfied, but the crisis had been averted for the moment, at least. Hatzis sensed a flurry of electromagnetic communications as hole ships were summoned. She left the room, happy to leave the logistics of docking and loading passengers to her various selves on Sothis and off. Opening a link to Gou Mang, she said, I WANT EVERY SPARE HOLE SHIP HERE WITHIN THE DAY. HOW MANY DO WE HAVE NOW?

SEVEN.

AND WHEN THE COLONIES GROUP HERE, WE SHOULD BE

ABLE TO MAKE THAT DOUBLE FIGURES AT LEAST.

She pondered how Axford had created a larger hole ship by merging two into one. Using that sort of technique, moving whole colonies around would be a lot simpler.

BROADCAST A REQUEST TO ALL COLONIES TO CONSIDER THE FOLLOWING SYSTEMS FOR RECOLONIZATION: UPSILON AQUARIUS, HD194640, 94 AQUARIUS, AND BSC8477.

THE FIRST ONES ATTACKED?

AND THE FARTHEST AWAY. WE MIGHT BE PUTTING OUR EGGS IN ONE OR TWO BASKETS, BUT AT LEAST THOSE BASKETS WILL BE A GOOD DISTANCE APART. WE'LL KEEP A BARE MINIMUM OF HOLE SHIPS STATIONED IN EACH REFUGEE SYSTEM: ENOUGH TO PULL OUT IF SOMETHING DOES HAPPEN, PLUS A COUPLE TO PROVIDE COMMUNICATIONS RELAYS. THAT SHOULD INCREASE THE NUMBER AT OUR DISPOSAL.

THE NEWER COLONIES WON'T BE EASY TO MOVE: PERENDI, HERA, MEDEINE, JUMIS . . .

I KNOW.

Sol pondered this all the way back to *Arachne*. The novelty of the gifts inevitably led to an increased feeling of invulnerability. It was hard to believe, with so many age-old questions being answered everywhere they looked, that the ultimate one—of killing or being killed—was still being asked.

They'll learn, she thought to herself. *They'll have to. One can only take baby-sitting so far.*

By the time the next midday deadline arrived, she had pre-pared a long report detailing her experiences with Francis Axford and the Yuhl. It told the colonies everything they needed to know about the situation and closed with a personal plea for both calm and levelheadedness. The last thing the survivors needed was to panic or to cut themselves off from the support networks they would need in order to survive the coming weeks.

Preparations for the evacuations were already under

way. Hole ships had been sent to the four proposed refugee systems to ensure they were still fallow. Dormant
facilities on and around Sothis were coming back to full
operation in readiness for an influx of colonists in both
physical and virtual form. Hatzis expected around a third
of the remaining colonies to take up her offer of sanctuary. About half would opt for hiding out in the refugee
systems. The rest would either do as Wyra suggested—
hunker down and hope no one noticed them—or they
would follow some other scheme. She wouldn't be surprised if more than one fell apart under the strain, either
from internal conflict within the colony or from engram
failure. Such losses would be regretted, but there was little
she could do about them except make sure no resources
were lost in the process.

One of the first things she did was send an envoy to
Juno in Gamma Serpens to discuss the establishment of
an intensive library search in the system. She doubted
she'd meet much resistance; it did mean more resources
for the colony, after all, even if it did also slightly increase
the risk of a Starfish attack (with so much flowing through
the system, the chances of a slipup would be higher). But
she wasn't worried about a sneak attack at the moment.
The Starfish front was still seventy to eighty light-years
behind that of the Spinners. If everyone was careful, they
should be safe for a couple of weeks yet.

The hard-to-shift recent colonies weren't a problem for
the same reason, although it did make things difficult in
other ways. While she had no doubt that colonies like
Aretia in Van Maanen 2, which had been buzzed by the
Yuhl, would be more than happy to contribute to the effort, they were also farther away from the action than she
would have liked them to be. Supply lines would be
stretched as a result. But, again, they would manage. She
could bring in nongift resources from senescent colonies
like New France in Tau Ceti. Some of them had nanofactured a great deal of equipment, as the colonists had on
Sothis, that was otherwise lying around rotting or being
stolen by the Yuhl.

Only one thing irked her. During the broadcast of the last midday message, a short report had arrived from Thor. Sol had assumed that her engram was still with Axford and Alander, but the report indicated otherwise. Thor had left them planning to investigate the site of a possible alien staging point. Why she had left them wasn't exactly clear, but she did say where she was going. She was heading to pi-1 Ursa Major to see if she could find any concrete evidence of Yuhl aggression. As Sol herself had reasoned, they couldn't take Axford's word carte blanche. She personally thought the aliens were as guilty as hell, but until she had a smoking gun, she couldn't very well expect anyone to believe her, either.

It all made a kind of sense. The trouble was, though, that Sol had already sent someone to pi-1 Ursa Major. Her engram from Tatenen, flying a hole ship liberated from the destruction of the colony in HD113283, had been happy to check out what had happened to her engram from Eos. The likelihood of both missions arriving at the same time was reasonably high, so *Oosphere* and Tatenen would most likely find nothing but *Pearl* and Thor, and both trips would have been a waste of time.

When Thor finally did return, she would have words with her in regards to wasting valuable resources. She could understand her engram's grief at the loss of her home colony, but still, if humanity was to survive, then everyone was going to have to put aside their personal needs and remain rational at all times. This type of impulsive behavior had the potential to put others at risk. If Sol realized that, why didn't Thor?

Perhaps, she thought, something had gone wrong in Thor's simulation. One of Sol's experimental alterations, designed to assist the stability of her virtual copies, might have inadvertently had the opposite effect in a stressful situation.

She paced the interior of *Arachne*, wishing there was an easier way to coordinate her engrams. They were primitive, stubborn, and inclined to be flaky the older they became. But they were all she had. They were all *her*, so how could she blame them for shortcomings that stemmed from her own personality in the first place?

WE'VE LOST A RELAY.

Gou Mang was gradually getting used to using the Overseer channels for private communications. Operating at a level below conSense, they were much harder for an external source to access and interpret.

WHICH ONE?

ADAMMAS IN *KOYOTE*. SHE WAS BROADCASTING FROM ETA LEPUS WHEN HER SIGNAL WAS CUT OFF.

STARFISH?

I'M GUESSING YES. THEY MUST HAVE TRACKED HER DOWN AND SURPRISED HER, OTHERWISE SHE WOULD'VE SAID SOMETHING IN THE MESSAGE. BUT IT JUST STOPPED DEAD.

Sol pondered the loss. One less hole ship; one less facet of herself. She shook her head firmly. She couldn't allow herself to be sentimental.

SEND OUT DIANA IN HER PLACE. HALVE THE TIME THE RELAYS STAY IN POSITION. IF THE STARFISH ARE COTTON-ING ON TO WHAT WE'RE DOING, WE'RE GOING TO HAVE TO START BEING CAREFUL.

It was the relays' job to move among the systems, collecting data and then jumping elsewhere to broadcast it. They also ferried equipment and people. As the evacuation began, their distribution and movement would be critical. The necessity for fine control of the process gave her an extra reason to encourage her engrams to pilot the alien vessels, thus giving her an even tighter stranglehold on communications and transportation.

SHOULD WE SEND SOMEONE TO VEGA?

Sol dismissed the suggestion out of hand. NO. AXFORD CAN HEAR WHAT WE'RE BROADCASTING. HE'LL RESPOND IF HE WANTS TO.

YOU DON'T THINK HE'LL WANT TO JOIN FORCES?

I GUARANTEE HE WON'T. THE ONLY WAY HE'LL JOIN US IS AS CONQUEROR. HE'LL NEVER FIT IN.

BESIDES WHICH, HE MIGHT BE USEFUL JUST WHERE HE IS, RIGHT?

Sol smiled. THAT, TOO. WE NEED SOMEONE TO DO THE
DIRTY WORK.

But the smile was short-lived. Neither Axford nor Alander had reported back from their encounter with the Yuhl,
if it had in fact gone ahead as Thor had suggested. The
hole ship sent to investigate Alsafi had returned to report
that the system was empty. A feeling of frustration rolled
through her. Despite being at the center of such an enormous flow of information, it was still easy to be very
much isolated.

Another midday broadcast came and went. The Library re-
search team was coming together on Juno and had already
reported some progress in the area of hole ship amalga-
mation: once they knew the data was there, it was much
easier to find. Two refugee colonies had been established
in 94 Aquarius and BSC8477. Seven colonies had indicated that they would like to relocate to Sirius, once a
safe way to move their core survey resources was found.
Somehow, in among the chaos, two new colonies were
found on the forward edge of the Spinner advance. That
was still a priority: preserving lives from the stupid mistakes of the early days. Just because there were new
threats to deal with didn't mean that the old ones had gone
away.

Meanwhile, a rush of information crisscrossed surveyed
space via the Overseer channels from all the manifold
versions of herself visiting dozens of systems: Yuhl vessels raided five senescent colonies whose resources had
been earmarked for Sothis; another relay hole ship was
targeted by the Starfish but managed to escape unscathed;
covert software that Sol had devised for installation in the
colony Overseers was spreading as expected, bypassing
virus checkers and firewalls that were a hundred years out
of date by the Vincula's standards. The Congress of Orphans was falling into place, even if, as yet, there was no
mention in the broadcasts of what it would ultimately be
used for. The secret transmissions had always been cir-

cumspect about that. Since Axford had let the secret out to Alander, Sol had even more need to be careful.

When the transmissions ended, Thor didn't move for half an hour. She lay on *Pearl*'s couch, still wary of her bruised abdomen, thinking long and hard about what she was doing. There had been a request from Sol for her and Tatenen to report in. Earlier, she had actually recorded a message and had *Pearl* queue it, ready to transmit the moment midday arrived. But she didn't send it. She had regretted leaving Alander and Axford the way she had, and hearing Sol's annoyance in her message only compounded that regret. But that, in turn, only added to the urgency with which she felt she needed to redeem herself. It was why she had volunteered for the pi-1 Ursa Major mission in the first place, although she was aware that not telling Sol in advance what she intended to do would have undoubtedly negated the value of her effort. But she hadn't been thinking rationally after the loss of her home colony. And now it was too late: now she couldn't call in without giving herself away.

In the end, staying hidden was more important than letting Sol know what she was doing. The moment she used her ftl communicator, it would be obvious to anyone who knew how to track such technology where she was going. She didn't doubt that the people who had killed the version of her from Tatenen knew all about that sort of stuff; they had certainly dispensed with her hole ship quick enough. Or at least they appeared to have. Whoever they were, Thor knew too little about them to take any chances. She knew just enough to be afraid.

Damn you, Peter. This is all your fault!

Briefly, she considered turning around. The screen glowed with the dull light of the red dwarf known as 4130-697-1. In the previous hours, she had visited numerous similar systems: 4134-318-1, Hipp43534, 4130-580-1, 4130-915-1. She was twenty-five light-years from pi-1 Ursa Major and seventy light-years from Sol. She had run out of likely targets in the range she was

searching, but she wasn't giving up yet. She still had a
number of leads she could try:

Hipp40918	G0	119 ly
Hipp41308	K2V	122 ly
Hipp43477	G0	133 ly
2 Ursa Major	A2m	158 ly
Muscida	K2III	252 ly

All were possibilities, and *Pearl* had calculated the
most fuel-efficient trajectories to follow to each of them.
She knew roughly how far away to look, and the hole
ship's senses were uncannily precise.

Still, it was hard not to be daunted. In fact, she might
have even given it all up for a lost cause, had it not been
for that one, single clue she had picked up in 4130-580-
1.

"*Pearl,* take route four, please," she said, picking the
one leading to Hipp40918. In her hand she jingled a small
metal disk; in her head she heard a distant voice: her own
from another mouth in another time: "This is Caryl Hatzis
of UNESSPRO Mission 805, *Paul Davies,* hailing UNES-
SPRO Mission 391. *Andrei Linde,* are you receiving me?"

Thor had detected the faint echoes of the transmission
from the fringes of pi-1 Ursa Major the previous day,
when she arrived in the system. A quick glance over the
system showed nothing out of the ordinary, but Thor
wasn't taking any chances. The engram of herself from
Tatenen had obviously been sent to look over pi-1 UMA
as well, and she was dutifully following the next step of
trying to hail the mission sent to that system. Tatenen
broadcast the message several times while Thor triangu-
lated on her. Then, following a lengthy pause: "Eos, this
is Tatenen. If you're reading me, please respond." Eos
had been on the first mission Sol had sent. *Pearl* found
Oosphere, Tatenen's hole ship, on the far side of the system's primary and, at Thor's request, locked in the destination. She fought the urge to send a reply, since it
would take some hours to arrive at electromagnetic

speeds. Once she was certain it was safe, she would jump across and greet her copy in person.

The standard transmission used near the Spinner and Starfish fronts followed: "This is an open broadcast to all vessels within range of this transmitter. I represent the sole survivors of the race known as human through whose territories you are traveling. We request the opening of diplomatic channels as a matter of some urgency. We desire nothing but peace. Please respond. I repeat: this is an open broadcast . . ."

Thor had only half listened to the broadcast while scanning through the data. There was no sign of the other hole ship sent to explore the system, and no sign at all of the original survey mission. If the *Andrei Linde* had ever made it, something very bad had gone wrong since.

"—request the opening of diplomatic channels as a matter of some urgency. We desire nothing but peace. Please—no, wait. I—"

The transmission had ended in mid-sentence.

Thor stopped what she was doing with a frown.

"What happened, *Pearl*?"

"The transmission has ceased."

She rolled her eyes at the AI's pedantry. "I realize that," she said. "Play the ending again."

She heard her own voice repeat the familiar words, exclaim in alarm, and then suddenly fall silent.

A chill tingled Thor's spine. "Do you have an image yet?"

"Yes, but the quality is very poor," said *Pearl*.

"Show me anyway."

On the screen a white dot appeared against a grainy black background. As the end of the message played through again, something streaked across the screen from the left side and struck the white dot. There was a red flash, then both were gone.

"They were *attacked?*"

"It would appear so," said the hole ship emotionlessly.

"Can you tell who did it?"

"No."

"Show it to me again," she instructed. "This time give a wider angle."

The attack repeated at a slightly decreased magnification. The streak of light that struck the *Oosphere* and destroyed it appeared to come out of nowhere. There was nothing visible at its source.

"Take us closer," she said, recognizing in her tone the uncertainty she felt about taking such an action. "But be as careful as you can—and stay ready to get the hell out of there if whatever hit her comes at us. Understood?"

"Understood."

The view of pi-1 Ursa Major faded from view. Thor worried at a hangnail while waiting for *Pearl* to arrive. Something was definitely up. They needed to know what it was, but Sol had already lost two hole ships and two copies of herself in pi-1 Ursa Major trying to find out. Thor was determined not to make it three.

The short hop seemed to take forever. When she finally arrived, she conducted a quick scan of the area. It was empty, apart from the billowing particulate residue of what had once been the *Oosphere*, still warm despite the hours that had passed since it had been destroyed. An itch in her back spread to become a stabbing fear in her gut as she found nothing suspicious that might explain the hole ship's destruction: no strange artifacts, no threats. *Nothing.*

That should have reassured her—that, and the modifications Axford had applied to *Pearl*, giving it a means of defending itself. But . . .

No, she thought. *There is something here. Something nearby. I can feel it. It killed Eos and it killed Tatenen and it's going to kill me, too, if I sit around here much longer.*

"Take us out of here, *Pearl*." The order came out as a whisper but, as the apprehension grew, she repeated it as a shout: "Get us the hell away from here! Now! Move it!"

Her fear peaked at the same time as the floor lurched under her. A searing white light burst out of the screen an instant before it went completely black. She fell sideways onto the couch, then onto the floor, jarring her left arm beneath her as she heavily hit the ground. There was a noise like tearing paper magnified a thousand times. She might have screamed, but she couldn't tell beneath the sound.

Then, abruptly, everything went quiet. She held herself still for a moment, barely breathing, expecting more to follow. When she was confident that nothing would, she rolled over and sat up.

"What happened, *Pearl*?"

"We were attacked."

"No shit?" she muttered, clambering to her feet. "Who by?"

"I can't answer that question, Caryl."

"But we're okay, right? We didn't sustain any damage?"

"Yes, Caryl. Minor damage has already been repaired."

"Where are we going?"

"To our previous location."

"No, wait," she said slowly, thoughtfully. "Don't relocate anywhere near the system. It's—"

It's what? she wondered. *Not safe* was the obvious answer, but she had to have something to support her suspicions. And she knew that Sol wouldn't be happy without hard data. There *had* to be a way to find out what was going on in the system without putting herself in any more danger.

A day later, she was still cursing Peter Alander for putting the idea in her head. Lucia Benck, had her exploratory mission succeeded, *should* have passed by pi-1 Ursa Major some forty years earlier. That was a long time ago, but she was still the closest thing to a local observer there was. All Thor had to do was track her down, find out if she had seen anything, then report back to Sol. It was that simple.

Or so it had seemed in theory. The problem, of course, was that Lucia Benck had been piloting a probe 25 percent the size of a normal survey probe. Even if the engine were running, *Chung-5* would be very hard to find. And even if Thor *did* find her, Lucia might not be able to tell her anything, anyway.

Thor knew an avoidance tactic when she saw it. Something about going back was bothering her. It wasn't just Sol's anger, or the death of her colony. It was a thought that Axford had placed in her head. Vega was a hive populated by one person. Was that what Sol wanted survey space to become? She could understand—intellectually, at least—that Sol had been just one of the many parts of a distributed intellect that Thor could not even hope to comprehend. She could also appreciate the simplicity of the Congress of Orphans program: the traitors in each survey mission had been programmed to obey the orders of UNESSPRO, and since Sol was the sole surviving remainder of the original organization, they should obey her just as readily. Sol now had a chink in the armor of every colony in survey space. This, combined with the many versions of her, put her in an excellent position to take over.

Sol didn't need to listen to anyone. She could do whatever she wanted, once everything was in place. Thor should be glad about that, since she was part of it. She knew she *should* be happy to contribute. But something nagged at her; doubt tickled at the back of her mind. What made Caryl Hatzis so special that she should decide what happened to everyone? Especially when everyone literally meant *everyone*. The future of humanity would rest in her hands.

Until she knew exactly how she felt about that, Thor suspected that continued avoidance would be for the best. Even if all the other Caryl Hatzis engrams signed up without question, she could be the odd one out. There had to be some random variation in every group. Maybe she was the freak in this case.

But, then again, maybe all her selves were feeling the same way about their highly evolved original. Maybe *that* was the real reason for the Congress. If her own engrams revolted against herself, Sol would still hold the reins. She would still be at the center of the web holding humanity together.

Pearl arrived at the center of the latest search area and began scanning. At least she knew she wasn't chasing shadows. The metal disk she had found in Hipp43534 sustained her and urged her on; the quote from Nietzsche molded on one side confirming that Lucia Benck was both alive and, apparently, in good humor. Who else would still believe that "the love of truth has its reward in Heaven"?

Whatever Lucia Benck had seen or not seen might be irrelevant, but at least the search was giving her time to think. And that was the most important thing. Behind her, in surveyed space, engrams were dying, whether by being taken by surprise by the Starfish or ambushed by the Yuhl. For the time being, Thor felt she was probably in the safest place around. Unless the thing in pi-1 Ursa Major was hunting her, too, in which case it might just prove to be the most dangerous place of all.

2.0.1

EXCERPTS FROM THE PID (PERSONAL INFORMATION DIRECTORY) OF ROB SINGH, UNESSPRO MISSION 639, TESS NELSON (PSI CAPRICORNUS).

2160.9.11–13

Disaster: it turns out that the Starfish have a more thorough cleansing program than we gave them credit for. Apparently, trailing behind the stealth front is a kind of mop-up crew that is guaranteed to find us and wipe us out, in time. How anyone knows this I can't imagine, but we have to move, nonetheless. Maybe it has something to do with the new aliens—the Yuhl/Goel. I've heard a rumor that they worship the Spinners like a god. Maybe there's room for my secondary specialty, after all.

My first is still a devalued commodity, though. Our hole ship came back from Sothis today. Hatzis told us about the problem, and we voted to evacuate to Sothis. We'll be downloaded into solid-state data storage, then physically loaded into the hole ship for transportation. The hole ship will do all the navigation required for the jump through unspace. They need pilots like our survey ships need hand cranks to get them going. Just for the record, I voted against the move. Personally, I'd rather take my chances in one of the dead systems—like some of the other missions. When I told Hatzis that, she called a vote, and we lost. We didn't stand a chance, and she knew it. The majority decides to drag us with them to an illusion of safety and warmth, and we all have to tag along. It's too inefficient to split the mission at this stage; too complicated.

Fuck that, as Hatzis might say. Were our positions reversed, I'm sure she'd endure a little inefficiency to get what she wanted.

But I guess I shouldn't complain. There'll be plenty of data at Sothis to lose myself in. Even without the gifts, there'll still be work to do. It'll be interesting, in fact, to compare my findings regarding the Esch'm and the X-ray sources with information from the other colonies. If they don't have the same error, I'll be even more confused.

*In transit. Nothing to do now but wait. The trip is unremark-*able, endured in quarter time so as not to overload the processors we have available. The hole ships make it too easy, almost boring. But at least I can say, now, that I've traveled faster than light. It'll take us less time to cross the fifty-odd light years between psi Capricornus and Sirius than it would've to circumnavigate Inari. Amazing.

Before we left, I got the chance to ask the Gifts about the Map Room data. Everyone else was preparing for the journey to Sothis (packing their suitcases, so to speak), newly afraid that the Starfish might drop out of the sky on us at any moment. Neil was free for a short time, and he passed on my question. It wasn't anything too tricky, just a simple request for clarification regarding the X-ray glitches. Did the Gifts know anything about where the mistakes might have come from?

"No," they said. "We don't."

No great surprises there. But Neil took it upon himself to pursue the matter further.

"Could they have been deliberately planted?"

"They could have been," the Gifts replied.

"What about the Yuhl?" Neil asked. "Why aren't they in the Library?"

"We are not familiar with that race."

"Why not? They were contacted by the Spinners. They must have been, or else they wouldn't have hole ships. So why aren't they in the Library?"

"We are not familiar with that race," came the flat response again.

"If I ask you a third time, am I going to get the same answer?"

There was a brief silence. I saw the recording, so I know it happened. I've never seen the Gifts hesitate before.

"Our knowledge is obviously not complete," the Gifts finally admitted. "We cannot explain why."

End of conversation. Neil has had enough experience with the alien AIs to know when to give up.

Still, good on him. That's hole number three. We're no closer to knowing what the errors mean, of course, if anything, but at least they're mounting up.

I thought I was ready for Sothis, but I wasn't. It's so crowded. Not physically, but electronically. We're not the only colony that's been evacuated and plugged into the network they're building here. Where before I'd only forty-odd people to talk to, now there are over two hundred within easy reach. We've been thrust face-to-face with the reality of engram duplication. I have met three Caryl Hatzises so far, and two other Ali Genoveses. Four of myself have come to visit, also—virtually, that is. We have taken to wearing green name tags on our chests, not displaying our names, but rather the names of our origin colonies. It's the only way to keep track.

They expect thirteen colonies to join up all told. I'm not superstitious, but I find myself hoping that it's not unlucky.

Still settling in. There was plenty to do when we arrived, but that's slowing now. We've been playing catch-up— not just with the other missions and other versions of ourselves, but with what's been going on in general. The other versions of myself who have been here longer are no clearer on what's happening behind the scenes, even the ones who are survey managers. The Hatzises are a closed court. Sometimes I think they're as bad as the Gifts.

But we have resources here, at least. I can think as fast as I want, even if it does mean using Overseers from destroyed colonies. That's like thinking with someone else's dead brain cells and struck me as a bit distasteful at first. But there's no denying the need we have for it, and it doesn't make sense letting good hardware go to waste. In a sense, it gives us a little *too much* time to play with. There's an air of expectancy through the refugee camp. The Starfish are more dangerous than ever. Giving us time to muse on that thought is not helping.

But it has given Ali more time to visit. Although she's still nominal SMC of our mission, now that she's chucked our lot in with the Hatzises she's delegated the greater part of her responsibility to them. She looks relieved about that, too. Mostly.

"There's been no talk of what happens *after*," she complained to me yesterday. "If we survive the Starfish, I mean. Do we go back to our colonies and finish what we started, or do we stick together in one big group and try to recolonize Sol System or something?"

"Is that what you'd like to do, Ali?"

"I don't know, Rob. But it'd be good to discuss our options."

"Perhaps they're not even thinking about options until they're sure we'll have any."

"Perhaps. And I suppose there's always the senescence problem. That'll be with us, no matter what we do."

"I've been thinking about that," I said, looking to lighten the mood a little. "I think the Vincula could have fixed the engrams back in Sol if it wanted to. It'd be like fixing a steam engine for someone from our time. But it didn't need to. Who repairs steam engines when everyone uses fuel cells? They'd be museum pieces, not worth serious attention. So the Vincula didn't even try.

"Sol, on the other hand, has nothing *but* us. Her options are limited. She can let us fade away, which we know we'll do in time, or she can work out how to fix us. It might not be that hard. Even if it is, she can just freeze batches of us in SSDS memory until she has the problem nutted out. All she needs is time, and she could have plenty of that."

"Assuming we survive the Starfish," Ali repeated.

"If we don't, the point is moot."

"True." After a slight pause, she asked, "Do you ever wonder how your original died?"

"Of course." I gave in to her gloominess. "I can't help it. I'd always hoped to meet him again, somehow."

"Ever the optimist." She smiled sadly. "I wonder what mine would have made of all this."

"The same as you, surely?"

"Maybe not. She wouldn't have stayed like she was when I left forever."

"She might have become like Sol, you mean?"

"Perhaps. I don't know if she survived the Spike, but if she did and she was here now—"

"Would she be doing the same?"

"As Sol, yes." She shrugged, sending her hair swaying. I had upgraded my virtual quarters to include floor-to-ceiling windows with views of San Francisco Bay outside. Sunlight suited her skin.

I put a hand on her shoulder. "You would have done the right thing, I'm sure."

She looked grateful, even though she knew I was being carefully noncommittal. "I like to think we all would," she said.

She stayed longer than I expected. I guess we all need a little closeness, now, when things are really getting tight. I know I'm grateful for it, if only because it takes my mind off things. It certainly makes the move to Sothis that much easier to bear. If this is to be our last stand, at least I'll be there to see it.

2.0.2

The darkness surprised her. Lucia Benck knew who she was, where she was, and what had happened to her. She knew what the date should have been when the manual switch tripped her Overseer back into life. But she couldn't see. She couldn't feel. Had she died during her long transit through the system? Was this formless, empty nothingness Hell? Then the dusty pathways of her moth-balled mind reassembled completely, and she remem-bered. She had programmed a discontinuity so she would *know* when the jump was over. It would have been all too easy to program the Overseer to suspend her operations and then revive them without any perceptible break at all, but she wanted more than that. She wanted something that would remind her, at least, of the risk she had taken. Something that would make her appreciate making it out the other side in one piece.

Let there be light, she thought wryly. It was a cliché but what the hell. No one was there to hear it, anyway, but her.

At the command, her conSense modules came on-line one by one, gradually building a virtual world for her to slot into. As yet she had had no direct contact with *Chung-5*, since the probe was inert, apart from her and the nanofacturing plant. The latter was rebuilding her and itself at the same time from the raw materials she had stored near the core of the probe. Her clock rate was very slow to compensate for low energy reserves as it extended tendrils through the inert shield encasing the probe's ac-tive core. She imagined molecular drill heads burrowing in and out of cracks, heading for the outside. When they reached vacuum, they would sprout roots and petals like elegant, microscopic flowers and begin to grow.

Two days after her awakening—barely an hour her time—she received her first visuals from the outside. She saw stars and, at the sight of them, her nerves eased instantly. *Chung-5* was rotating with a different period from the one she had given it before flipping the switch: slightly faster and with more of a tumbling feel. She could correct it later, once she had attitudes again. Training her miniature sensors around her, she caught sight of pi-1 Ursa Major as it rolled into view. The star was still there, apparently unchanged, but for the moment she could tell little more than that.

Her first impulse was to check the camera to see if it had operated correctly. When she had actuators in place, she dragged the film into view. The process appeared to have worked, but she had forgotten that she would need to develop the negatives before viewing them properly. Creating a chemical bath was, temporarily, less important than getting the power on and ensuring her own safety. The pictures would have to wait. Other than that, though, everything appeared to be going well, so far. The plant was busy building all of the many components she would need to continue her mission. It would probably take weeks before she was back to full capacity, if she could ever reach that level again. Depending on how much shielding had been ablated away by her passage through pi-1 Ursa Major's solar atmosphere, she might have to wait many years as her magnetic shielding accrued mass from interstellar dust before she could have everything she wanted. But it didn't look as though she was going to be crippled, and that was the main thing.

It was only while considering where she would go next that she realized she hadn't dropped her customary souvenir on the way through the system. She'd even had a quote prepared, but the disturbing events leading up to her arrival had distracted her from routine. Only now, with time to spare, did she have the chance to remember it. Maybe, when things were back to normal, she could build something smaller and fire it back at the system; she might even be able to nudge it along with a laser for a while, to give it some extra delta-v. It might take a century or two to arrive, but at least the chain would be unbroken.

She wondered if her other selves had stuck to the deal. UNESSPRO wouldn't approve, of course: she was wasting resources, for one thing, as well as polluting pristine environments. She preferred to think of it as disseminating the wisdom of humanity one sound bite—or meme—at a time, while at the same time creating a legacy that she could truly call her own. If all went well, there might be tens of thousands of her word disks already scattered throughout the expanding bubble of surveyed space surrounding Sol. She didn't need to do anything, really, while *Chung-5* went about its repairs. The decision of where to go next could wait. So she kept herself in a very slow-mo state as she settled back to watch the star behind her shrink.

There goes Jian Lao, she thought to herself. *There goes Peter.*

After a while, she turned her sensors forward and pondered the stars ahead.

Hipp40918, Hipp41308, Hipp43477, 2 Ursa Major, Muscida . . .

And, farther ahead still: *Bode's Nebula, M82, NGC3077, NGC2976, IC2574* . . .

Then: *infinity* . . .

She shivered—or, at least, her virtual body shivered. Normally, the thought of flying forever filled her with a powerful sense of wonder. This time, though, there was an uneasy edge to it, as if that sense of wonder had been corrupted by something else. She didn't know what it was, either. All she did know was that there was something dogging at her, something that left her feeling oddly anxious.

A moment later, however, it passed, and she was left wondering whether she hadn't simply imagined the whole thing. The sense of wonder was as pure and powerful as it had ever been at any point in her light-years of traveling. If there was one thing she was sure of after twenty subjective years, it was that she would never regret her decision to join UNESSPRO, to explore the universe. It was who she was; it defined her. As Peter had said, she was a tourist through and through.

Sometimes it struck her as strange that it *had* been twenty years. She hadn't changed at all. Her memories, her sense of self were as strong as ever. Even though in the past she had regarded the boffins at UNESSPRO as penny-pinching, shortsighted, and complacent, there could be no denying that they did a good job when they put their mind to it. She was proof of that. As were all the other engrams.

To hell with the memes I'm leaving behind, she thought to the universe at large. *The way I'm feeling, I reckon I can outlast the lot of you.*

The probe alerted her with a fair imitation of a cake timer when the photos were ready. She woke herself out of her deep-time thoughts and brought herself back to the present.

There were seventy-three pictures in all, and she turned her cameras on each of them with a fair degree of nervousness. What if there was nothing to see? What if the entire exercise had been a complete waste of time?

Plates one through twenty chronicled her approach to the system. The tumble of the probe along with its motion through space rendered many of the details as little more than streaks, but some had come out quite clearly. The gas giants were in the right places, and neither of them changed dramatically as she streaked toward them. She glimpsed rings, satellites, atmospheric storms: details she would have loved to have studied further had the opportunity not been over three quarter trillion kilometers behind her.

The next thirty plates concentrated on the inner system, Jian Lao in particular. The world was as blue as she had dreamed, with a crystal clarity to its cloud systems and landmasses that reminded her of Earth. It had three small moons. It was easy to add them to her dream of her and

Peter, surveying the paradise they claimed together, in the back of her mind.

None of the first fifty plates showed anything out of the ordinary. No odd streaks or flashes; no unexpected blobs. No *Andrei Linde*, either. In fact, there was no evidence that anyone had ever even been in the system—which was impossible, because she had seen it arrive.

The remainder of the plates had been taken as she left the system. The images of pi-1 Ursa Major's planets and primary shrank steadily as they receded from her, and they told her little that she didn't already know. The last one had been taken only a day before her awakening and showed exactly the same view she had herself seen upon burrowing out of her cocoon.

Nothing. They told her nothing. With a sinking heart, she knew that her misgivings had been fully realized: it had all been a waste of time.

She couldn't believe it. There *had* to be something going on. She couldn't have imagined the whole thing. The flashes she had seen must have been immensely powerful for her dishes to pick them up. They must have left some sort of record, if only on the atmosphere of Jian Lao. If a natural phenomenon had caused them—like a comet strike—it must have been so large as to nearly crack the planet in two!

But it didn't matter what logic dictated. The fact was, there was nothing. The motion-streaked images were blurry but not so ambiguous as to hide the evidence of a catastrophe on that scale. She checked every image minutely, hunting for the slightest unaccounted-for photon. She plotted the trajectories of every major body in the system to make sure that what she saw really was natural. She even ran them forward and backward across her vision like a brief time-lapse movie.

And that, in the end, was how she noticed it. As the probe had tumbled its way through the system, the shutter on its mechanical camera had clicked open once every ten hours or so. The mechanism had been as simple as she could devise, given her self-imposed limitations on technology and emissions. If there really had been nothing in the system but herself, then the metronomic click of the camera would have been the only regular sound, ticking like a very slow clock.

When she riffled through the photos, however, she noticed that there was a discontinuity. The smooth progression jumped just before the probe flashed past the fourth terrestrial planet. It was slight, just one frame, barely enough to be noticeable, and for a long while she couldn't decide whether or not she had simply imagined it. It was only after she had double-checked the probe's trajectory and replotted the various points at which the camera should have fired that she was able to dispel her doubts.

There was no question about it: there was a plate missing. Not unexposed, either, but actually *missing*—as though it had never existed. The plates formed a clear, uninterrupted sequence, so it didn't make sense that the shutter should fail to open at that moment and no other. And it hadn't become jammed in the camera mechanism, otherwise all the photographs after it would have failed or emerged damaged.

She could think of only one explanation for the loss, and that was that the plate had been stolen.

A cold feeling washed through her at the thought, as though her virtual world in the heart of the probe had somehow been invaded by the iciness of space. If someone *had* stolen the plate, there was only one way they could have gone about it. They must have scanned the probe and realized what the camera was for; they must have snipped out the plate and covered up the loss so that, barring a close inspection, it wouldn't be noticed. For the plate to be stolen, she knew, the probe must have been physically infiltrated.

She tried shaking the idea from her mind, telling herself that she was making a mountain out of a molehill. But she couldn't stop following the thought through. Had whoever was responsible for this known that she was inside the probe, in a state of suspended process, waiting to look at the plates when she awoke? Or had they simply thought the probe a simple, mechanical artifact flung from a distant star?

No. The latter didn't make sense, because if that were the case, then why remove just one plate and then send the probe on its way again?

All of this paled into insignificance compared to the one troubling thought that continued to niggle at the back of her mind: this had to have been done by something other than human. There was no sign of the *Linde* in any of the surviving photos, and no evidence that humans had been to the system, advanced or otherwise. The theft had to have been performed by aliens.

And this unsettling notion, assuming it was correct, gave rise to an even more troubling thought: from her trajectory, could these aliens have then guessed where she came from? Could they have traced her origins back to Earth? What would they do if they did?

The awful uncertainty of her situation galled her. The whole point of going into deep storage and waiting out the trip past Jian Lao had been to gain hard data on what was going on. But in the end it had done the exact opposite. If something had approached the tumbling probe and been caught on film, then she would have preferred that either the film had been left intact or that she had been destroyed outright.

But in a way she could understand why these aliens had gone to the lengths they had. If they didn't want to be found, then destroying a probe that might be intermittently reporting back home would be the worst thing they could do. Destroying it would only draw attention to them, whereas the ambiguous concealment of data might simply be ignored.

A large part of her was wishing she had never analyzed the data in the first place. It would certainly have been easier that way. After all, in the end there was nothing she could do about it, whatever she found. It wasn't as if she could turn the probe around and go back to reprimand the aliens. If they wanted anonymity and had been prepared to destroy the *Linde* to achieve it, then they'd have no hesitation in swatting her like an irritating bug. She couldn't even call Earth to let them know what she might have stumbled upon, for her transmitter wasn't powerful enough, and the time lag made the gesture pointless. She was truly alone.

For the first time, as she coasted through space at a substantial percentage of the speed of light, she regretted her decision to remain alone. She needed someone to talk to—someone to offer another opinion, someone off whom she could bounce ideas and thoughts. Even someone just to shout at would have been good.

Where are you, Peter? she mused as she studied the vast spread of stars. *If you were here, what would you be telling me to do right now?*

"I want to find answers," he had said that last night they'd spent together before their copies—before *she*— came on-line, "explanations for the things we still don't understand."

Could she spend eternity not knowing what had happened to the *Andrei Linde?* Could she stand the possibility that an alien had merely interfered with the probe instead of making any form of contact whatsoever? Could she live with the thought that her friends and her dream of paradise had died meaningless deaths that would never be acknowledged by their loved ones back home?

She would have to. That was the short and brutal answer. She would have to and, therefore, she would. Maybe someone else would have thought of something to do, but she couldn't. The only choice open to her was her next destination.

Hipp40918, Hipp41308, Hipp43477, 2 Ursa Major, Muscida? Bode's Nebula, M82, NGC3077, NGC2976, IC2574?

Opening her magnetic vanes to their maximum extent, she directed her dishes forward and her low-g thrusters backward. Then, with only her thoughts and the stars to keep her company, she continued her lonely journey into the vast tourist's playground of space.

2.1

FEARFUL SYMMETRY

2160.9.13 Standard Mission Time
(12 August, 2163 UT)

2.1.1

Alander paced the confines of the cockpit, counting each step as a means of distraction from his growing anxiety. There was no sensation of movement to suggest that the hole ship was docking with the giant craft the aliens had referred to as *Mantissa*. For all he knew, *Silent Liquidity* could have been performing a simple hop from one side of the system to the other. Then again, it might not have been going anywhere at all. It was impossible to say one way or the other.

His only companion was Ueh, the Yuhl "priest," but he had done little to allay Alander's worries. He just sat motionless throughout the wait on his side of the boundary, his alien features fixed and unreadable as he stared unflinchingly at Alander.

"Do you know what's going to happen to us?" Alander asked him at one point. He had settled on a male gender for the alien because his mind needed something to hang onto. Calling the Yuhl "it" was too depersonalizing.

"No," Ueh said in reply.

"Do you know who we might talk to?"

"No."

"Are we likely to talk to the person in charge? The captain?"

"*I don't know/The Praxis decides.*"

"Decides what? Who we meet or what to do with us?"

"Both." The alien's jaw clicked shut then open again.

THERE IS NO [UNKNOWN] BETWEEN US,
PETER/ALANDER.

Alander examined the missing term, deciphering it as:
we/unity. Was Ueh trying to say that they weren't allies?
If so, it was understandable. Nevertheless, as they were
quite literally stuck in the same boat for the moment,
Alander felt he should use the time to gain some local
knowledge. Or try to, anyway. It surprised him, though,
that Ueh didn't do likewise. This was a perfect opportunity to learn about an alien species, yet he just sat there,
silent and staring. Maybe the Yuhl didn't have the same
sense of curiosity that humans did. Or perhaps the aliens
were just too damned arrogant and simply presumed that
there was nothing about humanity they particularly
needed to know.

"Was there we-slash-unity between you and your companion?"

Ueh's expression was utterly unreadable. "Yes."

Alander remembered the results of the scan showing
that they had been of different genders. "Were you lovers
or—" He sought another term. "Or breeding partners?"

"*We are* helots *do not breed.*"

Ah. That was an insight Alander hadn't hoped to get so
early. The existence of reproductive rights within Yuhl
society—or the fragment that remained of it, at least—
might indicate a heavily stratified regime, as the existence
of the helots themselves suggested.

"Are there children aboard the *Mantissa*?"

OUR CHILDREN ARE [UNKNOWN].

Alander couldn't decipher the missing words. There
were more than one, and each had multiple meanings.
Lost? Unborn? In suspended animation? He couldn't decide.

"Who speaks for the Praxis?" he asked, pulling at that
thread instead. If the Praxis was some kind of governing

body, the equivalent of a chairperson was who he would be looking for.

"*The Praxis* speaks *for itself.*"

"Is it a sort of group mind, then?"

"No."

Alander sighed. "I would really like to learn more about your people," he said. "Will there be someone else in the *Mantissa* that could answer my questions?"

"*I am answering when* I can *not understand your questions,*" said Ueh. Then, in a double vocal cord ululation that made Alander wince, the alien added: "Strange."

Strange? Why would the alien think his question strange? He imagined it to be the type of thing any alien culture might ask another. But again, perhaps this was something missing from or different in the Yuhl's intellectual makeup. Perhaps their only focus was on themselves and their own survival. Maybe after living so long as scavengers in the Starfish's shadow, they had learned to curb their curiosity and concern themselves *only* with themselves.

On the other hand, he had never spoken to an alien before. For all he knew, there might be a detailed protocol when it came to first contacts, protocol he was failing to follow. If that protocol involved stealing a species' resources and wiping out entire colonies, then the Yuhl certainly had a long way to go in regards to diplomatic relations.

Alander's train of thought was interrupted when the hole ship suddenly shuddered, and the screen came to life. It took him a moment to work out exactly what he was looking at. He appeared to be flying low over a smooth cloud bank, ascending slowly into a black sky. Then something round and darker still cut across his view, and he realized that it was another hole ship: a modified one shaped like a stubby *Y* in cross section with growths sprouting from the center.

"You have returned *Silent Liquidity*," came a voice through the cockpit's speakers.

"Only temporarily," he replied quickly. "It will leave

with me, I assure you. I am here to offer you Ueh Ellil in exchange for information."

There was a slight pause. Another alien cockpit swept past, then another. He felt as though he was trapped in an old classical model of the atom: one electron of many orbiting a fat uranium nucleus.

"Information is the most valuable commodity you could ask for," said the voice, "whereas life is expensive to maintain in space." It spoke slowly, carefully, as if to ensure that both vocal streams worked in unison. The Yuhl wanted to make sure, Alander thought, that he would not misunderstand what they were saying. The effect, however, was still high-pitched and dissonant in his ears.

"You're saying you're not interested in trading?"

"Such an arrangement is not confluent. You will not fare well from it."

"Then I guess I might as well leave," he said evenly. "Is that what you want?"

"Do you think leaving is an option?"

"You tell me," he said. "*Is* it?"

The pause was longer this time. "The helots are valuable to *me/us*. Your leader has promised to kill the other half of this operating pair if we do not deal fairly with you. *I/we* do not want this." There was another pause of a few seconds. "*I/we* will let you leave unharmed, should you so wish."

"But you're not prepared to bargain for the return of the helots?"

"*I/we* are prepared to bargain."

Alander felt like he was going around in circles. "All right," he said. "That's progress. What we would like is any information you have on the beings you refer to as the Ambivalence."

"*I/we* do not know them," was the instantaneous response.

"You must," Alander insisted. "You've been following them for over two thousand years! You'd have to know *something*."

"The Ambivalence does not reveal itself to *we/us*," came the reply. "*I/we* know only its works."

"Can you tell us what you know about *that*, then?"

"It will make no difference."

"Because we're the already-dead, right?"

There was no immediate reply to this.

A trio of cockpits, one comprising at least two dozen units linked in a fat ring, swooped past, but instead of vanishing into the distance, the formation swung around in a tight arc and came back to approach *Silent Liquidity*.

"The Praxis will talk to you," the alien voice finally announced.

Alander frowned. "I assumed you *were* the Praxis."

The alien's reply translated as: "I am Conjugator *Vaise/Ashu*." The name came from a difficult double meaning with connotations of mediation and bringing about change.

The ringlike structure approached. Clearly they wanted him to dock his cockpit in the middle.

"General, are you hearing all this?"

"Loud and clear," came the reply from Axford. His voice was so clear that it seemed to Alander as if the man was right there in the cockpit with him. Strangely, the thought gave him comfort. The ex-general was dangerous, but at least his motives were immediately comprehensible.

"You approve of docking the cockpits?" he asked.

"In for a penny, as they say."

"As they *used* to say," returned Alander.

"How very cynical of you," Axford said with a dry laugh.

"Just being realistic." Alander nodded to himself as though he had nothing to worry about. As long as he stayed in two-way electronic contact with *Silent Liquidity*, he would be able to communicate with Axford and take advantage of the translator. But the thought of leaving the cockpit made him nervous. He would be completely vulnerable.

His captive sang a series of overlapping syllables that the hole ship was only able to translate in part. Whatever

the alien said, it had something to do with a notion of
congruity that Alander couldn't get his head around. Perhaps, he thought, it sprang from the innate concept of
superposition that Axford thought might have sprung from
possessing two sets of vocal cords and such pronounced
symmetry. If the aliens did indeed have a better grasp of
quantum states, their entire philosophy might reflect this.
Such a philosophy would conflict strongly with the mech-
anistic, Western worldview under which Alander had been
raised. Hence his failure to understand.

But he didn't doubt that there would be some things
their separate philosophies had in common, and if they
could just discover what that was, then there was always
a chance that a meaningful arrangement could be reached
between the two species. After all, both had more in common with each other than either did with the Spinners or
the Starfish, who hadn't attempted to communicate at all.

The ring structure descended over *Silent Liquidity*.
When asked for authorization to dock, he gave it without
hesitation. Despite his apprehensions, there was no point
holding back now.

The cockpit experienced a series of very faint nudges,
then the maneuver was complete. The airlock opened.
Alander instinctively stepped away from it. A bubble of
yellowish atmosphere bulged into the room like an inflat-
ing balloon. Stepping into that bubble, seconds later, was
the third Yuhl Alander had physically met. Of them all,
this one was by far the most imposing.

It stood well over two meters tall, and its body was
much more solid than those of the two captives. Its skin
exhibited pronounced ridges as though it had been teased
into shape and left to dry. Where the helots had worn
simple kilts and vests, this one was wrapped in a complicated pattern of bandages and cloths from which hung
ribbons in deep purple and black. Its face was painted in
similar colors, giving it an even more masklike effect. It
wore flared boots on its long, tapering shins that clicked
like a Geiger counter with every step it took.

"Conjugator Vaise-Ashu, I'm guessing?" Alander said,

refusing to be intimidated by the alien's size or presence.

The alien looked briefly at him, then faced Ueh.

"*Have you/been harmed?*" it asked Ueh.

"No," Alander's captive replied. "*Although I am* hungry *for our food.*"

"Food shall be brought." The black eyes turned once again to Alander.

"Oh, yes, of course," Alander said after a moment, when he realized that the alien was waiting to see if he would allow this. "My culture has strict rules for the care of prisoners. I don't wish any of you harm."

The conjugator didn't respond to Alander's comment. Instead, he pointed toward the cockpit entrance while at the same time two small plates between his eyes clicked twice in quick succession. Almost instantly, another alien walked into the cockpit carrying a small, flat package. When the yellowish bubble of energy expanded and merged with Ueh's, the package was silently delivered to him. Then the courier alien exited without so much as a word of thanks from either Ueh or the conjugator.

Alander watched as Ueh hurriedly opened the package and greedily devoured the contents. He took to the food in tiny, quick bites—too quick, in fact, for Alander to discern exactly what was being eaten. A dark-colored tissue of some kind, possibly vegetable in origin.

"The Praxis waits," said the conjugator, raising an arm in a disarmingly human *this way* gesture.

Alander turned to the alien. "What guarantee do I have that I'll be allowed to return to my hole ship once I've left it?

"None," said the Yuhl bluntly and without apology. The alien tilted its head. "All things happen."

"As long as they don't happen to *me*," he snapped. Resigning himself, he walked forward, through the cockpit exit corridor. *Silent Liquidity*'s atmosphere folded around him as he left the hole ship, giving him, along with his I-suit, added protection. Even so, he still felt incredibly exposed.

Conjugator Vaise fell in behind him. Alander instructed

Silent Liquidity to collapse the force wall as Ueh brought up the rear. The three of them filed through the corridor and out of the airlock. What awaited them there surprised Alander, for he had been preparing himself for something completely alien. But there was just a simple umbilical made out of ribbed, opaque material that gave slightly when he walked over it. The artificial gravity that oriented him in the hole ship didn't even flicker.

At the end of the umbilical was another airlock identical to *Silent Liquidity*'s. It opened smoothly before them. The far side held a small antechamber not dissimilar to the usual cockpit. It was sparsely furnished and barely large enough for the three of them. This, he assumed, was where they would talk to the Praxis—but he was wrong.

The conjugator walked ahead of him and placed one narrow hand on the wall before them. It irised open with a hiss, and Alander took his first look at a Yuhl habitat. It was crowded. That was his initial impression. Everywhere he looked there were furniture or people or equipment or objects that could have been works of art, for all he could tell. The lighting was orange-tinged and dim, and the noise was overwhelming, with dozens of double throats competing for attention. The space containing it all consisted of an intestine-like tube curving to either side, obviously following the center of the ringlike design of the vessel. Some of the structures extended up the wall and onto the ceiling. A single step across the threshold demonstrated an abruptly reduced ambient gravity in the habitat: much less than that of Earth: possibly as low as half.

A closer look revealed that the habitat wasn't as crowded as he'd first thought. It was just arranged differently from how he was used to. Instead of keeping things around the edges of working space, the Yuhl spread out in all directions. There were no clear paths; the jagged angularity of workstations and other equipment overtook everything. That there *were* clear spaces he was certain, for the Yuhl moved through the habitat with graceful ease;

but he, as a human used to straight lines and well defined corridors, had trouble finding them.

The conjugator led the way, his long legs much more lithe and graceful in the reduced gravity as he wove through the chaos. Alander followed as best he could, afraid that he would overstep and break something. Everything looked so fragile—and sharp. Masklike faces turned to follow him as he went, their expressions primordial and eerie. He felt like he was passing through a peculiarly Oriental vision of hell.

"Where are you taking me?" he asked, ducking under a fan of pointed glass sticks that emitted light from each end. *Silent Liquidity* translated his words into the Yuhl language and used the membrane keeping his air in as a vibrating medium to repeat them.

"To the Praxis," the conjugator replied without turning.

"I'm still not really clear on this," said Alander. "What is the Praxis, exactly? A person? A thing? A type of government?"

"*It is* all of this *and more.*" The conjugator made a pointing gesture at one of the Yuhl they passed. The Yuhl reciprocated the action. Alander had seen the signal before; it seemed to be one of respect or perhaps even a salute.

"I don't understand," he said, starting to feel frustrated that the conjugator wouldn't even face Alander as he spoke.

"You are not required to."

"Look," he said tiredly. "If we're ever going to come to any sort of agreement, then *my* people will need to understand *yours.* We have to be able to reach some kind of agreement that—"

"There *can/will* be no agreement," said the conjugator. "You are the *already/dead.*"

Alander sighed wearily. "Yes, so we've been told. But we refuse to accept that role. We intend to fight."

The conjugator reacted to the word by jerking his head back and uttering a sequence of strange squeaking sounds. A laugh, perhaps? Alander wondered.

From behind him, Ueh said: "The *already/dead* do not fight."

"Exactly. So we're not them."

"*Silence* helot *has no voice here!*" There was no mistaking the command in the conjugator's voice.

Glancing back briefly, Alander saw Ueh's expression change to one of crosshatched diagonal lines, and he fell back a pace in deference. Alander felt vaguely sorry for the alien.

"If you're not going to allow him to speak," said Alander to the Yuhl ahead of him, "then why is he here at all?"

"His voice is half," the conjugator said. "*He has been separated by* you *must assume responsibility for him.*"

Alander pondered this, wondering where in the conversation with either Ueh or the conjugator he had missed this important point. "Are you telling me he's my ward— or my slave?"

"He is your conscience."

"What?"

Conjugator Vaise didn't answer. Instead, he raised a hand in an unmistakable *stop* gesture. They had reached a frosted glass wall that stretched the entire width of the habitat. Beyond it on the far side, Alander could see shapes moving to and fro, although he couldn't quite make them out.

"*These subjects protect* this vessel *protects the Praxis,*" said the conjugator. "You *try to harm the Praxis/they will stop* you."

"Who's going to stop it from trying to harm me?" said Alander.

Again, the conjugator didn't reply. Instead, he stepped back as the wall before them dissolved into a startlingly beautiful waterfall of tiny glass beads that gently washed down and disappeared into the floor. A mass of organic tissue—far too vast to take in with one glance—waited on the far side, arranged in fleshy pseudopods that stirred and lifted with constant, incomprehensible motion.

Alander took an uneasy step back. "What the hell is this?"

Ueh stepped up beside him, his alien hand on Alander's
back preventing him from moving any farther away.

"*The Praxis will not harm you will only be eaton,*" said the conjugator.

Alander barely had time to register the alien's words
before one of the pseudopods suddenly opened like a
flower—a *mouth*—and rushed forward to engulf him.
Powerful, ropelike muscles seized his body and pulled
him effortlessly into the fleshy maw. He experienced a
brief, sickening feeling of being crushed and suffocated,
and then everything went black.

Why didn't the I-suit save me? was Alander's first thought
on the other side of the blackness. Then a second, confusing notion: *How can I be thinking if I'm dead?*

"You cannot be dead," said a voice, "if you were never
really alive to begin with."

The voice, although whispered and soft, startled Alander.

"What? Who—?"

"I am the Praxis."

The darkness peeled back to reveal something Alander
automatically thought of as a face, even though it bore no
resemblance to anything he had ever seen before. It was
red and moist-looking, with a wide central cavity. It was
open at the top, sloping back and out of sight down the
creature's back. Sensory organs, including numerous compound eyes, lined the left and right sides of the cavity.
The image faded into darkness in all directions, so Alander couldn't see where the face truly ended or even began.

"You're not a Yuhl," Alander said.

"I am from another species altogether," the Praxis replied. "I am the caretaker of the *Yuhl/Goel.*" The creature's
mellifluous voice divided easily to pronounce the alien
term.

"You tell them what to do?"

"I find out what it is they want to do and help them do
it," it said. "In return, they keep me alive."

"They feed you?" Alander pressed. "Things like me?"

The edges of the cavity lifted, then sagged. "I am a physical being as well as a mental one, and as such require sustenance in both areas. But I assure you, had my goal been simply to devour you, we would not be talking now."

Alander felt no sense of intimidation or threat in the Praxis's words. If anything, he felt himself encased in a strange and seductive calm. He felt at peace with himself and everything around him.

"I guess I've been absorbed, then," he said after a moment's reflection. He nodded to himself at the realization. The concept didn't trouble him as much as he felt it should. "Is that why the Yuhl will only talk to people with physical bodies?"

The huge creature remained silent for more than thirty seconds, the edges of its cavity shifting in a subtle and almost hypnotic undulating motion.

"Your friend wishes to speak with you," the alien said finally. "He requires reassurance that you are all right."

"My friend . . . ?"

Axford's voice erupted into the darkness, his anger unnatural in the calm Alander had found since awakening.

"If I don't hear from him in the next sixty seconds, then I'm leaving," Axford snarled. "And you can damn well say good-bye to your pal here, too."

"Can I speak to him?" Alander asked the Praxis. If Axford said he was going to leave in sixty seconds, then he meant it. And he would stand by his threat to execute the Yuhl hostage, as well.

It wasn't the alien who replied, however.

"Peter?" said Axford with some surprise, some relief. "Is that really you?"

"Yes," said Alander, his gaze roaming aimlessly about the darkness, not sure where to direct his response. "Don't do anything rash, Frank. Don't do anything at all just yet. I'm fine." He resisted an impulse to add, *I think*.

"Where the hell have you been?" Surprise and relief

were quickly exchanged for anger. "First I lose your feed, then *Liquidity* can't locate you—"

"I can't explain right now," he said, thinking, *I couldn't even if I wanted to.* "But I think everything is going well enough."

"Are you sure?" Axford sounded uncertain, as though he was ready to leave even though he had received a reply.

"Fairly sure," said Alander. "I'm going to need a little longer. You're going to have to be patient, okay?"

There was a pause before Axford said anything. "Okay," he said. "But if I don't hear from you in ten minutes, then every ten minutes thereafter, I'm assuming you're no longer a viable proposition and clearing out."

"Understood," said Alander. "I'll be in touch."

Turning his attention back to the Praxis, he said, "You didn't need me to do that, did you? You could have faked my voice to offer him the reassurance he needed."

"We have nothing to hide, Peter," said the Praxis. "But if it would have been beneficial to our cause to deceive your friend, then yes, your voice—and image if need be—could be emulated."

Alander nodded thoughtfully. "And you can do this because I've been . . . absorbed?"

"I now possess in me everything there is to know about you."

Again, he felt that this should have troubled him, but he had been anaesthetized against any form of anxiety.

"So let me get this straight," he said. "Having absorbed me, you've modeled me inside you?"

"I am keeping it simple, though," said the alien, "because I am aware of your conSense-related disorientation."

"But this is *you* I'm seeing right now?"

The face flexed again. "I'm an artificial intelligence housed in a biological construct." Its voice swept across Alander like a gentle breeze. "My creators based me on their own forms, but only loosely, and I have been modified extensively since. The last of my kind, I am even more of an individual than I ever was."

"Someone *made* you?"

"A long time ago, now," it replied with something like sadness in its tone. Alander had no doubt it was there purely for his benefit.

"But why?" he asked. "What for?"

"Many things," the Praxis said. "Tasks so complex that what I do for the *Yuhl/Goel* seems like child's play in comparison."

Alander pondered this. "I'm guessing the Yuhl came across you during their scouting raids in another region of space. They say they've been traveling for twenty-five hundred years. In that time they would have undoubtedly come across other species. You're just one of them, and they've put you to good use, right?"

"On the contrary," said the Praxis. "It was I who adopted them. I have ridden the coattails of the Ambivalence far longer than either your or their species has been recording history."

"Then you know things about the Spinners and Starfish that even the Yuhl don't?"

"Perhaps." The word was a sigh. "But that is something we can discuss at a later date. For now, I simply wish to meet you."

For a fleeting moment Alander wasn't sure whether the creature had actually said "to eat you." But whatever was said, he felt no threat inherent to the words. If anything, the voice of the alien had a faintly amused edge to it.

"Are you going to let me go?" he asked.

Amusement became disdain. "You believe I would kill you, having absorbed your body and gone to so much trouble to re-create you?"

"It would hardly be regarded as killing," said Alander. "Not in your eyes, anyway. What was it you said when I awoke? Something about me not being alive in the first place?"

A sound, deep and bassy, rolled and echoed through

the darkness. Alander had no doubt the creature had just laughed.

"You are offended by my observations?" the creature asked.

"Not particularly," Alander said. "Although as an intelligent life-form, I feel I *should* be."

"You cannot reproduce and you cannot change," said the Praxis. "Two prerequisites for intelligent life, in my opinion."

"I can change," Alander defended himself.

"Fundamentally, you cannot. That is what it means to be an engram. You are defined by who you were, not by who you might be now. The slight randomization you experience only alleviates the symptoms, never the problem."

"I *feel* alive."

"And in most respects you are. The distinction between a conscious, rational, intelligent being and one that has the capacity for life in the biological sense is arguably a small one. It is one you might care to dismiss as irrelevant, in the present circumstances. Your priority is survival, as it should be. Reproduction and change can come later."

The massive, alien face didn't move, but Alander sensed that he was being tested, toyed with.

"What is it you want from me?" he asked. "Why am I here?"

"I could well ask you the same questions. What do *you* want from *me?* Why have *you* come *here?*"

"You've absorbed me," he said sardonically. "I would have thought you'd know the answer to both those questions."

There was a slight hesitation before it said, "Your impatient and angry friend, Francis Axford, wants us to ally with you against the creatures you call the Starfish. Your other friend, the one who goes by the name Caryl Hatzis, would want you to ask us how we have survived for so long. There you have the fundamental dichotomy between your two major allies: offense and defense. And you are

stuck in the middle, Peter Alander: you who could well
be the only *singular* person left in all of humanity."

Alander would have flushed, had he had a body to do
it in. "Remember, though, you're picking up these
thoughts from me. I undoubtedly have a biased view-
point."

"I prefer bias. Its flavors are that much more . . . interesting." The Praxis managed a convincing interpretation
of a throaty human chuckle. "Caryl Hatzis sounds like an
interesting person, someone I would very much like to eat
one day."

This time Alander had no doubt what the alien had said.

"I doubt she'd let you anywhere near her, especially if
she knew *that.*"

"When you speak to her next, tell her from me that she
is unlikely to fix the engrams by the methods she has
chosen. They are clumsy and skirt the major design flaws.
Attempting fundamental repairs without the awareness of
the patient is never going to work. She needs consent in
order to succeed."

"Consent?" The implications of what the Praxis was
saying sent distant alarm bells ringing through Alander's
mind. "She's been tinkering with the engrams? With *me?*"

"Ten minutes has elapsed," the Praxis said. "Your
friend will become anxious if you don't call him soon."

"Answer my question," Alander demanded. "Has Caryl
tampered with me?"

"You already know the answer to that," said the Praxis
calmly. "If I know it, then so, too, do you."

No, he wanted to say. *You can see my head from the
outside, see how my mind operates, like taking an engine
apart with a spanner.* But he knew that wasn't what the
Praxis meant. He had been feeling much more stable
within himself since the arrival of the Starfish. He had
presumed that stability had come from the need for de-
cisive action—but it had also come with the arrival of
Caryl Hatzis from Sol, who had once overwhelmed his
mind with her own thoughts in order to knock him out.

He had warned her then that if she tried anything like

that again—invaded him, compromised who he thought he was—he would kill her.

He could feel anger welling up inside him, railing against the calm that the alien creature generated. If the Praxis was right, he *should* be angry with his so-called ally. But if the alien was wrong, however, or just lying to manipulate him into being angry, then it would be a mistake to go off half cocked.

"Peter?" Axford's voice spilled into the darkness once again. "Peter? Can you still hear me?"

"I'm still here," he answered, feeling the anger slip away.

"What's going on?"

"I'm talking with the Praxis," he said, looking the immense creature up and down once more. "It seems to be the one running the show down here."

"Directing," interrupted the alien with a firm but friendly tone. "Not running, Peter. There's a difference."

"That's the Praxis?" said Axford following a pause. "It doesn't sound anything like the Yuhl we've spoken to so far."

"That's because it isn't Yuhl," he explained. "It's—something else altogether, actually."

"You're kidding," Axford muttered. *"Another* alien species?"

"Another alien species," confirmed Alander.

"So, is this one prepared to come to the party?" Axford went on, his bluster returning. This was a new factor in the equation, one the ex-general hadn't counted on.

"Too early to say," said Alander. "But I think—"

"May I make a suggestion?" said the Praxis.

Neither Alander nor Axford spoke for a few seconds. Then, from the ex-general: "Go on."

"This installation is not the appropriate place to conduct any sort of strategic meeting. We would be better served choosing another location."

"Such as?" said Axford.

"The system you call Rana in Becvar."

"That's half a day away," said Axford. "Are you sure

you're not trying to get rid of me while you get up to no good?"

"You have my word that Vega will not be approached."

"You know about that, huh?" Axford sounded disapproving, as though he thought Alander had revealed everything to the aliens. "Well, if you want to relocate to Rana in Becvar, that's fine, but I'm swinging by Vega on the way—*and* I'm taking my guest with me, too. That's just my mistrusting nature, I'm afraid. I'm sure you understand."

"Of course." The Praxis's voice expressed understanding and a willingness to cooperate. It *had* to be artificial, Alander knew, given the alien's nonhuman origins. "We shall meet you there in your own time."

"Wait," Frank the Ax said suddenly. "What's there, anyway? I mean, why the need to leave here?"

"That's just *my* mistrusting nature," said the Praxis. "I'm sure you understand."

Axford laughed gently. "See you in ten hours."

Alander sensed rather than heard the line to Axford close. A moment later, before he even had the chance to feel uneasy about being separated from the ex-general for so long, the alien's face suddenly vanished. Then, abruptly, with a violent, sucking wrench, his mind was snuffed out like a match dropped into a whirlpool.

2.1.2

For a moment or two following the dream, Alander found he couldn't move. The dream of his mother held him suffocatingly close. It was strange; he hadn't thought of her for years. She had died in a car accident when he was a child, along with his unborn sister. His original had spared him any memories of the accident and the nightmares that had followed, but just for an instant, among the blood and gore in the belly of the Yuhl vessel, he thought he had glimpsed his sister's face. Her eyes had been shut, her lips slightly parted, as though reaching for that first breath that would never come.

He opened his eyes to find himself lying in a hollow like the crook of an elbow, half submerged in clear fluid. It was warm and slightly sticky.

A shudder of revulsion ran through him as he stood up and tried to wipe the slime from his skin. He was naked and found the substance sluiced easily away beneath his hands. Flicking the last droplets from his body, Alander stepped away from the pool he'd been lying in. There were no lights about the area, yet somehow he was able to see quite clearly. Given his surroundings, that in itself wasn't necessarily a good thing. All around him—the walls, the floor, the ceiling—was the reddish pink hue of the monster's flesh. Soft, wet, and veined with blue, it heaved rhythmically like the sides of some immense whale.

And the *smell* . . .

Two intestine-like tubes, one to his right, the other off to his left, led from the fleshy cradle in which he had woken. He stood between them for a moment, running his hand across his scalp as he considered his options. The veined, undulating surface around him pulsed as though he was caught in a gigantic bowel. Neither way looked particularly appealing.

He froze suddenly at the unfamiliar roughness under his fingers. *Hair?*

He felt again to check. Sure enough, there was stubble on his head.

"My God," he mumbled, slowly checking out the rest of his body: arms, legs, belly, face, groin . . .

It was real. It was *all* real. The vat-grown android shell was growing hair! His body was—he was . . .

"What is this?" he asked aloud.

"Are you not satisfied?"

The voice of the Praxis issued from all around him— or possibly from inside himself. He couldn't tell which.

"It's not that. I just . . ." He ran the flat of one hand along his upper arm, feeling the firmness of the muscles there. He seemed smaller but so much more substantial. "What have you done to me?"

"I have remade you," said the alien. "I have remade you in your own image."

He was touching skin that was precisely the right color and texture, not the olive smoothness he was used to. And with that came another realization.

"My I-suit?" he said, patting his body to confirm its absence. "What have you done with my I-suit?"

"Your personal effects are waiting for you outside," said the Praxis. "They will be returned shortly. But first I want you to appreciate this moment of vulnerability for what it is. You are what you are made of, Peter. As a computer program dictated by rules of logic and grammar, no matter how much you dressed it up, you were never anything more than dead electrons. As creatures of flesh and tissue, however, you dance at the whim of biological uncertainty." It paused long enough for the flesh around him to pulse half a dozen times. Then: "Welcome back to the real world, Peter."

Alander continued to examine his body as best he could. It wasn't the same as the one he had known on Earth, before engram activation. This body was in its healthy thirties and lacked none of the added extras the artificial body had enjoyed. He could feel implanted capacities lying dormant at the edge of his consciousness. There was no feeling of breathlessness or imbalance he might have expected from his alien environment. But most of all . . .

He took a deep breath. *Yes.* Most of all, there was still the disturbing feeling of fragility underlying everything, as though his mind was a house of cards the slightest of breezes might knock down. That feeling had ebbed in recent weeks—his anger at Caryl Hatzis flared briefly at that thought—but it was always there. And it was *still* there, despite his new home. Perhaps it would always be part of him: the new him, the one created by UNESSPRO and sent out to the stars.

Still, what the Praxis had done, if the alien was indeed telling the truth, was impressive. Not only had it ingested his old body and rebuilt his mind in a virtual world, but it had then rebuilt that body a different way and returned him to it.

I doubt even Vincula technology could have done that, he mused.

"In the long run," said the Praxis, "I believe you will find this body more beneficial than the one you were using. New times call for new beginnings, after all."

Alander nodded as he continued to look himself over—as though he were examining a new suit. "Thank you," he said finally. "I think."

"I trust you will see this act for what it is."

Alander frowned (and noted that even the smallest expressions felt different with his new skin). "What do you mean?"

"I have provided this service freely," explained the Praxis. "As a gesture of goodwill between our species."

"And because you happen to have devoured my old body," said Alander. "Let's not forget *that.*"

The Praxis emitted another of its disturbingly human-like chuckles. "If you walk some distance to your left," it said, "you will find an exit."

Alander did as he was told, his naked feet recoiling slightly from the moist and spongy surface. He forced himself not to be squeamish. This was, after all, probably nothing but the alien version of a bioreactor. His old body had slid in a shroud out of a machine the size of an old family sedan designed to build everything from paper plates to people. There was nothing organic about the process. At least this way the experience of rebirth had a genuinely visceral component.

He passed another of the fluid-filled hollows like the one in which he had awoken, and was surprised to see another body lying there. It was a Yuhl, curled up with its great, triangular thighs pressed hard against its chest. Its eyes were shut, and the lines on its yellow and black face were set in a mask of random asymmetry, but Alander thought he recognized it.

"Ueh?" he said incredulously.

The alien's eyes snapped open, and it sprang upright in

one lightning-fast motion. Both hands came out, pushing with all the strength of those mighty legs behind them, and shoved Alander away. Unbalanced by the low gravity, Alander let himself take the tumble, rolling as he did so.

"No, wait!" he called out, clambering to get to his feet again. The combination of the new body and the springy surface made it difficult, but he finally managed to get upright.

The Yuhl faced him squarely, eyes blinking black-white, black-white.

"I didn't mean to startle you," he insisted, trying to mollify the alien. Although its arms were dangling inoffensively at its side, Alander's inability to read the alien's expressions made it impossible to determine if Ueh was angry or not. "I don't mean you any harm, I promise."

The Yuhl's head seemed to retreat on its neck, then it fluted a dissonant reply.

"He says that he is sorry, too," said the Praxis. "He regrets having used force to fend you off."

The alien ran both hands over its smooth, leathery scalp and blinked several times in quick succession. Naked, Alander could see every aspect of its anatomy in perfect relief; its musculature was ropy and clearly defined around its chest and limbs but hidden behind layers of fat around its torso. There were none of the strange flanges that adorned the conjugator's body, but there were strips of darker discoloration across its skin, like primitive body paint or less-defined examples of the pigment on its face. Its genitals were mostly retracted, but he could clearly see the petal-like tips of its double penis between its legs. The Praxis had referred to Ueh as a male, but Alander still suspected that issue of gender among the Yuhl was more complicated than humans took for granted.

Alander wondered if Ueh was as curious about *his* body as he was about the alien's. In their long travels, the Yuhl might have encountered many alien species, in many different forms, so their interest might have been long sated. Ueh seemed more interested in examining himself than Alander, touching his body in several places and staring at both sides of his hands for several seconds. He emitted several short phrases the Praxis didn't translate.

"You ate him, too?" he asked the Praxis.

"It is my habit to keep a regular check on the mood of the people in my care," it replied. "This way there can be no deceptions."

Ueh seemed to have finished examining his body. Whether he was satisfied by what he found, Alander couldn't tell. The Yuhl emitted a string of sounds like two flautists playing the same phrase a semitone apart, and pointing at the same time at Alander.

"He says that you should get moving," supplied the Praxis. "As honored as he is to share this process with you, he knows that the conjugator will be waiting for you both out the other side."

"What's he so worried about?"

"Maintaining the proper display of obedience. The Yuhl belonged to a relatively primitive culture before the Ambivalence favored them and I tamed them. The more useful aspects of that culture remain today. The conjugators do my will primarily because that puts them in a position of dominance over their own kind. *Ueh/Ellil* is on the cusp of either advancement or further dishonor. The Yuhl have more in common with humans than you suspect."

Alander smiled at the implication. "If you think for a moment that we would allow ourselves to be *tamed*—"

"I never said that was my intention," the Praxis said.

"No, you didn't," said Alander. "But *is* it your intention?"

"Of course not." There was almost a hint of indignation in the alien's tone. "Now, I suggest you do as Ueh says before he becomes agitated."

Alander nodded and let the Yuhl guide him out of the insides of the Praxis. He wasn't reassured by the alien's assurance that humanity was safe from its manipulations. *No deceptions,* it had said. What was there, he thought, to keep it honest?

*   *   *

Getting out of the Praxis involved sliding feetfirst through a series of well-lubricated sphincters and being messily deposited into a bath of acrid-smelling water. Attendants were on hand to clean them off. Alander gathered that this was a fairly regular procedure, one the Yuhl had become accustomed to over time. Certainly no one expressed surprise at Alander's new appearance.

Then it was to a dry antechamber where Alander found his belongings waiting for him, as promised. His shipsuit was bunched up on the floor, none the worse for wear after his old body's ingestion. In the middle of it was the coiled-up chain from which hung Lucia's disk. *Bliss indeed,* he thought. His I-suit rested beside them, collapsed into a translucent ball. When he touched it with his right hand, it spread up his arm and over his body with one liquid motion. Its presence was almost unnoticeable, but he was glad it was there. For all the Praxis's rhetoric about coming to terms with the flesh of his new self, he felt much better knowing that he was safe again, even though the Spinner device hadn't exactly protected him from the Praxis.

He was also back in touch with the hole ship. The Praxis may have remade his old body, but it had, thankfully, left the implants he'd become used to in the android. While he didn't know if the Yuhl had tried to merge AIs and take the data it contained, he supposed it didn't make much difference, seeing that the Praxis had already picked through his brain and discovered everything there, anyway.

He was looking forward to getting back to *Silent Liquidity,* where he could take a closer look at the new body he inhabited. But there was no way he was going to return to the others until he was absolutely certain he wasn't carrying the seeds of their enslavement with him.

"Has anyone tried to interfere with you?" he asked the ship's AI. Even as he asked it, he knew that he wouldn't necessarily be able to believe what it said in reply.

"I have experienced no invasive attempts," it said smoothly. "Overt or covert."

"And where are we?" He realized only then that he had no idea how long he had even been in the belly of the Praxis. "Are we still in transit?

"We are in Beid system."

"*Beid?* I thought we were going to Rana in Becvar."

"We have already been there, Peter," announced the Praxis, breaking into the link between him and the hole ship. "We stopped at Rana in Becvar long enough to drop a simple navigation buoy. Your friend will find the buoy when he arrives, and it will instruct him to come to Beid. If he is not here in six hours, then we will move on."

Alander sighed heavily. "This is going to make the man suspicious," he said. "If you aren't where you said you'd be, then he's going to—"

"We cannot take the risk of him surprising us," the Praxis cut in softly.

"Surprising you? How?"

"He is an unknown quantity, Peter. I know from your memories that he has successfully attacked at least one of our scouts in his home system. And he is not above using the Ambivalence against us, should he deem it necessary."

"If he did, you could hardly complain," said Alander. "He'd just be using your own tactics against you."

"You believe him uncritically, then," the Praxis said evenly, "when he tells you it was us who destroyed your colonies, not him?"

This caught Alander off guard. He hadn't even considered the possibility that Axford might be lying. "That doesn't make sense," he said. But even he could hear his own doubts creeping into his voice. "He has footage showing—"

"Footage can be faked," the Praxis pointed out.

"But he has only the one hole ship," he said with more conviction. "If he *was* raiding the gifts from our colonies and calling the Starfish to hide the evidence, where's all the stuff he's stolen?"

The mighty alien paused meaningfully. "Where, indeed?"

The conjugator entered the antechamber at that moment. It didn't seem to concern him that Alander was still only half dressed. The hole ship translated his words into English while Alander picked at the disturbing thought the Praxis had planted in his head.

"The Praxis has determined that you must meet with the Fit immediately," said the conjugator, indicating the door through which he had entered. Alander hesitated, then walked through it. Ueh followed closely behind, with the conjugator bringing up the rear.

"The Fit?" Alander asked, thinking: *Now what?* After his experience with the Praxis, he was wary of taking anything for granted. Once eaten, twice shy.

"I have chosen that word from your language carefully," said the Praxis. "It combines notions of connectedness as well as superior adaptation."

"The Fit are a sort of council, then," he ventured. "The top Yuhl echelon?"

"Crudely speaking, yes. Decisions that affect everyone should not be made in isolation, even by me," said the Praxis sagely. "There has to be a chain of command, and that chain must be flexible. The Fit are the first link in that chain. The conjugators comprise another. The organic progression of information, misinformation, and disinformation enables *Yuhl/Goel* society to mimic a living system. I would not have it any other way. Totalitarianism reeks of those stale electrons, Peter."

Alander nodded: he could see that. "But why did we have to come all this way to talk to them? Why couldn't we have just stayed in Alsafi?"

"Take a moment to look around you, Peter. It will explain many things."

Alander assumed the Praxis didn't mean the empty, curving corridor through which they were walking. "*Liquidity*, give me an overview of the system we're in." A 3-D map appeared before him containing a complex mix of symbols. He probed deeper, ignoring the tug of dis-

orientation as he walked. Beid was an F2II-III star with
a rapid variability. Also called 38 omicron 1 Eridani, it
wasn't on the UNESSPRO lists because no oxygen or
water signatures had been detected around it. Its solar system consisted of one medium-sized gas giant in a highly
elliptical orbit, currently around the same distance as Mars
was from Sol, plus two terrestrial worlds in the process
of being knocked out of orbit by gravitational perturba-
tions. The gas giant had no intact rings left, but there
appeared to be an asteroid belt in close around the sun,
where *Silent Liquidity* itself was stationed. The odd thing
was that Alander wouldn't have expected such a feature
to remain in such a perturbed system—and asteroids
didn't normally move on their own.

It was then that he realized what the Praxis had meant.
The *Mantissa* was a planetoid-sized craft made of many
thousands of individual hole ships. Orbiting Beid were, in
turn, many thousands of such craft. What looked like an
asteroid belt from a distance turned out, in fact, to be
millions of hole ships in a chaotic yet contained swarm.

"What is this?" he asked, awestruck. "The Yuhl migration fleet?"

"*This* is the *Mantissa*."

"But—?"

"The *Mantissa* is much more than the fragment that you
encountered in Alsafi," the Praxis explained. "Since the
possible combinations of so many hole ships is almost
infinite, the usual notions of independent vessels and the
boundaries between them do not apply. The hole ships
that comprised my bier this morning might by this eve-
ning be part of an exploratory mission to a far-flung system. The *Mantissa* as a whole is never entirely in one
place."

Hence the name, I guess, mused Alander, still stunned
by the vast number of hole ships present in the system.

"There are always pieces coming and going," the Praxis
was saying. "It is a dynamic process that is very difficult
to control."

"And organic, again."

"You are grasping the essential difference between my species and yours. While you seek to transcend the flesh in which you evolved, I embrace it wholeheartedly. The Yuhl are my protégés. The arrangement serves us both quite well."

What if it didn't? Alander wanted to ask. *And what if it doesn't serve humanity?* He imagined the *Mantissa* swarming through space at the cusp between the Spinner/ Starfish migrations, seizing what resources they could: both physical, in terms of the gifts and other valuable materials, and mental, in the form of new species happened across along the way. *Will we be eaten, too, if we can't see eye to eye?*

"The Fit are *waiting/ready*," said the conjugator impatiently.

Alander wrenched himself from the hole ship's feed and back into the long, curving corridor.

"Everything you need to know will be explained to you in due course," the Praxis assured him.

Alander glanced at Ueh, who still stood by him and whose alien body language suggested patient subservience. A full head taller than Alander, the situation was ludicrous, and it highlighted just how little he knew about any of the species currently impacting on his life. Just because he could exchange words with the Yuhl and the Praxis didn't necessarily mean he understood them any better than the Spinners or the Starfish.

But there was no reason not to try, he knew, even if the risk of making mistakes was high. He owed it to the surviving humans, if not to himself. After being eaten, he supposed, he could deal with anything.

He took a deep and steadying breath. "Let's get it over with, then."

Encased in his bubble of Earth-like air, he continued along the corridor to where the Fit waited.

He had imagined the Fit gathering in a tiered amphitheater, all shouting at once, but only the latter part turned out to be the case. The Fit as a whole didn't gather physically, although they did congregate in one place when possible. Alander was shown to a room partitioned into many small areas, not dissimilar to the intestinal corridor along which he had been led to meet the Praxis. Among the increasingly familiar tangle of ornamental and functional installations—he was still unable to tell which was which—he saw many spine-encrusted Yuhl sitting at low desks, bent forward with their heads encased in fleshy helmets.

Conjugator Vaise led him to an empty cubicle and gestured that he should sit.

"Once more into the breach?" he said, his stomach sinking.

"This is not like conSense," said the Praxis.

"What is it like, then?"

"You'll see."

Alander suppressed his misgivings and sat down in front of the desk. The helmet hung before him, and he felt as eager to slip his head into it as he would a crocodile's mouth. Its interior wasn't fleshy and veined like the interior of the Praxis but lined instead with millions of slender cilia that stirred in strange, geometric patterns. There was no obvious way for air to get in or out, which only exacerbated his apprehensions.

He ran a hand nervously across his newly stubbled scalp. He felt Ueh come up behind him as though to protect his back, and he felt the stare of the conjugator watching him.

Damn it, he thought. Then, without allowing himself the opportunity for second thoughts, he closed his eyes and thrust his head firmly into the helmet. He almost gagged as the cilia enfolded him, squirming against his skin like a flesh-eating anemone. It was much colder than he expected, and he flinched and tried to pull away as something pressed against his mouth and nose. But there was no way he could pull out of the helmet. A fleshy sphincter had closed around his neck, trapping him inside the squelching darkness. When the breath he held could sustain him no more, he opened his mouth to gasp for air,

but found instead a torrent pouring down his throat. He
wanted to scream out at the disgusting violation, but he
was no more able to do that than he was able to wriggle
free. He could feel alien hands on his back and arms,
restraining his flailing body.

He choked and spasmed for what seemed like an eternity, until, abruptly, everything cleared. The cilia were
gone; the helmet seemed to have vanished. The pressure
on his back and arms and neck and throat had simply
evaporated, and he felt instead as though he was floating
face-forward in free fall, his eyes closed and arms outstretched.

"I am moderating this experience to a certain extent,
including translation," the Praxis's voice intruded easily
into the illusion. "But I assure you I'm not interfering with
it in any way."

"*What* experience?" Alander asked. His voice sounded
strangely muted and lonely. "There's nothing here."

"I was just giving you a moment to adjust," said the
Praxis. "But if you are ready—"

"I'm ready," said Alander. He wanted to sound confident, but even he could detect his repressed panic in his
words. "I guess . . ."

It started, oddly, as an odor: a combination of many
smells, both sweet and caustic. At first he put it down to
the aroma from the helmet his head was encased in, but
then he heard a faint noise in the distance, as though he
was standing outside a theater in which a large number
of people were shouting to drown out a concert. The noise
became louder, and he began to identify different strands
within it, individual voices that stood apart from the rest
by virtue of their volume or their eloquence. When the
combined cacophony became louder still, he focused on
one of those strands and realized as he did that he could
discern words within it. Gradually it became clear that
what he was hearing was the babble of the Fit, their linked
minds all shouting simultaneously at one another.

At first the rousing rabble frightened him, being as it
was a new and, indeed, completely alien experience. He

felt for a moment that he would drown in the flood of voices but was thankful, at least, that the Praxis was keeping the translations free of any double vocal streams, which would have only added confusion to the already overwhelming event.

He also realized that he had some control over the situation. He was able to maintain some distance from the incessant and headache-inducing babble. For the first few minutes, he tried teasing apart the various voices and the threads of their conversations. Although what they were talking about didn't make much sense—making him wonder if the Praxis's translation was designed to obfuscate information he wasn't privy to—he felt confident afterward of at least hearing any replies they offered him.

"Can you hear me?" He found himself instinctively shouting to be heard over the racket.

Voices and smells swirled around him like a fine, snakelike mist. From the writhing fog, a reply emerged, angry and indignant, and smelling of gunpowder: "Of course we can."

"I want to thank you for allowing me—"

"What is it you want?" another voice shot from the rabble.

"I—I want . . ." He faltered for a moment, wondering for whom he was actually speaking. What *he* wanted surely differed from what Axford or Hatzis wanted. "We want—humanity, that is, wants—to form an alliance with the *Yuhl/Goel* against the common threat we all face."

A barrage of replies erupted from the mist:

"Alliance?"

"He is *already/dead*!"

"How can you help *us?*"

He withdrew for a moment from the onslaught of voices and emotion, his entire being feeling as if he were trembling. But he knew he couldn't afford to show any sign of weakness with these aliens and so quickly reimmersed himself into the almost impenetrable vapor of their protests, snatching at the comment he felt to be the most important.

"I'm referring to the threat of the Starfish," he said. He realized also that he didn't need to shout at all; his voice would come across as a shout regardless of how much effort he put into it. "You regard them as part of the Ambivalence. It—"

"THE AMBIVALENCE IS INDIVISIBLE!"

The response clearly came from many voices at once, and their combined protest was a painful and disorienting shriek. A smell like sulfur accosted his senses. For a moment he was confused, wanting to withdraw again from the voices.

"What—?" he started, not knowing how to respond to such a unified outburst.

"The Ambivalence gives—"

"The Ambivalence takes away."

"One cannot exist without the other!"

Flustered, Alander struggled for words. He had inadvertently given rise to a religious argument.

"But surely it takes more than it gives," he interjected. "Surely *lives* are more important than technological trinkets."

"Lives are lives," said another voice. "Before the Ambivalence, we were a profligate race. We didn't truly understand the gift of life."

"We squandered it," said another.

"We warred."

"But there is no more war now," the first voice went on, their words carried on a subtle scent of cinnamon. "We have achieved a refined state."

A general hubbub rose at the pronouncement, like a cheer. Then: *"PRAISE AND THANKS TO THE AMBIVALENCE!"*

"We are the *Yuhl/Goel!*" roared a familiar voice.

"You are just *humanity/riil*," put in another.

"You are the *already/dead*."

"Yes, we are," said Alander defiantly. "But we are also living creatures like yourselves. Surely the Praxis has taught you the importance of the flesh. Did you spurn *it* because it was not Yuhl/Goel?"

"The Praxis is many things to us," came a new voice, deep and measured. "It guides us."

"It teaches us."

"It tells us that you are *not* creatures of the flesh, but that you have spurned your bodies."

"It is true," said Alander. "We *did* abandon our bodies—but only so that our species could explore space. We never abandoned the *idea* of our bodies. We carried our sense of physical self as an anchor to keep us sane, to protect who we are. Some of us, like me, have been unable to survive without it, and we returned to the flesh as soon as we were able. You must see that these are *not* the actions of a species that spurns the flesh; but rather they are the actions of one that has made a mistake and learned from it."

The mist settled momentarily, as did the various aromas. Then, bursting from the calm: "You seek exoneration for your actions?"

"I didn't know I had to," said Alander.

"We are not forcing you to do anything."

"You are coming to us for help."

"We merely seek to understand what it is you want."

Alander felt like he was being played with but forced himself not to rise to the bait.

"We want many things," he said. "But first and foremost, we want peace with all aspects of the Ambivalence. We do not want war; we do not want destruction. We want coexistence, not predation."

"And how do you hope to achieve this?"

"The only way to achieve it is to cooperate," he said firmly. "The details are not as important as that fundamental impetus. If we can agree to work together, the details will fall into place of their own accord, I am sure."

"We are not so sure," one voice replied.

"We already have peace with the Ambivalence."

"Why should we jeopardize that?"

Alander was surprised when another voice from the mist answered for him: "We do not have peace with the Ambivalence," it said, with the smell of freshly cut grass accompanying its words. "We have peaceful coexistence."

"They amount to the same thing."

"No, they are different! We survive because we exist in the fringes. If we stray beyond those boundaries, we risk upsetting the balance we have striven so long to maintain."

"Perhaps that would be a good thing," said another voice.

It occurred to Alander that he was starting to tell the voices apart. The strident voice with the near-fanatical interest in preserving the status quo was *Zealot/Shrieking*; the more measured but equally conservative tones of the one who had argued for peaceful coexistence was called *Status Quo/Mellifluous*. The new voice deservedly had the name *Radical/Provocative*.

That wasn't their real names, he assumed; these were simply titles that identified the individual's character. Equally, he was sure that the names weren't of his own creation. They were being given to him by the Praxis.

"I think we have stifled in this niche, this rut we have dug for ourselves, long enough," said the new voice. "It's time for a change."

"What? And put our lot in with this bodiless rabble?" retorted *Zealot/Shrieking*. "With *prey*?"

"And attack the Ambivalence?"

"Is that gratitude?"

"Attack is not the only option," said *Radical/Provocative*. "There was a time when the *Yuhl/Goel* aspired to more than the parasitic lifestyle we currently enjoy."

A wave of shouting almost drowned out *Radical/Provocative*, but the alien persisted.

"Yes, parasitic! Be outraged at the notion of what we *do* rather than what I say!"

"You are talking about the Species Dream," broke in *Status Quo/Mellifluous*.

The hubbub eased, allowing *Radical/Provocative* to speak more freely. "That is what I am referring to," he said. "Yes. But it doesn't have to be a fantasy. We have the resources and the opportunity to make it all real. The only thing we lack is the will."

"The will to survive remains strong in us," said a new voice: *Stoic/Enduring*. This voice had a hint of caramel lifting from it. "Perhaps too strong to take such a risk."

"It *is* a risk, but it's a glorious one. This envoy from *humanity/riil* is proof of that. See how he defies what we regard to be self-evident? See how he challenges us to reinvent ourselves? He shames us with his very presence."

"What is the Species Dream?" Alander asked over the voices building in response to *Radical/Provocative's* challenge.

"It is an ancient aspiration of the *Yuhl/Goel*," said *Status Quo/Mellifluous*. "When our people were first visited by the Ambivalence and were swept up in its journey through space, we very nearly did not survive. We adopted many of our current practices in order to ensure that what remained *would* survive. With the help of the Praxis, we formed a stable society that could outlive the eons yet was capable also of adapting to constant change. We no longer needed a home system in which to live. We are nomads, crossing the gulfs between the stars and scouring the universe for knowledge.

"But some said that wasn't enough," he went on. "There were some who advocated that this was only a short-term solution, that the *Yuhl/Goel* need more than just survival in order to thrive. They argued that we needed a goal, an aspiration, and that that aspiration should be a new home somewhere, a permanent settlement in the wake of the Ambivalence, where we can establish ourselves as an independent civilization. That is the Species Dream."

"But time has demonstrated that we can live without it," said *Radical/Provocative*, picking up the story with bitterness. "Time has seen us grow in strength. I say that this strength is only illusory. We have sown the seeds of our downfall with the very crops that keep us alive! We need the Dream—and now might be the perfect time to embrace it."

"What need have we for a home planet now?" snapped

Zealot/Shrieking. "You would have us halt our progress! You would have us turn back and reenter the aeries!"

"Your lies in my mouth!" *Radical/Provocative* spat.

"I see no possible advantage to leaving the Ambivalence."

"We have everything we need right here."

"Minerals, resources, space—the Ambivalence gives all!"

"What about freedom? What about pride?"

"You mustn't be hard on yourselves," Alander interjected, wanting desperately to shift the subject away from the Yuhl's shortcomings and back to humanity. "You have done what you needed to do in order to survive."

"There are limits," said *Radical/Provocative*. "If the method is abhorrent, the results cannot be justified. And what might have been morally justifiable thousands of years ago no longer applies today. The simple fact is that we are able, now, to choose for ourselves. We have accumulated the resources to settle down. The only reason we continue as we do is in order to give us more space to expand—and creating more of something abhorrent hardly makes us better as a species."

Hatzis should be here, Alander thought. *Radical/Provocative* was definitely thinking along her lines.

"I look at you," Alander said, "and I see us. Humanity is facing the same choices you were when you first encountered the Ambivalence. If we choose the same as you, then in two thousand years or so, we might be in the same position you are now. Our species may be very different, but we face the same choices. Humanity, Yuhl, the Praxis—the Ambivalence forces us to decide what we as a species want and what we are prepared to do in order to obtain it."

"The Ambivalence tests us," said *Zealot/Shrieking*, in a tone of agreement and a scent of tea tree oil. "It refines us."

"It distills from us the qualities that make us worthy," said *Radical/Provocative*. "What about the species that didn't survive? How many of those have we seen? They weren't inferior to us; they simply made different choices."

"And we honor their passing," said *Zealot/Shrieking.* "We honor *all* those who fall in the Ambivalence's path. What more can we do?"

"Help them," said *Radical/Provocative.* "*Join* them."

"You would die with these humans rather than continue as we are?"

"Our existence is already a form of death," said *Radical/Provocative.*

"I don't think dying will be necessary," Alander said. "I'm certain that cooperation needn't necessitate mutual destruction."

"Not if you were to join us here," said *Status Quo/Mellifluous,* "in our great venture."

"Become humanity/goel?" Alander asked, remembering the derision that Axford's hostage had shown the idea.

"Interspecies cooperation is the norm, here, and the Praxis has let you come this far. It is an option you should consider."

And Alander did consider it—very carefully. If Hatzis would agree with *Radical/Provocative* in calling for a permanent settlement in the wake of the Spinner/Starfish advance, Frank the Ax would undoubtedly go for the second option, of joining the ragtag fleet that were attending the superior aliens like birds picking ticks off hippopotami. That would give him time to collect resources, study the advanced technology, and gather allies for a retaliatory attack against the Starfish.

But where do I stand? Alander wondered.

He could see sense in both sides just as readily as he could see the faults. If they opted for Hatzis's plan and founded a permanent settlement, the remnants of humanity would be vulnerable to outside attack for a long time to come. And if Axford had his way and they joined the *Yuhl/Goel,* there was a very real risk that humanity would end up exactly the same: feeding off the weak in the wake of the strong.

"Surely there must be a third option?" he asked. "Couldn't some of the Yuhl/Goel join with the humans who want to settle, while the rest of humanity joins the migration? I can understand that the travelers wouldn't want to lose resources to the settlers, but with what we could bring to replace it—"

The mist of sound billowed with objection and the smell of burning wood:

"Impossible!"

"Unthinkable!"

"Absurd!"

"*Why* impossible?" asked *Radical/Provocative*, his dissenting voice loud and forceful in the storm of protest.

"How can we trust these creatures?"

"We know nothing about them."

"Then we must *learn*," he returned quickly.

"And if the *Yuhl/Goel* splits, what then? Our paths will no longer be concurrent. We will be divided; we will be weakened."

"We are already weak," said *Radical/Provocative*. "Better to be divided in fact rather than essence. I suggest we put the proposal to a vote."

"Now?" The single word from *Zealot/Shrieking* was clearly an objection. "We need time to think about the issues and—"

"We all know the issues; we have been living with them for millennia," said *Radical/Provocative*. "There is an opportunity here for change. We must act before it slips through our fingers."

"You mean before humanity is extinct?" asked *Status Quo/Mellifluous*.

"Yes."

"Then we must move quickly."

"Wait," said Alander. "Why is that the only alternative we have to allying with you?"

"Because if you do not join the migration," said *Status Quo/Mellifluous*, "then you will be cleansed by the Ambivalence. It leaves nothing in its wake."

"The Starfish," he said, feeling cold. "The sneak attacks. Is that what you're talking about?"

"We have seen this many times before."

"Perhaps some survivors manage to escape, but you have never encountered them."

"None can hide where the Ambivalence passes. Your species must be fully aware of the risks it faces, should it choose to remain behind."

Alander's hopes fell as the murmuring of the Fit rose around him again. What hope was there when one path promised destruction and the other a life of scavenging? If staying put meant they would be destroyed, then clearly they had to move, and that left them only three options. The obvious one was to join the Yuhl, but they could also jump ahead and ride the front of the Spinner migration forever, afraid to slow down or stop; or they could jump backward, past the Starfish, and see what the wake held. Alander didn't much like that idea, either; he imagined it full of dead worlds and less sophisticated scavengers still.

It all seemed hopeless. He wondered how many species had faced the same choice. If the Yuhl and the Praxis were all that remained, maybe the number was small. Or maybe they balked at the end and chose death rather than dishonor. Or they had simply run out of time.

The hubbub eased for a second.

"We vote," said *Radical/Provocative*.

Alander wondered how they would go about it when they couldn't even see each other in the darkness. He didn't have to wait long to find out.

The sound of many mingled voices ebbed even further until there was nothing but silence and the mist receded completely. Then every one of them shouted at once, creating a blast of noise that left Alander reeling. It sounded as though all the Fit had cast their vote in the same instant, but with such a dissonant roar, how could anyone tell which side had won?

Yet, strangely, he *could* tell. There was something in the combined noise that indicated that the ayes outweighed the nays. He didn't know what it was, beyond a gut feeling, but he knew what *Status Quo/Mellifluous* was going to say before the alien's words reached him.

"We agree to explore the possibility of a strategic al-

liance with *humanity/riil*. If the Praxis allows it, we will
divert resources to ensuring the survival of those who
wish to join us. We will hear alternative proposals when
they are presented to us in detailed form. Is there anything
else we wish to agree to?"

"To live," said *Radical/Provocative*, a sentiment *Zealot/Shriek-ing* instantly seconded.

"It is our duty."

Then the babble of the Fit receded, and Alander felt
himself being drawn out of the organic helmet and back
into the seat. Senses other than sound and smells rushed
over him: he was shivering from the cold, and the skin of
his face felt slimy when he raised his hands to touch it.
Someone pressed a cloth into his hands and wiped at the
slime so he could see. Everything was yellow; none of
the faces looked quite right. Despite the relative youth of
his body, he felt haggard.

"Did it go as you hoped, Peter?" asked a voice.

Only he didn't hear it that way. He heard it direct from
the original Yuhl language, with its overtones of com-
mingled realities and overlapping wave fronts. The aliens
expressed the concepts of hope and eventuality very differently from humans, with less emphasis on finality and
certainty. All things changed; all things happened, somewhere; the issue was, did *this Peter/Alander* find himself in
the universe he wanted to be?

"Maybe," he said, and he was relieved to hear his words
translated into Yuhl by the I-suit membrane around him.
He might have suddenly been able to understand their
language, but he certainly didn't have any idea how to
speak it. Or the extra vocal cords.

What he'd wanted to say, though, was, *Yes. This is
what I came here to find: answers, a direction, hope.*

The alien who had spoken—Ueh—leaned closer. He
retrieved the circular cloth Alander had used to wipe his
face and placed it on the desk.

"We kept you in as long as we could," the Yuhl said.

"What's going on?" The Rorschach patterns on Ueh's
face shifted into an expression of concern. *Christ, I can*

read their expressions, too? he thought. *What the hell did the Praxis do to me?*

"Francis Axford has arrived," said Ueh. "He *needs to talk/ says it's urgent.*"

Alander was confused for a moment. "Frank's arrived? Already? How long was I in there?"

"*Five/hours.*"

That would explain why he was feeling so weak, he imagined, and why an intense headache was pounding behind his eyes. "Put me through to him. Can you do that from here?"

"I am opening a line," said the Praxis.

Alander leaned back to compose himself, wondering what on Earth he was going to tell Axford. He hadn't exactly secured anything for humanity except a willingness on the behalf of the Yuhl to talk. Hopefully that would be enough.

"Peter!" A life-size image of Francis Axford appeared beside him. His expression was one of concern mixed with relief. And, carefully buried even deeper, there was something else, too. Nervousness, perhaps? "I'm relieved you're back—more so than you imagine, probably. We need to talk."

"What is it?"

"Not here," said Axford. "Not like this. I'd prefer it if you'd join me in *Mercury.*"

Alander nodded. "All right," he said and closed the line. Axford's image instantly disappeared.

He turned his attention to Ueh and the conjugator.

"I have to go," he said apologetically. He was going to have to get to *Silent Liquidity* and relocate to Axford's position; he just wasn't sure whether the Yuhl would let him. "I assure you I shan't be away long."

Ueh helped Alander up as he struggled to his feet; he still found himself adjusting to his new body. "You *are free to move among us/we will not prevent* you," he said.

"The Praxis grants you the status," said the conjugator, but he spoke in a way that suggested to Alander that he didn't necessarily approve. "You are *envoy/catechist.*"

"Thanks," he said with an acknowledging nod. "I guess."

He urged his legs to carry him in a straight line past the rows of tables, each with a Yuhl hunched over, heads lost in their grotesque biological helmets. He wondered which one of them might be *Radical/Provocative* or *Zealot/ Shrieking*, but he had no real way of telling. Once they all might have looked the same to him, but as he moved among the aliens now, he realized he was starting to perceive differences in skin colors and other features.

The conjugator fell behind when they reached the hole ship dry dock but Ueh kept coming. Alander stopped at the entrance to *Silent Liquidity* and put a hand on the alien's chest. The interaction of their I-suits made his fingers skate slightly, as though he was pressing on ice.

"You can stay here if you like," said Alander. "I really will be coming back soon."

"I am *envoy/catechist* as is *Peter/Alander*," said the alien cryptically. Then, seeing Alander's puzzlement, he added: "I am remade."

"The Praxis?" said Alander.

"I am remade," Ueh repeated, the plates on its face shifting back and forth, "to perform this function."

Alander shook his head.

New times for new beginnings . . . ?

"Okay," he said with a sigh, glancing past Ueh to where the conjugator stood watching on from the entrance to the dry dock. "But don't try anything."

"*That's not* my role *is to observe and mediate*," said Ueh.

Alander studied the Yuhl for a moment. There was something in the alien's manner that was different, and it was more than just an improvement in his own ability to observe the aliens' nuances. Ueh was becoming more self-confident.

A bizarre thought struck him. He had received a number of hints that the Yuhl were of avian origin. Some birds on Earth had been known to grow new sections of their brains when new talents were required—such as singing during mating season—then lose them again when the need for those skills went away. What if the Yuhl did something like that, and he was looking at an individual who was literally more than he had been only a few hours earlier?

It didn't matter right now. All he needed to be sure of was that the Yuhl wouldn't jump when he had the chance, and for the moment, Alander was as sure of that as he could be.

He led the way into *Silent Liquidity* and instructed it to match positions with *Mercury*. Axford was lurking on the edge of the system, well away from the "asteroid belt" full of Yuhl vessels. With half the cockpit restored to a human-suitable atmosphere and the impermeable barrier dividing it in two again, Alander allowed himself to relax slightly. He might have been eaten, tinkered with, and perhaps even taken advantage of, but he had come out of it all ahead. That was something, at least.

When they arrived seconds later, *Silent Liquidity* quickly docked with *Mercury*. The airlock connecting them opened, and Alander walked unhesitatingly through, leaving Ueh behind without an explanation. When the airlock shut again, he was finally alone with Axford.

On seeing Alander, the ex-general started and took a hasty step back.

"Holy Hades!" he said, looking Alander over in amazement. "I thought there was something different about you, but it wasn't clear via conSense." He took a hesitant step forward and reached out to touch Alander's new body. "What did they *do* to you?"

Chewed me up and spat me out, Alander thought wryly, but he said, "You wouldn't believe me if I told you."

Axford pinched the skin between his fingers, testing it. "This looks as good as new," he said, unable to lose the astonishment from his tone.

"Better, I suspect," said Alander. Axford's android body looked green-skinned and blunt-featured, now that he could allow himself to observe it objectively. "But we'll have time for that later. What was so important that

I had to drop everything and come all the way across-system to hear it?"

"You missed the latest midday report from Sothis."

Alander shrugged. "I was a little busy at the time."

"Getting refitted?" Axford gestured to Alander's body.

"And trying to strike a deal," he replied. "I was talking to the Yuhl's equivalent of a senate or parliament. I've made some progress. But again, this can wait."

"I'm not sure it *can* wait," said Frank the Ax. "It's vitally important to know just how far we can push these guys, Peter. It might be the only hope we have left."

"What do you mean? What the hell is going on?"

"It's the news from home," he said. "It's not good."

"More sneak attacks?"

"Of course," he said. "But that's not it. It's our friend Hatzis; she's declared war."

Alander frowned. "On the Starfish?"

"No," he said, his expression and body language taut. "She's declared war on the Yuhl."

2.1.3

THE DELEGATION FROM JUNO IS HERE, SOL.

The words failed to register. Caryl Hatzis sat staring into space in *Arachne* and didn't consciously notice the world around her.

Am I doing the right thing? she asked herself. *Am I accepting a convenient target in exchange for one I can't even see?*

A roll call of lost hole ships and their pilots scrolled through her mind. The colonies she couldn't help, but these she had sent to their death. Adammas, Tatenen, Eos, Rama . . . The list was getting longer every day. She may not have been directly responsible for their deaths, but she still felt complicity. She couldn't shake the thought that maybe opting out, seceding from her own dream, might well be the simplest way to keep them safe.

But no, she couldn't allow herself to believe that. The

dissenters are dreamers, she told herself, and likely to die as a consequence, too.

But that didn't necessarily make *her* right.

SOL?

Convenience be damned, she thought. It wasn't so much that the Yuhl were *there;* it was that they were fighting over the same things. The Yuhl needed the resources as much as she did; the gifts were the only things keeping humanity alive at the moment, and having them stolen from under her nose galled her more than she could say.

While a hole ship stolen from its rightful recipient was bad enough, having one *destroyed* for simply being in the wrong place at the wrong time was utterly devastating. But there was nothing she could do about the Starfish. They were becoming increasingly machinelike in her mind, jumping from transmission to transmission, then spreading out in circles from each locus, scouring every sign of humanity when they found it. They were unstoppable and incommunicable.

Some people were beginning to blame the Spinners, suggesting that the silence of the alien benefactors belied their generosity in providing the gifts in the first place. What sort of person, went the argument, gives a savage a shotgun, then ignores the resulting carnage? Is that the sign of a caring society? But Hatzis didn't accept this; she was reluctant to believe that all the wonders of the gifts could comprise such a trivial, throwaway item in the eyes of their makers. She might not be able to explain the aliens' silence, but she refused to assign blame indiscriminately.

The Yuhl, though, they were something else altogether. Here was a tangible enemy. Calling for retaliation wasn't indiscriminate soapboxing. It was a matter of survival.

A hand touched her shoulder, and she started out of her thoughts.

I'M SORRY, SOL.

THAT'S ALL RIGHT. MY MIND WAS JUST ELSEWHERE. IS IT JUNO?

YES.
SEND THEM IN.

Three android bodies filed into the cockpit, waved on by Gou Mang. The space seemed crowded as Sol stood up to greet them. The meeting could have been conducted virtually, but where possible, she preferred physical contact with the engrams. It reminded them who was boss, she felt. And right now, that was something needing constant reinforcement.

"Thank you for coming," she said, nodding in turn to Kingsley Oborn, Materials Specialist Owen Norsworthy, and the colony's own version of herself. She came straight to the point. "I want to know what sort of progress you're making."

Norsworthy glanced at Oborn and swallowed nervously. "Some," he said. "I have files on several promising weapons systems we've found in the Library, as well as a variant on the I-suit envelope, which could cover a much larger volume."

"Anything we can use right now?"

"Not really. But then, it has only been—"

She didn't give him time to finish his excuse. "Things can move very quickly when they have to," she said. "And believe me when I say that right now I expect them to. I've given you extra Overseer resources so you can run as fast as necessary. I've given you as many Spinner contacts as we can spare, to ensure communications flow smoothly. If you pushed hard enough, Owen, three days could equate to a month."

"We *have* been pushing, Sol," he objected.

"Then is it a problem of cooperation, perhaps? Is someone getting in the way?"

Her android copy stepped forward. "Everything is running as smoothly as can be expected," she said. "The facility will reach optimum efficiency within eight hours. After then, progress will be rapid, I assure you."

"As rapid as Francis Axford's?"

"More so, actually. He is only one man, Sol, no matter how many times he's copied himself. We have the advantage of diversity. We can tackle many fronts at once. Now we know what to look for, we'll find it much faster than he did." Juno looked almost smug. "And building the results should be simple, too. We have dozens of nano-facturing plants now, and we can spread designs to other colonies once we finalize them. We could equip the hole ship fleet with what we already know in less than a day."

Sol nodded. "Excellent," she said. "The news did go some way to easing her uncertainty. The maneuvering around Hera had demonstrated just how little they knew about the hole ships and how vulnerable they were to outside attack. She needed to know that her pilots were safe before she lost any more. In the bigger scheme of things, she needed her hole ships to ensure that the remnants of humanity could stick together.

Oborn cleared his throat. "I hate to sound critical," he said, "but I feel that we could be working faster if I'd stayed behind. I'm the contact with the Gifts in Hera, after all, and my not being there is essentially slowing things down. Was there any reason in particular you wanted me here?"

She ignored the slight scold to his tone. He was right: things would be slower on Hera while he was away, but he would only be gone a few hours. She could afford it.

"There is, actually," she said. "Juno, Owen, if you would give us a moment. See to those plans while I talk with Kingsley."

The other two filed outside the hole ship, and she closed the airlock behind them.

"Take a seat." She remained standing as the biotechnician eased himself onto the couch.

"I wanted to discuss a delicate matter that must remain between you and me, for the moment. It concerns security on Juno—and in the colonies in general, actually. It's important that I know who I can trust." She paused meaningfully. "Can I trust you, Kingsley?"

As difficult as it was to rattle an artificial metabolism, she was surprised to see sweat beading the man's brow. "You know you can, Caryl."

"You're aware of what I've done to you, aren't you?"

He nodded slowly. "You've altered my Overseer settings in order to emphasize the UNESSPRO monitoring program," he said, swallowing thickly. "You've brought that program to the fore and made yourself the sole surviving UNESSPRO representative."

She watched his reactions carefully. "And how do you feel about that, Kingsley?" she asked. When she saw the anxiety in his expression, she added, "It's all right. You can be totally honest with me."

"I feel . . . I feel conflicted, I guess," he stammered. "Your colony statutes are different from the original ones I was given, and I know that my reasoning has been corrupted in some ways. There are layers within layers, but—" He leaned forward, reaching out almost pleadingly. "But I know that the core is stable. I *can* see the reasons for what you're doing, Caryl, and I'm not going to let you down."

She dipped into his Overseer simulation—into the actual working of his thoughts—and saw enough to confirm the sincerity of his words. His mind was racing along at a feverish pace, using twice as much capacity as an ordinary engram as he checked and double-checked every thought. But it seemed to be functioning well enough. His original engram was reasonably fresh, so she wasn't building on sand.

Slipping out of his mind, she nodded and sat down next to him. He shifted uncomfortably and averted his eyes. Something about his behavior was bothering her, but she couldn't quite put her finger on it. It was more than nervousness or stress.

"I'm glad that I can trust you," she said. "Your job on Juno is very important. It might make the difference between life and death." She paused again to look him firmly in the eye. "Do you understand that, Kingsley?"

"All too well," he replied.

"I'm sorry to have to put you under such pressure," she went on smoothly. "I only do it because I know I can rely on you. Hopefully it will be over soon, and we can all rest." *But not in peace,* she hoped. "The current estimates put the Spinner advance on the far edge of surveyed space in about ten days. The Starfish front will hit that same edge in approximately twenty, leaving, we presume, nothing behind. That, therefore, is the outermost limit on ensuring the safety of the colonies. With the Yuhl active within those two extremes, we have to find a way to fight back now, before we lose any more good people."

Oborn nodded emphatically. "We'll do it, Caryl," he said. "I know we can."

"So do I," she agreed. "The biggest problem we originally faced was knowing where the Yuhl were hiding. Since the experts think that tracing the hole ship movements isn't possible, I feared we might be dead in the water. But that problem seems to be solving itself." *The hard way,* she added silently to herself. "There are signs that something is going on in pi-1 Ursa Major. I presume it's the Yuhl. We need, therefore, to find a way to attack them there. But we can't just hand them weapons on a plate. We know less about the hole ships than they do; we'll always be at risk of them taking over our ships."

"So you'd like to find a way to make sure a captured hole ship won't obey the enemy," he said, again nodding. "There may be something in the Library relating to the AIs that pilot them. They're not as sophisticated as Gifts, after all, so we might be able to add something to their programming, which—"

"Just do it, Kingsley," she interrupted. "It's very important. In the meantime, though, we're working on a way to move the gifts. That way we can put them back in the destroyed systems and out of the firing line. If we can do that, we can move you, too—make you safe behind the Starfish lines. Like I said, I don't want to lose any more good people. You understand that too, don't you?"

"Fully, Caryl," he said. "I have nothing but complete confidence in your decisions." That sounded like his subversive UNESSPRO program talking. She turned away from his intense regard.

"Thank you, Kingsley," she said. "For coming here, I

mean. I'm glad we had the chance to talk." *I'm glad I got to peel back the layers and see how far I really can trust you Orphans.* "I'd appreciate it if you could keep this conversation and the things we've decided to do a secret. There are some who wouldn't appreciate my reasoning the way you do."

"I won't say a thing, Caryl. You have my word."

"Good." She stood. "Now, you'd better go find the others and see how they're doing. I want you in *Cue Ball* and on the way home within the hour. If you need anything, here or there, talk to Juno. She'll give you all the assistance you need."

Oborn rose to his feet also. He hesitated for a second, then, much to her amazement, he took her right hand in both of his and brought it to his lips, kissing it lightly. She let it fall to her side as he turned and walked out of the cockpit, moving rapidly as though he thought he had made a grave mistake.

It was then she understood what his behavior had signified. *Is that how he justifies it?* she wondered, sitting back down on the couch, feeling as though she had been sucker-punched. *Does he betray his friends out of love, not programming?*

Whatever gets results, she told herself, but she couldn't write it off quite as callously as that. It was a reminder that, no matter how unsophisticated they might be, the engrams still thought of themselves as people. From their point of view, their emotions were very real, and she admired Oborn's persistence with it—especially when he knew she was using him. All that separated her from them was just a matter of scale.

But that scale was important. She was over 150 years old. When she loved—and it had been a long time since she had let herself love in the old-fashioned, human way—there was a mountain of baggage that came with it. She had seen too many loved ones die in too many ways. It was one aspect of her psyche she had learned to keep very under control, even if, ultimately, she'd never had the courage to excise it completely.

*   *   *

Although she stayed in Arachne *mentally she was pacing.*
Her mind roamed the corridors of McKenzie Base—both
real and virtual—observing the work going on there. One
meeting contained strategic planners from all the refugee
colonies, trying to rationalize resource allocation in Sirius.
Another brought her up to date on progress on a shield
design that one of the other colonies had found in the
Gifts' Library. A third was discussing a detailed map of
the Spinner and Starfish fronts, trying to pin down exactly
which systems were safe for the moment and which colonists and their gifts would need to be moved as soon as
possible.

She observed the activity of that working group longer
than she'd intended. One of her team had confirmed that
the Starfish were concentrating their stealth attacks around
the loci of most recent communicator uses. That had given
her the idea of drawing the Starfish away from colonies
by pinpointing the least vulnerable areas and broadcasting
from there, rather than from wherever was convenient.
While it was too early to know for sure if the tactic would
work, she was eager to find out. They had to find a way
to reduce their losses from the Starfish—and fast, before
they lost any more ground than they already had.

The news from the previous day that one of the five
"ostrich" colonies had been attacked had briefly shaken
the fragile optimism of the human surveyors. Officially,
the systems that chose to opt out of the survivor network
were supposed to be left alone, but Hatzis had organized
a single hole ship to survey each of them once a day. The
discovery that one of them had been destroyed despite
having no advanced technology at all had struck her
deeply, and she had debated for a long time whether or
not to make the knowledge public or not. The next debate
had been over whether to let the remaining four know. If
she did, that would reveal that the ostriches had been
monitored from the outside and would only arouse cries
of betrayal. Hatzis didn't believe that a simple visit or two

could have led the Starfish to the destroyed system; if that was possible, Sothis would have been destroyed a long time ago. Surely, she told herself, it had to have been nothing more than a simple case of bad luck.

In the end it was decided to leave the ostriches in peace—a decision that Hatzis hadn't been entirely happy with, either. It felt like locking her children in a room full of pedophiles. Her hopes of finding them untouched afterward were slim, to say the least.

But there was nothing she could do about that now. If the Starfish and the Spinners steadfastly refused to communicate, she could only try to survive around them—or despite them. And that was why the Yuhl were her biggest problem.

Six hours after Kingsley Oborn left to return to Juno, a message came from Gou Mang alerting her to the arrival of Francis Axford.

HERE? NOW?

HE'S IN ORBIT AND IS REQUESTING PERMISSION TO DRY DOCK.

Sol thought very carefully before she replied. Having seen the tricks his hole ship could perform, she wasn't going to let it any closer to *Arachne* than she had to. Who knew what else the man had learned to do with his craft?

PUT HIM IN C DOCK AND TELL HIM THAT IF WANTS TO TALK TO ME IN PERSON, HE'S GOING TO HAVE TO WALK ACROSS HERE TO DO IT. ASSUMING HE EVEN HAS A BODY, OF COURSE.

C dock was on the far side of the station in a newly opened section. By the time Axford had docked and walked the distance, almost half an hour had passed. She watched him walk up the ramp into *Arachne* through external sensors linked to conSense. His android body was smaller than most but no less crude in appearance. Its resemblance to the original was quite poor. Its green, blunt, and hairless face displayed no outward emotion whatsoever and gave nothing away as to his reasons for coming. He had rebuffed all attempts to communicate, in person or otherwise, until he reached Sol.

"So," she said, rising when he entered but not offering him any more welcome than that. "You're back from Alsafi."

He folded his arms in front of him and smiled slightly. "Actually, that wasn't me."

Her self-assurance faltered. "But—?"

"Ten twenty-two went to Alsafi. I'm seven seventy-four."

"Then what happened to ten twenty-two?" she asked, a little confused. "He must've come back for you to be here, surely."

"And why is that, Caryl?"

"Because you said that *Mercury* was the only hole ship you had." She could already feel herself starting to bristle at the superior-than-thou smugness his expression hinted at.

His smile widened. "That's not *Mercury*."

She suppressed another startled double take. "What do you mean, it's not *Mercury*?" she asked with some irritation. Clearly he was enjoying putting her off guard. "You told me—"

"Situations change, Caryl," he interjected casually. "This one is called *Orcus*."

"And would you care to tell me how you came by it?"

"Not particularly," he said. "You see, the thing is, I've never really been one for laying all my cards on the table at once."

"So it would seem," she said.

"Listen, Caryl," he said, swinging himself onto the couch. His movements were surprisingly smooth and graceful. "I'm going to be blunt here. Your last missive to the masses has left me a little confused. As far as I'm aware, you've had no direct engagement with the Roaches. Why, then, are you declaring war on them?"

"According to your data, Frank, we've had numerous encounters with the Yuhl," she said. "I've seen footage of at least one colony destroyed by the Starfish as a result of their interference, and I have no doubt that there have been more. On top of that, we've lost three scouts sent to investigate one particular system in the last few days. If this doesn't count as direct engagement, then I don't know what does."

He shrugged. "I think you're overreacting."

"Why? You're ex-military, aren't you? You know a threat when you see one."

"And I know an opportunity when I see one, too. Caryl, you're jeopardizing the future of all of us by jumping the gun. The Yuhl *could* be a valuable ally."

"But they're already a powerful enemy," she said soberly.

He nodded thoughtfully for a moment. "Do you want to know what I think, Caryl?" He didn't wait for her to respond. "I think you want this battle."

"That's absurd," she said with disdain. "Why would I *want* a war?"

"Because you feel its one you have a chance of winning."

She was about to protest, but he silenced her.

"This is a knee-jerk reaction at best, Caryl, and you know it. In the face of the Spinners and the Starfish technology, you feel small—hell, we *all* do. But a victory against the Yuhl—well, that will make you feel just that little bit bigger, won't it? You won't feel so insignificant."

Hatzis snorted her contempt of his suggestion. "And I suppose you would rather make allies with them."

"It's an option."

"For exactly the same reason," she pointed out, standing. She took a couple of steps away and faced him. "You have no hope of achieving it with the Starfish, because they ignore you as though you were little more than an insect. But the Yuhl at least talk to you."

"My way we don't lose as many people," he said. "When you tally up the lives lost in a war with the Yuhl along with those being wiped out by the Starfish, how many will be left by the end? But if we can ally ourselves with the Yuhl, then maybe, just *maybe*, we'd stand a chance against the Starfish."

"That's a big maybe, Frank."

He shrugged. "It's a big enemy," he said. "But the Star-fish are going to keep eating away at us until there's noth-ing left, Caryl. Of that you can be sure. We need another solution. The Yuhl, with all their years of experience deal-ing with the threat, are the only one I've found."

She could see the sense in his words, but there were too many facts backing her side of the argument. Wishing was all very well, but at the end of the day, wishing would never stop the ax from falling.

"No solution can make up for the colonies we've lost because of these aliens," she said. "Not to mention the scouts in pi-1 Ursa Major—or even Peter and Axford 1022, for that matter. How can you casually sit here and talk about negotiation when they might have been de-stroyed the moment they arrived in Alsafi?"

"They weren't." Axford's self-satisfied smile returned.

Another curve ball that caught her off guard. "How could you possibly know that?" she asked.

"Yesterday I received a short, coded message from ten twenty-two," he explained. "He was in Rana in Becvar, en route to another system where he intended to rendez-vous with the Yuhl fleet. At the time of the transmission, he seemed fairly optimistic. He felt that progress was be-ing made."

"And Peter?" She was surprised at her concern for Alander, but she justified it by telling herself that he was her only hope of keeping Axford on the straight and nar-row when she wasn't around. "What about him?"

"I'm not sure," he admitted. "He went on ahead of ten twenty-two in *Silent Liquidity*, the hole ship we liberated from the Yuhl around Hera."

"Why did they separate?"

"It was a hostage swap, as I understand it. He went to open negotiations with one of the prisoners while ten twenty-two held the other as ransom. What exactly hap-pened then, I'm not sure. The transmission was brief, and I wouldn't like to speculate in the absence of hard data."

Hatzis imagined Alander killed and dissected by the aliens once they had got him away from Axford, and a

warm anger flowed through. How could Axford have let
something like that happen to him? Why hadn't Axford
gone in his place? After all, *he* was the one who was
disposable, not Alander.

"So basically we don't know much more than we did
before," she said, making an effort to keep her voice level.
"Peter could be dead by now, and whatever negotiations
he was trying get under way may have ground to a halt
before they even had a chance to get started. Frank, you
haven't given me a single reason to trust the Yuhl. There
are plenty to justify defending myself."

"I'm not saying you shouldn't defend yourself," Axford
jumped in quickly. "I'm all for you expending energy and
resources on ways to fight back. I'm just saying you
shouldn't fight back unless you have to, that's all. You
could end up doing us more harm than good. Try to remember, it's the Starfish who are our real enemies."

Hatzis snorted derisively. "But as you said, we don't
have much hope of defeating them, do we? Technologi-
cally speaking, they are so far ahead of us that they're
effectively invincible."

"Which is exactly why talking to the Yuhl makes more
sense than fighting with them."

"If the Yuhl knew how to defeat the Starfish, don't you
think they would have done it by now?"

"Maybe they lack the will," he said, shrugging. "Or
they're still building up their strength. Combined, we
might be enough to do the job."

She stared at him, trying to see past the android façade
to get a glimpse into what he was really thinking. "You
don't honestly believe that, do you?"

"I believe we need to try something more than picking
fights with the smallest kid in the schoolyard just to make
us feel better about ourselves."

"And when you're a bug about to be stepped on, you
don't hang around to philosophize and make poor schoolyard analogies! In the end, as always, it comes down to
practicalities. I'd give up ever knowing what the Spinners
and Starfish are in exchange for simply staying alive. And

I don't believe you'd willingly sacrifice yourself just to make a point, either."

"Not all of me, perhaps," he said.

SOL, I'M SORRY TO BOTHER YOU AGAIN, BUT WE HAVE ANOTHER REQUEST TO DOCK.

She turned away from her argument with Axford with a sigh of frustration.

WHO THIS TIME?

IT'S PETER ALANDER.

WHAT?

She didn't believe it at first. On the one hand, the timing was remarkably fortuitous, for it would allow her to see if his story matched Axford's. But on the other, the timing was unsettlingly suspicious.

TELL HIM TO PARK *SILENT LIQUIDITY* IN THE MAIN DOCK AND COME DOWN STRAIGHTAWAY.

I WILL, BUT THAT'S NOT THE NAME OF HIS HOLE SHIP. ACCORDING TO AXFORD—

THIS ISN'T PETER ALANDER FROM ADRASTEIA, SOL. THIS ONE'S FROM VAHAGN IN CHI HERCULES.

VAHAGN? I'VE NEVER HEARD OF THAT COLONY.

NEITHER HAD WE UNTIL HE ARRIVED. IT'S NEW. CHI HERCULES IS RIGHT ON THE SPINNER FRONT; THE COLONY WAS CONTACTED ONLY TWO DAYS AGO. HE WANTS TO TALK TO YOU ABOUT THE LAST BROADCAST WE SENT.

Hatzis closed her eyes and sighed. Clearly it was going to be one of those days.

"Welcome to Sothis, Peter," she said as, half an hour later, the chi Hercules version of Alander entered *Arachne*'s cockpit. She had been expecting to see Alander's face but instead saw an android wearing general-purpose features, the sort of average face that looked like no one in particular, employed when an android was used by many people either at once or in series. He obviously hadn't had his own body grown before leaving Vahagn. She made sure her surprise was kept in check as she extended a hand

toward him. "It's always a pleasure to meet a representative from a new colony."

"Spare me the bullshit, Caryl," he said, his hands at his sides, refusing to take hers in greeting. "I haven't come all this way for a pleasant chat." His gaze shifted to Axford. "And I certainly wasn't expecting to see Frank the Ax here, either. I wouldn't have thought you the type to indulge in hand-holding and banner waving."

"I assure you, I'm not," Axford responded with a slight inclination of his head.

"Then—" Alander hesitated for a split second, his eyes becoming vacant. Then he was back, clearly annoyed with himself. "I'm sorry," he said. "Something's not going quite right with me. Cleo, our SMC, says they had problems with my engram during the voyage out, and they had to put me on ice. But I don't remember any of that. All I know is that the Spinners woke me up when the gifts came. They brought me back from the dead."

Not quite, Hatzis thought, taking a microsecond out of the conversation to dip into his Overseer. There she found the same elegant yet roughshod technique that the Gifts had used in senescent colonies to give a nonviable engram a kind of life. His mind was fundamentally unstable, careering from thought to thought with all the control of a drunk driver on one of Earth's old freeways; his thoughts reached a gridlock every few minutes, unable to sustain the illusion that all the conflicting processes that comprised them belonged to one mind. Every time he failed, however, instead of crashing to a halt, his initial state was reloaded from the Overseer, deleting any minor changes that might have built up in that time. This initial state would only run for another few minutes before needing to be rebooted but, combined with the memories it had laid down in those few minutes, it was at least enough to create the illusion of continuity. That's all it was, though: an illusion. Alander's mind was like a short loop of film going around and around, redrawing over the frames as it went to make it appear as though the action was changing.

Hatzis knew that this couldn't be maintained forever. It didn't address the problem, only the symptoms.

She withdrew, satisfied he hadn't noticed her intrusion. She didn't like having to rely on this crude method to revive nonviable engrams. But as she hadn't yet been able to find a more effective technique, it was just going to have to do for now. She didn't want to spend the rest of eternity with a bunch of tape loops, endlessly repeating the same emotions, over and over again.

"You're not the only engram who's had that problem," she said as diplomatically as she could.

"Well, I've had a couple of days to sort myself out," he said, "and I'm sure I'll feel better in a couple more."

"That's the spirit," said Axford.

Alander shot him an impatient look but said nothing in response. His lack of curiosity was puzzling. Instead, he turned back to Hatzis and said, "We picked up your message on the ftl communicator. Everyone in the *Marcy* is stunned by what's been going on. They've been there for over forty years, now, and there's never been any hint of life. Then suddenly, *this*. It's pulled everything out from under them: the Earth is gone, humanity is practically dead, and it looks as though you're the only real one of us left." He shook his head slowly. "I can't believe it either. Two days ago I woke up thinking we'd just broken orbit, and here I am, a century in the future, and aliens are fighting over the scraps of what we've become."

"Trust me when I say I can appreciate your bewilderment," Hatzis said. "Having an extra century on you doesn't make it any easier."

"It obviously hasn't made you any wiser, either," said Alander pointedly. "Frankly, I can't believe what I'm hearing in your broadcasts. We finally find evidence of intelligent alien life—sentient beings we can actually *talk* to—and you're declaring *war* on them? Jesus Christ, Caryl. Are you insane?"

She felt herself stiffen and was unable to repress it. "If you came all this way to abuse me, then you can damn well—"

"What do you expect, Caryl? You think I'm going to sit back and say nothing?"

She took a brief moment to control her rising anger. "I gather you came with Cleo's approval." Cleo Samson, according to Sol's records, was the civilian survey manager of the Geoffrey Marcy, core vessel dispatched to explore chi Hercules.

Alander looked uncomfortable. "Actually, they voted against it. But I came anyway; the Gifts listen to me, not the others, and I recognize a con-con-con-conspiracy of silence when I see one."

He nodded as though perfectly satisfied with the point he'd made. Hatzis didn't say anything, and neither did Axford. She wondered if Alander even suspected the resetting of his Overseer functions and the slight glitch it had caused.

Axford's android couldn't hide a slight smirk, though. "Tell me, Peter, how it feels to be proven wrong."

Alander frowned. "About what?"

"About us being the only intelligent life in the universe, of course. That was your theory, wasn't it? Back on Earth? I can't imagine it being invalidated in a less subtle way."

"Who says it's been in-invalidated?"

"The facts speak for themselves, surely?"

"It depends on how you define intelligence." Alander bristled. "Or, more importantly, what sort of observer is required to collapse the state vector."

"I don't understand," said Axford, looking at Hatzis as though for explanation.

"It's simple," said Alander, speaking quickly, almost desperately. "My theory states that the early universe functioned as a quantum computer, existing as a combination of near-infinite but slightly different versions of itself, all overlapped. Under such conditions, the chances of molecules and atoms combining in just the right way to kick-start self-replication are greatly increased. That's the first hurdle. The second hurdle is evolving this basic form of life up to something conscious, and it's as big a hurdle as the first. The trouble is, once this new form of life becomes conscious, it collapses the universe back to one version of itself, so it no longer has the advantages of using quantum processing to create life elsewhere. It's like setting your computer to finding prime numbers, then telling it to reduce its capacity by a million once it has found just one. The existence of one intelligent life form in the universe, therefore, reduces the odds of finding another one to almost zero."

Axford opened his mouth to say something, but Alander talked right over him. "I assume you're raising the Starfish as evidence of intelligent life existing concurrently with humanity, thereby either disproving the theory or requiring an extremely unlikely coincidence to explain it away. But neither is the case. You see, according to your daily broadcast, the Starfish and the Spinners both exhibit behavioral traits indicative of machine intelligence. They perform limited functions, such as depositing the Gifts—themselves machine intelligences—and destroying colonies, while at the same time refusing to acknowledge any form of external communication. They could easily be robotic benefactors and planet smashers locked in blind, automatic ritual by their makers, millennia ago. Would such minds have true consciousness? Would they be enough on their own to cancel out the quantum-computing function of the universe? I don't think we can assume that."

"What about the Yuhl, Peter?" Hatzis managed to get in. "How do you explain them?"

"What about them? Has anyone apart from yourself even seen them?"

"Yes," put in Axford. "I have, actually."

"You or another *version* of you?" said Alander.

"What are you suggesting? That these aliens were made up?"

"Why not? The illusion of a common enemy would be just what you'd need to draw people together under you."

"Make up your mind, Peter," Hatzis said. "First you

come here to berate me for declaring war on them, and
now you don't believe they exist at all. Which is it to
be?"

"I—I . . ." He fell silent as his eyes became vacant once
more, his expression touched by the inner turmoil vexing
him. Then, just as suddenly, confusion vanished and was
replaced by anger. "My point is the same either way," he
announced.

"Which is what, Peter?"

"That you're completely mishandling this situation. It's
time someone else took over. Someone more level-
headed."

"Like who?"

"Let the people decide," he said. "The way it's supposed to be."

Coming from him, the accusation of incompetence was
like a slap in the face, and for a long while all she could
do was stare at him in silence. But, she reminded herself,
it wasn't *really* coming from him. It was coming from the
old him, the one she remembered from entrainment camp
back on Earth. Arrogant, self-confident, and bitingly intelligent, he had been automatically dismissive of anyone
he regarded as inferior. The only person close to him had
been Lucia; somehow she had seen past the façade and
found the person underneath, the one who had emerged
after months of struggling to keep his mind together, the
fragile, more tolerant Peter Alander who had returned
from Adrasteia to report the coming of the Spinners.

That was the Alander Sol had come to know, which
this Alander patently wasn't. From his point of view, entrainment camp had only been days ago. He was still on
a high from the launch, buoyed by the knowledge that
more copies of him had been sent to the stars than of any
other human. He hadn't yet had to confront the knowledge
that none of those copies had worked beyond a few days,
and that for all his cutting intellect, he would be regarded
as the failure of the engram program.

She waited as his Overseer cycled through once again.
He blinked, then shook his head.

"Well?" he snapped. "Don't you have anything to say?"

She shrugged. "What am I supposed to say, Peter? 'Thanks for pointing out my failings; how about you take over?' "

He turned away from her sarcasm to Axford. "And what about you? Are you going to let her run the show?"

"I have my own show to run, Peter." Frank the Ax gestured with apparent nonchalance. "Survival is the game, and I'll accept any means to that end."

"Even if she gets us killed in a war we don't need to fight?"

"*You* don't have to fight it, Peter," she said. "Opt out, or don't sign up. Other colonies have seceded. No one's forcing you onto the front line."

"Don't treat me like an idiot, Caryl!" He turned on her, and for the first time the undercurrent of hysteria running beneath his surface behavior showed clearly through. His eyes showed too much white and his hands shook. Alander knew he wasn't in control, but he refused to give in to his weakness. He would maintain the pretense until he fell apart completely.

"We *are* the front line," he went on heatedly. "Vahagn will be dragged in whether it wants to be or not. If you don't get us, the Yuhl will. And if the Yuhl don't, then the Starfish will. How do you think we feel facing such possibilities? You can't blame us for wanting an alternative."

But there is no us, she wanted to say. *You stole your crew's hole ship and came here to vent your tensions to the one person who's trying to do something constructive.*

"No one's treating you like an idiot, Peter," she said calmly, not wanting to aggravate his growing hysteria any further.

He stared at her with tight lips, as though biting back the urge to contradict her.

GOU MANG.

YES, SOL?

I WANT YOU TO SEND SOMEONE TO HIS HOLE SHIP— WHAT WAS IT CALLED?

BETTY.

GET INSIDE AND PUT IT IN ORBIT. HE OBVIOUSLY DOESN'T REALIZE THAT THE HOLE SHIPS WILL TALK TO ANYONE, UNLIKE THE GIFTS.

Gou Mang hesitated.

ARE YOU SURE THIS IS A GOOD IDEA, SOL?

POSITIVE. IT'S ABOUT TIME SOMEONE TAUGHT THIS ARROGANT PRICK A LESSON IN HUMILITY.

2.1.4

In cosmological terms, Beid and Sirius were close neigh-bors, with only ten light-years separating the two. The trip between them took just five subjective hours—half that in the real universe. Nevertheless, for Alander it felt like forever.

In the pre-Spinner relativistic universe, Einstein's laws had promised interstellar travel in the blink of an eye, no matter how many decades they actually took. Becoming an engram with UNESSPRO had offered another way to solve that problem. An impatient traveler could slow down their thought processes or even halt them completely, so that a century could pass in a few seconds for them. Alander knew of very few people, personally or secondhand, who had decided to sit out the journey in real time. He supposed if they had, they would never have arrived intact. According to Hatzis, engram senescence became a problem between fifty and seventy years, and most of the survey missions were that long. In his darker moments, he imagined what a disaster it would have been had the option to abbreviate the journey not been open to the engrams. What would the Spinners have made of a fleet of probes orbiting a thousand different stars around Sol, all completely dead?

After his own experiences with engram breakdown, he was reluctant to tinker with his time sense unless he had to. Without knowing exactly what the Praxis had done to him—or what Hatzis herself had done, for that matter—

he wasn't taking any chances with his sanity. Just because he felt perfectly fine didn't mean that something wouldn't suddenly trip him up and take him all the way back to where he had been on Adrasteia, picking up the pieces of his personality and trying to put them back together in a way that made sense. Any sort of sense.

So he sat out the trip in real time, thinking over his experiences with the Yuhl and the Praxis, and wondering what he was going to do when he arrived at Sothis. Of course, *that* depended on what state of mind Hatzis was in and how far her network had advanced. Or degraded, he supposed. If the Starfish sneak attacks had taken as deep a bite into the colonies as he sometimes feared, panic and self-preservation could tear apart what little remained of the old UNESSPRO team spirit.

Sometimes, when the silence grew too loud, he talked to Ueh. His fellow *envoy/catechist* was back behind *Silent Liquidity*'s invisible barrier, comfortable in his own atmosphere and gravity. From what Alander could make out, the alien didn't seem to mind the journey or the isolation. If anything, he took the isolation much as Alander did, only venturing out of it when his thoughts became too much.

"*Peter/Alander* and *Francis/Axford*," Ueh said at one point. "What is the relation?"

"Relation?"

"Between *Peter/Alander* and *Francis/Axford*."

Alander thought his answer through carefully, presuming that Ueh didn't mean relation in the physical sense. The Yuhl had a strong sense of hierarchy—as did humanity, with its various ranks, titles, and power plays— but Alander hadn't quite managed to grasp the subtleties of it yet.

"Frank was part of a razor gang for the military," he said. "A cost-cutter. He had a reputation for being ruthless and interested in only one thing: the bottom line. A real throwback to the 1980s." Remembering who he was talking to, he tried to put it in more objective terms. "He and my original moved in different circles. Their paths—or swords—only crossed over budgets, so in that sense I guess he did have some sort of power over . . ."

He stopped, realizing only then that he had been talking about his original in the third person. Saying "me" felt wrong, and there was no other word in the English language for it. He needed a new pronoun.

"That's all in the past, of course," he went on. "Now it's different. He has his world, and I have mine. We're only working together because each of us has something the other wants. It wouldn't surprise me to learn that he thinks he's got the upper hand, but I think it's in his nature to assume that, anyway—while at the same time building contingency plans in case it ever changes."

Ueh's head tilted. At the same time his facial plates shifted in a way that Alander recognized to be a nod of acknowledgment. "Your *genders/relationships* are unclear to *me/us. There were three of you* when we first met *I was confused.* I thought one was the *bearer/favored* to the others, but I could not decide which."

Alander sympathized. "*Bearer/favored*" was a notion the Praxis had implanted in him, and one he was still trying to unravel. His guess about the implantation of egg and sperm by both genders of the Yuhl seemed to be correct, but the identity of the third sex implied by the new term eluded him. Clusters of identical organs in both aliens he had studied so far might have been dormant wombs, waiting for implantation. In that case, either sex could gestate a child implanted by one or two others, which meant that maybe the third gender might not exist at all. It wasn't so different to the surrogate parent technique employed by infertile couples back on Earth.

If that was the case, Alander could understand Ueh's confusion. Supposing that humanity sent its frontier pilots out in reproductive pairs to ensure the continuity of the species, should the pair become separated from the Mantissa, then Ueh had been faced with the difficult decision of who had been what. Was Alander the male, Axford the female and Hatzis the *bearer/favored*? The question could only have been complicated by the fact that there had actually been *four* of them, counting the copy of Hatzis from Thor. Alander noted that Ueh made no distinction between the two Hatzises, either assuming that they shared the same mind or that Thor did not exist in her own right. Both Yuhl had, after all, refused to talk to Axford at first because he didn't have a body. Maybe that bias extended to copies when the original was present.

"Are you any clearer now?" Alander asked the alien, unsure that he himself was.

"The data *you have given/is helping*." The Yuhl had access to the abbreviated information Axford had left in *Silent Liquidity*. "*I/we* are still *learning/growing*."

"Well, don't kill yourself over it." He was about to say that Ueh had plenty of time to catch up, but that wasn't the case. If humanity didn't find a way to survive the Starfish, the last of them could be gone within weeks.

"Will *Francis/Axford* join us *at Sothis/soon*?"

"I don't know." Axford had returned to Vega to impart what they had learned to the rest of his collective. Alander had no idea what he would do with the information. Or his captive, for that matter. So far neither the Praxis nor any of the Yuhl had shown much interest in the half of the helot pairing that Axford held captive, and that made Alander curious.

When he asked about it, all Ueh said was: "*Asi/Holina* is no longer favored."

"In the sense of bearer-slash-favored?"

The alien's facial markings became sharply triangular, an expression that meant irritation—although Alander sensed it wasn't at him or his question. "In the sense of *multifurcate/isometry*."

And there they hit a brick wall of incomprehension that Alander didn't have the energy to climb over. He had too many problems with members of his own species to worry about conflicts within another. If it came up later, he might pursue it. Otherwise, it was something that would simply have to wait.

*   *   *

They came into Sirius cautiously, not certain what would await them there. The rocky ball of Sothis had changed in recent weeks. McKenzie Base had expanded, and there were numerous hot spots on the surface suggesting that some of the previously dormant installations were up and running again. The number of satellites in orbit had quadrupled. Some of them comprised little more than hardware excised from the UNESSPRO core survey vessels, fitted with attitude jets and shielding, and placed out of the way.

There was a cluster point in geosynchronous orbit above McKenzie Base. Over a dozen hole ships were docked there, looking like a bunch of sun-bleached grapes.

Running home to Mama, Alander thought. He hoped that was all it was.

"Take us there," he instructed *Silent Liquidity.* "We'll hail them when we arrive."

"Yes, Peter." He heard the hole ship echo its response in Ueh's language as the screen faded to black.

"You *cling to planets/are not safe here.*" The alien's face seemed to fold in on itself in an ascending series of black and white *M*s, indicating thoughtfulness.

"The Spinners ignored Sothis," said Alander. "Why wouldn't the Starfish?"

"The Ambivalence obeys its own logic," he said in accented but comprehensible English. Just as Alander had learned to understand the Yuhl language, so, too, was Ueh becoming more proficient at the human tongues.

"Aren't you curious about the rules of that logic?" Alander asked. "Wouldn't understanding it make survival easier?"

"*We are/I am* already surviving, *Peter/Alander.* What *I/we* see as the Ambivalence, you call the *Spinner/Starfish.* The Praxis sees it a third way. But there is no *wrong/right.* There are only degrees of aptness."

"What the Yuhl call aptness, we humans might call truth."

"*I/we* do not believe in truth."

Alander laughed at this. "Does that mean you never lie?" he asked. "Or that you *always* lie?"

"The universe *is the only true thing/cannot be completely known. We perceive the universe through* our senses *are then interpreted through our minds.*"

Even though the statements were somewhat jumbled, Alander thought he understood what the alien was trying to say. "Therefore all experiences of reality are at least partially false, right?"

"*Since we cannot see* the truth *cannot be spoken.*"

Alander mulled this over. If such an opinion was hard-wired into the Yuhl, that set them at odds with humanity's automatic black/white perception of the universe. He couldn't help but think that the people he knew could benefit from perceiving a little more of the uncertainty of the world. But at the same time he wondered if the Yuhl would envy humanity's ability to take moral stands and make quick decisions, even if they were wrong.

"I'd keep that thought under your hat for a while," he told Ueh. "I'm not sure Caryl would understand."

Ueh acquiesced with the Yuhl equivalent of a nod, its faceplates moving back and forth. "But the fact remains, *Peter/Alander,*" he said, indicating the screen where the image of Sothis had been, "that *you/they* are not safe *here/near* planets. *You/they* should forego them as *I/we* have done."

"So where *do* you suggest we go, Ueh?"

"Stars *are not safe/are valuable sources of energy,*" said the alien. "We are not so distant from ourselves that we hide in the deeps as *others have/some say we should.* We brave the light, for now, as we pass through."

"And later?"

Before Ueh had a chance to respond to this, the screen came alive with a close-up view of the grape formation. They had barely been there a second when Caryl Hatzis's voice came over the cockpit speakers:

"Please identify yourself and state your business." She didn't reveal her face. Even via conSense, Hatzis had always been shy of doing that.

"It's Peter Alander, Caryl," he answered. "I'd like to dock in McKenzie Base and—"

"Which Peter Alander am I talking to, exactly?" Hatzis cut in quickly.

He found himself frowning at the screen and biting back an impatient retort. Sol, via whichever drone addressing him, was no doubt playing games because he was late reporting in. "The one from Adrasteia, of course. And yourself?"

"Yu-quiang."

"Well, Yu-quiang, are you going to let me through or not?"

"Just awaiting confirmation from McKenzie Base." There was a slight pause. "Okay, Peter. Please proceed to A dock—your usual berth. But Sol requests that you leave any biological specimens in isolation for the time being."

"Tell her she'll have to come to me, then," he replied. "If the specimens I have *are* dangerous, I'm already infected, aren't I?" *In more ways than one,* he added to himself.

Another pause, longer this time. "Understood," she said finally. "They'll be ready for you."

One final quick jump took them down to the surface of Sothis where they proceeded to dock. No sooner had *Silent Liquidity*'s airlock opened than Sol strolled in with a look of superiority, entering the hole ship as if she owned the thing. She stopped dead in her tracks, however, when she saw Alander.

"What—?" Her mouth opened as she examined his new appearance. Finally, she managed: "What the hell happened to you?"

He shrugged. "New times call for new beginnings," he said. "Apparently."

She was about to ask something else when Ueh moved forward in his half of the hole ship. He acknowledged Hatzis with the simple pointing gesture that Alander now knew indicated respect.

"Hello again *Caryl/Hatzis*," he said. "I am *Ueh/Ellil, envoy/ catechist* of the *Yuhl/Goel*."

"We've met before?" she said, frowning as she faced the alien. "In *Mercury*? You were the quiet one?"

"Quiet no longer." Ueh's teeth made a rare appearance from between his thin, shell-like lips. "The Praxis now demands that I talk."

"The what?" she said. Before he could reply, however, she raised a hand and, shaking her head, said, "No, that can wait. We'll interview you in due course. Thank you, Peter," she added, turning to face Alander, "for finally bringing us some valuable intelligence. I'll take it from here."

"I don't think so, Caryl," Alander said. He wanted to place himself between Hatzis and his Yuhl companion. There was something about her—an edge, perhaps—that hadn't been there before. He didn't know what she would do next or even what her Vincula-modified body was capable of. "I'm not your delivery boy," he said steadily. "And Ueh here is not your prisoner."

"Wordplay." Her gaze was cold as it met his. "We both know how the land lies, Peter."

"I don't care," he insisted. "You so much as lay a finger on him, and I'm leaving—and I take him with me, too."

"So you'd rather we just sat around and had a little chat?" she said with a slight and humorless laugh. "Is that it? The three of us chewing the fat like we're old friends?" Her expression tightened noticeably as she said: "For fuck's sake, Peter, we're at *war*."

"No, Caryl. *You're* at war. *I'm* not."

She folded her arms across her stomach. "Really? You're turning traitor, then?"

"No," he said. "I'm doing the sensible thing. Look, we have an opportunity here, and we'd be insane to waste it. If it's intelligence you're after, the Yuhl are a gold mine. They could be our allies against the *real* enemy."

Sol rolled her eyes. "Not you, too, please," she said with annoyance. "That's not what I wanted to hear."

"Well, I'm happy to disappoint you," he said. "Forgive me for not jumping on your bandwagon, this time, Caryl.

If you intend to fight the Yuhl, then you'll be doing it without me."

She sighed through her nose and looked away briefly. When she looked up again, some of the coldness had gone from her expression. Nevertheless, she still looked a little frustrated, as though out on a limb. "Well, before you go and ride off into the sunset like some dark avenger," she said, "I have a situation I need you to help me with."

"What do you mean? What situation?"

"Just come with me, and you'll see," she said. Then, glancing at Ueh, she added, "And I give you my word your friend here won't be harmed."

"I don't need your word," Alander said. "He has joint control over *Silent Liquidity*. He can escape any time he wants."

Hatzis looked Ueh up and down as the alien's wing sheaths quickly snapped out and back in. Alander recognized it as a gesture of satisfaction; he was clearly okay with the arrangement.

"How very cozy," she said. She took one final look at him, then turned and led the way out of the cockpit. "Come on. Let's get this over with."

"You bitch!"

Peter Alander paced the stateroom in which he'd been placed by the copy of Hatzis from the colony called Gou Mang. His anger was pure and driving; it overrode everything else. It gave him a line he could cling to when everything else was slipping away. *Continuity.* That was what he needed to keep himself together. The terrible mindless moments when his thoughts seemed to trip up like an athlete with his sneakers tied together were happening more and more—and the more they happened, the closer to madness he felt himself slip. It was starting to feel as though the world was being pulled out from under him—as though *he* was being pulled out from under him. Nothing was certain anymore.

But he couldn't maintain the rage indefinitely. It had to

give way eventually, and when it did, despair would rush over him. He didn't want to lose his mind. It was the one thing he could be certain of. He would rather lose his sense of self than his faculties. Or so he thought, anyway. He'd been told on Earth that his engrams would be able to think as well as his original, for the rational processes of thought were the one thing that could be copied with absolute precision. Memories and emotions, those nebulous, erratic ephemera that did little more than differentiate one dysfunctional personality from another, were the hard stuff. Sometimes he wondered why they'd even bothered trying to copy it at all. The exercise was futile; he was proof of *that*.

They're not really us, Lucia. He'd told her that the night before his engrams had been activated. Or rather his *original* had told her and had bequeathed the memory to his other selves.

They're not really us, Lucia, he'd said. *They're just copies.*

At that moment, his pain was more real than anything else. More real than the bland android body they had siphoned his mind into. When he looked into the mirror, he saw no sign of the self within it. All he saw was a blank, hideous visage with eyes empty of everything but tears.

"Where's Lucia? Why isn't she here? Where have you taken her?"

It made sense that Hatzis had taken Lucia away, along with everything else. They'd taken *Betty*. They'd taken his freedom. But why? Because he'd spoken his mind? Was voicing his thoughts a crime in this terrible new age? Apparently it was, and he—

—he—

He was gone for a moment. Then the anger pulled him back.

"Goddamn you, Caryl! Let me out of here!"

Pounding on the door did nothing but rattle the seals. No one responded. He prowled the room again, his feet disturbing the wreckage of the chair he'd broken earlier.

He remembered doing it but couldn't remember why. He bent down now and picked up the splintered remains of one of its legs and flung it viciously at the wall. Apart from leaving a slight silver scratch, it didn't make any impact. But the release of energy did enliven him for a moment, flooding his body with endorphins and other chemicals.

The biological high wouldn't last—no more than his rage could. Either simulated by the Overseer or genuinely felt by his android body, a fatigue rolled powerfully over him, as though a truck had hit him. He fell into a crouch with his back against the door, fighting the irrational urge to sob. What was *wrong* with him? Why couldn't he think straight? It wasn't fair that he should be suffering like this. He'd been the bright one, the golden boy, and now he was a wreck. Why couldn't it have happened to one of the others?

"Why couldn't this have happened to *you*, Caryl? You *bitch!*"

A thought caught him momentarily, then slipped away. Something about Lucia. What was it she'd said? *Shit*. It had been in his mind only a moment ago. Yes, that was it: *This conversation is being recorded for your copies' memories, and* they'll *think they're real enough.*

Oh yes. He thought he was real, all right. There was no getting around that. He was programmed to think that way.

"Is Lucia here?" he called out. "Just let me talk to her, won't you? She'll understand. Caryl? Can you hear me?"

No one answered. He shook his head. No. Hatzis wasn't stupid. His memories—the memories of his original—from entrainment camp were clear on that. She was capable and strong. She was just wrong, that was all, and someone had to stop her before she dragged humanity down with her. It was either that or—

—or—

—or something he could no longer remember. A flash of anger burned the thought completely out of his mind.

"Open this bloody door before I go out of my goddamn mind!"

He continued to stalk the interior of his cell, striking out angrily at the walls and door and furniture—or what he hadn't destroyed of it, anyway. Not that it would do any good. He knew that. No one was ever going to respond to him or help him. That Hatzis bitch would make sure of *that.*

When the door did open moments later, he was so surprised that he took a few cautious steps back from it. He stared at the figure walking into the room, confusion wrestling with his anger. Then the door closed again, and the two of them were alone.

"You?" His thoughts logjammed; the cycle flew apart under centripetal stress, sending fragments spinning into the far corners of his mind. "It can't be. It's not possible. They tell me you're dead."

Doubt flickered across the face before him. "I'm not our original, if that's what you're thinking." The flesh-colored, life-sized Peter Alander took a wary step closer. "I'm just like you—except, perhaps, that I've been around a little longer. I was on Mission 842 to Upsilon Aquarius."

"I . . ." The pieces of his mind were in a tangle, and he couldn't put them back together. His legs found a chair behind them, and he collapsed gratefully into it. "We . . ."

"I know how you're feeling. Believe me. I went through it myself."

The version of himself from Upsilon Aquarius—*the ghost,* he thought feverishly—came closer still, almost near enough to touch.

"It's hard to see from the inside."

"There's nothing wrong with me," he managed slowly.

"Yes, there is. You're in the final stages of engram breakdown. You're unstable, not thinking clearly. Right now you're not even really *you.* The Overseer is patching up so many software errors that you're more its work than your own. No amount of willpower can make up for the fact that what lies underneath is falling apart."

He glared at the ghost, thinking, *If he's right, then this*

SEAN WILLIAMS & SHANE DIX

could all be a dream. But if he's a dream, then how could he be right? "How do I know that you're not something that Hatzis sent to finish me off? She's the one behind my engram failures. I'm sure of it."

"I'm not a conSense illusion." The ghost smiled and offered his hand. "Here. Touch me." The ghost's flesh was warm and pliable. "Listen to me, Peter: you've been locked in a cycle for some hours, now. Are you aware of that? Your android body badly needs maintenance, and you're not getting the sleep you need. If you keep on like this, you're going to end up psychotic. Or worse."

He snorted his derision at the idea. "What could be worse than losing my mind?"

"Shutdown," the ghost said simply as it took back its hand. Alander realized that he might have been gripping it a touch too tightly. "Being switched off is a big risk for an unstable engram. Sometimes it never comes back together again. If your pattern won't reboot, you're as good as dead. You know that."

Dead. Alander couldn't look the ghost in the eye. *He* already *was* the ghost, not the revitalized, impossibly organic creature sitting in front of him. Everything was around the wrong way.

"Why isn't it happening to you?" he asked. "Why aren't you like me?"

The ghost looked uncertain for a moment. It was strange to watch himself openly display something he himself rarely admitted to.

"Well," the ghost said, "for starters, I've had longer to deal with it. It's not something you can fix overnight; I went through a lot of difficult times at first, back on Adrasteia." The ghost was looking at him but clearly seeing somewhere else. "You've no idea what it was like. But I was lucky, too. Someone came up with the idea of personalizing an android body just for me. It looked as much like me as they could make it, and they gave it the ability to run me on its own, if it had to. Some of its subroutines were still distributed through the Overseers, but I was always aware that I could exist apart, as an independent creature. It made me feel more real to be in my own body, with my own mind. It gave me an anchor to hang on to while I pulled myself together." The ghost's attention returned to the present. "They tried the same trick with another version of me in Head of Hydrus, a colony called Athena, and it worked, too. They must've caught him in time, before the instabilities really dug in. But it wasn't easy for him, either. For months I felt like I was balancing on the edge every moment I was awake—not dissimilar to how everyone feels today, I guess. I never knew whether I was thinking right. For all I knew, I might have slipped back into dysfunction without noticing."

"And the others," he said. "They accepted that you—got better? You showed them, right?"

"Actually, no," said the ghost sadly. "They died before I got the chance. And even then, they hadn't finished the job. It was Caryl Hatzis—the Hatzis from Earth, the one you talked to when you arrived—who took my recovery one step further. I don't know what she did exactly." The ghost's expression was sour, even if its words were intended to be gracious. "But she did *something* to me—something to my mind. It seemed to stop the thoughts piling up. I wasn't as trapped as I was before, by what I'd *been*."

"She killed me," he said, his mind skating over the concept as though it was ice, then plunging through a crack. "She killed our original?"

The ghost shook his head firmly. A faint dusting of stubble caught the light, emphasizing his biological higher ground. "No, Peter," it said. "She killed the crippled, wounded creature I had become, and she allowed it to become something else. I've put the past behind me. I've become *me*."

"Is that why you came? To show that you've made it? To rub it in?" He couldn't help the bitterness.

"No, Peter." The ghost's voice was tinged with sadness, but the firmness was still there. "I can't offer you the same thing I have. I've gone another stage further, and I don't know where that's going to take me. The most I can offer you is another body, one built to approximate who we used to be rather than just something off the rack. That won't be a miracle cure, I know, but it's a start. Caryl can make the same alteration to you that she did to me. It will help, too. Once the pressure is off, you can start putting everything back together."

Alander remembered the rage he had felt for Hatzis. The rage, the self-pity, his longing for Lucia—all mixed up in some murky emotional cocktail. "Is there an alternative?" he asked.

The ghost nodded. "Of course," it said. "There are three. Firstly, we can leave you exactly as you are and watch you break down."

"That's a certainty?"

"Yes." The blankness of the answer convinced him. "Moreover, you won't be allowed out into the compound because we don't know what you might do. At the very least, you'll upset people. We're all facing the specter of senescence, and the last thing any of us need at the moment is a reminder of it."

Alander nodded. He could understand that. "Go on," he said after a few moments. "What's the next option?"

"We shut you down temporarily with the intention of starting you up later," said the ghost. "When we have more resources and, perhaps, a better understanding of the problem. It'd be like the cryogenics programs back home: putting you on ice until we find a cure for cancer."

"And with just as little hope for success, I imagine," he scoffed. "You said yourself you might not be able to start my simulation again."

"That's right."

"Okay, then I'm guessing you have to be saving the best option until last," he said. "It certainly couldn't be worse than the first two."

The ghost didn't say anything for a moment. "The third option is to voluntarily accept immersion into my personality," it said eventually. "Your patterns might be faulty, but your memories are intact. I can take those and incorporate them into mine. Caryl insists it can be done; she's been doing it with herselves for—"

"But what about me?" he interrupted. "What happens to *me?*"

"Nothing," said the ghost. "You'll still have to choose between the first two options. But this way, you'll know that what you've done and felt will go on in *some* form, at least. In that sense, you will survive." The ghost's expression was blank, as though trying not to give an opinion either way, but his eyes were eager.

Alander couldn't face it. He turned away, thinking of chi Hercules, the fiery F-type variable around which he had awoken just a handful of days before, when the Spinners had revived him to talk to the Gifts. He thought of Vahagn, the colony his fellow colonists had founded on a boiling rock of a world, still pounded by rubble left over from the formation of the system. Did any of those memories really belong to him? To the *real* him, back on Earth? But that Peter Alander was dead, apparently, and so was Earth. He was all that remained—he and all the other copies of him scattered throughout the survey missions. And the ghost.

If not for us, then for whom?

"Do you believe her?" he asked.

"Who, Caryl?"

"Yes. Do you believe her when she says she can save the part of me that's unique, which doesn't exist anywhere else?"

"Yes," it said somberly. "Actually, I do."

"And what about everything else she says? How far do you trust her?"

The ghost took a long time responding, and when it did, it was obvious that a lot of thought had gone into the answer.

"I trust her to do what she thinks is right," it said. "That's as much as I trust anyone. You know that."

He did. It was written in the rules that made him who he was. He didn't trust anyone absolutely, and he had found plenty of justification for that stance. It was the only rational one to take.

Yet here he was, being asked to put his faith in someone else's words with no way at all to test the outcome. If he was being lied to, he might never know. But then, he thought, that they were taking the effort to lie to him might actually be a good sign. They could have erased him more easily than convinced him to believe them. A solid magnetic pulse anywhere near his head would knock out his Overseer and effectively be the end of him, memories and all. Caryl Hatzis could do that to all of them at any time. She'd already done it to the ghost twice, metaphorically speaking, anyway. She'd stuck him in a body when he was falling apart, and then she'd messed with his head later. He didn't know how anyone could live with that. . . .

"Shut me down," he said after some consideration. "I'll take my chances in the dark."

The ghost frowned. "Are you sure?" There was disappointment in its voice. "Your memories—"

"I doubt I have anything unique to add to the Peter Alander collective, he said. "Another planet; another sun. What's that to you?"

The ghost looked unnerved. "I'm surprised. That's not the decision I would've made."

"Well, I had a choice. I wonder which way you would have gone if they'd stopped to ask you first. Would you risk losing your mind when it's the only thing you have left? Would *you*?"

The ghost hesitated. "I'm not sure."

"No, but I am," he said. "I'll pin my faith on your survival instead, thanks. I'm sure you'll fix the problem one of these days and bring me back." He forced a smile, although it felt awful. "You are me, after all, right? Nominally."

The ghost looked down, then nodded. "All right," it said. "If that's what you want, we'll shut you down and put you into hard storage."

"That's what I want." He grimaced. "And tell her I said hello, won't you?"

"Who?"

"Lucia, of course," he said.

The ghost didn't say anything. There was something going on in that stubbled fleshy head, and he couldn't read it for the life of him. It wasn't like looking into a mirror at all. It was more like looking at the face of a complete stranger.

When the silence had stretched on a moment too long, he said, "Okay. Do it."

The ghost didn't wish him good luck or farewell; he just nodded, once, and then blackness rushed in.

2.1.5

FUCK.

WHAT HAPPENED, SOL?

HE TOOK THE SHUTDOWN OPTION, THAT'S WHAT.

DOES IT REALLY MAKE A DIFFERENCE?

MAYBE NOT, BUT I WAS HOPING HE'D SET A GOOD EXAMPLE. DAMN HIM!

Sol felt Gou Mang reach in via conSense to take control of the sagging android body inside the room. In the seconds before Alander emerged, Sol took the faltering engram's memories anyway. Just in case. If he thought he was going to take any secrets with him, he would be sorely mistaken. There were none, but that didn't reassure her. It certainly didn't solve her problem.

The door opened, and Alander from Adrasteia stepped through it. She tried software probes again to penetrate the interfaces connecting him to the outside world, but they encountered the same blocks she had run up against in *Silent Liquidity*. His mind was a blank wall. It was totally frustrating. Just when she really needed to, she couldn't gain access to the information within him.

"You saw how it went?" he asked unnecessarily. He knew she would have been watching.

She nodded. "I can't say I'm unhappy," she lied. "He was a disruptive influence and a waste of resources. I know that's putting it bluntly, but we're not running a resort here."

He was about to say something when the android nudged him from behind.

WHERE WOULD YOU LIKE ME TO TAKE IT, SOL?

"J Habitat," she said aloud, for Alander's benefit.

The android headed off along the hallway. It would be used to house a new mind as soon as its diagnostics could be properly checked. There were plenty of colonists on and around Sothis who wanted to dirty their hands on reality while they still could.

Alander watched with an indefinable expression as it lumbered away under Gou Mang's control, clearly unnerved by the experience. The impact of seeing the old version of him had been dramatic enough for her. She couldn't even begin to understand how it must have made him feel. For a moment there, he had been like the others, a multiplicity rather than a sole individual. Then to see that old version being shut down, to be alone once more . . .

Hatzis cursed the failure of her gambit yet again. She had sent him in to deal with the faulty engram in the hope that he might be able to convince it to voluntarily give up its memories before being shut down. Had it worked, it would have set a precedent for what she wanted Alander to do for her. She needed to know as much as possible about the Yuhl, quickly, and he was her only trustworthy source. If she couldn't steal the information, then she would need him to hand it over willingly.

Her software, backed up by the twenty-second century know-how of the Vincula, bounced off his defenses like waves against a cliff face. She withdrew the probes with a mental wince. What had the Yuhl *done* to him?

He turned to face her.

"We need to talk," he said. "All of us: you, me, Ueh, and Axford—if we can find him, that is."

"He's here," she said.

Alander frowned. "So soon?"

"It's not the same one you were traveling with," she explained. "This one arrived earlier today. He came to tell me I was mad for declaring war."

"Just like me."

She half smiled. "Only you did it twice."

He almost laughed. "Are you getting the hint yet, Caryl?"

"This isn't a democracy, Peter," she said, suddenly serious again.

"I realize that only too well, Caryl," he said soberly.

"One of you does, at least," she said, turning away from him to avoid the bitterness in his eyes. "It might surprise you to know that I don't want it to be this way. I wish I didn't feel like I was the only one with the capacity to run things properly. I don't like the things I have to do just to keep what little there is left together. I'd rather hand it all over to someone else so I can retreat into a corner and wait for it all to blow over." She faced him again. "Do you want the job?"

The question obviously startled him. Even if he'd never considered it before, he was certainly doing so now—and very carefully, too. "Me? I don't think so. I might've taken it, once, if you'd meant the offer seriously. But now?" He shook his head. "I'm not interested in being in charge."

"Then what do you want, Peter?"

"I want to make sure people do the right thing," he said. "That's all. But that takes sacrifices, too, I guess." He took a deep breath as though steeling himself for something. "I can't blame you for the decision you've made, since you've arrived at it in the absence of what I've learned about the Yuhl. The only way I can hope to change your mind is to give you what I know. And the best way to do *that* is to let you in. Into my head, I mean." He paused, fixing her with a steady gaze. "I'm going to let you take what you need, and then we can talk."

For almost a second, Hatzis wondered if he was enacting some twisted revenge upon her by handing her what she wanted when all her manipulations had failed, knowing full well that she couldn't take advantage of it because of the barriers the Yuhl had installed in his new mind. But when she sent a tentative probe to test the waters, she found that the barriers had gone. His mind was as clear and transparent as it had been before. She saw changes there that she was aching to explore.

But she forced herself to retreat. The other possibility was that he had been sent to her containing destructive viruses or other software traps: a smart weapon from the Yuhl, targeted squarely at her. Any exploration of his mind would have to be conducted most carefully.

"Thank you, Peter," she said, nodding graciously. "Not here, though. Come to Arachne. It shouldn't take long."

"And afterward?"

"Afterward, we'll talk—you, me, and Ueh and Axford. I promise. I can't guarantee I'll change my mind, but—"

"I know," he put in quickly. "It's a start."

She nodded. "That it is," she said.

They stared awkwardly at each other for a long moment, then looked away.

Fuck, she thought. *I've got what I wanted, so why the second thoughts?*

Indicating that he should move ahead of her through the cramped habitat corridors, she told herself not to be so stupid. He was just another mind to pick through, no different in essence from his version from Vahagn, from his old self. There was no reason to be nervous.

It was the Yuhl, she decided. It had to be. The Yuhl, and nothing else. It had nothing to do with him, per se. Nothing at all.

The first thing she did when they reached Arachne *was* check to make sure *Silent Liquidity* was still sealed and docked. It was. Alander's alien friend appeared to be waiting calmly and patiently for his return.

Then she sealed *Arachne*'s own airlock in turn.

GOU MANG? I'M GOING TO BE OUT OF CONTACT FOR A

WHILE. YOU'RE IN CHARGE UNTIL I COME OUT.

UNDERSTOOD, SOL.

IF I *DON'T* COME OUT . . .

She wasn't sure how to finish the sentence. What *could* Gou Mang do if she didn't? There was only one thing she could think of.

SPEAK TO AXFORD. HE'LL KNOW WHAT TO DO.

Gou Mang hesitated, then said, UNDERSTOOD, SOL.

Then, with some apprehensions niggling at the back of her mind, she cut all connections with the outside world. If the Yuhl *had* prepared a surprise for her, then it would end here, in *Arachne*. She wasn't going to take everyone down with her.

She turned to Alander, who had seated himself on the couch. She sat facing him and tested the edges of his mind for anything untoward. For all intents and purposes, it seemed perfectly clear.

"Here," he said, offering her his hand.

At first she didn't know what he meant. When it came to her, however, she suddenly felt embarrassed on his behalf. The first time she had invaded him in *Arachne*, she had gained access via infrared ports in his android body's palms. He wasn't aware that she had already trawled extensively through his mind in Sol System, and he had clearly assumed that she would use the same route. His naïveté disarmed and disturbed her. She decided to humor it, taking his hand and continuing her exploration. He closed his eyes as though preparing himself for an injection.

She probed gently—too gently for him to notice. The difference between this time and the previous time he remembered was that then she had been trying to hurt him. Her world had just been destroyed, and he had been about to blindly rush both of them to their deaths. Stopping him had been a priority, and dumping her grief onto him had been a fitting method of achieving that. Or so it had seemed at the time. Later, when the crisis had passed, she had lifted the bulk of the memories from his mind to ease the load on his already burdened psyche. As a result he remembered little of the actual experience, just the distress it had caused him.

She visualized this intrusion less as a hammer blow and more as though her thoughts were comprised of a school of tiny, darting fish infiltrating the nooks and crannies of a giant coral outcropping. The fish spread in an expanding cloud around and through the coral, penetrating the inner layers with increasing caution. Soon enough, she had its broad structure mapped out, and she paused to study it before taking in the details she was looking for.

His mind had definitely changed. The Yuhl had done more to him than just transfer his Overseer into a body of genuine flesh. For one thing, the distinction between his engram and the Overseer that ran it seemed markedly blurred. They embraced each other in a tangle of hard- and software that looked like something grown rather than built. She thought she could probably unravel it, given time, but for the moment she had to content herself with only the briefest of passes. There didn't seem to be any obvious Yuhl traps lurking in the strange operating structure, and she had to be satisfied with that for now.

She needed his memories, though, not the finer points of his thought-to-thought processes. She sent her "fish" in search of the conceptual markers corresponding to the Yuhl which, she assumed, should be relatively fresh, given that all his experiences with them had occurred in only a few days. Results came in quickly, and she began to scan the flagged loci. That was when she encountered her next hurdle.

Memories in engrams were laid down in an extensive but functionally simple register, associating gross experiential data with their emotional tags and saving them, one after the other, in various dedicated locations. In the human brain, the process was much more complicated and had not been cracked at the time of the UNESSPRO probes. The rough engram analog had worked well enough to simulate human behavior and therefore allow the engrams to function, to a point, but it contained the seeds that ultimately led to senescence. The memories

Alander had inherited from his original had come with internal conflicts that resulted in instability and dysfunction. She recognized the signatures of those conflicts, even if she didn't know exactly how to erase them without erasing him at the same time.

What she saw when she looked into him now was not that the conflicts were gone but rather that they had been absorbed. They were part of a new and very complex tapestry that wove everything together in a fashion not dissimilar to the memories in her own mind. It was difficult to pull at one thread without teasing out another with it.

Structure and memories . . . The realization of how deeply he had been altered brought to mind something his version from Vahagn had said to him: "You are me, after all. Nominally."

But *was* he, anymore? She didn't even know which version of Alander she should compare this one to. The original, the dysfunctional engram, the fragile cripple she had first met, or the slightly randomized version she had turned him into? She wondered if it made any difference. An outdated, primeval part of her wanted to know who exactly she was talking to, but did it really matter?

Putting aside the problem for the time being, she began searching for the information she required. She found Axford first, and the encounter in Vega. She saw herself through Alander's eyes, not in her original form but as Thor. She saw Thor's attack on the Yuhl prisoners and gained an insight into the trauma her copy had undergone upon learning of the destruction of her colony. She earmarked that information for future consideration: the subtle adjustments she'd made to Thor's engram had clearly destabilized that aspect of her personality instead of fixing it.

The Yuhl loomed large in Alander's mind, once she found them. She followed their thread and found everything she needed. She saw the *Mantissa* in Alsafi, and its much larger counterpart in Beid—the "asteroid belt" of ships; she experienced being eaten by the Praxis and swallowed by the organic helmet by which he had communicated with the Fit; she followed the negotiations between Alander and the aliens, noting the conflicts within the Yuhl and understanding for the first time that they weren't a unified group as she had assumed them to be. She had perceived a front, based on a few interactions, but they were actually as fractured and divisive behind it as the human survivors. The arguments between the Yuhl that Alander had perceived as *Zealot/Shrieking, Status Quo/Mellifluous, Stoic/Enduring*, and *Radical/Provocative* were proof of that.

But there was also the Praxis to take into account. This she hadn't anticipated. The vast alien being was difficult to fathom, and she didn't kid herself that she was even close to understanding it. The exact relationship between the Praxis, the conjugators, and the Fit had not been clearly drawn. It had avoided Alander's questions about the Starfish and the Spinners, too. The Praxis had read from his mind the standoff between her and Axford, and it placed him even more firmly in the middle by giving him a new body and naming him *envoy/catechist*. It had also indicated that it would like to absorb her in the same way it had absorbed Alander.

Hatzis shuddered at the thought. She hadn't lived over one and a half centuries only to end up being swallowed by a giant slug. But she hadn't imagined herself in this position, either: sifting through the mind of a man rebuilt by aliens, trying desperately to find a way to keep the human race alive, and in the process picking up other thoughts along the way.

She felt Alander's outrage at learning that she had been tinkering with the engrams. But he didn't seem to have made the connection between such modification and her actually reading his thoughts. Maybe, she thought, he believed she would honor her promise and just stick to mechanical interference and not snoop around. Or maybe he just didn't want to believe it.

She felt the same coldness as he had when the Yuhl revealed that the Ambivalence had a scorched-Earth policy, that they would leave nothing of humanity behind in its wake.

She felt Alander's puzzlement at realizing that the Praxis had given him a measure of Yuhl-ness as well as granting him a second biological start.

And she felt his dismay at learning from Axford that she had declared war on the Yuhl and understood his fear that a single, unfortunate incident might unravel all the work he had done to bring the various alien species in surveyed space together.

That brought her up to date with everything he had done with the Yuhl since they had been apart. But, having come that far, she found that she couldn't stop. There was a strange familiar *un*familiarity about his thoughts that intrigued her, drew her to the encounter with himself upon his return to Sothis. She had already tasted the fringes of that incident; it was too wrapped up in his sense of self— and how it had been changed by the Praxis—for her to avoid it completely. Through his eyes, it was an enormously challenging event, one he would take some time to recover from. The shock of meeting his old self had firmly underlined the growing realization that he had changed. He wasn't who he used to be. This was more than just disliking the title *doctor* because he felt that it was no longer relevant. This was making him question the very core of his being.

From there, she roamed freely. A thousand thought images flashed across his mind as she dove even deeper into him. A score of worlds around a dozen suns; the changing expressions of *Ueh/Ellil's* face; the shock of feeling stubble on his scalp and seeing the fleshy pinkness of his new skin. She saw herself through his eyes in among the rush, not as an individual but as the center of a vast kaleidoscope of identical faces. The impression she received of herself was of a chaotic fracturing of identity, multiplied ad nauseam until he felt as though he was drowning. When he looked at her, he didn't see *her;* in fact, he hadn't really seen her as a person since Adrasteia, when her engram had sent him back to Earth to report the com-

ing of the Spinners to what remained of UNESSPRO.
Even in Sol System, she had been subsumed by the concept of the Vincula and had become a kind of cipher, a
mask behind which incomprehensible forces hid. And he
still saw her that way.

She could understand that, even though it left her feeling slightly hurt. After all, she was a person, too. She
wasn't a machine. Shit, he gave the Praxis more credit for
basic humanity. Just because she was different from anyone he had known didn't mean she had turned her back
on everything human.

She found a deep vein of loneliness and, feeling it strike
a sympathetic note in her, followed it right into the heart
of him, tugging at it even though there was a good chance
he would feel her doing so. Along the way, she felt the
hurt of rejection as the colonists on Adrasteia had rele-
gated him to the status of a crippled outsider. Once the
renowned generalist, he had been outcast and sent to do
menial jobs on the surface of the planet. Only Cleo Samson had had time for him, had seen how a new Peter
Alander took the pieces of the old one and molded himself
into something different. Or tried to, anyway. By the time
he had proven himself capable of doing something on his
own, the colony had been destroyed by the Starfish.

And then . . .

Hatzis felt Alander's delight at seeing how his relationship with Samson had become something deeper on
Athena, where the only other functional version of him
had lived. She felt his pain at learning that his copy had
died, the death of his vicarious happiness.

At least one of him had been happy.

Underlying his feeling of isolation, though, was another
hurt. It was a hurt that owed much to his old self, the
person on which his original engram had been based, but
which his new persona had embraced as proof positive of
his deservingness to be lonely. She heard Thor's words
in *Silent Liquidity*: "Lucia was enjoying being a tourist
too much. She didn't want to stop." She sensed his feeling
of abandonment at the realization that Lucia had never

intended to see him again after their affair on Earth.

You fool, she thought—not knowing if she meant Thor, Alander, Lucia, or herself—and he thought it with her. Their minds were so deeply entangled by then that it was becoming hard to tell who was who. She was swept up in a tornado of self-loathing and despair, shot through with grief. A sob escaped her as the emotions called up echoes within her own mind, rising from deep recesses that she hadn't touched for decades. She knew how he was feeling all too well, even if the source of her emotions wasn't the same.

They were the odd ones out at the post-Starfish party. Everyone else had copies except for him, while she was the only surviving member of the Vincula, profoundly isolated, surrounded by fragments of minds squabbling over territory that might be eroding under their very feet. But at least he was one of them. In his mind she was a hyper-advanced, humanoid robot, with all the tricks of an old sci-fi monster. She wasn't real.

Did everyone else see her that way? Was that how they all thought of her?

She realized with a shock that she was crying. Somehow, even though she had gone into Alander hoping to learn more about him, she had ended up uncovering vulnerability in herself that she hadn't suspected. She had been feeling lonely and isolated, even from her own copies, but she hadn't realized just how deeply it was motivating her.

If they won't accept me of their own free will, she thought, *then I'll* make *them accept me.* The Congress of Orphans carried the same emotional payload as a child's attempt at blackmail. They both had the same need—to belong, to be wanted, to be loved—and the shared ache created a resonance that drew them together like magnets. She felt Alander physically holding her at the same time as he accepted her mental embrace. They clutched each other like mourners at a funeral. Her body was shaking in his arms. She felt drained and weak, profoundly weary, yet strangely comforted at the same time. She felt almost as though they had physically coupled, taken solace in base physical needs in the face of emotional and intellectual distress.

But they hadn't. It was all in her mind—literally. And that was enough. Perhaps too much, in fact. The prospect of such intimacy, with *anyone,* would ordinarily have terrified her.

Even his own engram had rejected him . . .

"I'm sorry," she said as she physically and mentally pulled away from him. She was unable to look him in the eye. "I hadn't meant to dig so deep. Not at first, anyway."

"It's . . ." He hesitated over the word *okay*; she was still inside him enough to feel that. "It's understandable."

"I'm sorry anyway."

Forgive me, she wanted to say. *Tell me I'm not a bad person!*

But that was just stupid. She couldn't let what she had seen in both of them affect her decisions. She couldn't let her emotions override what she knew made sense. They still had work to do.

His expression was guarded and puzzled at the same time. "What does this mean, Caryl?" he asked. "What happens next?"

"I found what I needed," she said. *And more,* she added to herself. "I guess we talk. All of us."

"No, I mean to *me.* An hour ago, I shut down a version of Peter Alander on the grounds that I had the right to do that to myself. But does that make me a murderer? What right did I have to do that to him? If I'm not who I used to be, then who *am* I?"

"Remember what the Praxis said." She kept his hand in hers, squeezing it tightly. "Change is life. You are the superior version that has grown out of what Vahagn was . . . because you *have* changed. You had to let him go, Peter. Clinging to him was driving you crazy."

Alander nodded miserably. She wasn't sure if he was agreeing with her or just indicating that he'd heard her point.

"I went through something like this after the Spike,"

she went on. "I was changing, evolving, growing into something else. Each step challenged my perception of who I was, and sometimes it seemed that the only thing separating me from the other povs were the few kilograms of tissue that had been with me ever since my family died on Io. What basis was that to found a hierarchy? When it became obvious that I was no longer the strongest link in the chain, I had to let go of the reins. As much as I didn't want to admit it, I was no longer the core of the being I had become. It was somewhere else. In a sense, it was some*one* else, too, even though it shared continuity with me. I was part of it, and I learned to accept that role. It was an important role, but it wasn't *the* role, you know?" The decades she had existed as part of her distributed, greater self had been the most challenging and exciting in her life, but she didn't know how to get that across to Alander. The loss of the rest of her still burned in her mind like the cauterized stumps of vestigial limbs. The gradual connection of her engrams was in no way sufficient to ease that hurt, but she hoped that it might evolve into an alternative. "I knew I had to accept the change or become redundant."

"That's not the same thing as dying," he said.

"No," she said. "It's worse." She held his gaze, defying him to disagree. "There can be no greater challenge to your identity than being cast out by your own self. It's more painful than losing a family or a home. Who are you, if the superior aspect of yourself is no longer part of you?"

He grimaced. "So you're saying the onus is on them—my engrams—to adjust to me, not the other way around?"

She hesitated for a second, balancing conflicting impulses, then said, "You weren't a very nice person, you know."

"What?"

"Back on Earth. You weren't popular. Respected, admired, even envied, yes; but not liked. You could be arrogant, impatient, and patronizing. You had special status, and you knew it. You took people for granted; you used them, even if you thought they were your friends. You could be entertaining, but that wasn't the main reason people associated with you. Your main attractions were your intellect and your status. But never your company."

"Don't hold back, Caryl," he said, wincing. "Give it to me straight."

"I'm only telling you this, Peter, because you need to know," she said without apology. "You are the better part. If your engram chose death over absorption, then that's his problem, not yours. Don't let his failure drag you down. You're no longer him, Peter. You're better than that. Let him go. Whatever you've become, you have an obligation to yourself to keep moving on."

"You make it sound easy."

"It is," she said. "The only thing holding us back is ourselves, and they only win if we *let* them."

He managed half a smile. "Nothing new there, then."

"Just a little more out in the open than before."

He tried to ease out of her grasp, but she held him firm.

"You need to have a clear idea of what it is you're clinging to," she said sternly. "If your ship is sinking, then you want to at least make sure you're clinging to a life raft, not part of the ship itself, right?"

"And you're my raft, Caryl?" He spoke with derision.

She laughed at this. "Good God, no! I'm having as much trouble trying to stay afloat as you are. Cling to me, and we might both go under."

"Now there's a cheery thought."

"It is, isn't it?" she said lightly, although she didn't smile. *If we go down,* she affirmed to herself, *humanity goes with us.*

"No wonder—" he started to say, then stopped. But she didn't need to read his mind to know what he had wanted to say: *No wonder Lucia didn't come back.*

He slipped his hand from hers, and she let him go. It seemed to take him a long time to stand up, as though he'd aged decades during the previous hour. He paused beside her for a few moments. Then: "Ueh will be waiting."

She nodded again. "And Axford."

"Another head case," he said with a slight smile and a roll of his eyes. Then, somberly, he looked down at her and asked, "Do you really think we can work this out, Caryl?"

"I think we can try," she said. "And that's what counts."

2.1.6

The first thing Hatzis did when they emerged from Arachne was check with Gou Mang to see what she'd missed. She was used to being at the hub, connected to everything, and even an hour away felt like too long. Not even sleep could keep her out of the loop that long, with her redesigned brain allowing her to keep up via catnaps and the occasional fifty-minute rest. Too many things were poised in the balance for her to assume that nothing would change, no matter how brief a time she'd been gone.

Ueh was still docked, as was Axford. The latter waited in an antechamber not far away, chatting with some of the other colonists. She dreaded to think what seeds of dissent he was sowing.

TELL HIM WE'RE MEETING IN *SILENT LIQUIDITY* IN TWO MINUTES.

I'LL MAKE SURE HE'S THERE, SOL.

As she stood and brushed herself down, Gou Mang filled her in on the most disturbing new detail.

WE HAVE A NEW KILL REPORT FROM TAU CETI. INARI REPORTED THAT THE SUPPLY RECLAMATION MISSION TO NEW FRANCE BARELY GOT AWAY WITH THEIR LIVES WHEN THE STARFISH SHOWED UP.

Hatzis thought this through before replying. Inari was the version of herself from psi Capricornus who had been put in charge of reclaiming material from senescent colonies like New France, in Tau Ceti.

DOES INARI KNOW WHAT TIPPED THEM OFF?

NO. IT MIGHT HAVE BEEN A RANDOM SEARCH. THE

FRONT IS DUE TO HIT AROUND THERE ANY TIME NOW.

EITHER WAY, THEY'RE IN THE AREA NOW, SO WE NEED TO BE CAREFUL HERE, TOO.

OF COURSE.

Was that a note of annoyance in Gou Mang's voice? Hatzis wondered if some of her criticism of Alander might not apply to herself, too.

YOU KNOW, I APPRECIATE ALL OF THE WORK YOU'VE BEEN DOING LATELY, GOU MANG. IT'S BEEN DIFFICULT ENOUGH WITHOUT ME DISAPPEARING FOR ODD PERIODS AND LEAVING YOU WITH IT. YOU'VE HANDLED IT WELL.

WE'RE ALL DOING THE BEST WE CAN, SOL.

If it had been annoyance, it was replaced by pride in Gou Mang's reply.

Hatzis arranged for a feed from the inside of Silent Liquidity to be spread across the base and all the installations in the system. When the four of them met, it would be either the beginning or end of something important. She wanted everyone to see it, so there could be no claims of a cover-up afterward. For many in her care, also, it would be their first chance to actually see a Yuhl.

They made an odd foursome: posthuman Hatzis, android Axford, Yuhl-modified Alander, and the long-legged alien. There was an extended silence as they looked one another over, each hoping someone else would start the proceedings. Hatzis didn't want to be seen to be trying to take charge of the meeting, but when the silence stretched past a minute, she decided that someone should say *something*. Thankfully, before she spoke, the alien's high-pitched voice broke the quiet.

"Our paths are concurrent once again." He spoke slowly, carefully working to ensure that both vocal chords worked in synch. He obviously recognized the difficulty humans had with the double vocal streams and wanted to minimize any chance of communication breakdown. "I am pleased."

"Well, I'm just sorry you were kept waiting," said Axford with a sidelong glance at Hatzis. "I hope that won't impact upon the diplomatic process."

"The issue isn't promptness, Frank," said Hatzis.

"Then what is it, Caryl?"

"You tell me." She faced him squarely. "I seem to be the only one unconvinced of the need to talk."

Ueh pointed both his index fingers at Hatzis. Although she knew from Alander's mind that this was a sign of respect, she couldn't help feeling unduly singled out. *The finger of suspicion points at me,* she thought.

"The free flow of information is always desirable," the alien continued slowly, "no matter where it leads us. I am here to facilitate discussion between our species. If we come away from this meeting still at war, then I will not have failed."

"In your eyes, perhaps," said Axford.

The patterns on Ueh's face shifted suddenly. *"By what/ with whose* other eyes can I see?"

Hatzis smiled to herself at the alien's response. She was amazed at the Yuhl's transformation since their first encounter. Then he had been silent and passive while his companion cast aspersions at humanity. Whatever had happened to him in the belly of the Praxis, it certainly had changed him.

Perhaps, she thought, Alander should count himself lucky that he still recognized himself.

"We all want different things," Alander put in, "but in the end we all want the *same* thing as well. We want to survive this. At this point in time, humanity's options are both grim and limited. If the Yuhl are right, we have only a matter of weeks before the Starfish wipe all traces of our colonies from the space we occupy. We can either stay, or we can flee. If we flee, we have only one obvious direction in which to run, and that's with the Yuhl. But if we stay, we're going to need all the information about the Starfish we can lay our hands on—and the obvious place to look for that is with the Yuhl. Talking to the Yuhl seems to me not only the sensible option right now, but also our *only* option."

"I agree," said Axford.

Hatzis confronted the three pairs of eyes looking at her. "I think you're being naïve, Peter," she said. "And as for you, Frank, well, I don't trust your motives." She didn't give either of them the chance to respond. "We have no evidence that the Yuhl would ever be willing to deal honestly with us. The destruction of innocent colonies forces me to treat them as hostiles." She fixed the alien with an unflinching gaze. "I'm sorry, but where I come from, actions speak louder than words."

"They are not *my/our* actions," said Ueh.

"How can you *say* that?" She took a step closer, her body language unquestionably challenging in a human context. She wanted him to be certain of her intentions. "You yourself were actually captured during a raid on Hera."

"It was *not a raid/a reconnaissance mission*," the Yuhl responded. "*We/I* admit to stealing *your resources/on occasions*, but only from those colonies you refer to as senescent."

The more emotional the alien became, the less he was able to keep his vocal streams synchronized.

"We have footage," she said. "I saw you—"

"Caryl," Alander interrupted. "The Praxis said—"

"I *know* what the Praxis said," she interrupted him in turn. "But what would you have me believe, Peter? That Frank was responsible for it? Or maybe even another alien race?"

"There could be more," said Axford affably. "Space is a big, empty place, after all, and the Spinners have been traveling a long time. There could be dozens of species going along for the ride."

"Well, I've no intention of becoming another one," she said, letting the certainty she felt speak through her voice as much as her words. "This is our home, and I'm going to fight for it."

"And I agree, Caryl," Axford said quickly. "I just want to make sure we're fighting the right people."

Ueh made a noise like a hoarse whistle from both his windpipes, as though clearing his throat.

"The Praxis does not believe in aggression as a substitute for resolution," he said with more control.

"So what does it believe in?" Hatzis asked.

"Nature," was the short answer.

"Red in tooth and nail?"

The alien looked to Alander, its facial patterns shifting again.

"He doesn't understand the metaphor," said Alander.

"Really?" she said. "That surprises me." Then, to the alien: "It's all about predators and prey—who's highest on the food chain and who's being eaten, that kind of thing. You call us the already-dead and pick out our leftovers. You know, just because you profess to avoid aggression doesn't necessarily mean you're in a higher moral state than us."

"There is no *up/down* to morality." The lines around the alien's eyes formed inverted *V*s of almost comical surprise. "There is a multidimensional landscape of *peaks/troughs*. It benefits no one to compare absolutes in isolation. My species' willingness to talk, in some minds, might place us above you and perhaps even justify a firm response to your aggressive stance."

She placed her hands on her hips as she faced off with the alien. "Are you threatening us?"

"The Yuhl act," said Ueh. "*I/we* do not threaten. Were we to attack, you would not know until it had already happened."

It sounded like a threat, but she had to give him the benefit of the doubt. She shouldn't take human behavior into account when trying to interpret the words of an alien.

"What would you have us do, then? Just talk?"

"Yes, but not here. I *cannot decide/only listen.* You should come to the *Mantissa* and put your case to the Fit."

Hatzis thought of the cilia-filled helmets and shivered. "You want me to come to you?"

"The Praxis instructed me to consider this my goal: to get *humanity/riil* to agree to this. It is the only way our species will ever truly negotiate."

Again, the Yuhl's announcement sounded like an ultimatum, but she had to admit it made sense. If Ueh couldn't negotiate, there was little point going over the arguments with him. He was nothing more than bait to get her to agree.

She was tired of trying to work out who meant what. It felt like she was going around in circles, cycling over and over through the same old arguments and coming to the same decisions—decisions that never seemed to make anyone happy. There had to be another way. But she wasn't about to hand power over to Axford or the Yuhl, and she believed Alander when he said he didn't want it. The only alternative was to hand it over to one of the ordinary engrams, which, although she knew the idea was crazy, was perhaps halfway there.

GOU MANG, I CAN'T DECIDE THIS ON MY OWN; IT'S TOO IMPORTANT. I WANT TO CALL A VOTE. CONTACT EVERYONE WHO'S BEEN WATCHING THIS FROM THE START AND POLL FOR THEIR OPINION. I'LL GO WITH THAT RATHER THAN TRUST MY OWN DECISION.

OKAY, SOL. IT'S GOING TO TAKE A MINUTE OR TWO.

THEN YOU'D BETTER GET STARTED.

"What do you think, Caryl?" Alander studied her closely. Their moment of closeness had passed. She had no idea what was going through his mind now.

"Wait," she said, her raised hand motioning him to silence. "I'm calling for a second opinion."

She walked around the cockpit, worrying at a thumbnail until Gou Mang came through with the results. She could feel an energetic buzzing around her as the population of Sothis voted on their fate, but she didn't intervene or even observe. She wanted to stay completely out of it. *Let them decide their own fate,* she thought to herself. *If I don't like it, I can always leave.*

WE HAVE A RESULT, SOL.

TELL ME.

OUT OF 100: AYE, 54; NAY, 32. THE BALANCE CONSISTS OF ABSTENTIONS.

WHICH WAY IS WHICH?

AYE MEANS TO GO.

Hatzis took a deep breath. THEN I GUESS I GO.

Hatzis felt an immediate lightening of the load. Absolving herself of the decision was making all the difference.

"If we're to go," she said aloud, "would we need to call ahead?"

"No," said Ueh, again speaking slowly to keep his speech in a single stream. "*Yuhl/Goel* do not make announcements about what we intend to do. *I/we* just do them."

"Okay, then let's not waste any time. The sooner we have an answer, the better." She looked at Ueh, Axford, and Alander in turn. The alien was inscrutable; Axford looked cautiously pleased; Alander smiled openly. "We can continue this conversation on the way."

"Let's not go as beggars, either," said Axford. "I suggest docking *Arachne*, *Orcus*, and *Silent Liquidity* together and taking all three. It demonstrates a certain amount of knowledge and resourcefulness. It also shows how we can work together when it really counts."

Hatzis stared at him. "Next you'll be suggesting we should give *Silent Liquidity* back as a sign of goodwill."

"I may be many things, Caryl," he said, "but crazy isn't one of them."

As soon as the three cockpits were in a stable configura-tion around their new, combined central body, Hatzis called the order to relocate. The new vessel answered to the name *Triumvirate* and had more than enough room for its four occupants. For the first hour or so, they talked in general terms over what would happen when they arrived in Beid. Soon enough, though, she called a break to rest and rethink. It might, she thought, be the last chance any of them had to do this for some time.

Alander took himself off to a private berth the hole ship provided for him. Ueh blacked out his section of the cockpit so he couldn't be watched. Axford put his feet up on one of the couches and closed his eyes. He didn't sleep, though. He simply rested, breathing evenly with his hands folded in his lap.

Caryl wondered what Axford thought about when he was on his own. Did he miss the company of his fellow copies? Even though they weren't part of a gestalt, there had to be some sort of empathy, even if it was only based on body language and shared knowledge. She wondered if a person like Frank the Ax ever got lonely. If he did, she doubted he would ever admit it.

She watched him for fifteen minutes or so as Sothis receded behind her and the decision she had to make drew steadily closer.

"You think we should attack the Starfish, don't you?" she said aloud.

A faint smile played across his lips as though he had been waiting for her to ask. "Yes," he said, keeping his eyes closed, as if continuing to meditate even as he spoke. "I do."

"Why?"

He opened his eyes now and fixed her with an even stare. "That becomes obvious if you exchange the word *attack* for *resist*."

"But do you really think we stand a chance against them?"

"Better than none at all, which is what we have if we do nothing." Axford remained calm and untroubled, as though they were talking about nothing more than the stellar forecasts in Vega. "I do know we need the Yuhl to do it."

"I don't understand your certainty over this. If I did, I might reconsider."

"Perhaps it's a statement of faith. Or hope." He shrugged. "I once pinned that hope on the Gifts and the Spinners. But we obviously don't have time to dig through the Library to find out what we need, and we can't take the Gifts with us if we run. The next largest repository of knowledge is the Yuhl, so . . ." He left the sentence dangling between them.

She finished it for him: "Once they're gone, we've lost our last chance."

He nodded. "I believe so. And they will leave, once the Starfish front comes too close. If chi Hercules has been contacted, that means the Spinners are more than three quarters through surveyed space. Rho Corona Borealis could be next, followed by Asellus Primus or iota Boötis—"

"Then the Alkaid systems," she interrupted him. "Yes, I know. Trust me, the maps are burned into my mind."

"Do you know that Alkaid derives its name from the Arabic for 'chief of the mourners'?" he asked.

"Very fitting," she said. The big, blue variable lay ninety-eight light-years from Sol and appeared to lie right in the Spinners' path. Clustered around and before it were five target systems which, assuming their missions had been successful, would be the last colonies the Spinners would encounter before leaving human space forever.

"Especially when you consider that the Starfish are creeping past halfway," Axford said.

"Only eighty light-years or so behind."

They were silent for a moment. He didn't close his eyes, and he didn't retreat inward again. His gaze stayed firmly with hers.

She thought of 6 Ceti, the ostrich colony that recently had been destroyed. Once she had hoped that something might be left behind if they hid well enough. Now she wasn't sure—not even about the resettled refugee colonies like Adrasteia. All the Starfish had to do was leave monitors behind in the systems they had visited, and they would know if any of these systems had been reclaimed. She couldn't just sit back and simply rely on the Starfish not taking precautions.

She looked down at her hands, at her seamless, impossibly smooth skin, and felt a wave of sadness rush through her. Not anger, as usually struck her when she thought about the cruel stupidity of their situation. Just sadness. It would be a terrible waste if no one remained to know the human name of Alkaid when the Starfish finally swept by.

"What are you fishing for, Axford?"

"Me? I'm not fishing. We're just talking."

"Crap. We're going around in circles until you get what you want."

"And what would that be, exactly, Caryl?"

"You tell me."

He didn't say anything at first. His eyes didn't look away from her, and the rest of him didn't move. He was like a statue, motionless except for his mouth and the slow rise and fall of his android chest.

"All right," he eventually said. "I'll give you a few things to think about, and then I'll leave you alone for a while. Deal?"

She nodded affirmative in response.

"It's about the Starfish," he said. "You asked me if I wanted to attack them, and when I said that I did, you asked the wrong question. You asked *why*, not *how*."

"Would you tell me how if I asked?"

"Not really, but I do have part of an answer," he replied. "First: the Starfish are behaving like machines, searching as though they're following a simple algorithm. They detect a signal; they home in on it. Once the source is destroyed, they jump around at random in increasingly large jumps from their starting point until they find something. Or they hear another signal, at which point they start all over again in a new location. Sure, they're filling in the gaps eventually, but initially at least, their behavior isn't terribly complicated. Got it?"

She nodded again. "Go on."

"Second: we've never seen the Starfish strike in two places at once, so maybe their resources are limited."

"It's possible," she said. "You're not telling me anything I don't already know, Frank."

"I know that," he said, leaning forward. "But have you considered this: what happens if you present the Starfish with multiple targets at once? Perhaps they'd split their resources to try and take both at the same time."

"Haven't we already tried that? My engrams sent data back to me under cover of the midday broadcasts. That counts as simultaneous broadcasting. So far, this hasn't had any effect on the Starfish whatsoever—that we can measure."

"Then maybe you're not measuring it the right way," Axford shot back. "Or maybe it's simply because your scouts are broadcasting from interstellar space. The Starfish might be machines, as the other Alander thought, but they're not stupid. I think by now they know we have a penchant for G-type stars."

"So what are you saying? That we sacrifice a colony or two to find out?"

"Empty ones, yes. Failed missions. You must have enough of those to spare by now."

His stare was a challenge, daring her to bring up the pronoun he had used. To him it was still a case of Axford and the rest. They weren't on the same side yet, and perhaps would never be.

"Was that what you wanted to tell me?" she asked evenly.

"Not entirely," he answered, leaning back into his seat. "There is something else I think you've missed."

"Which is?"

"We're concentrating on what happens when the Starfish notice us," he said. "But where are they for the rest of the time?"

"Well, I imagine they have some sort of base or mother ship somewhere," she mused. "The same as the Spinners probably do."

"But where?"

"Fuck, Axford, how the hell should I know?" She met his challenge irritably, knowing he couldn't possibly have the answer to the question, either. "We don't think of surveyed space as *space,* really. We think of it as an array of points, with each point a system or colony, depending on your preference. We ignore the gaps. Ueh told Peter that we should consider hiding in the gaps if we decided to follow the Spinners, but maybe that's where the Starfish are. It would make sense, if they really wanted to stay hidden."

"Who from?" asked Axford. *"Us?"*

She nodded. "Okay, point taken," she said. "What's your take on the situation, then?"

"Me, I think they've got some sort of command center somewhere—as do the Spinners. I don't know what these centers would look like, mind you. Maybe they're nothing like we can imagine. But I reckon they exist. The fact that everything is proceeding in such a well-defined, linear fashion suggests that. If there wasn't *something* to follow, the Spinners wouldn't be leaving such a large wake. And if the Starfish aren't much more advanced that the Spinners, then they'll be doing the same."

"Okay," she said. "I'm partly convinced. But that still doesn't help us find it."

"Doesn't it? It'd be well defended, wouldn't you think?"

"Of course. But that would only make it harder to find, surely?"

"Not necessarily. Think about it, Caryl: we already have one prospective target, and you're already keen to attack it, even if it is for the wrong reasons: pi-1 Ursa Major."

"What?" She stared at him, unable to see how he'd come to that conclusion.

"We've lost three hole ships around that area, so something's going on in there."

"Why not the Yuhl?"

"Simple: the three systems they've led us to have been K-type primaries. Pi-1 Ursa Major is a G."

And Alander had already seen the massed Yuhl fleet in Beid, she belatedly realized. The fleet therefore couldn't be in pi-1 Ursa Major as well. Unless there was a second Yuhl fleet lurking there, her assumption had been wrong all along. She felt like slapping her forehead.

"I think you've got something there, Frank."

"I know I have, Caryl. And now you have it, too."

"Thanks," she said, half expecting a request to reciprocate at any moment, or a long, pointed gloat. But he surprised her.

"I'll give you some peace, now," he said. "I need to

think." He closed his eyes and folded his arms across his chest. Frowning, she watched as he settled back into the same state he had been in earlier, apparently oblivious to the outside world.

Think about what? she wondered. He had given her something, but she received the distinct impression that the reverse might actually have been the case. What had he got in return without her knowing? She didn't know, and it worried her that she didn't know. She was momentarily tempted to hack into his Overseer to find out what he was thinking, but she had no doubt that he had defenses in place that would stop her from prying. She would have to use old-fashioned guesswork to try to discover what he was up to.

The cockpit was suddenly silent. She wished she could relax like the others while they hung in the unspace void between locations, but she was too consumed with thoughts to rest. She kept turning over what might happen when they arrived at their destination.

What if it was a trap? Or the Yuhl weren't interested in negotiating? The trip would have been wasted, and the fragile beginnings of cooperation might dissolve forever, along, perhaps, with the few scattered remnants of humanity that remained in the universe. But she wasn't about to allow that to happen. No matter what it took, she would keep her species alive. Even if it meant abandoning her home and becoming a gypsy race, at least there would be *something* left. Anything was better than extinction.

2.1.7

An ftl communication rang through the combined hole ship ten minutes after they arrived in Beid. Sounding like a high-speed recording of a percussion ensemble played backward, it rapid-fired through the cockpit, making Alander wince.

"Sorry about that," said Axford. "It's for me. A message from home."

"Want to tell us what it's about?" Hatzis asked.

"Not really." Frank the Ax turned his attention back to the main screen, on which was displayed the tremendous assembly of the Yuhl. "Everything's falling into place nicely, though."

Alander followed the brief exchange with interest. The tension between Hatzis and Axford wasn't ebbing. If anything, it was increasing. And she still wasn't talking to Ueh properly. Hatzis was like a very compact hurricane, wrapping around itself tighter and tighter, never letting up.

He'd caught a glimpse of her when she had dived into his mind. He had a greater understanding of her fear of letting go, of not being in control, but at the same time she knew that she *wanted* to let go. She had a love-hate relationship with power, either pushing it away or pulling it in toward her. *That* was the dynamo that fueled her tension; it wasn't just the desire to be in charge all the time. She had simply yet to find the balance between accepting and delegating responsibility.

Not that he was one to talk. The academic life had been fine for his old self, back on Earth. Independently wealthy, he had been able to leap from interest to interest as the whim took him. He'd never had to answer to anyone but himself. As his stocks had risen in academic circles, then outside, he had enjoyed the influence he'd been able to wield while sitting comfortably safe behind glass, able to walk away whenever he wanted. He'd always learned from mistakes intellectually, never viscerally. He had been protected from the consequences, and thus thought himself immune.

He rejected me . . .

He wondered if his old self would have been any better adjusted than Hatzis after 150 years of life. Perhaps her greater self had been, the sum of the distributed Hatzis of which she had only been a small part. *That* Hatzis might have been completely incomprehensible to him, as far above the engrams as the engrams were above pocket calculators.

The Hatzis before him was afraid to surrender the control she had over the small universe she was rebuilding out of humanity's ashes. But if she was going to breathe life into those dying embers, if they were to survive, then she needed to realize that relinquishing control might be exactly what she needed to do. He couldn't tell which way she would jump—to join the Yuhl in running or Axford in fighting back—but he knew she couldn't solve it, this time, by calling for a vote. Whether she liked it or not, the decision was up to her.

Axford wasn't given another chance to explain about the message (not that Alander thought he was going to, anyway) because a transmission from the Yuhl arrived shortly thereafter, responding to Ueh's hail upon arriving in the system.

"The Praxis welcomes your return, *envoy/catechist Ueh/ Ellil*." The voice came with an image of a Yuhl adorned with the accoutrements of conjugator. It wasn't *Vaise/Ashu*, the first one Alander had met. This one seemed narrower and taller, its yellow and striped head reminding him of a pencil eraser.

"I bring *envoy/catechist Peter/Alander*," Ueh responded, "and representatives of *humanity/riil. We/they* request permission to speak to the Fit."

This time the reply came almost immediately. They were close enough to the *Mantissa* that transmission delays were less than a few seconds. The massive accumulation of hole ships and others structures made from ordinary matter still looked from a distance like an asteroid belt, but the more he looked at it, the more it appeared to teem with life and activity. Its component parts were in constant, chaotic motion, as though jiggled by Brownian motion on an infinitely larger scale.

"Permission is granted to dock," said the conjugator. "*Further eventualities/will then be considered.*"

The screen went blank.

Ueh turned his black eyes on his companions in the cockpit. "Does this satisfy you?"

Alander turned to Hatzis. "Caryl? Are you going to go through with it?"

She shot him a faint glare, knowing that he was throwing her a challenge. "If we have to do it, Peter, then we have to do it, I guess. But I don't like putting all our eggs in one basket."

"It will be seen as a sign of confidence," Ueh explained slowly.

She cast the alien a baleful glare. "Is that what you tell everyone as you lead them down the Praxis's maw?"

"Leave it, Caryl," said Alander. This was no time for squabbling, nerves or no. "We'll be going nowhere near the Praxis, will we, Ueh?"

"*Peter/Alander* is correct."

"So you don't need to be worried about being eaten or anything," he said. "Not straightaway, at least."

She didn't acknowledge his attempt at humor. "Okay, but once negotiations fail, then all bets are off."

"If negotiations fail," Alander said, "then we're as good as dead anyway, so being eaten is a redundant concern, wouldn't you say?"

She took his point with a curt, reluctant nod. "All right," she said, facing the alien, "tell them we're coming in. All of us."

The alien gave the Yuhl equivalent of a nod and confirmed the arrangement with his superiors on the *Mantissa*. Alander received an impression from Ueh's voice or body language that he was relieved to be going home. There hadn't been much for him to do on Sothis, really. The hard work of getting Hatzis to agree to talk had pretty much been accomplished before the meeting had even started.

The hole ship jumped. They were committed. Hatzis walked around the cockpit once, glanced at Alander twice, but said nothing.

They docked with a graceful polygon made out of what must have been at least a hundred cockpits rotating lazily over the white bulge of a giant hole ship. The simple triangle of *Triumvirate* was dwarfed by it. When its air-lock slid open, the yellowish atmosphere of the Yuhl flowed into the cockpit and merged with Ueh's isolated bubble. Once again, Alander was contained within a force field of the gifts' making. If it failed . . .

If it fails, he told himself, *there's still my I-suit. And if that fails, then I won't have to worry about anything anymore, anyway.*

The same conjugator who had hailed them walked in, flanked by two other Yuhl whose broad stockiness suggested to Alander that they might be guards. The conjugator acknowledged Hatzis, Axford, and Alander individually, his wing sheaths twitching with something akin to nervousness. Or perhaps distaste. Alander couldn't decide which.

"The Praxis is pleased that you have come," said the Yuhl. "I am Conjugator *Seria/Hile. Please follow me/I will escort you* to the Fit."

The conjugator turned and walked out of the cockpit, intending them to follow. Ueh and Axford went first, then Alander and Hatzis, with the guards falling in closely behind. Hatzis's lips were pressed tightly and anxiously together.

They were led into the sort of cramped, apparently disordered habitat Alander had come to expect among the Yuhl. He could see patterns to it now that hadn't been there before, and he wondered how much of that he owed to the Praxis. The attitude and presentation of each work-station displayed information about the status of the person behind it or the sort of work they did. The layout of each chamber followed information flows and decision-making chains rather than hierarchical order, so it was possible to trace a bureaucratic process from one end of the room to the other without missing a link in the chain.

Alander also found that he didn't need the conjugator to guide him. It was a lot easier, second time around, to tell where to go. The Yuhl used a complicated phonetic written language with symbols comprised of circles and

intersecting lines, uncannily like cloud diagrams from particle accelerators. He recognized about one word in three,
but he could have found his way to the Fit and back to
Triumvirate without much difficulty, if he'd had to.

He learned that the helmets by which they would interact with the Fit were called ingurgitation ports, but he
kept that to himself. Conjugator *Seria/Hile* led them to four
empty ports and indicated that they should sit. Hatzis's
expression was sour as she confronted the cilia-lined
mouth of the helmet. Attendants moved into position behind them to make sure they didn't break free during the
ingurgitation process.

Alander didn't want to see it from the outside. "On
three," he said, hoping he didn't look as nervous as he
felt. Axford nodded sharply and counted down. Alander
bent forward with the others, thrusting his head blindly
into the glistening mouth before him, while at the same
time hearing what might have been a faint moan from
Hatzis beside him. The last thing he saw was the gleam-
ing, marked dome of Ueh joining them in the maneuver.
It didn't reassure him to see that the Yuhl's expression
carried as much apprehension and distaste as his own face
displayed.

Then he was being smothered again, and he was unable
to resist flailing, physically and mentally, as the darkness
enfolded him.

"I'm pleased you returned, Peter," said a voice in the
void. He recognized it immediately as belonging to the
Praxis.

"Did I have any choice?" he said.

"Always," said the Praxis smoothly. "And, conversely,
never." It paused for a few seconds before continuing.
"Many things could have conspired to prevent this moment. The Ambivalence strikes swiftly and cruelly at
times."

Alander wondered how many times the Praxis had seen
potential allies wiped out before negotiations could proceed very far. "I don't understand what you're hoping to

get out of this," he said. "Do you want to join forces with us?"

"I want what is best for the *Yuhl/Goel*. That is all."

"You have no desires for yourself?"

"Beyond survival, there are few," it replied. "To learn, perhaps; to be kept occupied. Provided I am fed, my needs are small."

Alander instinctively distrusted such a blithe statement, but he was given no time to pursue it further. He felt a familiar thickening of the darkness around him as the minds and voices of the Fit rose out of the void. This time, though, the nonauditory component that came with the voices was stronger. Apart from odors, he saw flashes of faces and felt odd textures brushing against him. He didn't know whether they were the result of a closer meshing with the Fit, thanks to the Praxis's modifications, or whether his mind was triggering the sensations in order to make up for the absence of input.

"It is an honor," said a voice out of the darkness. In this environment, without the dual vocal streams, Alander almost didn't recognize the smooth, measured tones of Ueh.

"Speak now, while we will listen," came the dismissive reply. "Why are you here?"

"For the same reason as last time," Alander answered. "Humanity wishes to ally itself with the *Yuhl/Goel*."

"Why?" The word was called out by three or more voices, coming across as an ear-piercing shriek.

"So that we can be free to pursue the Species Dream," he said.

"How?" the shrieking voices continued.

"That's not important," he said defensively. "Freedom is in an end to itself."

"But you are already free to pursue the Species Dream," put in a voice Alander recognized as belonging to the Yuhl called *Status Quo/Mellifluous*. "No one is holding you back."

"But it is something we cannot achieve on our own. We need your help. And it's just possible, judging by what I heard last time, that you need our help in return."

A sound not unlike hail rattling on a metallic roof resounded throughout the dark. Alander put it down to a number of the Fit laughing.

One voice lifted from the noise: "We have already heard this one's preposterous prattle!"

"Who are the others?" asked another. "What do they want with us?"

"*Envoy/catechist Ueh/Ellil*," said *Status Quo/Mellifluous*, the alien's voice coming with a suggestion of cumin, "tell us what you have learned about these people."

"They are stubborn," said the Yuhl. "But they are also resourceful. At the time of First Contact with the Ambivalence, their primary system was more advanced than ours, despite having suffered significant losses in recent decades. Their societies experience great conflict as a matter of course, and this fuels a cycle of boom and bust that on the whole projects technology and knowledge in an upward direction. Their social structures lean toward central leadership, but once achieved finds that the equilibrium is unstable and quickly fractures. Again, this cyclic pattern tends to result in an overall improvement in quality of life, but at some cost. They are not natural cooperators. Issues of dominance and genetic relationships still color much of their interactions. Even among those they call engrams, who have dispensed with physical bodies in order to achieve sublight interstellar travel, there exists a strong tendency to retain corporeal urges. They impersonate the flesh, unwilling to let go."

Alander was impressed. So much, he thought, for Ueh not having much to do on Sothis.

"The Praxis would approve of this," said *Status Quo/Mellifluous*. "That explains why it has us consort with the *bodiless/prey* on this occasion."

He recognized the term *bodiless/prey* even though he had not heard it since his first encounter with the Yuhl, when *Asi/Holina*, the other half of the helot pair Ueh had belonged to, had used it to describe the disembodied Axford.

"If we didn't have bodies," he said, "would you have ignored us?"

"Yes," said *Status Quo/Mellifluous.* "That which has no flesh is of no concern to us. Our paths do not overlap."

"Your needs don't overlap, you mean." Hatzis spoke for the first time, her voice accompanied by the faint but unmistakable sensation of human skin touching. "If you're not competing for the same resources, you can safely ignore them."

"Should this not be so?"

"Humanity has concepts such as altruism and sympathy," she said. "We would help you, under those circumstances."

"It would be safer to say that you would help unless it hurt you too much," clarified Ueh. "All generosity has its limits. And we know our limitations."

"So you're saying it's easier to watch us die than help us live?"

"In social terms, it could be argued that the cost is much higher," said a new voice. Alander was glad to hear from *Radical/Provocative* again, even though he came with a strange aftertaste, like vinegar. "Our conscience weighs heavily enough as it is. When our resources were limited and our survival precarious, then we could justify standing aside while other species fell under the Ambivalence. But now we are strong and confident; perhaps now we should seek allies and make them strong, too. As the Praxis has said in the past, variety promotes life."

"But this is not the Praxis's decision," said *Status Quo/ Mellifluous.* "It is ours."

"Are you seeking to trigger one of your cycles of violence with us?" asked a new voice, needle sharp and cutting. Alander knew instinctively that its name was *Probing/Inquisitive.* "Would that be what you intend by declaring war upon us?"

"You decoded our broadcasts, then," Hatzis said.

"It was no trivial matter to find the quantum key you used, but not beyond us." *Probing/Inquisitive* seemed to enjoy her discomfort. "We have been wondering how to respond to your announcement."

"And have you decided?" asked Hatzis. She sounded calm and unperturbed, which surprised Alander. Given her current position among aliens, and given that these aliens were aware of her intention to wage war upon them, he would have expected her to be a little more apprehensive.

"To do no more than we already have. You hardly comprise a military threat. Now that you have lost the element of surprise, you will find our scouts vulnerable no longer."

"Perhaps a cycle of violence is just what you need," said Axford, all gunpowder and smoke.

"Ah, the warrior speaks." *Probing/Inquisitive* made the rasping noise that broadly correlated to a Yuhl's chuckle. "But what does he mean?"

"I mean that you've been stable for too long. You've lost the edge."

"What edge is this? We are vital, thriving, and versatile. How could we not be, when every few days see us in a new system, a new section of the galaxy, confronting new challenges and reaping new rewards?"

"You're scavengers," Axford put in sharply. "You live off the scraps that fall from the Spinners' table."

"It is a rich and fertile niche," the alien defended. "If we didn't occupy it, someone else soon would."

"To their detriment, too."

"You seem very sure of yourself, *Francis/Axford*, and yet you did not know us before. How can you say that the *Yuhl/Goel* are in any way lessened?"

Probing/Inquisitive was beginning to sound annoyed, and Alander stepped in before Axford could do any permanent diplomatic damage. "We cannot help but be followers of the Species Dream," he said. "Never having known an alternative, we seek that with which we are familiar. But that doesn't mean the idea is foolish, just because it comes automatically. It might be that we, like most plants, require a firm foundation on which to grow. A life of constant travel in the company of the Ambivalence might not be the right environment for us to thrive."

"I understand what you say," said *Probing/Inquisitive* after a moment's pause. "But you don't need our permission to follow the Dream."

"It would certainly be easier to do that if you weren't so busy attacking our colonies," said Hatzis. "As you said, *you're* thriving. We're not. If a cycle of violence is what it takes to safeguard our resources, then that's what you'll get."

"To your detriment, surely," said *Status Quo/Mellifluous*. "Such a war would be pointless. We don't want it, and you can't win it."

"So we might as well cooperate," said *Radical/Provocative*. "There must be another option besides conflict and avoidance."

"To what end?" asked *Status Quo/Mellifluous*.

"Change is an end unto itself," *Radical/Provocative* argued. "The Praxis would agree—"

"And again I say that this is not a matter concerning the Praxis. What happens to us has little bearing on its fate." *Status Quo/Mellifluous*'s voice was firm and rich with exotic spices. "It will find other feeders, just as it had others before us."

"Then why do we place such importance on what it thinks?"

"Because that *is* important. While our lives are entwined, its opinions are supremely relevant. It has served us well, just as we have served it. Our mutual dependency is synergistic."

"It's a parasite!" exclaimed *Radical/Provocative*, provoking a collective gasp from the assembled Yuhl that startled Alander. "And we are parasites, too. The Praxis is not so much a *bearer/favored* to the *Yuhl/Goel*, but a cancer sucking us dry!"

Amid the rising hubbub of the Fit, Axford's voice rang out: "I think we're arguing about the wrong thing. The Praxis isn't your problem. If anything, it is the solution.

Your problems began the day your species encountered the Ambivalence."

"*PRAISE AND THANKS TO THE AMBIVALENCE!*" came an answering chant from the Fit, but it sounded halfhearted. Doubt had been sown.

"From your point of view, it must seems so," said *Status Quo/Mellifluous* after the echoes of the chant faded.

"Of course it does, because right now we are where you were two and a half thousand years ago. People are dying every day; whole colonies are being destroyed. In a week or two we might not even *exist*. How can we look at it any other way?"

"We are different," said Ueh. "I have observed consistent deterministic tendencies among your people: you look for reasons, for something to blame. We do not think that way. For us, some things happen by a confluence of events, many of them seemingly irrelevant. The universe follows its own path, and we are swept up in it. Sometimes there *are* reasons and we do not see them, just as sometimes there are no reasons and you invent them."

"We didn't invent the attacks on our colonies," said Hatzis.

"But that's not the point." Axford sounded exasperated, and Alander wondered how genuine it was. "The attacks are minor, and we could argue from here to eternity about who crossed the line first. In the end it doesn't matter. It is irrelevant. What does matter is the Starfish. We're not inventing *that*."

"No, you are not." The voice of *Status Quo/Mellifluous* was soft, but it rose with perfect clarity out of a sudden silence. "Before the Ambivalence, the Yuhl possessed just two worlds and several satellite colonies. The Ambivalence brought us riches unimagined. Then it brought death." *Status Quo/Mellifluous* paused, and a brief, hollow silence fell.

"You were there?" Alander asked, amazed.

"A few of us have been kept alive well beyond our natural years by the gift you call I-suits. We have endured more than you can imagine."

"No doubt," Axford said. "But this underlies the point I'm trying to make. You *know* what it feels like to watch your civilization die."

"And I know that *humanity/riil* will die also, unless it follows the path of the *Yuhl/Goel*. There are no other options."

"None at all?"

"The number of futures open to anyone within the influence of the Ambivalence is just two: death or assimilation."

Startled by the fatalist sentiments, Alander realized only then that the nature of the Ambivalence had been fundamentally mistranslated. The Yuhl didn't think of it as a god, a deity with aspects of good and evil in whose shadow they crawled and by whose grace they lived or died. The notion of *decision* in this case had more to do with the results of a coin toss than conscious will. The Ambivalence was to them more like a physical phenomenon than a god, at most a giant machine, clunking and rattling its way through the universe completely oblivious to the creatures that lived among its cogs and levers. Whether it was comprised of one species or two, or even a thousand, was irrelevant. The Ambivalence was taken as a single, incomprehensible whole rather than any number of equally incomprehensible component parts.

"There are in fact three options," put in *Radical/Provocative*. "We have the Species Dream."

"We would gladly adopt the Species Dream if we could only find somewhere to live," *Status Quo/Mellifluous* said, more for the benefit of the Fit's human guests than *Radical/Provocative*. "The fact is that none of our deep scouts have ever succeeded in their quest to find a safe location. The few that return from their reconnaissance have brought inconclusive data. Remember: the Ambivalence is traveling through space at a sizable multiple of the speed of light, and we must maintain that velocity if we are to remain in our niche. Also, the scouts cannot use the ftl communicators for fear of exposing themselves. They must explore potential systems quickly, then return in time for the *Mantissa* to mobilize. It is a difficult task."

"Perhaps too difficult," said Alander. "Perhaps you are setting your standards too high."

"Our standards must be high. If we make the wrong decision, we will be destroyed by the Ambivalence. Just because a probe or two explored a tiny percentage of the wake and survived does not mean that a permanent settlement will. Who knows what might follow the Ambivalence?"

"You think the Starfish could be just the vanguard of something larger?" Hatzis asked uneasily. Alander could understand that unease, too. The thought was truly a disturbing one. If it was true, then it didn't matter what the *Yuhl/Goel* or humanity did; ultimately, the very last trace that they had ever existed would soon be cleaned away.

"It is not something I would like to put to the test," said *Status Quo/Mellifluous*. "To move from the shadow of the Ambivalence could mean our death."

"No more than staying here!" There was a bitter and smoky edge to *Radical/Provocative's* voice. "I have spent my entire existence in the underbelly of the Ambivalence. I am tired. Sometimes I think that I would rather risk death than an eternity in such a limbo."

"That is your choice," said *Status Quo/Mellifluous* severely.

"Is it?" asked *Radical/Provocative*. "I propose that those who wish to should be allowed to attempt the Species Dream. Perhaps you're right, and we can't do it alone. But here we have allies who are eager to assist! We may never have such a chance again."

"The Fit will never agree to—"

"Does it need to?" cut in *Radical/Provocative*. "Why can't those who wish to leave do so? We would demand only the resources due to us, in proportion to our numbers. Once gone, you would never have to worry about us again."

"Split the *Mantissa*?" Again, the Fit sounded collectively mortified. A fragrance not unlike fear accosted Alander's senses. At the same time, a number of Yuhl simultaneously spoke. It was impossible for a moment to tease out individual concerns, but the general feel was one of incredulity.

"Do you propose such a thing in seriousness or simply to get a reaction?" demanded *Status Quo/Mellifluous*.

"I wouldn't propose it if I wasn't serious," said *Radical/Provocative*.

"Exactly how many of you *are* there?"

"You would become *yuhl/riil!*" protested a voice from the crowd.

"We must not split the *Mantissa*" said another.

"It would be madness!" from yet another.

"Perhaps it is *time* for some madness, then!" said *Radical/Provocative*.

Alander found himself being seduced by the insidious pessimism of the conversation. He struggled to lift himself out of it, not knowing if it was natural or something to do with his modification by the Praxis. Centuries of hiding and predation were hard to resist.

"None of this helps us," he said, shouting to be heard over the hubbub. "If we wanted to commit suicide, we'd just throw ourselves at the Starfish and be done with it!"

"Perhaps we *can't* help you," said *Status Quo/Mellifluous* firmly. "Which brings us back to where we started, when you first spoke to us. I said then as I say now: why should we jeopardize our peaceful coexistence with the Ambivalence for the sake of *humanity/riil?*"

"And why should it be suicide?" spoke up Axford. "I can understand the Yuhl being uneasy about disturbing their precious peace with the Ambivalence—even if I disagree with it. But have you ever *seriously* considered the alternative?"

"Attack the *Ambivalence*?" *Status Quo/Mellifluous* sounded truly outraged by the suggestion.

"Listen: we've been trying to communicate with the Spinners and the Starfish at either end, ever since they first arrived. And I daresay that you once did the same until you gave up and decided to simply go along for the ride. But we need to try something different. They're already decimating us, so we certainly have nothing to lose by showing some resistance. And who knows? Maybe hurting them is just the way to get their attention. And once we have it, that changes *everything*."

"Or we have done nothing except waste lives," said *Status Quo/Mellifluous*.

"Our lives are wasted living this way, anyway," said *Radical/Provocative*.

"I think it's an acceptable risk," Axford jumped in quickly. Like Alander, he clearly didn't want the heated argument between these two Yuhl to dominate the proceedings. "Given time, I might have tried it myself. But I'd need to beef up my know-how a little in order to increase my chances, and I'd go into it expecting to get my ass kicked—but if nothing else, at least I'd have tried. And who's to say it won't work?"

"I am," said *Status Quo/Mellifluous* against a backdrop of agreement. "How do you know where to attack it? Are you planning to flail about blindly, hoping to hit something?"

"We have a target," said Axford evenly. "The system we call pi-1 Ursa Major is proving a problem for us. Something's in there—something that wants to stay hidden. I think it's the Starfish, and I think that we should attack them while we still have the opportunity to do so. This could be our chance to break the pattern."

"It still won't work," *Status Quo/Mellifluous* continued pessimistically. "The Ambivalence either destroys or ignores; there is no middle ground. Attacking it will only bring about our destruction!"

"How do you *know* that? Have you ever tried?"

"Of course not! To do so would—"

"You've never even *tried*?" Axford's voice expressed unrestrained scorn. "In all the centuries you've been living in the Ambivalence's armpit, you've never once tried to tickle it? No wonder some of you are calling this a kind of living death. You losers gave up and now expect everyone else to—"

"Frank, hold it." Hatzis cut across a wave of angry protest that was spreading throughout the Fit. "We're not here to throw stones—at the Yuhl *or* the Ambivalence. We're here to explore options."

"Not all the options, obviously," he grumbled.

"The *realistic* options, then," she countered. "You said it yourself: *given time,* you'd attack. You couldn't do it at the moment, and you can't reasonably expect the Yuhl to do your dirty work, either. So let's just try to find a way to *make* time shall we? Whether it's about the Species Dream or something else we haven't thought of, we should be talking, not arguing. Okay?"

"You've changed your tune," he said.

"That's what rational creatures do when they encounter a brick wall." Again Alander felt the sensation of skin sliding softly against skin when she talked. It wasn't an erotic feeling, though. Hatzis's voice was full of weary resignation, as though she was steeling herself to do something she still disagreed with. "If staying in surveyed space isn't an option, we need to work out where to go instead. And if that means negotiating a treaty, then I'm just going to have to bite the bullet."

"You're suggesting we join the Yuhl?" Axford didn't sound as happy as Alander had thought he might.

"If they'll have us, yes," she responded with some hesitation. "Then, one day when we're stronger, we can return here and—"

"And *what*?" he snapped. "Jesus, Caryl, we didn't come here to join *them*! We came to see if they would join us in a stand against the Starfish. You can't expect us to blindly throw our fate in with this lot of skulking scavengers!"

"That's not what I'm suggesting!"

"No? Well, it sure as hell sounds like it to me," he said. "How do we know we'll be safe if we do join up? Just because you've survived isn't enough reassurance, I'm afraid. I want more. I'm a military man, and I'd like to know exactly what it is that I'm stepping into."

"We take precautions depending on the environment in which we find ourselves," said *Status Quo/Mellifluous*. "Each time the Ambivalence encounters a species, there is a certain pattern to its distribution. We determine that pattern and avoid it. For instance, your species favors G-type stars, so we place the bulk of the *Mantissa* elsewhere for the middle phase of the Ambivalence. When the trailing edge—which scours all systems—approaches, we move forward again."

"How often do you move?" pressed Axford.

"Every four of your days," replied Ueh.

"And how long does it take to move the *Mantissa*?"

"Approximately five hours."

"That's under normal circumstances, I assume?" said Axford. "But what if the Starfish stumble across you? How quickly can you get away?"

"This has happened on occasions in the past," conceded *Status Quo/Mellifluous*. "The *Mantissa* is equipped for emergency dissipation. We can disengage the bulk of our hole ships in ten of your minutes. Since a large proportion of our infrastructure comprises ordinary matter and needs to be ferried through unspace, a complete evacuation can take anything up to two hours. Reassembling the *Mantissa* takes much longer, of course. It is not something we attempt lightly."

"No doubt," said Hatzis. "I can see now why you're so nervous about kicking the anthill."

A confused chatter peppered the dark with a variety of aromas.

"We do not understand your metaphor," said Ueh after a moment.

"You're careful not to upset the equilibrium," Hatzis explained. "And why should you, when life is so comfortable for you?"

"It's comfortable only on the surface," said *Radical/Provocative*. "It hides a rot that will eventually consume us all."

"I agree," Axford said. "But how far would you go to prevent that rot? Would you be prepared to provoke the Starfish? I mean, the Ambivalence?"

"Such a venture would be costly and probably futile," answered *Radical/Provocative*. I am for a peaceful solution.

Neither immolation nor slow decay is acceptable."

"I'm sorry to hear that," said Axford. There was a hint of amusement to his tone that Alander found strangely unnerving. "Because you're not going to appreciate what I've done."

"What are you talking about?" asked Hatzis.

"I've kicked the anthill for you," explained the ex-general matter-of-factly.

"You're not making any sense," said Hatzis. "What exactly are you saying?"

"You remember that ftl transmission when we arrived here?"

"The one you said was from—" She stopped. "Oh, fuck. Tell me you're joking, Frank."

"I don't know how long we've been sitting here talking," said Axford calmly, "but I'm guessing that a couple of hours have passed in the real world. Without knowing exactly where the Starfish were when I called them, we can't know just how quickly they'll get here. It could be hours. On the other hand, they might be here right now, targeting us even as we speak."

He paused. Nothing happened. "Well, guess I was wrong on that score," he said with a laugh that chilled Alander. "But I still think you should get moving. I'm pulling out of here myself so I can get to higher ground, and I suggest you do the same."

The presence of Axford disappeared from the communion of minds. In his wake, complete chaos ensued. The Fit dissolved into a violent tumble of voices, all of them shouting. Alander winced as the void fragmented into a storm of sensations, painfully overloading his senses. He wanted to cover his eyes and ears, but he had no hands in this environment with which to do this.

He could hear Hatzis calling shrilly for everyone to settle down, but it was *Status Quo/Mellifluous* who finally brought a semblance of order to the proceedings.

"He's not going anywhere! The conjugators will see to that. Ueh, tell us what you think. Is he telling the truth? What is he trying to do?"

"I think it would be best, this time," said Ueh, "for those who know him to answer."

"How can we trust *them*?" shouted one of the Fit.

"One of their own has brought destruction upon us!"

"We had nothing to do with this," protested Hatzis. "You have to believe me."

"We should have seen it," said Alander, mentally cursing. "We should have known how far he would go to get what he wanted."

"Could he be bluffing?" she asked.

"It's possible," he said. Then, to the Fit in general: "Is there any way that you know of to trace an ftl transmission?"

"No," a voice replied. "The space-time flexure caused by the communicator acts simultaneously on every point within its range. There are no delay times, no potential gradients."

"So without any means of detecting its source," said Hatzis, "we have only Axford's word to go on."

Hatzis sounded like she was only barely keeping calm, and Alander could empathize with her. Not only had Axford almost certainly sabotaged any hope of forming a treaty with the Yuhl, but he'd called the Starfish down on their heads, too. If they didn't move quickly, they might not escape.

"That is sufficient," said *Status Quo/Mellifluous*. "We have no choice but to call for evacuation."

"It's going to take time," said Alander. "What if the Starfish come before you can get away?"

"We will worry about that if it happens." The voice of the Yuhl conveyed taut resignation, as though its owner was steeled for a difficult and positively futile task. "We have a great deal of work to do. We must disband."

"What about us?"

"Leave these creatures to their fates!" shouted one of the Fit.

"They deserve what's coming to them!" called out another.

Alander felt minds falling out of the void around him.

"Wait," he pleaded. "We can't just leave it like this! Remember, if his intention was to wipe you out then he wouldn't have said anything. We should try to at least work out why he has done this—what he hopes to achieve."

"Isn't it obvious?" said Hatzis frostily. "He wants us to fight back, of course."

2.1.8

With a sickening sucking noise, Hatzis removed the helmet from her head and tossed it aside. She was gently but firmly eased back into her seat and a thin cloth placed into her flailing hands. She coughed violently, hacking up mouthfuls of viscous fluid. Once the fit subsided and she was able to breathe properly again, she took the cloth and wiped at her watering eyes. When she felt vaguely human, she stood up on wobbly legs and looked around her.

"Where is he?" she croaked dryly, then coughed again. "Where is that fucker?" Her blood felt as though jets of steam were bubbling through it. "I'm going to kill the bastard!"

One of the spike-studded conjugators attending Alander's emergence from the Fit pointed to a human form lying sprawled faced down on the floor. Shrugging off her own attendants and forcing her way through a gathering knot of Yuhl, she looked down at Axford's body. A trickle of black fluid issued from one ear; his eyes were red with blood.

"You beat me to it," she said with disappointment. She had to force herself to resist the urge to kick the prostrate figure. Then, turning to the conjugator, she asked: "Was he trying to escape?"

A warble of Yuhl-speak issued from the alien, and *Triumvirate* instantly translated it via the I-suit:

"He *wasn't trying to escape/did it to himself*. His body was simply removed from the *ingurgitation port/matrix*."

She could have kicked herself. Of course he would

commit suicide. There was no way he would allow himself to be captured and fed to the Praxis so that it could learn all of his secrets. His military training simply wouldn't have allowed it.

"Damn it!" she cursed, starting to pace. "That son of a bitch!"

"Easy, Caryl." Alander came up beside her and put a hand on her shoulder. Ueh hovered behind him, his zebra-striped face unreadable. "Did he say anything to you about what he thinks we should do? He wouldn't just dump us in the shit like this without believing we could fight our way out of it."

"Wouldn't he?" she snapped. "The man's a fucking sociopath, Peter."

"But he's not stupid, Caryl. He's right about needing the Yuhl to fight the Starfish. I don't think he'd wipe them out in a fit of spite. You said he wanted us to fight, not die."

She ran a hand across her face, breathing in deeply to calm herself. *Why am I so upset?* she wondered. Alander was the one who'd been fighting for peace; he was the one who'd had everything thrown back in his face. If anyone had a right to be angry, it was him. She had no reason to be upset at the way the Yuhl had been used.

No, she thought firmly, isolating her anger. *It's not just the Yuhl who have been used. It's us, too.*

So what was Axford up to? Alander was right. A military problem required a military solution, and Axford's was undoubtedly a military mind. He needed the Yuhl to beat the Starfish; he wouldn't just destroy them out of hand. There had to be a way they could get out of this, and that was the point he was trying to make.

There had been moments on the way to Beid during which she had sensed him trying to extract information from her. Perhaps, she thought, it had in fact been the other way around: he had been hinting at what was to come.

She pondered the question with all the resources of her post-Spike body. Before Alander's flawed copy had arrived on Sothis, they had been talking about whether humanity and the Yuhl would be enough combined to take on the Starfish. She had said, *I'd give up ever knowing what the Spinners and Starfish are in exchange for simply staying alive. And I don't believe you'd willingly sacrifice yourself just to make a point, either.*

He had replied, *Not all of me, perhaps.*

Then there was the journey to Beid, and the last private conversation she'd had with him. *The Starfish aren't stupid,* he'd said. *I think by now they know we have a penchant for G-type stars.*

So what are you saying? That we sacrifice a colony or two to find out?

Empty ones, yes. Failed ones. You must have enough of those to spare by now.

It fell into place like an ice sheet collapsing into the sea.

"Triumvirate?" she said. "I need you to send an ftl communication. Can I do that from here?"

"Yes, Caryl."

"Okay." She was silently relieved that Axford hadn't sabotaged the hole ship in any way. The fact that he hadn't done so convinced her she must be on the right track. Ignoring Alander's look of concern, she said, "I'm going to send you an Overseer file, and I want you to transmit that on its own."

She prepared the message and sent it to the hole ship.

GOU MANG, THIS IS SOL. I WANT YOU TO RESPOND IMMEDIATELY. DON'T WORRY ABOUT THE STARFISH. DO YOU UNDERSTAND? SOUND THE EVACUATION ALERT AND RESPOND IMMEDIATELY. THIS IS AN EMERGENCY.

She waited. There was no evidence that the message had even been sent, but presumably all the hole ships in the *Mantissa* and everyone with Spinner technology within 200 light-years was hearing it. The Starfish would be hearing it, too, but if Axford wasn't bluffing, then it really didn't matter—and she had no reason to suspect he was.

Alander edged closer to her as a sudden rush of activity

swept around them. "What's going on, Caryl?"

"I'm—" She got no further, for a large gel-covered alien had forced its way through the crowd and confronted her directly. Its wing sheaths were at full extension and vibrating agitatedly. A piercingly loud string of syllables made her wince. The translation, when it came from *Triumvirate* was mostly incomprehensible.

"This is one of the Fit," said Ueh, pushing forward to translate, again speaking slowly and precisely to synchronize his two vocal streams. "She wonders if this how you intend to start your cycle of violence, with the Yuhl as bait."

"This has nothing to do with me," Hatzis protested.

"That is how it looks to her." Another shrill spiel from the member of the Fit made Ueh blink rapidly. "She feels you have brought the Ambivalence down upon us."

"Look, I'm trying to help," she said, wondering what the hell was taking Gou Mang so long. "For God's sake, tell her I'm not Axford, okay? *He* did this to us, not me."

"She wishes that the Praxis never allowed any of you here," Ueh stammered under the barrage of another tirade, "that the usual policy of avoiding the *bodiless/prey* remained in place. Many will die because of you and—"

"Wait," said Hatzis, holding up her hand. The reply from Sothis had finally arrived.

THIS IS GOU MANG. I'VE HAD TO HACK MY WAY PAST THE SAFEGUARDS YOU INSTALLED TO STOP ANYONE USING THE COMMUNICATORS. I'M GOING TO BE IN TROUBLE FOR USING THEM, SO THIS HAD BETTER BE GOOD, SOL.

Hatzis winced. She had forgotten the safeguards.

GOU MANG, I NEED YOU TO LISTEN CAREFULLY AND DO EXACTLY AS I SAY. THERE'S NO TIME FOR EXPLANATIONS. I NEED YOU TO BROADCAST A REQUEST. I WANT ALL THE FREE HOLE SHIPS TO BROADCAST AS LOUD AND AS LONG AS POSSIBLE. I DON'T CARE WHAT THEY SAY; JUST KEEP THEM TALKING, OKAY? THE ONES THAT AREN'T FREE, I WANT THEM TO JUMP ONE REAL-TIME HOUR FROM THEIR COLONIES AND DO THE SAME FROM THERE.

"Okay, *Triumvirate*," she said, "send that one, but there's more to come."

"Yes, Caryl."

She took a deep breath.

GOU MANG, THIS IS THE MOST IMPORTANT PART. I WANT YOU TO PICK THE COLONIES YOU THINK CAN BE MOST EASILY EVACUATED OR HAVE THE LEAST TO LOSE. SENESCENT, EVACUATED, MOBILE — WHATEVER. IF THEY HAVE GIFTS, TELL THEM TO BROADCAST, TOO. SET A RECORDING GOING AND THEN GET THE HELL OUT OF THERE. I DON'T WANT TO SEE PEOPLE NEEDLESSLY KILLED, BUT I DO NEED THOSE TRANSMISSIONS — AND I NEED THEM FAST. USE THE CONGRESS OVERRIDES IF PEOPLE ARGUE. DO YOU UNDERSTAND?

She rocked back on her heels, hoping the urgency she felt would come through in her message.

"*Caryl/Hatzis*," said Ueh, softly, leaning in close. He smelled like figs. "The Fit have called for an immediate cessation of diplomatic relations with *humanity/riil*. You will no longer be allowed to join the migration. There may be retaliatory strikes should anyone attempt to join."

Alander looked pale and shaken. When Hatzis met his gaze, all he could do was stare back.

"I am to be demoted," said Ueh. "Communication has wrought dissolution. I have failed."

"No," she said, clutching him by the front of his coarse tunic and remembering Alander's insight that Ueh had probably grown the parts of his brain required to be a diplomat. Demotion to the Yuhl would mean the same thing as a lobotomy. "We need you now more than ever— and you need us. Please, tell them I'm doing my best to give us all a chance. Can you do that? Will they at least listen?"

"The Praxis wants to know how, Caryl," said Alander.

Before she could speak, Gou Mang responded:

I'M GOING TO FACE A LYNCH MOB IF I DO THAT WITHOUT A GOOD REASON, SOL.

She gently pushed Ueh away. She was having difficulty juggling so many conversations at once, when what she

needed to be doing was concentrating on the problem at
hand. "If I promise to tell you," she said, "will you let
me finish this conversation with one of my other selves
in Sothis? Both of you should know what that means."

Alander hesitated only a second. His face went even
paler. "The Praxis says it will wait."

Gratefully, she turned away, ignoring the shouts from
the member of the Fit, as well as the growing babble from
the crowd gathering around her.

OKAY, GOU MANG: LISTEN CAREFULLY. THIS IS WHAT I
WANT YOU TO SAY . . .

Quadrille *angled smoothly out of the tangle of vessels pull-*
ing away from the main body of the Yuhl fleet. Hatzis
watched with barely restrained anxiety as hole ships
seemed to pass within inches of her point of view, as seen
through a wraparound screen that left only the floor beneath her visible. She felt as though she was rocketing
through the stars surrounded by a dissipating cloud of
milky droplets. And, sounding constantly around her, the
incessant ringing and buzzing of the ftl communicator.

"You know that you've signed Sothis's death warrant,
don't you?" said Alander from the other side of the cockpit. He was sitting on the lip of two new flight couches
that the ship's AI had installed for them.

"Maybe," she said. Then, meeting his accusatory glare:
"But now the Starfish have lots of targets. They might not
be able to get to all of them at once."

"Do you honestly think that?"

"I wouldn't have done it if I didn't," she said, then
returned her attention to the incoming messages. Most of
the voices sounded puzzled and scared, but there were
plenty among them that were berating her for her idiocy.
Oh well, she thought, *I did tell Gou Mang that I didn't
care what they said.*

The activation of the Congress and her assumption of
control via her engrams and the UNESSPRO traitors had
caused a wave of outrage, but the truth was slowly spread-

ing, all the same—and she *was* effectively in charge. There was nothing anybody could do for the moment to wrest that away from her. Gou Mang was silent for the time being, getting the evacuation under way. If the Starfish followed the transmissions to Sirius too quickly, they would find a large percentage of the human survivors still putting their boots on.

"What are you going to do if—?"

"Be quiet, Peter," she cut him off sharply. "I'm trying to think." That was a lie. If anything, she was trying desperately *not* to think. There was no point in thinking about it at all now. Everything was in motion, and all she could do was sit back and watch and marvel at the scale of the endeavor unfolding around her.

The *Mantissa* was evacuating in dribs and drabs, breaking into fragments and beginning an exodus to a location she hadn't been told about. Some of the liberated hole ships disappeared straightaway. Others joined working gangs engaged in dismantling the large amount of infrastructure that couldn't be transported in one piece. Larger conglomerations of hole ships appeared to be acting as ftl cargo haulers, while others combined to form mass movers in real space, using globular alien thrusters to nudge the large chunks into position. She was slowly becoming accustomed to the various sizes and shapes of the Yuhl vessels, although at times their uniform color and textures made it difficult to tell them apart.

Triumvirate itself had merged with a fourth hole ship to create a new vessel that had the double advantage of being both an elegant regular tetrahedron as well as armed with the best weaponry and defenses the Yuhl had to offer. The Praxis had granted her that much, along with a pilot skilled in the use of the alien technology.

Ueh stood with his feet firmly planted on either side of the base of an organic-looking stalk growing out of the smooth cockpit floor; its summit, shoulder height for a human but at a comfortable reach for the taller Yuhl, sprouted numerous twigs and contact points. She didn't know whether the Praxis had implanted the skill in Ueh's mind biologically or electronically or if he had known how to use the attack systems all along, but he wielded the controls with both delicacy and quiet confidence.

Watching the breakup of the *Mantissa*, she saw many of the four-way hole ships mingling among swarms of single craft and dubbed them *tetrads*. When choosing a new name for their own tetrad, she had quickly opted for *Quadrille*, which meant either a dance or card game for four participants. Given that what was about to unfold was both a dance and a game, depending on whose point of view she took, it seemed oddly appropriate.

Some game, she thought wryly. The fate of thousands depended on so many factors beyond her control: how long the Starfish took to respond to Axford's call, how distracted the Starfish would be by the multiple signals flooding surveyed space; how able the Yuhl would be to repel the attacking vessels. Even en masse, she couldn't let herself expect too much, although for her sanity's sake she *had* to. She had seen the destructive power of the Starfish firsthand, as well as through many of her engrams' eyes. But she had to have some reason to hope, too. If the Yuhl couldn't do it, then no one could. Everything was riding on this gambit.

"When the battle begins," said Ueh, at the same time directing *Quadrille* in a smooth, sweeping arc around the fragmenting *Mantissa*, "I will be subsumed by the Praxis, which will *over/coordinate* the defense of the *Mantissa*. I will retain a degree of self, for I will need full access to my reflexes should the Praxis's prove not immediately tenable, but I might seem distracted. Please be encouraged to contribute to what I am doing. I am not like the Praxis; I cannot see in many directions at once, and I cannot think many things at the same time. It relies on my judgment as well as my senses, and you can be part of that."

"We will," said Alander. "I for one don't want to sit here watching while you do all the work."

"Should things go wrong," Ueh went on, "this vessel is programmed to fragment into unspace and remove you to a safe location."

"Will it have time to do that?" Hatzis asked, remembering the lightning-fast ferocity of the Starfish.

"If it doesn't, we will not know." Ueh's attention was focused on the task before him, which seemed to be nothing more than putting *Quadrille* into formation. She wondered how much of his mind had been taken over by the combat pilot he had become and what he had lost in the process.

"If Axford was lying . . ." Alander began, letting the sentiment go unexpressed.

"Either way, I'm going to wring his fucking neck," Caryl said. Even if Axford *had* been lying, the Starfish would still come, attracted now by her own ftl message. But it would at least give them a couple more hours to play around with, which would be plenty of time for the Yuhl to escape. That would be a relief, but it would still annoy her. The entire exercise would have been for nothing, and it would do nothing for human-Yuhl peace.

The worst thing about it was that it could have so easily been prevented. The Yuhl, she had learned, had been keeping an eye on Axford. After Alander and Ueh had left for Sothis, three days before, he had left almost immediately for Vega, Hatzis assumed. Barely a day later, *Mercury* had returned. The Yuhl had watched him as he lurked about the system, studying their activities. They'd regarded him to be no real threat, so they had let him be. But had they known the stunt he was capable of pulling, they could have destroyed him or at least forced him away. Clearly they had assumed that no one in their right mind would have actually *summoned* the Starfish.

Hatzis agreed with them. It was a tactic she had seen used only once before, in the recording Axford had shown them, supposedly of the Yuhl raiding a human colony. Now she was far from sure. It wouldn't surprise her at all if Axford and his private army had conducted at least some of those raids. It would certainly explain away the mystery of his extra hole ship, and he had quite openly wished for more.

She stood up and started pacing the cockpit again. The

wait was killing her. She was beginning to wish she hadn't volunteered to stay around to see what happened. So what if the Yuhl would have thought her cowardly? At least she would have been spared the waiting, as well as the possible death.

Then a new voice joined the babble through the ftl communicator, and Ueh's posture changed slightly.

"Someone is knocking on our door," the Praxis announced. It spoke in English for her benefit, but she assumed it was communicating with Ueh in other ways. "Tighten those sphincter muscles. This could be it."

She forced herself back onto the flight couch, and realized as she did so that she was trembling. From her seated position she studied the information pouring around and down the screens. Much of it was in the Yuhl language, but the diagrams were universal. On the far side of Beid was a winking light that signaled a new arrival in the system. As she watched, it split up into more than a dozen individual lights and spread out in an expanding disk. Many of them vanished in midflight—to jump closer to the *Mantissa*, she assumed, from there to attack.

Then another voice came over the cockpit speakers.

"This is Kingsley Oborn of Juno," it said. "Caryl, are you anywhere among this lot?

Ueh raised an arm to indicate that she should reply.

"Right here, Kingsley," she said. "What the hell are *you* doing here?"

"Thought you might need some reinforcements," he returned. "I know it's not much compared to what you've got here, but . . ."

"I'm glad you're here," she said softly, sincerely. It didn't ease her inner trembling, but the rallying together of both Yuhl and humans did fill her with a sense of hope. "Listen, Kingsley: the Praxis will give you instructions. Do as it says. If things get too rough, or if you're told to leave, then get the hell out of here *fast,* all right? I don't want you wasting the precious little resources we have."

"I understand, Caryl," he said. Six hole ships traveled in formation, their cockpits modified in ways quite dif-

ferent from the Yuhl's. She could hear something like
relief mingled with fear in Oborn's voice as he said,
"Let's hope it doesn't come to that, though."

Then, suddenly whispered into her mind, the Praxis
said, "Thank you, Caryl Hatzis."

She frowned. "For what?"

"For the contribution of your people," it replied. "It
might make little difference to the outcome, but we appreciate the gesture. It is a significant one."

She didn't know what to say in response to the alien's
gratitude, so she said nothing at all. Instead, she just nodded pensively to herself. *I know,* she thought.

The wait was interminable. It was all she could do to sit still
as the *Mantissa* slowly unraveled. Ueh took *Quadrille*
along a gentle, reconnoitering spiral around one of the
largest agglomerations of the alien hole ships, while Alander stared at the screens with a tightly focused expression.
The simultaneous broadcast from every available human
ftl communicator continued, blaringly loud and utterly
meaningless. She was just beginning to wonder if bore-
dom and unresolved tension were the worst they were
going to face this day when something flashed across the
face of Beid system's primary. Her heart sank as her worst
nightmare was suddenly realized.

"We have confirmation of contact," announced the
Praxis. Light blossomed, and dozens of spinning silver
shapes burst through it. "Abandon all remaining facilities.
All noncombat personnel should commence final evacuation immediately."

Quadrille abruptly changed course. The starscape rotated around them, but Hatzis felt no shift whatsoever in
momentum.

"What about us?" she said. "Are we going to fight for
what's left, or are we escaping, too?" Neither the Praxis
nor the Yuhl had made it entirely clear what their intentions were.

"We will attempt several defensive maneuvers," said

Ueh. His hands were buried up to the wrists in the stalk growing out of the floor of the cockpit; the muscles of his triangular thighs flexed agitatedly. Every time the hole ship performed a particularly striking swoop or roll, his wing sheaths snapped restlessly.

"We're not on the front line, are we?" she asked.

"It is not our intention for you to be," returned the Praxis.

On the screens, the enormous and impossibly fast Starfish vessels blinked into view, then out again, no doubt using something similar to the Spinner relocation drives to move to places in the system with greater tactical advantage. Once they had gone, there was no way of knowing just where they would reappear again.

Hatzis felt as though dry ice was evaporating in her gut.

"Tell them to spread out," she said. "The more locations they have to attack—" She stopped when she realized this was precisely what the hole ships were doing. Lightspeed delays were already making it hard to follow the battle. The Praxis had given its orders via the ftl communicators the moment the Starfish arrived, but only now were the effects of those orders being seen. Hole ships blinked out of sight throughout the crumbling ring of the *Mantissa*. For a moment, the battlefield seemed almost empty, as both aggressors and defenders leapt to new positions.

Then the Starfish were back, and space across the system was suddenly full of light.

Alander's gasp of surprise covered her own as the screens around them blazed white with energy. The Starfish vessels were knife-slim but kilometers across, and spun at relativistic velocities around their edges. Red darts and strange, curving lines of energy whipped through the hole ships and other structures that remained where the bulk of the *Mantissa* had been. Thousands of tapered blue lances, ten times thicker across than a single hole ship, issued from the underbellies of the giant Starfish vessels, engaging anything that fought back. They in turn emitted tiny yellow dots that blinked in and out as they traced through the space between combatants. When they struck, they, too, exploded, bursting with a spray of energy that belied their size.

Hatzis couldn't believe what she was seeing. It was carnage, pure and simple. Wherever the Starfish appeared, they left only destruction in their wake. The Yuhl had erected defensive screens around some of their installations that deflected the red darts, but the whipping lines and yellow dots cut effortlessly through them. Single hole ships and tetrads could only avoid the weapons by relocating elsewhere, and that left the installations they were trying to protect open to attack.

Only when the initial wave of relocations was over and the Yuhl numbers tripled in size did the carnage momentarily ebb.

Hole ships in ones and fours and larger configurations appeared all over the system, all wielding the very best weaponry the Yuhl had at their disposal. Invisible beams cut sporadically visible lines through dust clouds and debris, painting black lines on the sides of the blue lances that interfered with the snapping of the destructive whips. *Quadrille* danced through a close encounter between one of the yellow dots and a large Yuhl contingent. The screens clearly showed the dot blinking in and out of space as it zoomed in toward its target. When it struck, the Yuhl were blown apart. Half were destroyed completely; the rest were either were left drifting, presumably damaged, or managed to relocate to safety.

Safety? she thought. Such a concept didn't currently exist in Beid system. The Yuhl were fighting a losing battle.

It was only then, as the possibility of her own death began to look dismayingly real, that she thought to send a message to Gou Mang. THEY'VE ARRIVED. THE STARFISH ARE HERE! IF I DON'T MAKE IT, YOU'RE IN CHARGE.

Barely had she sent the message when something strange happened: clear spaces began to form in the map of the system as energy levels ebbed. Fierce pockets of conflict still burned around the Starfish vessels, but in other places, where the fighting had previously been just as intense, there was now a relative calm and stillness.

A new tactic? she wondered nervously. Perhaps the Starfish were about to employ a weapon that had the potential to wipe out everything in a volume of space in a single, horrible flash.

Then it occurred to her: this had nothing to do with any new weapon, or even a change in strategy. The Yuhl were still in those spaces. She could see single hole ships and tetrads re-forming and jumping elsewhere, battered, perhaps, but definitely willing to fight on. No, this was something else altogether.

"We have confirmation of withdrawal," said the Praxis, voicing her own realizations. "We have a seventy percent reduction in aggressor presence. It looks like they're heading elsewhere."

A cold feeling of joy swept through her. The plan had worked! The number of ftl transmissions blaring through surveyed space had distracted the Starfish. They had split their forces in order to deal with them, and that left—

Her joy was short-lived.

Oh, shit, she thought. That still left 30 percent of the initial strike force.

A total of nine giant Starfish ships remained in the system. The Yuhl forces had been reduced to barely half, and they had yet to make a significant dent in the Starfish. For every blue lance damaged, ten more took its place. And what made it worse was the fact that the missing Starfish had to be heading *somewhere* . . .

HEADS UP, GOU MANG. IT LOOKS LIKE OUR PLAN WORKED. A NUMBER OF THE STARFISH COULD BE COMING YOUR WAY. IF PEOPLE WANT TO STOP BROADCASTING NOW, I'LL UNDERSTAND. THEY'VE HAD THE EFFECT WE WERE LOOKING FOR.

Ueh relocated *Quadrille* to a position closer to the nearest battle. Hundreds of singles and tetrads appeared all around them, some of them shifting into a loose formation, others blinking out of existence to go elsewhere.

"We *are regrouping our forces/were spread out too thinly before*," said Ueh. Clearly distracted by the ensuing battle around him, he spoke hurriedly, lapsing into his species' normal double-streamed speech.

"You think a more focused response will make a difference?" asked Alander. Hatzis was about to warn the alien that having such an obvious concentration for too long might not be advisable when suddenly the Starfish were among them, breaking the loose formation apart with a flurry of energy. *Quadrille* bucked beneath her, and she clutched the arms of her flight couch. Its cushioned arms and seat automatically wrapped around her, keeping her safe, as Ueh ducked and wove through the wild energy storm around them. Sheets of light flashed and vanished. Soundless explosions rocked them from side to side. She didn't know if they were fighting back in any way, but she found herself grateful for every second she remained alive.

Then something yellow loomed large in the screen: one of the spiky balls the blue lances fired. Instinctively she pulled back into the seat with a cry of panic.

Quadrille relocated into absolute silence just in time. Ueh sagged at the cockpit stalk, his wing sheaths limp.

"We do not know how to hurt them," he admitted solemnly. "The Ambivalence will surely destroy us if we continue to fight."

Alander took a deep, shuddering breath. "I hope Axford can see this," he said. "I hope he can see what his stupidity has done."

"He should be *here*," Hatzis snarled. "He should be the cannon fodder, not us."

They reemerged into real space at a relatively safe distance from the battle. From their new position they could see the numerous battlefields at some remove. The perspective was illuminating. It looked like several small asteroids were exploding, and taking a long time about it. Apart from that, all resemblance to an asteroid belt had vanished. The *Mantissa* was in pieces.

"I've been watching the weapons they're using," Alander said, rising from the flight couch. "They seem to travel through unspace a lot more than we do. Whenever we get too close to them, they disappear and reappear somewhere else."

"Astute observation," Hatzis said sarcastically. "But it doesn't really make our job any easier. We're not designed to think in terms of three-dimensional conflicts—let alone *more* than that!"

"The *Yuhl/Goel* are accustomed to three dimensions," said Ueh. "But even for us this is too much."

Alander brought his attention back to the battle in the distance. "Have you noticed those little yellow bombs?" he said. "I think they're using unspace as well, blinking in and out until they hit a target."

"Wait a second," said Hatzis, herself standing now. "What would happen if we materialized inside something?"

"The hole ships are designed to push matter aside," said Ueh. "They start off small and grow large."

"Exactly. They reenter the universe as a point smaller than the Planck length and expand from there."

Alander shrugged, confused. "So?"

"So what would happen if we were to lob some dead matter into the heart of one of those big ships?" she asked.

Alander nodded his understanding. "That might be how the yellow bombs work."

"It is a technique we could not emulate," said Ueh. He straightened at his post and seemed to regain some of his lost vitality. "The Praxis calls. We must return."

"Couldn't we attack that way?" Alander refused to let go of the idea. "Jump into the big ships, drop some explosives or whatever, and get the hell out of there before they blow?"

"I shall convey your thoughts to the Praxis when we return," he said.

"But what happens if we can't think of anything else?" Hatzis asked. "Do we just fight until we die?"

"We will retreat and rebuild the *Mantissa* elsewhere,"

said Ueh, as though the answer was an obvious one. "Then our journey will resume."

"Much reduced, obviously," said Alander.

"There was no warning," the alien said, his wing sheaths snapping slightly in what might have been the equivalent of a human facial twitch. "Losses could be as high as fifty percent."

"I suppose that rules out the Species Dream for a while," Alander said.

Ueh turned to look at Alander, then Hatzis. "Tell me," he said. "Did you really not know about Axford's plan?"

"I swear, Ueh," Alander said soberly, "we didn't know." He returned to his seat, then, settling wearily into it with a tired sigh.

Hatzis couldn't blame the Yuhl for doubting their word, but she was at a loss to know how she could prove their innocence in the face of Axford's treachery. In the end she simply nodded at the Yuhl and said, "It's true. We honestly had no idea what Axford had in mind."

It was difficult to read the alien's expression as he looked at both her and Alander in turn. Possibly satisfied, he turned again to the ship's screen.

They relocated on the edge of the main battle. The activity was furious, and Ueh was hard-pressed to dodge a shower of strange new missiles fired their way. They looked similar to ones that had attacked *Arachne* in Sol, but these flew with less coordination, as though so many targets overloaded whatever guided them. For a dizzying moment, she felt as though she was scuba diving in a brilliant sea, swimming through the midst of a shoal of darting, silver fish that exploded at the slightest touch.

The fear of dying was still great in her, but a new one was quickly rising. Gou Mang was silent. She hadn't replied to any of Hatzis's transmissions since setting their plan in action. Either she had been ousted from power on Sothis or . . .

That was an *or* she didn't want to think about right then.

"We are disengaging to attempt your maneuver," Ueh

said after sending *Quadrille* back into unspace for a short distance. "The Praxis will give us a target when we are ready."

Hatzis had seen the alien's larger vessel briefly during the last skirmish. It had been in the process of evading crossfire laid down by three of the blue lances.

"It's still alive, then?"

"Yes. It will join us shortly."

They emerged in a pocket of empty space above the system's ecliptic. They were alone, but only for a second as more than fifty singles and tetrads blossomed around them, painting the starscape a brilliant white. A few of them, she noted with pride, were from Juno, but she didn't have a chance to find out if Kingsley Oborn was in any of them.

"We won't have long before the Starfish notice us," Alander said.

"The Praxis is aware of this," said Ueh.

Hatzis felt *Quadrille* shudder beneath her. "What are you doing?" she asked.

"I have volunteered to take part in the attack," Ueh said. On the screen, the numerous hole ships surrounding them began to divide. But they weren't dividing into singles. The white circles blossoming out of the void didn't become as large as that. They were much smaller, some of them barely three meters across.

"I don't understand," Alander began, staring dumbly.

"You have discovered that hole ships can join," Ueh went on, "but you may not have guessed that they can divide, as well. A single hole ship can split itself into three parts, and each part can support life. Some of their capacities are reduced, but they should have more than enough for what we intend to do."

"Which means they can be armed, I'm guessing?" said Alander. "Or at least fitted with automatic mines?"

The Yuhl hesitated for a moment, almost as if concentrating, then moved its head slowly up and down in a manner that approximated a nod—a human affectation the alien was consciously trying to emulate. "All we have to do is hold out long enough for them to get in place."

"Inside one of the Spinner ships, you mean?" Hatzis said.

Ueh nodded again. "The weapons have been programmed to arrive in different sections of the vessel. They will explode on arrival."

Hatzis flinched as something painfully bright burst at her out of the screens. *Quadrille* jolted beneath them. Ueh tugged at the controls and urged the vessel into a desperate spiral, away from whatever had attacked them. The space they were moving through was suddenly boiling with energy. Through it, visible only in glimpses, was the razor-edged hull of a Starfish disk. It blocked out half the universe, its surface blurred by rotation. The distortion in space-time it dragged around with it seemed to impart a vibration on everything nearby. Even through the inertia-dampening fields of the hole ship, she felt its presence as much as saw it.

Single hole ships and tetrads exploded when struck by the powerful weapons of the Starfish. Among them, she noted, were the smaller spheres they'd intended to attack this mighty ship with. They hadn't even left yet.

"Where the hell is the Praxis?" Alander asked anxiously, his voice raised. "Has it called the attack?"

"It hasn't arrived yet," said Ueh, clearly fighting to remain calm.

"Has it been destroyed?" Hatzis asked.

"I do not know."

Hatzis's stomach sank at the thought that the Praxis, the only creature capable of coordinating the Yuhl's attack, may have been blown out of the sky.

"Then hadn't you better launch the attack anyway?" she said. "This could be our last chance!"

Ueh stiffened at the controls.

She didn't hear him say anything, but a second later, the hundred or more smaller spheres vanished from the space around them. There was no way to monitor their progress. All she could do was cross her fingers and hope for the best.

Then her attention was taken by a new assault from the blue lances. Dozens of the things appeared from nowhere to attack the formation Ueh was flying within. The formation broke apart, and flash after flash of furious energy followed them as they raced away from a concentration of enemy fire, Ueh doing everything he could to dodge in three directions at once. Hatzis clutched the sides of her flight couch and wished there was something she could do other than just watch. She felt impotent, useless.

They evaded the lances only to fall foul of the red darts. One of them came so close that the screens went entirely red for a moment. A second came closer still. Hatzis only had enough time to think that a third might finish them off when it very nearly happened. A yellow bomb blinked into life directly in front of their tetrad and exploded with such force that Hatzis blacked out for a moment. She fought the blackness, fearing it was death, and dragged herself back into full consciousness. *I will not die here,* she told herself. *I will* not *die!*

When her eyes had recovered, she saw that the cockpit was filled with a white, powdery mist.

"I have sustained damage," she heard the voice of *Quadrille* announce quietly.

Ueh emitted a grating, close-pitched whistle as he fought controls that didn't respond as they were meant to. A close-hatched weave of red darts seemed to wrap itself around them as three of the blue lances closed in.

Something struck *Quadrille* a hammer blow, wrenching her seat onto its side and throwing Ueh across the room. Atmosphere boiled around her as one whole side of the cockpit disappeared in a single chunk. In the vacuum, she couldn't hear Alander shouting, but she could see him gripping his flight couch as it hung over the yawning void, exposed to the furious energy fire filling the space around them. She wanted to help him, to take his outstretched arm and pull him back to safety, but her couch wouldn't let her. It wrapped itself around her like an ameba, trying to keep her safe but in effect pinning her down. But for their I-suits, both of them would have been killed in-

stantly. That was simply delaying the inevitable, though.
They were exposed to the battle around them. There was
no hole ship to protect them, no Ueh to fly them to safety.
It wouldn't take a red dart or yellow bomb to finish them
off; a single piece of shrapnel or a radiation flash would
be enough, no matter how much she willed it to be otherwise.

This is it, she thought hopelessly. She would have
laughed at her predicament (160 years old and a casualty
in a battle with aliens!) had she not been so terrified.

Then, suddenly, everything went quiet. The blue lances
stopped firing; the yellow bombs blinked once and disappeared. The whipping arcs of energy snapped and went
out. There was a brief salvo that lasted a few seconds,
then faded as the hole ship pilots realized that no one was
firing back.

She craned her neck to find the massive Starfish craft.
It hung in the sky over her left shoulder. Violet light
boiled around its edges, and its previously spotless surface
had acquired a black line encircling the center of its rotation.

Damage? She almost didn't dare hope. But a sickening
new variability to the vibration rippling the space around
her suggested that all was not well with the alien vessel.
The purple light intensified until it became too blinding
to stare at directly. She looked away and felt a violent
pulse flex through space-time, like a shock wave radiating
out from the center of an explosion. She gasped as a second followed the first, only this one much more powerfully. There was a flash so bright that even its reflections
were blinding.

Quadrille began to tumble, and for a moment the Starfish vessel was lost to sight. When it hove back into view,
the light had ebbed and the vibration was barely a stutter.
It was still spinning, but it had lost its disk shape. Enormous chunks had been torn from its edges, and the newly
uneven mass distribution was tearing the rest of it apart,
piece by piece. Within a minute, more than half had been
torn away, leaving just the vessel's central hub and a

small percentage of the surrounding disk, from which
chunks were still flying. "My God," Hatzis muttered. At
the same time, the flight couch eased its grip and she slid
from it to help Alander. Her movements were slow and
cautious in the gravity-free environment, but she managed
to make it over to him safely. His couch was still hanging
in space, barely attached to the remains of the cockpit
floor. He clutched her gratefully as she pulled him back
to safety.

In the volume of space around them, the battle appeared
to be gradually stalling. The Yuhl hole ships moved
among the wreckage, absorbing damaged hole ships and
collecting survivors. The Starfish lances appeared to be
dead, killed along with their mother ship.

Quadrille was dead, too, and *Arachne* along with it, but
that was no reason to give up hope. They'd survived this
far, and there was no reason to think they wouldn't continue to do so.

Together, she and Alander took Ueh and put him onto
her couch. He was unconscious and bleeding yellowish
blood from various wounds across his body, but at least
he was still alive. She was surprised by how little he
seemed to weigh.

She waved to attract the attention of the nearest tetrad,
but it flew past without seeing her. She didn't notice the
shadows shifting around her until Alander tapped her on
the shoulder. She turned, and he silently pointed to a blaze
of light blossoming behind her.

"Now what?" she asked.

"Whatever it is," he said, "you can bet it's not going
to be good."

It wasn't. Out of the glaring light flew three more of
the enormous Starfish vessels relocated from elsewhere in
the system. The Yuhl contingent scattered before them
like krill confronted by a pod of whales. The destruction
of the Starfish ship had only postponed their defeat, not
avoided it entirely.

Still, they had destroyed one of the Starfish vessels. It
didn't make up for the destruction of the Vincula and all

the colonies, but it did give Hatzis a measure of satisfaction. Even though her ship had been incapacitated and three more of the huge craft were bearing down upon them, she would die knowing that with the destruction of that one Starfish ship, there was a chance that humanity would survive. The aliens *could* be hurt.

Her anger and frustration, however, quickly became puzzlement when the three disk-shaped cutters swept by the Yuhl contingent without so much as hesitating and gathered around their crippled comrade.

Comrade. The word came to her automatically and seemed increasingly appropriate the longer she watched. The two nearest swung into position above and below the damaged vessel, as if they were building a stack of giant pancakes, spinning in opposite directions. They docked with the damaged craft and gradually slowed its rotation. Where only minutes before there had been nothing but a blur, now she could make out strange chambers and tubes, all torn and distorted by the breakup of the vessel.

Light began to pulse around the three docked cutters as well as the one standing guard nearby. All of them seemed to vanish into the light, as though traveling down an endless corridor. When the light faded again a minute or so later, they were gone.

"What was *that*?" she muttered to no one in particular. The behavior of the giant vessels was perfectly explicable if she imagined them as living beings, tending a wounded fellow. But living beings *kilometers* across? It wasn't possible.

"We frightened them away," she said, breaking from her unlikely musings.

Alander emitted a guttural sound that might have been a laugh. "The ant biting the anteater on its nose, Caryl?"

"Well, how else do you explain it?"

"I don't," he replied. "I'm just glad to be alive."

She laughed uneasily as her hand found his arm and gripped it tightly. Unbelievably, they'd made it—against the odds, defying her expectations, and with a great deal of luck. But they'd come through it alive, and that was all that mattered.

They waited for what seemed like an interminably long time before a hole ship swooped in over the dead *Quadrille*, its cockpit swinging around to face them. They pushed Ueh through the open airlock first, then quickly followed. Inside, they found two Yuhl pilots who spoke to Alander in their native language. The ability to translate had gone with *Quadrille*, but he seemed to understand them well enough despite this. One of them indicated that they should take Ueh into one of the side quarters, where they laid him on a long, curving mattress.

Alander stood up when they were done and wiped his hands on his shipsuit. His expression was distant for a moment as he listened to a voice that Hatzis couldn't hear. For once, he was the better accessed of the two of them, plugged into some sort of Yuhl communications network she wasn't privy to.

"The Starfish have gone," he told her. "The Yuhl are gathering up what remains of the defense fleet and getting it out of here. There's not much left of anything else, though. What the *Mantissa* didn't take with it has been destroyed." Then he smiled with something approximating satisfaction. "They have a survival rate of forty percent. That's the highest ever recorded in a direct skirmish with the Ambivalence—I mean the Starfish."

She nodded, barely hearing his words and unable to respond emotionally to them anyway. There was nothing but emptiness inside of her right now. Yes, they'd hurt the Starfish, but her initial joy at that fact had quickly faded. She could no longer see it as the victory that Alander obviously thought it was.

He put a hand to his ear, listening again. "And they've found the Praxis," he said. "It was hit, but not fatally. It'll be at the regrouping point when we arrive."

"They're taking us with them?" she asked.

"You expected them to leave us here?"

"I . . . No, of course not," she stammered. "I just

thought we'd get a lift with someone from Juno, that's all, and . . ."

She stopped, not knowing what came after the *and*. She could feel the ringing of ftl communications all around her, but it was less strident than before. Whether people had given up broadcasting or been destroyed, she couldn't tell. Either way, she dreaded finding out.

"*Did* anyone survive from Juno?" she asked after a few moments.

"I'm not sure, Caryl," he said.

A commotion from the cockpit sent a look of alarm across Alander's face.

"What *now*?" He was out of the room at a run, and she followed right behind him.

The pilots were agitated, pointing at the screens and screeching in their own language. At first, Hatzis couldn't tell what they were pointing at. She saw something that looked like a giant, metallic claw hanging against the stars—but a claw that had been stretched impossibly thin, so that it looked more like a long, narrow rib tapering to a point at each end. There were three crossbars of irregular size toward the middle of the thing, and a faint glow surrounding one end.

"Jesus," gasped Alander. "Look at the size of it!"

Hatzis couldn't read the Yuhl figures, and was about to ask exactly just how big the thing was, when she saw an image that caused the breath to catch in her throat.

"That can't possibly be . . ." she started, staring in awe at the swarm of Starfish cutters arcing toward them from the belly of the strange, new craft, dwarfed by its size. She felt an overwhelming sense of dread and nauseous helplessness quickly take her over. "It's not possible." Her words were barely a whisper.

If the cutters themselves were kilometers across, then that made this new craft thousands of kilometers long. Maybe tens of thousands—as long as a planet was wide!

The swarm of cutters loomed large in the screen, splitting up or jumping through unspace to deal with the remnants of the *Mantissa*. Single hole ships and tetrads flew in all directions under the advancing enemy. She couldn't understand the words the Yuhl pilots were shouting, but she caught the gist of it.

"Get the hell out of here!" she yelled as the Starfish fleet—sufficient to destroy a thousand Vinculas—bore down on them. The glare of red and yellow energy weapons exploded from the screen.

Then the view from Beid disappeared, and they were relocating.

Hatzis felt herself physically sag. The battle had been exhausting enough, but *this* . . .

"Are you all right?" Alander asked, stepping between her and the screen, which she continued to stare at, despite there being nothing there to see.

"I'm . . ." She stopped, leaning back tiredly against the wall. "How the hell are we going to fight *this,* Peter?"

"I don't know," he admitted, shrugging. "But if we can destroy one—"

"*One?*" she spat. "That one took out almost everything we threw at it! How the fuck are we supposed to take on *hundreds* of the damn things? *How,* Peter?" Even as she said this, part of her was crying out, *But we have to!*

"So you're saying we should just give up?" he said incredulously. "After everything we've been through?"

"It has to be better than dying, surely?"

They'd fought, and they'd lost. No matter how hard she tried, she couldn't shake that simple fact. They'd tried and failed. Everything the Yuhl had said about the Starfish was true: they were unstoppable. The human race would have to flee, in much the same way the Yuhl had done, or it would be destroyed.

She felt tears of frustration well up inside her, but she refused to cry. She wouldn't give in to the emotions. Not here, not now. Instead, the emotions remained unexpressed. For a long moment she felt as though her entire insides were screaming.

When Alander put his arms around her and pulled her in close, she couldn't help but laugh. They were the last two humans left—the closest things *left* to human, anyway. They were alone against the stars. It seemed almost ridiculous that of all people, they should be here now, comforting each other.

But she didn't pull away, either, because regardless of how ludicrous it seemed, it *was* comforting, nonetheless. As their tetrad traversed the smooth safety of unspace, she realized just how foolish it would be to turn away what reassurance she could find. With so little of it remaining in the universe, God only knew when she'd be offered any again.

3.0.1

2160.9.18–19 Standard Mission Time

Two more holes, both cross-referencing errors between the Gallery, the Map Room, and the Library: the same as the first, in other words. They are otherwise dissimilar, however, and don't seem to be connected. I was hoping a pattern would have emerged by now. I can't decide if the absence of a pattern means there isn't one, or if I just don't have enough data.

The errors I've found appear in the other colonies' data, though. That was easy enough to check across the board, if a little time consuming. I'm the only one pursuing this topic at the moment. Everyone else is looking for weapons or defenses with which to fight the Yuhl. It strikes me as futile fighting another victim of the Starfish, no matter what they've done to us. Is this what we are to be reduced to?

The question of whether the gifts contain deliberately hidden clues has haunted me since I found the first one. The alternative is frightening. We have to believe that the Spinners are doing the right thing by us; otherwise the whole exercise becomes futile. If the gifts comprise one enormous pack of lies designed to throw us off the track of self-improvement, then it might even be worse *than futile. Are these errors, then, this evidence of the Spinners' infallibility, chinks in their armor or continuity errors arising out of fabricated data?*

There is a middle ground, and it is here I prefer to

balance my opinion at the moment. The Gifts are notorious for their avoidance of anything to do with their makers. Maybe this has something to do with them. They could be fudging the data to cover their origins. But I don't know. And that's the problem. No one really knows *anything*. We're like birds picking at stray seeds around a grain silo. And if some of those seeds are bad . . .

Only time will tell, I guess.

I don't know why, but the existence of the Tedesco bursts is bothering me again. Part of me believes that there's a way to fit everything together in a neat, sensible order. I hope that part of me proves to be right.

Today's theory is that the Spinners haven't been traveling in a straight line at all. Quite the opposite, in fact. If they're wandering drunkenly across the galaxy, or spiraling outward from the core, they could have passed near here once before. Assuming the transmissions came from iota Sculptor, say, it's quite conceivable that the Starfish destroyed the civilization that made them in its wake, provoking a short-lived scream for help we picked up 310 years later. Later still, the Spinners completed a circuit of the galaxy and came through our part of the universe again, very nearly returning to the scene of the crime. The close coincidence of our receiving the Tedesco bursts and the arrival of the Spinners was simply just that—a coincidence.

But that doesn't explain why the data is so vague in this area of the Map Room. If they've passed this way before, the data should be more complete. Or so I would've expected. And why travel in such a wandering manner, anyway? Once again, I am at a loss to explain the behavior of a species so mysterious and secretive that we don't even know what they *look* like.

If I'm getting somewhere with this investigation, it's impossible for me to tell. Maybe I'm just wasting my time. I keep thinking, *One day.* If I knew how many days were left, maybe I would let myself believe that this one would come. Far more likely, I think, that I will die with the questions entirely unanswered.

Today is a bad day. I miss my home. I miss Earth. I can't believe (*another* thing I can't believe) that it's really gone. Why don't we evacuate to Sol and live among the ruins? That's what I'd like to do. At least I'd gain a sense of completion, of coming home. It might not be much, but at least it would be *something*.

Sol is still gone. There's talk of a summit with the Yuhl, but I don't know who or what to believe anymore. Christ, I still can't believe that Frank the Ax is alive! He's the prick who cut the budget for the third-generation Euroshuttle by half in the midtwenties, effectively killing the project. Of the billions of people that once populated the Earth, what sort of perverse twist of fate was it that allowed a son of a bitch like *him* to be one of the handful to carry on humanity's legacy? If there is a God, then clearly he or she has a warped sense of humor.

*A little more has been released about the Yuhl. In particu-*lar, I know now that they don't actually worship the Starfish. That hasn't stopped me being intrigued by the notion of the Spinners and Starfish as diametrically opposed aspects of the same thing, though: the giver and the taker on a truly cosmic scale. It put me to thinking about double-headed gods from our own culture, the most obvious being Janus, Roman god of gateways, entrances, and exits. As the god who stood for the beginning of the new year and the end of the old—hence January—he would make a good analogy for this Ambivalence I keep hearing about. Ringing in new times, then smashing all the bells.

But Janus is not the most apt I can think of. There's Harihara, a Kampuchean representation of Vishnu and Shiva as a two-headed divinity: Vishnu the god of earth, atmosphere, and heaven, and Shiva the embodiment of cosmic power in all its aspects. We know Shiva best as the Destroyer, thanks to Oppenheimer's famous speech about the atomic bomb, two centuries ago. Even after all this time, those words still chill me to the bone.

Morbid thoughts, but not entirely fruitless. I wonder now if the Yuhl aren't in the Library because the Gifts are a standard care package put together millennia ago, well before the Starfish encountered them. We already assume that the Spinners are so advanced that they can easily afford to throw around dozens of Gift drops without even noticing; is it that much harder to believe that they are so far above us they don't care what's in them?

This might also explain the vagueness of the Map Room, as well as the presence of the communicators in the package. The ftl communicators have the capacity to summon all and sundry to our calls when we use them, but that means nothing to the Spinners. And why should it? After all, would *we* bother to stop to ensure that the crumbs we drop are used appropriately by the ants that found them? Of course not. It's not the Spinners' fault they're too advanced to care about us. In fact, it's no one's fault that we're too coarse to see the subtleties underlying the grand design of these advanced beings.

That damned subtlety. I remember thinking that knowing it existed put me halfway to understanding it. Now I realize how naïve that was. There's nothing more I can really do now except curse it. Even if it kills us, that's just too bad. It will just have to serve as a harsh lesson, I guess.

Ali's just left. We were together when word came over the communicator that Sol is going to use the empty colonies as decoys.

"She's *what*?" I was shocked.

Ali shushed me in order to hear the rest of the message. This was coming out raw, right from the horse's mouth. Sol's squaring up to fight the Starfish in Beid, which was where she went to negotiate with the Yuhl. I don't understand how it has come to this. I'm all for raging against the dying light and all, but Christ, you don't *invite* it in.

Ali went pale as the words echoed through my virtual space. There was no point arguing; we were committed. And besides, in a way, I could see the sense of it. Spreading the Starfish thin is the only tactic left open to us. But why Sothis, too? Why did they have to put *us* at risk? Haven't we lost enough already?

Gou Mang signed McKenzie Base's death the moment she responded to Sol's call for help. If she takes even one of us down with it, I'm going to hold her personally responsible.

"I'm sorry, Rob," Ali said, cupping my cheek in one hand. "But I have to go."

"I understand. Is there anything I can—?"

She shook her head quickly. "I don't know just yet. I'll call you, though, if I need you. I know I can rely on you."

She left, blinking back tears. I was struck then by the thought that we might never see each other again. I still am, to be honest. The possibility of my own death I can face squarely; it'll just be an end after all, a ceasing. But the death of a loved one cuts deep. Even the thought that if we go down at all we go down together is no comfort, since we're running on the same cannibalized processors. No comfort at all, in fact. Given the choice, I would deny her nothing.

Actually, given the choice, I wouldn't even be here. Evacuation procedures are getting into gear as I dictate this. People are panicking. The whole infrastructure is breaking down. We thought we were ready for anything. But we're not. We all hoped it wouldn't happen to us. People are never ready for this sort of thing.

Even I can't quite believe it yet. The Starfish are going to attack Sothis. Sooner or later, they'll come. They always do when a communicator is used. We know that. It's only a matter of when. It could be in an hour, it could be in a day. It could already be happening, and we simply haven't noticed yet.

Either way, it's time I ended this. In a second, I'll save

the file and store it in the reserve SSDS banks. They'll be backed up in triplicate and shipped out with the SSDS records of our colony. We go in the shipment after that. That makes sense, even if it is another harsh lesson. Our data are worth more than we are. But at least my investigation will be saved, even if in the end it doesn't mean anything.

I sit here watching my processing rate, waiting for it to drop. When it does, I'll know the upload to the evacuee ship has begun. If I could pray, I would—to either the old gods of Earth or the subtle new gods of the stars. Shit, I'd pray to the Ambivalence if I thought it would make a difference. But I doubt they'd even bother to listen.

But perhaps my belief in the method behind the Spinners' madness is not so foolish. It has sustained me this long; maybe it will sustain me longer. Maybe. We'll see. All I can do is wait, and it is the waiting that I find truly awful.

3.0.2

She had been dreaming. At least she thought she had. It was hard to say for sure. At the moment she didn't know where she was or how she had even come to be there, so who was to say that *this* wasn't the dream?

She remembered trying to recall something. Something had been missing. Some data? A memory, perhaps? Whatever it was, it had been troubling her for a long time. Something to do with Peter, maybe? A picture of the two of them, which she had misplaced?

She silently scolded herself, wanting to shake the idiotic thought from her head. But she didn't have a head with which to do this. Nor a body, for that matter. She extended to all directions in a new and strange environment. Whatever it was that held her, it certainly wasn't the *Chung-5*. It seemed to be a ship, albeit of a sort she hadn't even imagined before. It was constructed from principles she could barely begin to grasp, and the external structure appeared to have been recently modified, complicating the picture even further. She knew that there was another mind inside with her, coiled up among the strange pathways like a hibernating snake. Presumably the ship's mind, it ticked slowly over, maintaining esoteric processes she had no hope of understanding. The mind didn't object to her presence; she sensed that clearly. It gave her free rein to explore and experiment. Perhaps one day, she thought, given the chance, she could learn to fly the ship herself. For now, though, she just wanted to look.

With a simple effort of will, she utilized all of the ship's scanning equipment to see around her. Outside was a system in ruins, littered with radioactive dust and the residue of what must have once been ships like hers. A desert world sported several new craters beneath a haze of hot dust. The system's blinding white sun left nothing to the imagination. A war had been fought here. And someone had lost.

As she pondered who it might have been, a white dot disturbed the battlefield. A voice reached out to her.

"*Pearl?* Can you hear me?"

The voice prompted movement within her. Startled, she turned her attention back inside and realized only then that she had missed something absolutely fundamental about the ship's design. It had no heart, but it wrapped around itself in such a way as to leave a space. And inside that space, there was a person sitting on a narrow couch, staring at a display screen. She could see this person from various povs around the cockpit and even from the inside, and she soon realized that her first thought was wrong. This was no person, except in the broadest possible sense. With its unnaturally large build and its olive-green skin, the body was an android, not naturally born.

"Sol?" said the android, standing. It seemed oblivious to her presence. "Is that you?"

"Yeah, it's me. What are you doing here? We thought we'd lost you!"

The voice from outside spoke in reply to the android. She sensed the messages rushing along channels all around her, from the white speck to the chamber within and back again.

"Sol, I'm sorry. I was trying to . . ." The android stopped and shook its head. Its cheeks were wet. "I—I thought you were dead."

"Not quite. I wasn't here when the Starfish came. Gou Mang managed to get about half of the people away in time before they wiped her out with the base. We lost Rama, Hammon, Inari, and Hera as well, and we're pulling out of everywhere else just in case. I only came back to see if anyone else had turned up; otherwise, you would've missed us completely."

The names were unfamiliar to her, but the voice from

outside rang a faint bell. Something about the android looked familiar, too, in a blunt sort of way—although therein lay a paradox: both reminded her of the same person.

"But how did it happen? I thought we were safe here."

"You don't know?"

"I've been in transit. It was a long trip."

"Shit, Thor. So much has changed! We're based in iota Boötis now, an empty, binary system where no one will think of looking for us. It's a good place to retool and rethink, for us as well as the Yuhl. The Fit think we're lunatics, but the Praxis is on our side. It's listening to reason, and that's the main thing."

Swinging her pov to a lower angle, she saw the android frown. Thor seemed to understand what Sol was saying about as much as she did. And there was clearly a lot going unsaid, too.

"We were fighting them, the last I heard."

"Now we're either fighting with them or running with them." Sol paused for a second. "It's complicated. We're still trying to work out who's with who, and who's making the decisions."

"Not Axford, I hope."

"Definitely not. Or Peter."

The name grabbed her attention immediately. She felt a thrill start somewhere around her and work its way through all sections of her new, extended self. Peter was alive! Suddenly she didn't want to be a passive observer anymore. She wanted to become active in the conversation, take control of it, guide it to where she wanted it to go.

"Peter is alive?" she said, closing off the incoming message and taking over the communication channels it had used.

The android looked around, bewildered. "Lucia? Is that you?"

Lucia. Yes, that was her name. *Lucia Benck.* How long had it been since she had even thought of herself as that? So long that she'd almost forgotten it.

"You mentioned Peter," she said.

The android's eyes moved about the room, its green-hued face creased with perplexity. "Are you all right?"

"I'm not sure," she said. "I remember dreaming; I remember being scared. I forgot something, and then . . ."

Then there had been a strange white orb hanging off her stern, twice the length of the *Chung-5* in radius—the same sort of craft, she now realized that Sol was talking from. (Lucia had suppressed the transmission so the android couldn't hear her. She wanted Thor all to herself for the moment.) Images recorded by her ailing sensors revealed that it had literally appeared out of nowhere. Her processing speed accelerated from glacial slowness to the highest her Overseer could manage as another sphere emerged from the first one's side: black, orbiting like a miniature moon. This second sphere slowed to a halt so it seemed to point at *Chung-5*. Then a voice had spoken to her in English.

"You were experiencing brainlock when I found you," the android was saying, back in the present. "You would have experienced smaller events leading up to it: déjà vu, dissociation from your senses, things like that—all symptoms of engram senescence. *Chung-5* wasn't faring much better. I uploaded you to my hole ship, the only place I had to put you, but I wasn't sure it would work. I'm sorry if this is confusing for you—"

"I feel different," Lucia said. "I'm part this ship, now. This *Pearl*. It makes me feel good, knowing that I can do so many things."

"You feel that?" Something approximating disbelief glinted momentarily in the android's eyes. "You're part of the workings of *Pearl*?"

"I think so," Lucia said. "Most of it, anyway. Why should that surprise you? You put me in here."

"Yes, but I didn't expect that to happen. I don't think anyone's tried to do this before. Can I talk to—?"

"Caryl," Lucia interrupted, having reasoned with a fair degree of confidence that this was indeed the android's name (even though that meant that Sol had to be another

Hatzis, judging by the increasingly frustrated voice match). "You mentioned Peter. Where is he?"

Android Hatzis stopped, frowned. "He'd be in iota Boötis now, I guess. That's where Sol said the others were. But you should know that he's not the Alander from your mission. He comes from Mission 842, the one to Upsilon Aquarius. He's changed since you knew him."

Lucia stopped listening. It didn't matter to her which one he was. It just mattered that he was Peter.

"I want to go there," she said.

"Yes, we will, but—"

"I want to go there now."

"What's the hurry, Lucia? We only just got *here*."

"Where is here?"

"Sirius."

"*Sirius?* But that's . . ."

Her mind tripped over the absurdity of android Hatzis's statement and simultaneously accepted it without question. While she couldn't remember anything between blacking out in *Chung-5* and waking up in *Pearl*, she did have a sense of crossing an enormous gulf of space. She also had a feeling that time had passed, more time than could be accounted for by all the days and years she had been awake.

"What year is it, Caryl?"

"Twenty-one sixty, Mission Time."

She wanted to shout, *Impossible!* That made her 130 years old! But she was beginning to understand that she was very much out of her depth. For all the capacity of her new home—and her sudden age—she was like a newborn blinking to focus on a very puzzling world.

What's happened to us all? she wanted to ask. It would have been the beginning of a torrent of questions: *What are we doing in Sirius? Why did you come find me? Who is Axford, and why are we fighting? What are the Starfish and the Yuhl and the Praxis? How had Peter been changed?*

What came out, though, was, "Why did you bring me back?" The plaintive tone to her voice surprised even her.

Android Hatzis looked regretful. "We needed to know what's going on in pi-1 Ursa Major, and you were the closest person to it. I was hoping you might have seen something recently, but your memories were scrambled. I had no idea you'd be in such shape, and even when I did know, I couldn't very well leave you there. I'm sorry if I did the wrong thing."

The wrong thing? Lucia wasn't sure. The mention of pi-1 UMA did trigger an unexpected series of memories: a sunset; the name Jian Lao; the pressure of Peter's hand in hers; a strong pang of sadness. Was this what she had been trying to remember—or trying to forget?

Then another memory came. There had been photographs. The probe had absorbed them decades ago. The evidence was gone, except for her.

"There *was* something odd about pi-1 Ursa Major," she said. "It destroyed the *Linde*. It might have killed me, too, but I hid. It couldn't find me."

"It came after you, you mean?"

"No, when I flew through the system."

"But that was over forty years ago, Lucia. That can't be right."

She felt again the terrible gulf of time and space that she had crossed. Forty years since the *Linde* had died, since she had switched herself off to survive the flyby? It felt like hours. An eternity of seconds.

"I want know what's going on, Caryl," she told the android.

The android laughed low and uneasily. "To be honest, I feel the same way."

"I want you to explain it to me."

"All right. I'll try."

"And when you're finished, we'll go to iota Boötis."

There was a silence filled only by the persistent calling of Sol-Hatzis. ("For fuck's sake, Thor. Answer me!") Lucia switched off the part of *Pearl* that persisted in listening.

"Are you sure that's what you want to do?" the android asked, as though projecting her own uncertainty.

"Yes. I want to see Peter. I want to tell him . . ." She stopped, not sure *what* she wanted to say to her old lover, so many years after they had parted. Her thoughts moved in strange ways through the conduits of the ship, complicating every emotion. "I want to tell him that the tourist has come home," she finished after a moment.

And that she has changed.

APPENDIX ONE

THE ADJUSTED PLANCK STANDARD INTERNATIONAL UNIT

After several notable mission failures in the late twentieth and early twenty-first centuries, the United Near-Earth Stellar Survey Program (UNESSPRO) developed a single system of measurement to prevent conflict between data or software from nations contributing to joint space projects. The following charts summarize the results, as adopted by UNESSPRO in 2050, using Planck units and other physical constants as starting points.

1 new second		= 0.54 old second
1 new minute	= 100 new seconds	= 0.90 old minute (54 old seconds)
1 new hour	= 100 new minutes	= 1.5 old hours (90 old minutes)
1 new day	= 20 new hours	= 1.2 old days (30 old hours)
1 new week	− 5 new days	= 0.89 old week (6.2 old days)
1 new month	− 6 new weeks	= 1.2 old months (5.3 old weeks)

1 new year	= 10 new months	= 1.025 old years (12 old months)

1 new centimeter		= 1.6 old cm / 0.64 inch
1 new decimeter (dm)	= 10 new cm	= 6.5 inches
1 new meter	= 10 new dm	= 1.6 old m / 3.3 feet
3 new meters		= 10 feet
1 new kilometer	= 1,000 new meters	= 0.97 mile

1 new hectare	= 2.6 old hectares	= 6.4 acres
1 new liter (dm³)	= 4.2 old liter	= 1.1 gallons

1 new g		= 2.2 old g
1 new kg	= 1,000 new g	= 4.8 old pounds
1 new tonne	= 1,000 new kg	= 2.1 old tons

1 new ampere		= 2.972 old amperes

(new)	(Centigrade)	(Fahrenheit)	(Kelvin)
1°	= 1.415°	= 2.563°	= 1.415°
0°	=−273.15°	=−459.67°	= 0° (absolute zero)
193°	= 0°	= 32°	= 273.15° (freezing point of H_2O)
264°	= 100°	= 212°	= 373.15° (boiling point of H_2O)

c (the speed of light)	$= 1.00 \times 10^8$ ms^{-1}
1 light-year	$= 6.00 \times 10^{15}$ m
1 light-hour	$= 1.00 \times 10^{11}$m
1 parsec	$= 2.0 \times 10^{16}$ m
1 g	$= 1.0$ light-year/year^2
1 solar radius	$= 430,000$ km
1 Earth radius	$= 4,000$ km (equatorial)
geostationary orbit	$= 22,220$ km (Earth)

APPENDIX TWO

DRAMATIS PERSONAE

Human

Peter Alander (*S. V. Krasnikov*)
Peter Alander (*Geoffrey Marcy*)
Peter Alander (*Michel Mayor*)
Peter Alander (*Frank Tipler*)
Jene Avery (*Andrei Linde*)
Jene Avery (*Tess Nelson*)
Francis Axford (*Matthew Thornton*)
Lucia Benck (*S. V. Krasnikov*)
Lucia Benck (*Geoffrey Landis*)
Lucia Benck (*Andrei Linde*)
Ali Genovese (*Jack Lissauer*)
Ali Genovese (*Michel Mayor*)
Ali Genovese (*Tess Nelson*)
Caryl Hatzis (Sol)
Caryl Hatzis (*Miguel Alcubierre*)
Caryl Hatzis (*Roger Angel*)
Caryl Hatzis (*Robert Haberle*)
Caryl Hatzis (*Stephen Hawking*)
Caryl Hatzis (*Martin Heath*)
Caryl Hatzis (*S. V. Krasnikov*)
Caryl Hatzis (*Michel Mayor*)
Caryl Hatzis (*Tess Nelson*)
Caryl Hatzis (*Fred Rasio*)

Tarsem Jones (*Fred Adams*)
Faith Jong (*David Deutsche*)
Nalini Kovistra (*S. V. Krasnikov*)
Nalini Kovistra (*Tess Nelson*)
Vince Mohler (*Paul Davies*)
Vince Mohler (*S. V. Krasnikov*)
Vince Mohler (*Frank Shu*)
Owen Norsworthy (*Tess Nelson*)
Neil Russell (*Carl Sagan*)
Neil Russell (*Tess Nelson*)
Cleo Samson (*Geoffrey Marcy*)
Cleo Samson (*Michel Mayor*)
Cleo Samson (*Tess Nelson*)
Cleo Samson (*Steven Vogt*)
Donald Schievenin (*Ronald Bracewell*)
Donald Schievenin (*Stephen Hawking*)
Donald Schievenin (*S. V. Krasnikov*)
Rob Singh (*S. V. Krasnikov*)
Rob Singh (*Tess Nelson*)
Jayme Sivio (*Stephen Hawking*)
Jayme Sivio (*Andrei Linde*)
Angela Wu (*S. V. Krasnikov*)
Otto Wyra (*V. S. Safronov*)

Yuhl/Goel

Asi/Holina (helot)
Seria/Hile (conjugator)
Ueh/Ellil (helot, *envoy/catechist*)
Vaise/Ashu (conjugator)
Probing/Inquisitive (Fit)
Radical/Provocative (Fit)
Status Quo/Mellifluous (Fit)
Stoic/Enduring (Fit)
Zealot/Shrieking (Fit)

APPENDIX THREE

MISSION REGISTER

#	Target System	Core Survey Vessel	Primary Survey World	Hole Ships
13	23 Boötis	*Maroj Joshi*	(unknown)	
17	chi Hercules	*Geoffrey Marcy*	Vahagn	*Betty*
31	Beta Hydrus	*Carl Sagan*	Bright	
95	94 Aquarius	*Larry Lemke*	(unknown)	
154	HD92719	*S. V. Krasnikov*	Thor	*Pearl*
163	Tau Ceti	*Brian Chaboyer*	New France	
180	Dsiban	*Geoffrey Landis*	(unknown)	
182	Altair	*Didier Queloz*	(failed)	
183	Van Maanen 2	*Steven Weinberg*	Aretia	
219	BD+14 2621	*Douglas Lin*	Medeine	
253	Gamma Serpens	*Stephen Hawking*	Juno	*Cue Ball*
267	mu Ara	*V. S. Safronov*	Pan	*Prometheus*
278	HD113283	*Lee Smolin*	Fu-xi	*Oosphere*
340	HD165401	*Michio Kaku*	(unknown)	

344	BSC8477	Anna Jackson	(unknown)	
373	6 Ceti	Heather Hauser	Silvanus	
387	BSC8061	Jill Tarter	Heimdall	
391	pi-1 Ursa Major	Andrei Linde	Jian Lao	
400	BSC7914	Fred Rasio	Eos	
402	HD203244	Ronald Bracewell	Fujin	
416	Delta Pavonis	Martyn Fogg	Egeria	
477	Hipp1599	Roger Angel	Yu-quiang	
512	Head of Hydrus	Michel Mayor	Athena	
538	61 Ursa Major	Fred Adams	Hera	Kirsty
543	zeta Dorado	Steven Vogt	Hammon	
564	gamma Pavonis	Jack Lissauer	Diana	
639	psi Capricornus	Tess Nelson	Inari	
647	Procyon	Philip Armitage	(failed)	
648	Luyten's Star	Alan Boss	Jumis	
666	Vega	Matthew Thornton	(none)	Mercury
707	AC +48 1595-89	Frank Shu	Ea	
709	Sirius	David Deutsche	Sothis	
726	BD+14 2889	Norman Murray	(failed)	
754	Hipp101997	Amy Reines	Balder	
755	zeta Serpens	Henry Throop	Rama	
784	Hipp64583	Robert Haberle	Adammas	Koyote
805	Zeta-1/2 Reticuli	Paul Davies	Tatenen	
833	Mufrid	David Soderblom	(failed)	
835	HD194640	Carol Stoker	Varuna	
842	Upsilon Aquarius	Frank Tipler	Adrasteia	Arachne

861	Alpha Mensa	*Subrahmanyan Chandrasekhar*		
906	58 Eridani	*Martin Heath*	Gou Mang	
919	64 Pisces	*Miguel Alcubierre*	Ilmarinen	
950	Groombridge 1830	*Sarah Manly*	Perendi	

APPENDIX FOUR

TIMETABLE

Universal Time		Mission Time
1988, 17 Dec	Peter Stanmore Alander born	
2049, 26 Nov	UNESSPRO Engrams activated	2049.9.29
2050, 1 Jan	UNESSPRO launches commence	2050.1.1
	Frank Tipler launched	2051.2
2062, 8 Jul	Spike	2062.3.3
	McKenzie Base (Sothis) founded	2066
2081–82	Tedesco Bursts detected	
	Matthew Thornton arrives at Vega	2088.08
	Andrei Linde arrives at pi-1 Ursa Major	2115.5.5
	Andrei Linde destroyed	2117.1.17
	Chung-5 flyby of pi-1 Ursa Major	2117.3.18

	Frank Tipler arrives at Upsilon Aquarius	2151.1
	Breakdown of Peter Alander engram	2151.1
	Peter Alander engram revived	2160.2
	Spinners enter surveyed space	2160.8
2163, 10 Jul	Gifts arrive in Upsilon Aquarius	2160.8.17
	Adrasteia (Upsilon Aquarius) attacked	2160.8.26
2163, 24 Jul	Sol System attacked	2160.8.28
	Inari (psi Capricornus) contacted by	2160.9.1
	Spinners	
	Sothis recolonized	2160.9.3
	Athena (Head of Hydrus) destroyed	2160.9.3
	Vega contacted by Alander/ Hatzis	2160.9.10
	Hera (61 Ursa Major) attacked by Yuhl	2160.9.11
	Thor (HD92719) destroyed	
	Ilmarinen (64 Pisces) destroyed	
	Inari (psi Capricornus) evacuated	2160.9.14
	First contact with the Praxis	2160.9.15
	Tatenen (Zeta-1/2 Reticuli) destroyed	2160.9.16

Lucia Benck (Jian Lao) recovered by Caryl Hatzis (Thor)	2160.9.18
Starfish attack Beid	2160.9.19
Sothis (Sirius), Rama (zeta Serpens), Hammon (zeta Dorado), Hera (61 Ursa Major), Inari (psi Capricornus) destroyed	

AFTERWORD

Once again we are indebted to a large number of people for helping make this book possible. These include Simon Brown (to whom this book is gratefully dedicated) and Chris Lawson, who provided invaluable feedback at an early stage; Shaun Thomas; the real Neil Russell; everyone at Ace and HarperCollinsPublishers Australia, Ginjer Buchanan and Stephanie Smith in particular; Richard Curtis and Danny Baror for services rendered; Erik Max Francis, for first proposing a scale based on Planck units (see http://www.alcyone.com/max/writing/essays/planck-units.html); Winchell Chung, for his weird world of 3-D star maps and other resources http://allison.clark.net/pub/nyrath/starmap.html#contents); and Claus Bornich, author of the invaluable program *It's Full of Stars*, for putting our star maps on his site (http://www.geocities.com/CapeCanaveral/7472/). Other programs that came in handy were Cinegram Media's *Red Shift 4* and Pro-Fantasy's *Campaign Cartographer 2* and *Fractal Terrain*.

Finally, we would like to emphasize that any factual errors found in this novel are, despite the best efforts of those listed above, entirely our fault.